THE KNIGHT OF
MAISON-ROUGE

ALEXANDRE DUMAS

THE KNIGHT OF
MAISON-ROUGE

A NOVEL OF MARIE ANTOINETTE

A new translation by Julie Rose

Introduction by Lorenzo Carcaterra

THE MODERN LIBRARY

NEW YORK

2004 Modern Library Paperback Edition

Biographical note copyright © 1996 by Random House, Inc.
Introduction copyright © 2003 by Lorenzo Carcaterra
Translation copyright © 2003 by Random House, Inc.
Notes and glossary copyright © 2003 by Random House, Inc.

LIBRARY OF CONGRESS CATALOGING-IN-PUBLICATION DATA
Dumas, Alexandre, 1802–1870.
[Chevalier de Maison-Rouge. English]
The knight of Maison-Rouge: a novel of Marie Antoinette /
Alexandre Dumas; a new translation by Julie Rose.
p.   cm.
ISBN 0-8129-6963-4
1. France—History—Revolution, 1789–1799—Fiction.   2. Girondists—
Fiction.   3. Marie Antoinette, Queen, consort of Louis XVI, King of
France, 1755–1793—Fiction.   I. Rose, Julie.   II. Title.
PQ2225.C713 2003
843'.7—dc21

2003044577

Modern Library website address: www.modernlibrary.com

Printed in the United States of America

2 4 6 8 9 7 5 3 1

ALEXANDRE DUMAS

Alexandre Dumas, who lived a life as dramatic as any depicted in his more than three hundred volumes of plays, novels, travel books, and memoirs, was born on July 24, 1802, in the town of Villers-Cotterêts, some fifty miles from Paris. He was the third child of Thomas-Alexandre Davy de la Pailleterie (who took the name of Dumas), a nobleman who distinguished himself as one of Napoleon's most brilliant generals, and Marie-Louise-Elisabeth Labouret. Following General Dumas's death in 1806 the family faced precarious financial circumstances, yet Mme. Dumas scrimped to pay for her son's private schooling. Unfortunately he proved an indifferent student who excelled in but one subject: penmanship. In 1816, at the age of fourteen, Dumas found employment as a clerk with a local notary to help support the family. A growing interest in theater brought him to Paris in 1822, where he met François-Joseph Talma, the great French tragedian, and resolved to become a playwright. Meanwhile the passionate Dumas fell in love with Catherine Labay, a seamstress by whom he had a son. (Though he had numerous mistresses in his lifetime Dumas married only once, but the union did not last.) While working as a scribe for the duc d'Orléans (later King Louis-Philippe) Dumas collaborated on a one-act vaudeville, *La Chasse et l'amour* (*The Chase and Love*, 1825). But it was not until

1827, after attending a British performance of *Hamlet,* that Dumas discovered a direction for his dramas. "For the first time in the theater I was seeing true passions motivating men and women of flesh and blood," he recalled. "From this time on, but only then, did I have an idea of what the theater could be."

Dumas achieved instant fame on February 11, 1829, with the triumphant opening of *Henri III et sa cour* (*Henry III and His Court*). An innovative and influential play generally regarded as the first French drama of the Romantic movement, it broke with the staid precepts of Neoclassicism that had been imposed on the Paris stage for more than a century. Briefly involved as a republican partisan in the July Revolution of 1830, Dumas soon resumed playwriting and over the next decade turned out a number of historical melodramas that electrified audiences. Two of these works—*Antony* (1831) and *La Tour de Nesle* (*The Tower of Nesle,* 1832)—stand out as milestones in the history of nineteenth-century French theater. In disfavor with the new monarch, Louis-Philippe, because of his republican sympathies, Dumas left France for a time. In 1832 he set out on a tour of Switzerland, chronicling his adventures in *Impressions de voyage: En Suisse* (*Travels in Switzerland,* 1834–1837); over the years he produced many travelogues about subsequent journeys through France, Italy, Russia, and other countries.

Around 1840 Dumas embarked upon a series of historical romances inspired by both his love of French history and the novels of Sir Walter Scott. In collaboration with Auguste Maquet, he serialized *Le Chevalier d'Harmental* in the newspaper *Le Siècle* in 1842. Part history, intrigue, adventure, and romance, it is widely regarded as the first of Dumas's great novels. The two subsequently worked together on a steady stream of books, most of which were published serially in Parisian tabloids and eagerly read by the public. He is best known for the celebrated d'Artagnan trilogy—*Les trois mousquetaires* (*The Three Musketeers,* 1844), *Vingt ans après* (*Twenty Years After,* 1845), and *Dix ans plus tard ou le Vicomte de Bragelonne* (*Ten Years Later; or, The Viscount of Bragelonne,* 1848–1850)—and the so-called Valois romances—*La Reine Margot* (*Queen Margot,* 1845), *La Dame de Monsoreau* (*The Lady of Monsoreau,* 1846), and *Les Quarante-cinq* (*The Forty-Five Guardsmen,* 1848).

Yet perhaps his greatest success was *Le Comte de Monte Cristo* (*The Count of Monte Cristo*), which appeared in installments in *Le Journal des débats* from 1844 to 1845. *Le Chevalier du Maison-Rouge* (*The Knight of Maison-Rouge*, 1845–1846) was also a collaborative effort. A final tetralogy marked the end of their partnership: *Mémoires d'un médecin: Joseph Balsamo* (*Memoirs of a Physician*, 1846–1848), *Le Collier de la reine* (*The Queen's Necklace*, 1849–1850), *Ange Pitou* (*Taking the Bastille*, 1853), and *La Comtesse de Charny* (*The Countess de Charny*, 1852–1855).

In 1847, at the height of his fame, Dumas assumed the role of impresario. Hoping to reap huge profits, he inaugurated the new Théâtre Historique as a vehicle for staging dramatizations of his historical novels. The same year he completed construction of a lavish residence in the quiet hamlet of Marly-le-Roi. Called Le Château de Monte Cristo, it was home to a menagerie of exotic pets and a parade of freeloaders until 1850, when Dumas's theater failed and he faced bankruptcy. Fleeing temporarily to Belgium in order to avoid creditors, Dumas returned to Paris in 1853, shortly after the appearance of the initial volumes of *Mes Mémoires* (*My Memoirs*, 1852). Over the next years he founded the newspaper *Le Mousquetaire*, for which he wrote much of the copy, as well as the literary weekly *Le Monte Cristo*, but his finances never recovered. In 1858 he traveled to Russia, eventually publishing two new episodes of *Impressions de voyage: Le Caucase* (*Adventures in the Caucasus*, 1859) and *En Russie* (*Travels in Russia*, 1865).

The final decade of Dumas's life began with customary high adventure. In 1860 he met Garibaldi and was swept up into the cause of Italian independence. After four years in Naples publishing the bilingual paper *L'Indépendant/L'Indipendente*, Dumas returned to Paris in 1864. In 1867 he began a flamboyant liaison with Ada Menken, a young American actress who dubbed him "the king of romance." The same year marked the appearance of a last novel, *La Terreur Prussiene* (*The Prussian Terror*). Dumas's final play, *Les Blancs et les Bleus* (*The Whites and the Blues*), opened in Paris in 1869.

Alexandre Dumas died penniless but cheerful on December 5, 1870, saying of death: "I shall tell her a story, and she will be kind to me." One hundred years later his biographer André Maurois paid him this tribute: "Dumas was a hero out of Dumas. As strong as Porthos, as adroit as d'Artagnan, as generous as Edmond Dantès, this superb giant strode across the nineteenth century breaking down doors with his shoulder, sweeping women away in his arms, and earning fortunes only to squander them promptly in dissipation. For forty years he filled the newspapers with his prose, the stage with his dramas, the world with his clamor. Never did he know a moment of doubt or an instant of despair. He turned his own existence into the finest of his novels."

Contents

THE KNIGHT OF MAISON-ROUGE

INTRODUCTION

Lorenzo Carcaterra

Alexandre Dumas was already at the head of his class. Few writers, if any, could approach his masterful way of intertwining historical fact (layered, of course, by his own imagination) with high-octane action, adventure, and romance. He proved it again and again in his novels about revenge-seeking counts and sword-slashing musketeers. And now he does it once more, with an even more powerful voice, in his tale of a magical and heroic young knight.

The Knight of Maison-Rouge is one of those rare gifts that are all too seldom found in the book world. A work once thought lost in the dust-bins of a shuttered store, with few if any editions in circulation, is re-discovered, lavished with a fresh coat of paint and polish, and brought out to the front of the shop for all to see and grasp. Once the pages are cracked open, from that very minute we enter the streets of Paris in early March 1793, we are thrust back into another time, hurtling into a distant world. It may well be a place we have never seen or even heard about. But it is one that, through the many works of Alexandre Dumas, we have come to know so very well.

——

His world was always my escape route. As I read through each page of this wonderful new novel, crammed to the brim with fights, betrayals, deceit, friendships, and the quest for honor, it became a simple feat to drift back and remember all that Dumas has given me. I was raised in a violent household, my parents always within inches of taking that final plunge toward death. When the battles became too difficult to face, the shouts and screams too wrenching to hear, I would turn to Dumas and his books, and in their company I would always find the safest refuge.

I would sit in the rear of a small, quiet library in my New York City neighborhood, in a room that faced onto a busy and bustling avenue, a wood table with four chairs all to myself, the pages of one of his novels spread out before me. There, through many a long afternoon, I allowed Dumas to take me deep into his world, miles away from the anguish of my own. I have never been to Paris, but in the back room of that cramped library, I walked and fought my way through its streets with the best possible guide by my side.

—

All great writers offer a refuge through their work, speaking to us with words and tales they have chiseled with their own particular stamp. Dumas was a man of great wealth and high-end tastes who had spent his way through a fortune by the time he lay on the thick quilts of his deathbed, breathing his last. Yet, despite the money he spent so freely, his stories and his heart rested in the soul of the working man. His heroes are all colored with the flag of honor, each bred through the ranks of abject poverty. Dumas made himself so rich by writing so well about their adventures, each of their tales wrapped in the cloak of loyalty to king and queen, giving them the veneer of the respect each central character very often had to draw sword to obtain.

With this fresh and vibrant novel now reclaimed, the heroic Maurice and Lorin will soon be placed in the vaunted ranks of other Dumas stalwarts—from Dantès to D'Artagnan and the rest of the glorious Musketeers. Brave men who willingly flipped aside their thick robes to clash swords for a noble cause or a beautiful woman (and few are as luminous as our current heroine, Geneviève), or very often both at the same time. Dumas's characters all live through turbulent days, death always a mere flick of a blade away, romance ever elusive; they are men of power and wealth flaunting their riches in cities drowning in poverty and despair.

It is what helps make Dumas timeless—his Paris of 1793, with a mere shuffling of the deck, can be any other major city, with little care to decade or century. The turmoil faced by Lorin during the glory years of Marie Antoinette could easily be matched in today's world in many a city and any number of countries.

—

In *The Knight of Maison-Rouge*, as in all his other works, Dumas treats history with the casual indifference of the storyteller. He uses it not for accuracy but to propel his story forward, to turn its laws and abuses to suit the goals of his tale. His fictional creations mingle easily in the company of historical personages, fighting for their causes, bowing to their lineage, pledging fidelity to their reign. All of it done for the sake of story. Yet despite any quibbles historians may have with Dumas, his Parisian novels paint a more than accurate picture of an explosive time and a changing world.

In this enchanting book, the anger that percolates on the stone streets of Paris is felt through every page. The tension between the classes, between those casually dismissive of their wealth and the hands and faces of those one missed meal away from death, is as palpable as a baby's heartbeat. The seeds of a revolution are not merely planted in a careless manner but seem always to be on the brink of a bountiful harvest. Through his many novels, this latest just one more brilliant addition, Dumas has made the city and its history his own and is more than eager to share it with a willing world.

—

It is so very easy to get lost in the pages of a Dumas novel. To forget time and place and be engulfed by characters rich and full, battles one-sided and hopeless, promises that must be kept and deceptions that cannot be forgiven. There are dozens of unforgettable characters in *The Knight of Maison-Rouge*, each one of them a complete portrait, his strengths, weaknesses, foibles, and motives painted with a palette of many colors. The panorama is, as always, lush and layered, from the overview of a struggling nation to the turmoil of a small side street, all drawn down to the most precise detail. It is the work of a writer trolling within the full force of his powers, both the destiny and the direction of his story resting in his hands alone. The reader is merely a passenger venturing on a literary journey that will always be remembered.

———

After my childhood, I continued to turn to the works of Alexandre Dumas. As a troubled teen, I sought out his stories as a safe haven from the questions of a life that offered me so few answers. As a young man, I looked to his work as my template for the proper way to deliver a story, to coat it and coax it and bring it to a conclusion with the power and brilliance it so much deserved. I have always fallen short in my attempts, while Dumas never failed to succeed with his own. And now, as a middle-aged man, I read his works for the fond memories they never fail to bring. The time I've spent with those fine novels will always belong to no one else but me.

Ride with *The Knight of Maison-Rouge*. If you have never read Dumas before, let this be the first of many steps in his direction. If you've crossed his path, are familiar with his many sagas, then there should be no hesitation to journey on yet another adventure. Either way, once we are inside the pages, there is no escape, as we are again taken hostage and made this master's literary prisoners.

So allow Dumas to do what he does best—turn us all once again into quiet children sitting in the warmth of small libraries, at empty tables, our heads buried in one of his books, our imaginations filled with the raging battles and the fierce loves of another century and another place. As we turn each page, we are once again free to turn his adventures into our very own.

It is the truest gift any novelist can hope to give.

And none has been more generous than Alexandre Dumas.

———

LORENZO CARCATERRA is the bestselling author of five books, *A Safe Place, Sleepers, Apaches, Gangster,* and *Street Boys*. He has also written scripts for movies and television. He lives in New York.

THE KNIGHT OF
MAISON-ROUGE

1
The Recruits

It was the night of the tenth of March, 1793. The bell at Notre-Dame had just struck ten, and each stroke rang out clear and distinct, one after the other, before flying off into the ether like a night bird soaring from some bronze nest, sad, monotonous, and resonant.

Night had descended on Paris. But it was not the usual noisy, stormy Paris night, punctuated by lightning yet cold and misty. Paris itself was not the Paris we know today, dazzling by night with its thousands of lights reflected in its golden mire, the Paris of busy promeneurs, jubilant whisperings, and deliciously sleazy outskirts where fierce feuds and reckless crimes flourish, a wildly roaring furnace. It was a shabby little dive, tremulous, beetling, whose rarely seen inhabitants would run whenever they had to cross a street and scuttle away into their alleyways or under their porte-cochères, the way feral creatures pursued by hunters sink into their burrows.

It was, in a word, the Paris of the tenth of March, 1793, as I think I might have said. But first let me tell you a little bit about the extreme situation that made the capital so different from what it is today, and then we can start on the events that are the whole point of this story.

With the death of Louis XVI,[1] France cut its ties[2] with the rest of Europe. The three enemies it had already defeated[3]—Prussia, the Austro-Hungarian Empire,[4] and Piedmont—were then joined by England, Holland, and Spain. Sweden and Denmark alone maintained their former neutrality, busy as they were watching Catherine II tear up Poland,[5] as it happens.

The situation was alarming. Less looked down upon as a physical force, but also less esteemed as a moral one, since the September massacres[6] and the execution of Louis XVI on the twenty-first of January, France was literally surrounded, like a mere town, by the whole of Europe. England was at the coast, Spain along the Pyrenees, Piedmont and Austria across the Alps, Holland and Prussia to the north of the Netherlands, and at one single point, at Escaut, along the Upper Rhine, two hundred fifty thousand combatants marched against the Republic.

Our generals were thrust back at every turn. Maczinski had been forced to abandon Aix-la-Chapelle and to withdraw to Liège. Steingel and Neuilly were pushed back to the Limburg; Miranda, who had been laying siege to Maastricht, fell back on Tongres. Valence and Dampierre,[7] reduced to beating a hasty retreat, had let part of their supplies be spirited away. More than ten thousand deserters had already fled the army and scattered throughout the interior. Finally, the Convention,[8] putting all its hopes in Dumouriez[9] alone, had fired off letter after letter to the general ordering him to quit the banks of the Biesboos, where he was preparing a landing in Holland, and to return and take command of the army of the Meuse.

Vulnerable at the heart like a living body, France felt in its very heart—for that is what Paris was—every one of the blows that invasion, revolt, or treason leveled against its extremities. Every victory brought a riot of joy, every defeat an uprising of terror. It is not hard to imagine the tumult that broke out with the news of the successive defeats France had just suffered.

On the ninth of March, the day before, the meeting of the National Convention had been among the stormiest ever held; all officers had received the order to join their regiments at the same time. And Danton,[10] that undaunted proposer of things that were impossible but that nevertheless somehow got done, Danton, taking the stand, cried out: "There are not enough soldiers, you say? Let's give Paris a chance to save France! Let's ask Paris for thirty thousand men and send them to Dumouriez, and then not only will France be saved, but Belgium will be in the bag and Holland will be ours."

The proposal was greeted with cries of enthusiasm. Registers were opened in all the forty-eight sections[11] of Paris, which were invited to meet that night. Theaters and cabarets were shut down so that there would be no distractions, and the black flag was hoisted at the Hôtel de Ville as a distress signal.

Before midnight, thirty-five thousand names had been entered in those same registers. Yet what happened that night was a repeat of what had already happened in the bloody days of September: in every section, wherever volunteers signed up, they demanded that all traitors be punished before they themselves left for the front.

Traitors were, in effect, any counterrevolutionaries and secret conspirators who threatened from within a Revolution that was clearly threatened from without. But as you can well imagine, the term was as flexible as the extremist parties then tearing France apart wanted it to be. Traitors were whoever was the weakest. It so happened that the Girondins were the weakest, so the Montagnards[12]—the Mountain—decided the Girondins would be the traitors.

The next day—this particular next day being the tenth of March—all the Montagnard deputies made sure they turned up at the meeting of the Convention. The Jacobins[13] came armed and had just filled the stands after chasing the women away when the mayor of Paris[14] rose and presented himself alongside the council of the Commune.[15] He confirmed the report of the commissioners of the Convention about the general dedication of the citizens and reiterated the wish, expressed unanimously the day before, for an extraordinary tribunal to be set up expressly to judge traitors.

Immediately the cry went up for a committee report, and immediately the committee met. Ten minutes later, Robert Lindet[16] emerged to announce that a special tribunal composed of nine completely independent judges would be appointed and divided into two permanent sections, which would gain convictions by whatever means they chose and would pursue, either directly or at the request of the Convention, anyone and everyone attempting to lead the people astray.

As we know, the term "traitor" was most malleable, and the extension of these powers was far-reaching. The Girondins immediately understood that the whole point of the move was to make it easy to arrest them, and they rose as one.

"We'd rather die," they cried, "than consent to the setting up of this Venetian Inquisition."

In reply to this bit of invective, the Montagnards demanded the motion be put to the vote by a show of hands.

"Yes!" cried Féroud.[17] "Yes, let's vote and show the world who it is that seeks to assassinate innocence in the name of the law."

A vote was in fact taken and, contrary to all expectations, the majority declared, first, that there would be juries; second, that these juries would be made up of equal numbers from all the departments of France; and, third, that they would be handpicked by the Convention.

The moment these three proposals were accepted, a great roar was heard. The Convention was in the habit of visits from the general public. When they asked what the racket was all about, they learned that a delegation of recruits had turned up, after dining at the wheat market, and was demanding to now parade before them.

The doors were promptly flung open and six hundred men, armed with swords, pistols, and pikes, appeared, half drunk and calling deafeningly for death to all traitors as they trotted round to the sound of wild applause.

"Yes!" Collot d'Herbois[18] shouted back. "Yes, my friends, despite all the intrigues, we will save you, you—and liberty!"

With that he shot a deadly look at the Girondins, one that made it clear they were not out of the woods. Indeed, as soon as the meeting of the Convention was over, the Montagnards fanned out to the other revolutionary clubs, eagerly taking to the Cordeliers[19] and the Jacobins the proposition that traitors be declared outlaws and their throats cut that very night.

Louvet's wife was at home in the rue Saint-Honoré, close to the Jacobins' club. She came rushing downstairs when she heard the commotion and ran to the club to see what was going on. When she heard the proposal, she raced back upstairs as fast as her legs would carry her to warn her husband. Louvet swiftly armed himself and went running from door to door to warn his friends, all of whom were out. He learned from one of their servants that they were all over at Pétion's place and flew there himself, only to find his cronies sitting around quietly debating a bill they were planning to introduce the following day and which they flattered themselves would be adopted, lulled as they were by a chance majority. Louvet[20] told them what was afoot and that he feared the worst, since the Jacobins and Cordeliers were scheming against them even as they sat. He wound up by inviting them to take forceful measures of their own.

Pétion then rose, calm and imperturbable as ever, went to the window, and looked out at the sky. He stuck his hand out and whipped it back streaming with water.

"It's raining," he said. "Nothing will happen tonight."

Through the open window, the last ringing stroke of the clock told them it was ten o'clock.

And that is what happened in Paris on the day before the tenth and on the tenth; which is why, on the evening of the tenth, in the rainy darkness and the unnerving silence, houses built to shelter the living became as mute and somber as sepulchres peopled exclusively by the dead.

Long lines of wary National Guards, preceded by scouts with bayonets at the ready; troops of citizens belonging to the sections, armed with whatever they could find and sticking close together; gendarmes poking into every nook and cranny, every gaping alleyway: these were, indeed, the sole inhabitants of the town to venture out into the streets, such was the overwhelming feeling that something unfamiliar and terrible was about to happen.

A fine, icy rain was falling. The same rain that had reassured Pétion only intensified the bad mood and malaise of the militia, whose every encounter had the feel of a prelude to a fight, with a reluctant mutual acknowledgment leading to an exchange of the password only begrudgingly and ungraciously. You would have thought from the nervous way people separated and sidled off, looking back over their shoulders, that everyone was afraid of being jumped from behind.

On that same night, when Paris was in the grip of one of those panic attacks that were by now so frequent you'd think people would have gotten used to them, that night when everyone knew without saying that the lukewarm among the revolutionaries were about to be slaughtered, since they had voted mostly with misgivings for the death of the King and now shrank from the death of the Queen (a prisoner, locked up in the Temple[21] along with her children and the King's sister); that very night, a woman wrapped in a cloak of lilac calico with black fur trim, her head covered by, or rather buried in, the cloak's hood, glided noiselessly past the houses along the rue Saint-Honoré. She slipped out of sight in the odd doorway or in the shadow of a wall whenever a patrol appeared and stood as still as a statue, not daring to breathe until the patrol had passed; then she would dash frantically ahead again until danger once more presented itself and forced her to stop in her tracks, holding her breath.

The woman had already managed to make it part of the way down the rue Saint-Honoré, thanks to this uncommon stealth, when, at the corner of the rue de Grenelle she suddenly fell upon a troop—not one of the regular patrols but a small band of the brave volunteers who had dined at the wheat market and whose patriotism was further exalted by the number of toasts they had drunk to their future victories. The poor woman gave out a yelp and turned to flee down the rue du Coq.

"Hey, you! You there, citizeness!"[22] cried one of the volunteers, the chief, in fact, for already the need to be told what to do, so natural to human beings, had caused our worthy patriots to appoint chiefs to rule over them. "Hey! You! Where do you think you're going?"

The fugitive kept running without a word.

"Take aim!" said the chief. "That's got to be a man in disguise, some aristocrat hoping to escape!"

The sound of two or three guns going off in hands a little too unsteady to be accurate told the poor woman that the jig was up.

"No! No!" she cried, coming to an abrupt halt and retracing her steps. "No, citizen, you are mistaken. I am not a man."

"Well, then, come forward—and that's an order!" said the chief. "So tell me where you're going like that, my little night owl. And don't beat around the bush."

"But, citizen, I'm not going anywhere. . . . I'm going home."

"Ah! You're going home!"

"Yes."

"Going home a little late for an honest woman, citizeness."

"I've been visiting a sick relative."

"Poor little lamb," said the chief, with a movement of the hand that caused the woman to swiftly step back in fright. "So where's our card?"

"Card? What card, citizen? What are you talking about? What do you want?"

"Didn't you read the Commune decree?"

"No."

"You must have heard the town crier shouting about it?"

"No, I did not. What does it say, this decree? God!"

"First of all, we no longer say 'God'; we say 'Supreme Being.'"

"Sorry, I forgot. Old habits die hard."

"Bad habits, aristocratic habits."

"It won't happen again. But you were saying . . . ?"

"I was saying that the Commune decree bars any excursion after ten o'clock at night without an identity card. Do you have your identity card?"

"I'm afraid not."

"Did you leave it at your relative's?"

"I didn't know you had to have this card to go out."

"In that case, we'd better check in at the nearest station and you can have a nice little chat with the captain. If he's happy with you, he'll get a couple of lads to escort you home; if not, he'll keep you till we have more information. To the left, quick, march!"

Hearing the small shriek of terror that escaped the prisoner, the chief of the volunteers realized that the poor woman was more than a little alarmed at such a prospect.

"Oh, dear!" he said. "Something tells me we've caught us a most distinguished little bunny rabbit here. All right, my little *ci-devant*[23] aristocrat, let's move it!"

With that the chief grabbed the defendant's arm, clamped it under his own, and dragged her off, sobbing, in the direction of the police station at Palais-Egalité.[24] They had gone as far as the Sergeants' barrier when, suddenly, a young man of considerable stature, wrapped in a greatcoat, turned the corner of the rue Croix-des-Petits-Champs at the very moment the prisoner was begging to be set free. But the chief of the volunteers yanked her violently on without paying any heed, the young woman whimpering, half in fright, half in pain.

When the young man saw the woman struggling and heard her cry, he bounded from one side of the street to the other to face the troop.

"What gives? What are you doing with this woman?" he asked the man who appeared to be the chief.

"Why don't you mind your own business instead of asking me questions?"

"Who is this woman, citizens, and what do you want with her?" the young man repeated in an even more commanding tone.

"And who are you, might I ask, to question us?"

The young man threw open his coat to reveal a military uniform on which gleamed an epaulet. "I am an officer," he said, "as you can see."

"An officer? What in?"

"In the National Guard."[25]

"Well, well, well! And what's that to us, eh?" said one of the troop. "What are the officers of the National Guard to us?"

"What's he on about?" asked another of the troop in the special drawl and caustic, ironic tone of a true man of the people, or rather of the populace of Paris, beginning to be riled.

"What he's on about," the young man replied, "is that if the epaulet doesn't get respect for the officer, the sword will get respect for the epaulet."

With that the young woman's unidentified defender stepped back and swept aside the folds of his coat, allowing a broad and substantial infantry saber to shine brightly in the light of the streetlamp. Then, with a deft movement that spoke of a certain familiarity with armed combat, he seized the chief of the volunteers by the collar of his car-magnole.[26] Holding the point of the saber against the man's neck, he said, "Now, let's have a friendly chat."

"But, citizen . . ." stammered the chief of the volunteers, struggling to get free.

"I warn you: the slightest move you make, the slightest move your men make, and I'll run you through with my sword."

While this was going on, two of the volunteers continued to hold the woman. "You asked me who I was," the young man continued. "You had no right to ask since you don't command a regular patrol, but I'll tell you anyway. I am Maurice Lindey. I commanded a battery of gunners on the tenth of August.[27] I am a lieutenant in the National

Guard and secretary of the Frères et Amis section.[28] Is that enough for you?"

"Ah, citizen lieutenant," answered the chief, still threatened by the blade, the tip of which he could feel pressing sharper and deeper into his neck. "That's a different matter. If you really are who you say you are, that is, a good patriot . . ."

"There. I knew it wouldn't take much to come to an understanding," said the officer. "Now it's your turn. Tell me, why was this woman crying? What were you doing to her?"

"We were just taking her to the station."

"And why were you taking her to the station?"

"Because she doesn't have an identity card and the latest decree of the Commune states that anyone mad enough to be out in the streets of Paris after ten o'clock at night without an identity card is to be arrested. Have you forgotten our beloved homeland is in danger and that the black flag is flying over the Hôtel de Ville?"

"The black flag is flying over the Hôtel de Ville and our homeland is in danger because two hundred thousand slaves are marching[29] on France," the officer retorted. "And not because some woman is running around the streets of Paris after ten o'clock at night. But never mind, citizens, there's a Commune decree, so you're within your rights. If you'd only told me that straightaway, things would have been quicker and a lot less unpleasant. It's a fine thing to be a patriot, but it doesn't hurt to be polite. The first officer citizens should respect, it seems to me, should be the one they themselves elected. Now take this woman away if you want, you're free to go."

"Oh, citizen!" This time it was the woman. She lunged at the officer and took hold of his arm, having followed the debate in a state of profound anxiety. "Please don't abandon me to the mercy of these drunken barbarians."

"As you wish," said Maurice. "Take my arm; I'll escort you to the station with them."

"To the station," the woman repeated in fright. "To the station! But why take me to the station? I've done no harm to anyone."

"We are taking you to the station," said Maurice, "not because you have done any harm, not because we suppose you capable of doing any harm, but because a Commune decree prohibits anyone going out without a card and you don't seem to have one."

"But, monsieur, I didn't know."

"Citizeness, you will find decent men at the station who'll appreciate your reasons and from whom you have nothing to fear."

"Monsieur," said the young woman, squeezing the officer's arm. "It is not insult I fear at this point. It is death. If you take me to the station, I am finished."

2

THE STRANGER

In her voice there was such a note of fear and distinction combined that a shiver ran down Maurice's spine. Like a jab of electricity, that ringing voice pierced his heart.

He turned to the volunteers, who were busy conferring among themselves. Humiliated at having been brought to heel by a lone man, they were clearly working out how to regain lost ground. They numbered eight to one; three of them had guns, the others pistols and lances. Maurice had only his sword. The battle would hardly be equal.

The woman herself understood as much, for she dropped her head upon her chest with a heavy sigh. Maurice stood frowning, his upper lip curled in a disdainful sneer, his sword unsheathed, as he wavered between manly instincts that compelled him to defend this woman and his duties as a citizen, which urged him to hand her over.

Suddenly, at the corner of the rue des Bons-Enfants, several rifles flashed like streaks of lightning and the measured tread of a patrol on the march could be heard. At the sight of people gathered together, the patrol halted, roughly ten feet away, and the voice of their lance corporal sounded the cry: "Who goes there?"

"Friend! Friend!" cried Maurice. "Over here, Lorin." The man to whom this injunction was addressed sallied forth at the head of eight men, who followed hot on his heels.

"Ah! It's you, Maurice," said the corporal. "You devil! What are you doing gadding about the streets at this time of night?"

"As you can probably tell, I've just left the Frères et Amis section."

"Yes, only to hook up with the Sœurs et Amies.[1] I know all about that:

> Listen, *ma belle:*
> On the stroke of twelve
> An eager hand
> The hand of a lover
> Will silently glide
> Through the shadows
> And slide back the bolts
> That have locked you in
> Since nightfall.

"That about sums it up, *n'est-ce pas?*"

"No, my friend, you've got it wrong. I was heading straight home when I found this citizeness struggling in the hands of these citizen recruits. I ran over and asked them why they wanted to arrest her."

"That sounds like you," said Lorin. "Such is the nature of the French cavaliers,[2] as Voltaire said." The corporal-poet then turned toward the recruits. "And why were you arresting this woman?" he demanded.

"We already told the lieutenant," came the reply from the chief of the smaller troop. "Because she doesn't have an identity card."

"Oh, what poppycock!" said Lorin. "There's a juicy crime for you!"

"Don't you know about the Commune decree, then?" asked the chief of the volunteers.

"Yes, of course I do; but there's another decree that renders that one null and void."

"What decree?"

"It goes like this:

> On the Pindus and Parnassus[3]
> Love has decreed
> That Beauty, Youth, and Grace
> May, any hour of the day,

At their own pace
Pass without a pass.

"How do you like that as a decree, citizen? Sounds quite gallant to me."

"Yes, but it doesn't strike me as exactly decisive. For a start, it's not in that popular rag *Le Moniteur*;[4] second, we are not on the Pindus or Parnassus; further, this is night, not day; and lastly, the citizeness may well be neither young, beautiful, nor graceful."

"I bet you the opposite," said Lorin. "Let's have a look, citizeness. Prove to me that I am right. Take down your hood and let everyone see whether you meet the conditions of the decree."

"Oh, monsieur!" said the young woman, hiding behind Maurice. "You protected me from your enemies; please protect me from your friends."

"You see, you see!" cried the chief of the volunteers. "She's hiding. I reckon she's some kind of spy for the aristocrats, the little hussy, some kind of nocturnal man-eater."

"Oh, monsieur!" cried the young woman, pulling Maurice toward her and unveiling a face at once ravishingly beautiful, youthful, and distinguished, radiant in the light of the streetlamp. "Look at me! How do I look?"

Maurice was dazzled. Never had he dreamed of anything remotely resembling what he glimpsed. We say glimpsed, for the stranger covered her face up again almost as swiftly as she had uncovered it.

"Lorin," Maurice whispered. "You take charge of conducting the prisoner to the station. You have a right to, as head of the patrol."

"Right you are!" said the young corporal. "Say no more." Then, turning to the stranger, he said, "Follow me, *ma belle*; since you don't wish to offer us proof that you meet the conditions of the decree, you'll have to follow me."

"Follow you? How come?" asked the chief of the volunteers.

"We will, of course, conduct the citizeness to the station at the Hôtel de Ville where we are keeping guard, and we will take down any relevant information about her there."

"Not on your life!" said the chief of the original troop. "She's ours and we intend to hang on to her."

"Ah, citizens, we are starting to get annoyed," said Lorin.

"Get annoyed all you like; it's all the same to us. We're the real soldiers of the Republic. While you're out patrolling the streets of Paris, we'll be spilling our blood at the front."

"See that you don't spill it on the way, citizens. That's exactly what will happen if you don't show a bit more respect."

"Respect is an aristocratic virtue. We are the sans culottes,[5] don't you know!" retorted the volunteers.

"Bully for you!" Lorin shot back. "But let's not discuss such things in front of the lady. She may well be English for all we know. No offense, my lovely night owl," he added, turning gallantly toward the stranger.

> A poet has said, and we can only repeat
> After him, humble echo at best:
>> "I' the world's volume
>> Our Britain seems as of it, but not in it:
>> In a great pool, a swan's nest."

"Aha! You've given yourself away there!" cried the chief of the volunteers. "Admit you're one of Pitt's men,[6] in the payroll of England, a..."

"Do be quiet!" said Lorin. "Poetry is not your forte, my friend. I see I'll have to address you in prose. Listen, we may be nice polite National Guards, but we're still children of Paris: when someone really gets our goat, we come down hard."

"Madame," said Maurice. "You see what's happening and you can guess what's going to happen; in five minutes, ten or twelve men are going to cut each other's throats over you. The cause that those who wish to defend you have embraced—is it worth the blood that will be shed?"

"Monsieur," replied the mystery woman, bringing her hands together. "There is only one thing I can say, one single thing: if you allow me to be arrested, the consequences for me and others would be so catastrophic, I'd rather you ran my heart through with that weapon in your hand right now and threw my body into the Seine than abandon me."

"Say no more, madame," said Maurice. "I'll take full responsibility." And letting go the hands of the beautiful stranger, which he had clutched, he addressed the National Guards: "Citizens, as your officer, as a patriot, and as a Frenchman, I order you to protect this woman. And you, Lorin, if these guttersnipes utter a word, use your bayonet!"

"Ready! Aim!" cried Lorin.

"Oh God, oh God!" cried the stranger, swaddling her head in her hood and slumping onto a stone post for support. "God protect him."

The volunteers stumbled around trying to get into a defensive position. One of them even fired a shot from his pistol, and the bullet whistled straight through Maurice's hat.

"Cross bayonets," said Lorin. "Attack!"

In the shadows there followed a brief scuffle and momentary confusion during which one or two blasts from firearms rang out, followed by imprecations, cries, blasphemous shouts. Nobody came to help, for as we said at the beginning, the rumor of a massacre being about to take place had made the rounds, a massacre was therefore silently expected, and so it seemed the massacre had begun. Only two or three windows opened—only to promptly shut again.

Less numerous and less well armed, the volunteers were instantly out of the fight. Two of them were seriously injured, four others stood pinned against the wall with bayonets aimed at their chests.

"Right," said Lorin. "I hope you'll be as gentle as lambs from here on. As for you, citizen Maurice, I order you to take this woman to the station at the Hôtel de Ville. You understand that you will be held responsible."

"Yes," said Maurice, adding, under his breath, "What's the password?"

"Oh, damn!" said Lorin, scratching his ear. "The password . . . is . . . um."

"Aren't you worried I might put it to bad use?"

"Please!" said Lorin. "What you do with it is up to you."

"So you were saying?" Maurice said.

"I was saying I'd tell you in a moment. Let's get rid of these great lumps first. After that, I wouldn't mind giving you a few other words of advice before I bid you good night."

"Fine. I'll be waiting."

Lorin returned to his National Guards, who were still holding the volunteers at bay. "There now, have you had enough?" he asked.

"Yes, you Girondin dog," the chief answered.

"You've got it all wrong, my friend," said Lorin, calmly. "We are better sans culottes than you are, for we belong to the Thermopylae club,[7] and no one would question their patriotism, I hope. Let the citizens past, they're not putting up a fight."

"It remains the case that if this woman is a suspect . . ."

"If she were a suspect, she would have run away while we were fighting instead of waiting, as you see, for the fight to end."

"Hmm!" murmured one of the volunteers. "That's true enough, what he says, this Mister Thermopyle."

"Anyway, we'll hear all about it—because while my friend here is taking her to the station, the rest of us will go and drink to the health of the nation."

"We're going to go and have a drink?" asked the chief.

"Certainly. I'm as thirsty as anything, and I know a nice little tavern at the corner of the rue Thomas-du-Louvre!"

"Well, why didn't you say so in the first place, citizen? We're sorry to have doubted your patriotism; to prove the point, let's shake hands in the name of the nation and the law."

"Let's!" said Lorin.

And the recruits and the National Guards shook one another's hands heartily. In those days, they were as happy to kiss and make up as they were to cut one another's heads off.

"Off we go, friends," cried the two united troops. "To the corner of the rue Thomas-du-Louvre!"

"What about us?" wailed the wounded. "You're not just going to leave us here, are you?"

"I'm afraid so," said Lorin. "We are going to leave you, we're going to abandon you, you brave fellows who have fallen fighting for your country—against your fellow countrymen, it's true; and by mistake, truer still. But don't worry—we'll send stretchers for you. While you're waiting, why not sing the *Marseillaise*,[8] that'll keep your mind off things.

> *Allons, enfants de la Patrie,*
> *Le jour de gloire est arrivé."*

With that parting shot, Lorin walked over to Maurice, who was standing with his mysterious captive at the corner of the rue du Coq, while the National Guards and the recruits headed back arm in arm toward the place du Palais-Egalité.

"Maurice," he said. "I promised you a bit of advice, so here it is. Come with us—don't compromise yourself by protecting this citizeness. She seems to me to be a perfectly charming creature, but that doesn't make her any less suspect. After all, what is a charming woman doing running around the streets of Paris in the middle of the night . . . ?"

"Monsieur," the woman cut in, "do not judge me by appearances, please."

"First, you use the word *monsieur,* which is a big mistake, don't you know, citizeness? Notice you don't hear me using old, polite forms of address."

"All right, citizen; but why not just let your friend finish his kind deed?"

"How do you mean?"

"By taking me home and ensuring my safety until I get there."

"Maurice! Maurice!" said Lorin. "Think what you are about to do. You are compromising yourself horribly."

"Yes, I'm well aware," said the young man. "But what can I do? If I abandon the poor woman, she'll be stopped every step of the way by the patrols."

"Yes, I will! Whereas, if I'm with you, monsieur . . . monsieur, I mean citizen, I'll be saved."

"You hear that: saved!" said Lorin. "So she's in mortal danger?"

"My dear Lorin," said Maurice. "Let's be reasonable. Either she's a good patriot or she's an aristocrat. If she's an aristocrat, we would turn

out to be wrong to protect her; if she's a good patriot, it's our duty to
see she's safe."

"Forgive me, dear friend, and my apologies to Aristotle and all, but
your logic is pathetic. You're like the man who says:

> Iris has stolen my reason
> And demands that I be wise."

"Lorin, leave Dorat, Parny, and Gentil-Bernard[9] out of it, please.
Seriously, will you or will you not give me the password?"

"In other words, Maurice, you're putting me in a situation where I
have to sacrifice either my duty to my friend, or my friend to my duty.
And you know as well as I do that it'll be duty that goes."

"You decide what it's going to be, my friend. But for heaven's sake,
get on with it."

"You won't misuse the password?"

"I promise."

"That's not enough: swear!"

"On what?"

"Swear on the altar of the nation."

Lorin promptly took his hat off and handed it to Maurice with the
military insignia known as cockades[10] facing him. Maurice, who acted as
though the whole performance were perfectly normal, kept a straight
face as he swore the required oath on the improvised altar.

"And now," said Lorin, "here is the password: *Gaul and Lutetia.* . . .[11]
You might find people will say to you, as they have to me, 'Gaul and
Lucretia,' but who cares! Let them pass anyway. It's all Roman."

"Citizeness," said Maurice. "I am now at your service. Thank you,
Lorin."

"Safe trip!" said Lorin, clapping the altar of the nation back on his
head. Then, true to his anacreontic tastes, he sauntered away muttering:

> "At last, my dear Eleanor,
> You have done the delicious deed
> You feared, yet hoped for;

You tasted, still quivering,
So, tell me: what's so frightening?"

3

RUE DES FOSSÉS-SAINT-VICTOR

Maurice suddenly found himself alone with the young woman and was momentarily embarrassed. The fear of being played for a fool, the lure of her wondrous beauty, a vague feeling of remorse that grated on his pure, passionately republican conscience, held him back just as he was about to give the woman his arm.

"Where are we going, citizeness?" he asked.

"Alas, monsieur, quite a way," she replied.

"Yes, but . . ."

"Over near the Jardin des Plantes."

"So be it. Shall we go?"

"Oh, dear, monsieur!" said the stranger. "I can see I'm being a nuisance. Believe me, if it weren't for the terrible trouble I'm in, if I were only afraid of the usual dangers, I would not abuse your generosity like this."

"Yes, well, madame," said Maurice, suddenly forgetting the prescribed republican vocabulary in this tête-à-tête and swiftly reverting to everyday speech, "how is it, in all conscience, that you're out on the streets of Paris at this hour? You can see for yourself there isn't a soul about except you and me."

"Monsieur, I told you: I went to visit someone in the faubourg du Roule. I left at midday without hearing anything about the new decree and I was coming back none the wiser. I spent all my time in a fairly out-of-the-way place."

"Yes," murmured Maurice. "In the house of some *ci-devant* aristocrat, in some aristocrat's lair. Admit it, citizeness: while you're outwardly begging my support, you're inwardly laughing at me for giving it."

"I am!" she cried. "How do you mean?"

"It's pretty clear. You've managed to get a republican to serve you as a guide. Well, this republican happens to be betraying his cause: it's as simple as that."

"But, citizen," said the stranger with real verve, "you are mistaken. I love the Republic as much as you do."

"Well, then, citizeness, if you're such a good patriot, you have nothing to hide. Where were you coming from, where have you been?"

"Oh, monsieur, have some pity!" said the stranger.

In that *monsieur* there was such a deep and touching expression of propriety that Maurice felt certain he got her gist. "No doubt about it," he said to himself. "This woman's returning from some amorous tryst." And though he did not know why, the thought gave his heart a pang and caused him suddenly to clam up.

They headed off into the night, and when they had reached the rue de la Verrerie, having encountered three or four patrols who had let them continue freely on their way thanks to Maurice's use of the password, an officer of a fifth patrol seemed determined to make trouble. Maurice thought it best at this point to add his name and address to the password.

"Right," said the officer. "That's you taken care of, but what about the citizeness. . . ."

"Go on: the citizeness?"

"Who is she?"

"She is . . . my wife's sister."

The officer let them pass.

"So, you are married, monsieur?" the stranger murmured.

"No, madame, why do you ask?"

"Because," she laughed, "it would have been easier to say I was your wife."

"Madame," Maurice replied solemnly, "the word *wife* is a sacred title, one that should not be used lightly. I do not have the honor of knowing you."

It was the beautiful stranger's turn to feel a pang in the region of the heart; she said no more. By now, they were halfway across the pont-Marie. The young woman picked up the pace noticeably the closer they got to the end of the run. They zipped across the pont de la Tournelle[1] in a flash.

"Here we are in your neighborhood, I presume," Maurice said as he stepped onto the quai Saint-Bernard.

"Yes, citizen. But it is precisely here that I most need your help."

"Really, madame, you don't want me to be indiscreet but at the same time you're doing everything you can to excite my curiosity. That's not nice. Let's have a little trust; surely I've earned it. Won't you do me the honor of telling me to whom I am speaking?"

"You are speaking, monsieur, to a woman whom you have saved from the greatest danger she has ever experienced. One who will be grateful to you for the rest of her life."

"I'd settle for less, madame. Won't you be a little less grateful and a little more forthcoming and tell me your name?"

"I can't."

"Yet you'd have told the first police officer you met if we'd taken you to the station."

"No, never!" cried the stranger.

"But then you'd have been put in jail."

"I was ready for anything."

"But these days, jail . . ."

"Means the guillotine, I know."

"And you would have preferred the guillotine?"

"To betrayal . . . To say my name would have meant betrayal!"

"As I was saying, you're making me play a funny part for a republican!"

"You are playing the part of a man with a true heart. You find a poor woman being threatened but you don't turn your back on her even though she's a working-class girl, since she may easily be threatened again. So you snatch her from the jaws of death and bring her home to the poor slums where she lives. That's all."

"Yes, you're right; at least, that's what it looks like. I myself might have believed that story if I hadn't seen you, if you hadn't spoken to me. But your beauty, the way you speak, show you to be a woman of distinction, the absolute opposite of your getup and this slum. All of which proves to me that your little late-night foray is covering up some mystery. You don't say anything. . . . Well, don't say anything. Do we still have far to go, madame?"

At that point, they were entering the rue des Fossés-Saint-Victor.

"You see that small blackened building?" the mystery woman asked

Maurice, pointing to a house just visible beyond the walls of the Jardin des Plantes. "When we get there, you will leave me."

"As you like, madame. Your wish is my command."

"Are you annoyed with me?"

"Me? Not in the slightest. Besides, what does it matter to you?"

"It matters a lot to me, for I have one more favor to ask you."

"Which is?"

"I want us to say good-bye . . . like proper friends."

"Proper friends! Oh! You do me too great an honor, madame. Funny sort of friend who doesn't know his friend's name and from whom his friend conceals her address, no doubt dreading she'll see him again if she gives it to him."

The woman bowed her head and did not reply.

"As for that other business, madame," Maurice continued, "if I stumbled across your secret, you must not hold that against me. It was not my intention."

"Here we are, monsieur," said the stranger.

They were opposite the old rue Saint-Jacques, which was lined by tall black houses and pockmarked by dark alleys and lanes where factories and tanneries stood, for the Bièvre River[2] runs close by.

"Here?" said Maurice. "You're joking! This is where you live?"

"Yes."

"I don't believe it!"

"Yet there you have it. Adieu, adieu, then, my brave chevalier.[3] Adieu, generous protector."

"Adieu, madame," Maurice replied with gentle irony. "But tell me, humor me a little, you really are out of danger now?"

"I am."

"In that case, I'll be off."

And with that, Maurice took two steps back and coldly saluted. The stranger didn't move a muscle.

"This was not what I had in mind," she said. "Come now, monsieur Maurice, your hand." Maurice approached the woman and held out his hand, and as he did so he felt her slip a ring onto his finger.

"Citizeness, what do you think you're doing? You must know you've lost one of your rings?"

"Oh, monsieur, what you're doing now is wrong."

"So, the only vice I was lacking, eh, madame, was ingratitude?"

"Please, monsieur, please . . . my friend. Don't leave me this way. Please, what would you like? What do you need?"

"As payment, you mean?" said the young man savagely.

"No," said the stranger, flashing him a bewitching look. "But to pardon me for the secret I'm forced to keep from you."

Maurice saw her beautiful eyes glistening with tears in the dark and he felt her warm hand tremble in his, heard her voice, which was now as soft as a prayer, and he went instantly from anger to a feeling of wild excitement.

"What do I need?" he cried. "I need to see you again."

"Can't be done."

"Just once, for an hour, a minute, a second."

"Not possible, I tell you."

"What?" Maurice demanded. "You mean to tell me seriously that I'll never see you again?"

"Never!" said the woman in what sounded like a mournful echo.

"Oh, madame. You really are toying with me." And he raised his noble head and shook his long streaming hair in the manner of a man trying to break free of some power holding him against his will. The mystery woman watched him with an indefinable expression on her face. It was clear she had not gotten off scot-free from the feelings she had aroused.

"Listen to me," she said after a moment of silence, interrupted only by a sigh Maurice vainly sought to suppress. "Listen! Do you swear on your honor to close your eyes when I tell you and count to sixty? Cross your heart and hope to die. . . ."

"And if I do, what will happen to me?"

"I will prove my gratitude to you in a way I promise you I never will to anyone ever again, even if they do more for me than you have—which would be hard. . . . That is what will happen."

"Surely you can just tell me. . . ."

"No. Trust me, you'll see. . . ."

"Really, madame, I can't tell whether you're an angel or a fiend."

"Do you swear?"

"Oh, all right. I swear!"

"Whatever happens, you won't open your eyes? . . . Whatever happens, you understand, even if you felt yourself being stabbed?"

"This is the dizzy limit, madame."

"Swear, monsieur! It seems to me you have little to lose."

"All right, I swear, whatever happens," said Maurice, closing his eyes. But he opened them again.

"Let me see you one more time, just once, please," he begged.

The woman flipped back her hood with a smile not entirely free of coquetry. By the light of the moon, which slid out from between two clouds at that very moment, Maurice saw for a second time the long black curls hanging down, the perfect arc of the eyebrows, which looked painted on with India ink, two almond-shaped eyes, soft and velvety, an exquisitely chiseled nose, fresh lips gleaming like coral.

"Oh! You are beautiful, so beautiful, too beautiful!" cried Maurice.

"Close your eyes," whispered the stranger, and Maurice did as he was told. The woman took both his hands in hers and spun him round. Suddenly he felt something like perfumed heat waft toward his face and a mouth brushed his mouth, leaving the ring he had spurned between his lips.

The sensation was as fleeting as a thought and it burned like fire. Maurice felt something akin to pain, so unexpected and profound it shot to the bottom of his heart and set it singing. He lurched forward, stretching out his arms in front of him.

"You gave me your word!" cried a voice already remote.

Maurice pressed his palms to his eyes to resist the temptation to break his promise. He was no longer counting, he was no longer thinking; he stood silent, paralyzed yet unsteady on his legs. After a moment he heard what sounded like a door shutting fifty or sixty feet away, then everything fell silent once more. He spread his fingers, opened his eyes, looked around as though coming out of sleep; maybe he actually would have felt he was simply waking from a dream if the ring that made this incredible episode an incontestable reality were not lying there, hard between his burning lips.

4

THE CUSTOMS OF THE DAY

When Maurice Lindey came to and looked around, he saw nothing but dark alleys running left and right wherever he looked. He tried to get his bearings and work out where he was, but his mind was reeling, the night was dark; the moon, which had come out briefly to shed light on the stranger's haunting face, had gone back behind the clouds. After a moment of cruel uncertainty, he set off on the path that led to his home in the rue Roule.

When he reached the rue Sainte-Avoye, Maurice was surprised at the number of patrols circulating in the Temple quartier.

"What's the matter, then, Sergeant?" he asked the chief of a very busy patrol that had just carried out a search in the rue des Fontaines.

"The matter?" said the sergeant. "My dear officer, the matter is that they tried to break out the Capet woman[1] and her brood this very night."

"How's that?"

"Some patrol of ex-aristocrats managed to get ahold of the password and worm their way into the Temple dressed as chasseurs[2] of the National Guard, and they would have carted her off, too, except that, fortunately, the one who was supposed to be the corporal spoke to the officer in charge of the watch and called him 'monsieur'; gave himself away, he did, the dirty aristocrat!"

"I'll be damned!" Maurice let out. "And have the conspirators been arrested?"

"No. The patrol made it back out onto the street and scattered."

"Any chance of catching up with any of them?"

"Oh! There's only one worth catching and that's the chief, a great tall streak of a thing. He was introduced into the watch by one of the municipal officers on duty. Did he make us run, the mongrel! But he must have found a back door somewhere and he got away through the Madelonnettes prison."[3]

In any other circumstances, Maurice would have spent the rest of the night with the patriots keeping watch over the safety of the Republic. But for the last hour love of the nation was no longer his main concern, so he continued on his way, the news he had just learned gradually fading from his mind and evaporating behind the experience he had just been through. Besides, these so-called attempts at helping the Queen escape had become so frequent that even patriots knew that in certain circumstances they were more than handy as a political tool, so the news did not inspire any undue anxiety in our young republican.

When he got home, Maurice found his officieux waiting for him there. In those days people no longer had servants. Maurice, therefore, found his officieux waiting for him, indeed having fallen asleep waiting for him, and snoring fretfully.

He woke him with all the consideration due one's fellow, pulled his boots off for him, and sent him away so as not to have his thoughts disturbed, and then he went to bed and, since the hour was late and he was young, fell asleep in turn despite his preoccupied state.

The next day he found a letter on his night table—a letter written in a fine, elegant, and unfamiliar hand. He looked at the seal; as sole motto, it bore the English word: *Nothing*.

He opened the letter which contained these words: "Thank you! Eternal gratitude on my part in exchange for eternal forgetfulness on yours! . . ."

Maurice called his servant. True patriots no longer rang for them, bells being thought to recall past servility. Besides, lots of officieux made this a condition of employment in their master's service when they signed up.

Maurice's officieux had been given the name of Jean at the baptismal font some thirty years previously, but in 1792 he had had himself debaptized, by his own private authority, Jean smacking of aristocracy and of deism. He now went by the name of Agesilaus.[4]

"Agesilaus!" Maurice began. "Do you know anything about this letter?"

"No, citizen."

"Who gave it to you?"

"The concierge."

"Who gave it to him?"

"A messenger, no doubt, since there's no national stamp on it."

"Go down and ask the concierge to come up."

The concierge came up because it was Maurice who asked him to and because Maurice was very much loved by all the officieux associated with him; but when he came, it was not without declaring that if it had been any other tenant, he would have asked him to come down.

The concierge was called Aristides. Maurice questioned him and found that it was a stranger who had brought the letter at about eight in the morning. The young man could ask as many questions as he liked, put them any way he liked, but that was all the concierge could tell him. Maurice begged him to accept ten francs and invited him, should this strange man turn up again, to follow him without further ado and come back and tell Maurice where he had gone.

We hasten to add that, to the great relief of Aristides, a tad humiliated by the idea of following one of his own kind, the man never reappeared.

Left to his own devices, Maurice screwed up the letter in a fit of pique. He pulled the ring off his finger and put it with the crumpled letter on the night table and turned his face to the wall in the vain hope of going back to sleep. But when, after an hour, he'd recovered from this show of bravado, Maurice kissed the ring and reread the letter. The ring was set with a stunningly beautiful sapphire.

The letter was, as we have said, a beguiling little note that reeked of aristocracy a mile off.

While Maurice was lost in contemplation, the door opened. Maurice stuck the ring back on his finger and shoved the letter under his bolster. Could this be the shyness of dawning love? Was it the shame of a patriot who does not want it to get about that he has any kind of connection with someone reckless enough to write such a note, the perfume alone being enough to compromise both the hand that wrote it and the hand that broke its seal?

The man who burst in on Maurice was a young man in patriot's garb, but of the most supreme elegance. His carmagnole was made of fine fabric, his pants were of cashmere, and his chiné hose were of finest silk. As for his Phrygian cap[5] it would have put Paris himself[6] to shame with its elegant shape and its luscious purple hue.

On top of all this he wore at his belt a pair of pistols from the former royal manufacture of Versailles, and a short straight sword similar to that used by students at the Champs-de-Mars military academy.

"Ah! You sleep, Brutus,"[7] said the visitor, "while the homeland is in danger. For shame!"

"No, Lorin," Maurice said, smiling. "I'm not sleeping, I'm dreaming."

"Yes, I understand: you dream of your Eucharis."[8]

"I don't get it."

"You don't?"

"What are you talking about?"

"Well, the woman . . ."

"What woman?"

"The woman from the rue Saint-Honoré, the woman from the patrol, the mysterious stranger for whom we risked our necks, you and I, last night."

"Oh, yes!" said Maurice, who knew only too well what his friend was driving at, but had no intention of giving the game away. "The mystery woman!"

"Well, who was she?"

"I've got no idea."

"Was she pretty?"

"Phhuh!" said Maurice with a contemptuous sneer.

"Some poor woman abandoned after an amorous tryst.

> . . . Yes, weaklings as you see us, then,
> It's always love that torments us men."

"That may well be," Maurice muttered, now most put out by the very idea that he had at first had; he preferred to think of his beautiful mystery woman as a conspirator than as a woman in love.

"And where does she live?"

"I've got no idea."

"How amazing! You have no idea! Sorry, I don't believe you."

"Why not?"

"You took her home."

"She gave me the slip at the pont-Marie . . ."

"Gave you the slip—you!" cried Lorin, hooting with laughter. "A woman gave you the slip; pull the other one!

> Does the dove escape
> The vulture, that tyrant of the air,
> Or the gazelle the desert tiger
> When he has pinned her with his stare?"

"Lorin, can't you ever resign yourself to talking like everyone else does? You're really starting to get on my nerves with your atrocious poetry!"

"What! Talk like everyone else! But I talk better than everyone else, it seems to me. I talk like the citizen-poet Demoustier,[9] in prose and in verse. As for my poetry, dear boy, I know a woman called Emily who rather likes it; but let's get back to yours."

"To my poetry?"

"No. Your Emily."

"I have an Emily?"

"Oh, please! Your gazelle turned out to be a tigress in disguise; she showed you her teeth and now you're out of sorts, but in love."

"Me, in love!" cried Maurice, shaking his head.

"Yes, you, in love.

> Let's have no more mystery;
> The blows that rain down from Cythera[10]
> Hit the heart harder, you see,
> Than those of thundering Jupiter."

"Lorin," Maurice warned, grabbing a sort of whistle that was lying on the night table, "if you talk any more poetry at me I'm going to give you the whistle!"

"All right, so let's talk politics. Besides, that's what I came for. Have you heard the news?"

"I know the Widow Capet tried to escape."

"Oh! That's nothing."

"What else is there, then?"

"The famous Knight of Maison-Rouge[11] is in Paris."

"Really!" cried Maurice, sitting up.

"The very same, himself, in person."

"But when did he get here?"

"Early last night."

"How?"

"Disguised as a chasseur with the National Guard. A woman they think is an aristocrat, decked out like a woman of the people brought him the clothes at the city barrier, and a minute later they entered, arm in arm. It's only after they were through that the sentry had a few suspicions. He'd seen the woman go by one way with a parcel, then he sees her come back the other way with some sort of military type on her arm. It was fishy, so he gave the alarm and the chase was on. But they disappeared into a hotel on the rue Saint-Honoré when the door opened suddenly, as if by magic. The hotel had a back door on the Champs-Elysées, so that was that! The Knight of Maison-Rouge and his accomplice just vanished into thin air. They'll demolish the hotel and guillotine the owner, but that won't stop the Knight from trying again, just as he did the first time, four months ago, and the second time last night."

"And they haven't got him?" asked Maurice.

"Try and get Proteus,[12] dear boy, just try and get Proteus. You know how much trouble Aristides had when he tried.

Pastor Aristaeus fugiens Peneia Tempe . . ."[13]

"Look out!" said Maurice, bringing the whistle to his mouth.

"You look out! This time it's not me you'd be booing, it's Virgil."

"Ah, you're right. Well, as long as you don't try and translate it, I won't say a word. But getting back to the Knight of Maison-Rouge . . ."

"Yes, well, you can't say he doesn't cut a dashing figure."

"The fact is, to do what he does, you'd have to have a lot of courage."

"Or a lot of love."

"So you believe in the story of the Knight's love for the Queen?"

"I don't believe it; I'm just saying it like everyone else. Anyway, she's made plenty of others fall in love with her, so it wouldn't be surprising if she's seduced him too, would it? She certainly got to Barnave,[14] if you believe what you hear."

"However that may be, the Knight must have informers inside the Temple itself."

"That's possible:

> Love breaks bars
> And laughs at locks."

"Lorin!"

"Right."

"So, you go along with that like everyone else?"

"Why not?"

"Because, according to your count, the Queen would have to have had two hundred men pining after her."

"Two hundred, three hundred, four hundred. She's beautiful enough. I'm not saying she's been in love with them, but they've certainly been in love with her. Everyone looks at the sun but the sun doesn't look on everyone."

"So you were saying, the Knight of Maison-Rouge . . . ?"

"I was saying they're hunting him a bit seriously at the moment, and if he manages to get away from the bloodhounds of the Republic, then he must be a very clever fox."

"And what's the Commune doing in all this?"

"The Commune's about to issue a decree by which every house will put up a list of the names of all the men and women who live there on the outside for all the world to see, like an open register. The dream of the ancients has come to pass: 'If only there was a window into a man's heart so everyone could see what goes on there!'"

"What an excellent idea!" Maurice cried.

"What, to stick a window in men's hearts?"

"No, to stick a list on every door."

Maurice, of course, was thinking that this would be one way for him to track down his mystery woman, or at least to find a trace of her that could set him on the right track.

"Yes, it is, isn't it?" said Lorin. "I've already bet the measure will bring us in a nice batch of around five hundred aristocrats. Speaking of which, we had a delegation of recruits this morning at the club. They were brought in by our adversaries of last night, whom I left dead drunk. They came in, I'm not joking, with garlands of flowers and crowns of everlasting daisies."

"Really!" Maurice chuckled. "How many were there?"

"About thirty. They'd had themselves a shave and popped flowers in their buttonholes. 'Citizens of the Thermopylae club,' the orator said, 'like the good patriots we are, we don't want the French union to be disturbed by any misunderstanding, so we've come to fraternize again.'"

"And so? . . ."

"And so we started fraternizing pronto, by repeating ourselves, as Diafoirus[15] would say. We made an altar to the homeland out of the secretary's table and a couple of carafes someone had stuck flowers in. As you were the hero of the festivities, we called you three times to crown you; and as you didn't answer, since you weren't there, and as it's always important to crown something, we crowned the bust of Washington.[16] So there you have the marching and the order in which the ceremony took place."

As Lorin wound up his accurate account of the proceedings, which in those days had not a whiff of burlesque about them, a commotion was heard in the street and drums, at first distant then closer and closer, sounded the then-familiar note of the tocsin.

"What's that?" said Maurice.

"It's the proclamation of the Commune decree," said Lorin.

"I'm off to the section," said Maurice, leaping to the foot of the bed and calling his officieux to come and dress him.

"And I am going home to bed," said Lorin. "I only slept a couple of hours last night, thanks to the rabid recruits. If they just smack each other around a bit, let me sleep; if they smack each other around a lot, come and get me."

"Why have you got yourself all dolled up like that?" Maurice asked, eyeing Lorin as he rose to his feet to leave.

"Because to get to your place I have to go down the rue Béthisy, and down the rue Béthisy, on the third floor, there's a window that always shoots open whenever I go by."

"And you're not afraid people will take you for a muscadin?"[17]

"A muscadin, me? On the contrary, everyone knows I'm an honest to goodness sans culotte. But there are certain sacrifices you just have to make for the fair sex. Worship of the nation doesn't exclude worship of love. Far from it: one calls for the other:

> The Republic has decreed
> We are to follow in the Greeks' traces;
> And the altar of Liberty
> Is the twin of that of the Graces.

You dare hiss at that and I'll denounce you as an aristocrat and have you shaved so hard you can never wear a wig.[18] Adieu, dear friend."

Lorin gave Maurice his hand, tenderly, and the young secretary gave it a hearty shake; then Lorin spun on his heels, chewing over a stanza of gallant verse that was to be a bouquet for Chloris.[19]

5

What Sort of Man Maurice Lindey Was

Maurice Lindey threw on his clothes and reported to the section in the rue Lepelletier, where, as we know, he was secretary. While he is busy there, we might try and trace the ancestry of this man who burst on the scene as a result of one of those surges of the heart familiar to powerful and generous natures.

The young man was telling the whole truth and nothing but the truth when he told the mysterious stranger of the day before that his name was Maurice Lindey and that he lived in the rue Roule. He could have added that he was a child of that deminobility to which those belonging to the legal profession—the Robe[1]—had been promoted. For the past two hundred years, his ancestors had invariably belonged to the parliamentary opposition that had made the names Molé and Maupeou famous. His father, Lindey senior, had spent his life attacking despotism but when, suddenly, on 14 July 1789, the Bastille fell to the hands of the people, he died of shock and horror to see despotism replaced by a militant liberty. His death left his only son independent of fortune and republican by inclination.

The Revolution that followed hot on the heels of this momentous event thus found Maurice in the prime of that vigor and virility that are only right in an athlete ready and raring to enter the race, with republican education supplemented by fervent participation in the clubs and a heady dose of all the pamphlets of the times. God knows how many pamphlets Maurice must have read. A profound and reasoned contempt for hierarchy, philosophical pondering of the elements that compose the social body, absolute negation of the very notion of a nobility entailing anything other than a personal quality, impartial appreciation of the past, keenness for new ideas, sympathy for the people matched with the most aristocratic of temperaments—such was the nature, not of our hero, but of the newspaper portrait on which we have drawn to produce him.

Physically, Maurice Lindey was between twenty-five and twenty-six years old; he stood six feet tall and was as muscular as Hercules, and startlingly good-looking, with those peculiarly French looks that derive from a specific race of Franks that include a pure and noble forehead, blue eyes, wavy chestnut hair, ruddy cheeks, and a good set of pearly teeth.

That's the portrait of the man; and now for the status of the citizen. Maurice was not rich, but he was at least independent and bore a name that was not only respected but, more important, popular. Maurice was known for his liberal education and for his even more liberal stance, so it was only natural that he had more or less placed himself at the head of a party composed of all the young patriots of the bourgeoisie. You could no doubt argue that, next to the sans culottes, Maurice could look a bit of a wimp—"lukewarm"—and, next to the sectionaries, a bit of a fop. But he was forgiven his lukewarmness by the sans culottes by smashing to smithereens the most gnarled of cudgels as though they were fragile reeds; and he was forgiven his elegance by the sectionaries by sending them reeling twenty feet away with a well-aimed smack between the eyes if those eyes had looked at Maurice in a way he didn't like.

As for the physical, the moral, and the social combined, Maurice had taken part in the storming of the Bastille; he had joined in the expedition to Versailles on the fifth and sixth of October 1789;[2] he had fought like a lion on the tenth of August, and on that memorable day, to give him his due, he had killed as many patriots[3] as Swiss Guards,[4] for he was no more prepared to put up with the assassin in the carmagnole than the enemy of the Republic in the red livery.

It was Maurice who, exhorting the defenders of the Tuileries to give themselves up and prevent bloodshed, threw himself across the mouth of a cannon that a Parisian artilleryman was about to fire; it was Maurice who was first to enter the Louvre, through a window, despite the fusillade of fifty Swiss Guards and as many gentlemen behind the lines, and who already, by the time he saw the signals of capitulation, had torn open more than ten uniforms with his saber; it was Maurice who then, seeing his friends massacring at will prisoners who were throwing down their arms and holding out their hands and pleading for mercy and begging for their lives, began to furiously hack at his friends—all of which had helped to forge a reputation worthy of the great days of Rome or Greece.

When war was declared, Maurice signed up and left for the front with the rank of lieutenant, in the company of the first fifteen hundred volunteers that Paris pitted against the invaders, which were to be followed each day by fifteen hundred more.

In the first battle in which he fought, that is, at Jemmapes[5] on the sixth of November 1792, he took a bullet that first split open the steel-like muscles of his shoulder before lodging itself in the bone. The people's representative[6] knew Maurice and sent him back to Paris to recover. For a whole month, Maurice thrashed around in bed, devoured by fever and pain, but by January he was back on his feet commanding the Thermopylae club, if not in name then certainly in deed. The club was made up of a hundred young men from the bourgeoisie of Paris, armed to quell all support for the tyrant Capet. There is more: with his brow furrowed by a somber rage, his eyes wild, face pale, heart seized by a singular mix of moral hatred and physical pity, Maurice was there, sword in hand, at the execution of the King; and perhaps alone in all that crowd, he remained silent when the head of this son of Saint Louis,[7] whose soul rose to heaven, fell and all his friends cried out: "Long live liberty!" They did not notice that, though Maurice raised his fearsome sword in the air, this time, for once, his voice did not mingle with theirs.

That is the kind of man that was now making his way toward the rue Lepelletier on the morning of the eleventh of March and whose stormy life, a life typical enough for the times, we'll visit in detail in the course of our story.

At about ten o'clock, Maurice arrived at the section where he was secretary. Things were heating up. At issue was a vote on an address to the Convention with the aim of putting down the schemes of the Girondins. Maurice was impatiently awaited.

All anyone could talk about was the return of the Knight of Maison-Rouge and the audacity with which that dedicated conspirator had entered Paris for the second time, in defiance of the price on his head. The escape attempt at the Temple the day before was linked to his return to town, and each man expressed his hatred for and outrage over all traitors and aristocrats.

But to everyone's surprise, Maurice remained unmoved and silent, though he cleverly drew up the proclamation and got through all outstanding work in three hours flat before asking if the session was over; when told it was, he grabbed his hat and turned on his heels, heading for the rue Saint-Honoré.

Paris looked entirely different to Maurice from the rue Saint-Honoré. He saw once again the corner of the rue du Coq where the beautiful stranger had appeared to him the night before, struggling in the hands of soldiers. Then he followed the rue du Coq down to the pont Marie, as he had done at her side, stopping where the different patrols had stopped them, going over the words they had exchanged, as in those places the words came back to him like an echo; but it was one o'clock in the afternoon and the sun, shining bright as he strolled along, brought home these memories of the night before every step of the way. Maurice crossed over the Seine and was soon in the rue Victor, as it was then known.

"Poor woman!" murmured Maurice, who the day before hadn't considered that the night only lasts twelve hours, and that the woman's secret would probably not outlast the night. "In daylight I'll find the door she slipped through, and who knows if I won't spot the woman herself at a window somewhere?"

So he turned into the old rue Saint-Jacques, stood where the stranger had placed him the night before, and for a moment he closed his eyes, perhaps feeling—poor fool!—that last night's kiss would burn his lips once more. But all he felt was the memory of it—though it's true the memory of it was still burning.

When Maurice opened his eyes again, he saw two alleyways, one to the right, the other to the left. They were muddy, badly paved, lined with gates and broken up by little bridges thrown across a stream. You could make out arcades with wooden beams, sunless nooks and crannies, something like twenty dubious, rotting doors. It was destitution in all its ugliness. Here and there was a garden, enclosed either by hedges or by fences made of stakes, a few by walls, and there were skins drying out in sheds and giving off that nauseating tannery smell that makes you want to heave. Maurice poked around for two hours and found nothing, gleaned nothing. He retraced his steps a dozen times to reorient himself. But all his efforts were in vain, all his forays fruitless. All traces of the woman seemed to have been erased by fog and rain.

"So," Maurice said to himself, "I was dreaming. This cesspit can't have served my beautiful fairy of last night as a refuge for a single moment."

This fierce republican had a poetry in him different from, but just as real as, the poetry of his friend of the old-fashioned anacreontic quatrains, for he carried that idea home with him, so as not to dim the halo shimmering over his mystery woman's head. True, he went home in despair.

"Adieu," he sighed, "beautiful stranger. You've played me for a fool or a child. Would she have brought me here if she actually lived here!

Not on your life! She merely passed through like a swan on a foul bog. And like a bird on the wing, she's left no trace."

6

THE TEMPLE

That same day, while Maurice was going back over the pont de la Tournelle in acute disappointment, several municipal officers, accompanied by the commander of the National Guard of Paris, Santerre, were paying a grim visit to the tower of the Temple, which had been turned into a prison since the thirteenth of August 1792.

The visit was centered on the apartment on the third floor, comprising an antechamber and three rooms. One of these rooms was occupied by two women, a young girl, and a boy of nine, all dressed in mourning.

The elder of the two women could have been thirty-seven or thirty-eight years old. She was sitting reading a book. The second woman was sitting and working on a hoop of tapestry. She could have been twenty-eight or twenty-nine years old. The girl was fourteen and kept close to the boy, who was lying down sick with his eyes closed as though he were asleep, although it was obviously impossible to sleep with the racket the municipal officers were making.

A number of them were shoving the beds around, others were unfolding articles of linen; still others, having completed their search, were staring insolently at the unhappy female prisoners, who kept their eyes resolutely lowered, one on her book, the other on her tapestry, the third on her brother.

The elder of the two women was tall, pale, and beautiful. As she read, she seemed to be concentrating her attention entirely on her book, though no doubt her eyes alone were doing the reading, not her mind.

One of the municipal officers walked over to her, snatched the book out of her hands, and threw it on the floor in the middle of the room. The prisoner stretched her hand toward the table, took a second volume, and began reading that. The Montagnard made a furious move to tear this second volume from her, but as he did so, the prisoner busy embroidering next to the window started to tremble; the young girl shot forward, put her arms round the reader, and quietly sobbed, "Ah, my poor mother!" giving her mother a kiss.

The prisoner pressed her lips against the young girl's ear as though kissing her back, but instead she whispered, "Marie,[1] there is a note hidden in the mouth of the stove; get rid of it."

"That will do! Enough!" cried the municipal officer, jerking the girl away from her mother. "Enough canoodling for one day!"

"Monsieur," said the girl. "Has the Convention banned children from kissing their mothers?"

"No; but it has decreed that traitors, aristocrats, and former aristocrats will be punished. That's why we're here to conduct an interrogation. So let's get on with it, Antoinette. Answer."

The woman so grossly addressed did not even deign to look in her interrogator's direction. On the contrary, she turned her head away, her cheeks suddenly on fire, drained of color and streaked now with tears.

"It is not possible," the man continued, "that you don't know about the attempt to break you out made this very night. Who is behind it?"

Nothing but silence from the prisoner.

"Answer, Antoinette," Santerre[2] said, coming closer, without noticing the shiver of horror that gripped the young woman at the sight of this man who, on the morning of the twenty-first of January, had come to the Temple to take Louis XVI to the guillotine. "Answer. Last night someone conspired against the Republic, they tried to release you from a captivity that the will of the people has imposed upon you while you await punishment for your crimes. Tell us, did you know about this conspiracy?"

Marie Antoinette trembled on hearing this voice, which she seemed to be trying to escape by shrinking back to the very edge of her chair. But she no more answered this question than the previous ones, took no more notice of Santerre than she had of the municipal officer.

"So you don't feel like answering?" said Santerre, stamping his foot violently.

The prisoner took a third volume from the table.

Santerre spun on his heels. The brute power of this man, who commanded eighty thousand men and only needed to wave his hand to drown out the voice of the dying Louis XVI, was shattered by the dignity of a poor woman prisoner whose head he could also cause to roll but whose spirit he could not break.

Addressing the other woman, who had interrupted her tapestry for a moment to join her hands in prayer—prayer directed not to such men as these but to God—Santerre thundered, "What about you, Elisabeth,[3] will you answer?"

"I do not know what you are asking," she said. "So I cannot answer you."

"Oh, for pity's sake! Citizeness Capet,"[4] said Santerre getting hot under the collar now. "What I am saying is perfectly clear. I'm saying that during the night an attempt was made to break you out of here and that you must know who the guilty parties are."

"We have no communication with the outside world, monsieur; so we cannot know either what is being done for us or what is being done against us."

"All right, then; have it your way," said the municipal officer. "We'll see what your nephew has to say on the subject."

With that he walked over to the Dauphin's bed.[5] But Marie Antoinette shot to her feet at this threat. "Monsieur," she said. "My son is ill and he is sleeping. . . . Do not wake him."

"Well then, answer."

"I know nothing."

At that, the municipal officer leapt to the bed where, as we said earlier, the little captive was feigning sleep. "Snap out of it, Capet!" the man said, shaking him roughly. The child opened his eyes and smiled as the municipal officers surrounded his bed. Rocked by pain and fear, the Queen signaled to her daughter, who took advantage of the moment to slip unnoticed into the room next door, where she opened one of the stove doors, took out the note, and burned it before immediately returning to the main room and giving her mother a reassuring look.

"What do you want?" the little boy asked.

"We want to know if you heard anything last night."

"No. I was sleeping."

"You really like sleeping, it would seem."

"I do, because when I sleep I dream."

"And what do you dream about?"

"That I see my father again, even though you have killed him."

"So you heard nothing?" Santerre snapped.

"Nothing."

"The cubs are certainly in league with the wolf," said the officer, furious. "And yet there was definitely a plot."

The Queen smiled.

"She's laughing at us, the Austrian woman!"[6] cried the municipal officer. "I reckon, since that's how it is, we should carry out the Commune decree to the letter. Up you go, Capet."

"What are you going to do?" cried the Queen, forgetting herself completely. "Can't you see that my son is sick, that he has a fever? Do you want to kill him?"

"Your son," said the municipal officer, "is a constant cause for alarm for the Council of the Temple. He is the target of all the conspirators. They flatter themselves they'll get you all out of here. Well, let them try. Tison! . . . Call Tison."[7]

Tison was a sort of day laborer and general factotum whose job it was to do the heavy domestic work about the prison. He arrived, a man of about forty with a tanned complexion, a rough-hewn, Neanderthal face, and frizzy black hair that crept down to his eyebrows like a carpet.

"Tison," said Santerre. "Who came yesterday to bring the detainees' food?"

Tison cited a name.

"And their linen, who brought that?"

"My daughter."

"So your daughter does the laundry?"

"Certainly."

"And you got her the job of looking after the prisoners' laundry?"

"Why not? She might just as well do theirs as anyone else's. It's not tyrants' money anymore, it's the nation's money, since the nation's paying for them."

"You were told to examine the linen carefully."

"Well then, didn't I do my job? The proof is, yesterday there was a handkerchief someone had tied two knots in, so I took it to the Council, who ordered my wife to untie the knots and iron it and give it to Madame Capet without a word."

At this reference to two knots tied in a handkerchief, the Queen trembled; her eyes widened and she exchanged a look with Madame Elisabeth and the girl.

"Tison," said Santerre, "your daughter's patriotism is beyond doubt. But from today she will no longer set foot in the Temple."

"Oh, my God!" said Tison, frightened. "What are you trying to tell me? No! You mean I'll never see my daughter again until I get out of here?"

"You will no longer get out of here," Santerre retorted.

Tison looked around him, his haggard gaze not registering any one object. Then he suddenly erupted: "I'm no longer to leave the Temple? So, it's like that, is it? All right! I'll leave once and for all, right now! I'm handing in my resignation. I'm no traitor, no aristocrat, not me, to be kept in jail. I tell you I'm leaving this minute."

"Citizen," said Santerre. "Obey the orders of the Commune and hold your tongue or you could well be sorry. Stay here and watch whatever happens. We've got our eye on you, I'm warning you."

During this time the Queen, thinking she had been forgotten, had regained her composure and put her son back to bed.

"Get your wife up here," the municipal officer directed Tison— and Tison obeyed without a murmur. Santerre's threats had rendered him as docile as a lamb. Tison's wife stepped in.

"Come here, citizeness," said Santerre. "The rest of us are going into the antechamber, and while we're there you will search the detainees."

"Do you know," Tison said to his wife, "they won't let our daughter into the Temple anymore."

"What! They won't let our daughter come here anymore? But that means we won't see her again, doesn't it?"

Tison shook his head.

"What are you muttering about over there?"

"I'm saying that we'll file a report with the Council of the Temple and that the Council will decide. Meanwhile . . ."

"Meanwhile," said the wife, "I want to see my daughter."

"Quiet!" said Santerre. "We brought you up here to search the prisoners, so search them. We'll see what happens after that. . . ."

"But . . . I mean!"

"Oh, dear!" said Santerre, frowning furiously. "It looks like things are going to get nasty."

"Do what the citizen general asks you to! Go on, woman! Afterward, you heard him, he says we'll see." Tison turned an abject smile on Santerre.

"Very well," said the woman. "Off you go. I'm ready to search them." The men filed out of the room.

"My dear Madame Tison," said the Queen. "Please don't think . . ."

"I don't think anything, citizeness Capet," said the horrible woman, grinding her teeth. "Except that it's you who are the cause of all the people's misery. And if I find anything suspect on you, you'd better watch out."

Four men remained in the doorway to lend Madame Tison a hand should the Queen resist. The woman began with the Queen, on whom she found a handkerchief knotted in three places, unhappily looking like a prepared response to the one Tison had spoken of. She also found a pencil, a scapular, and sealing wax.

"Aha! I knew it!" crowed Madame Tison. "Didn't I tell the municipal officers that the Austrian woman was writing in secret! The other day I found a drop of wax on the ring around the candlestick."

"Oh, madame!" said the Queen in a tone of naked supplication. "Just show them the scapular."

"Oh, yes," said the woman. "Pity you, is it! . . . And who pities me, I ask you? . . . They're taking my daughter away from me."

Madame Elisabeth and Madame Royale[8] proved to have nothing on them, so Madame Tison called out to the municipal officers and they marched back into the room with Santerre at the helm. She handed them the objects she had found on the Queen, which were passed round from man to man, giving rise to numerous conjectures.

The handkerchief with its three knots in particular kept the imagination of the persecutors of the royal race busy for some time.

"Now," said Santerre, "we will read you the Commune decree."

"What decree?" the Queen demanded to know.

"The decree that orders you to be separated from your son."

"So it is true that this decree exists?"

"Yes. The Convention is too concerned with the care of a child entrusted to the nation to leave him in the company of a mother as depraved as you."

The Queen's eyes flashed fire. "Come up with an actual accusation, at least, tigers that you are!"

"That's not hard, for crying out loud," jeered one of the officers. "Let's see . . ." And he named the foul crime—the crime of incest!—Suetonius once accused Agrippina[9] of.

"Oh!" cried the Queen, on her feet, white and magnificent with indignation. "I appeal to any mother who has a heart."[10]

"Come! Come! All this is very well but we haven't got all day; we've already been here too long. Get up, Capet, and follow us."

"Never! Never!" cried the Queen, throwing herself between the municipal officers and the young Louis, ready to defend the approach to the bed as a tigress defends her lair. "I will never let anyone take my child away from me!"

"Oh, messieurs," Madame Elisabeth entreated, joining her hands in a moving attitude of prayer. "Messieurs, in the name of Heaven! Have pity on two poor mothers!"[11]

"Speak, then! Give us names!" said Santerre. "Confess to your accomplices' plans, explain what these knots mean tied in a handkerchief the Tison girl brought in with your linen and tied in the handkerchief found in your pocket, and we'll let you keep your son."

Madame Elisabeth shot the Queen a look that seemed to entreat her to make the terrible sacrifice demanded. But the Queen, proudly wiping a tear that glittered like a diamond at the corner of her eye, merely said, "Adieu, my son. Never forget your father, who is in heaven, and your mother, who will soon join him there; say the prayer I taught you, every night and every morning. Adieu, my son."

She gave her son one last kiss before straightening up, cold and unyielding. "I know nothing, messieurs. Do what you will."

But the Queen did not have the superhuman strength required, especially for a mother, to maintain her pose. She fell, utterly annihilated, onto a chair as they took the child away, sobbing and holding out his arms to her, though without uttering a single cry.

The door shut behind the municipal officers as they carried off the royal child, leaving the three women to themselves. There was a moment of desperate silence, interrupted only by a few stifled sobs. The Queen was the first to break the silence.

"My daughter, what did you do with the note?"

"I burned it, as you told me to do, Mother."

"Without reading it?"

"Without reading it."

"Adieu, then, last ray of light, supreme hope!" murmured Madame Elisabeth.

"Oh! You are right! You are right, my sister. This is too much for anyone to bear." She turned to her daughter again. "But you did see the writing, at least, Marie?"

"Yes, Mother, for a second."

The Queen stood and went to the door to check whether anyone was watching, and then she pulled a pin from her hair and walked over to a part of the wall where there was a crack, out of which she hooked a small piece of paper folded up like a note. She unfolded it. Showing the note to Madame Royale, she said, "Try to remember very carefully, my daughter, before you answer. Was the writing you saw the same as this?"

"Yes, yes, Mother," cried the princess. "Yes, I recognize it!"

"God be praised!" cried the Queen, falling to her knees in fervent thanks. "If he was able to write this morning, he must have been saved. Thank you, God! Thank you! Such a noble friend certainly merits one of your miracles!"

"Who are you talking about, Mother?" asked Madame Royale. "Who is this friend? Tell me his name so that I can commend him to God in my prayers."

"Yes, you are right, my darling. I will tell you. Never forget the name, for it is the name of a gentleman full of honor and bravery. This man is not committed out of ambition, he is not some fair-weather friend, for he only came forward when everything collapsed. He has never seen the Queen of France, or, rather, the Queen of France has never set eyes on him, and yet he dedicates his life to defending me. Perhaps he will be rewarded, as all virtue is rewarded these days, by a terrible death. . . . But . . . If he should die . . . Oh! Up there! Up there in heaven! I will thank him. . . . He is called . . ."

The Queen looked around anxiously and lowered her voice:

"He is the Knight of Maison-Rouge. . . . Pray for him!"

7

A GAMBLER'S OATH

The attempt to spirit away the Queen, as debatable as it was, since it hadn't actually gotten off the ground, had excited the wrath of some and the curiosity of others. Besides, this almost overwhelmingly probable event was corroborated, as the Committee of Public Safety[1] learned, by the fact that a host of emigrés[2] had been crossing back into France via different points on the border for the last three or four weeks. It was obvious that people who would risk their necks in this way would not do so without some intent and that this intent was, in all probability, to help get the royal family out.

Already, as proposed by Osselin,[3] a member of the Convention, a terrible decree had been promulgated condemning to death any emigré convicted of having set foot back on French soil, as well as any French person convicted of having plans to emigrate; any individual convicted of having aided and abetted such a person's flight or return; and, finally, any citizen convicted of having harbored an emigré. This terrible law ushered in the Terror.[4] All that was lacking after that was the law against "suspects."

The Knight of Maison-Rouge was too active and too bold an enemy for his reentry into Paris and his turning up at the Temple not to give rise to the gravest of measures. The most thorough searches ever undertaken had been carried out in a host of suspect houses. But apart from the discovery of a handful of emigré women who allowed themselves to be caught and of a few old men who couldn't be bothered fighting the executioners over the short time remaining to them to live, such searches were entirely fruitless.

As you can well imagine, the sections had their hands full for several days on end following this episode; as a result, the secretary of the Lepelletier section, one of the most influential in Paris, had little time to worry about his mystery woman. At first, as he had resolved walking away from the old rue Saint-Jacques, Maurice had tried to forget; but as his friend Lorin might have said:

> Just by thinking one should forget,
> One remembers—never fret.

Maurice, though, had said nothing and admitted nothing. He had locked away in his heart all the details of this adventure that managed to escape his friend's prying eye. But this friend knew Maurice too well, knew him to be joyful and expansive by nature; when he now found him endlessly dreaming and seeking to be alone, Lorin was in no doubt that, as he said, that little rascal Cupid had been by.

It must be noted that, in all its eighteen centuries of monarchy,[5] France has had few years as mythic as the year of grace 1793. Yet the Knight had not been caught, and so people stopped talking about him. The Queen, widowed of her husband and orphaned of her son, contented herself with crying when she was alone in the company of her daughter and her sister-in-law. The little Dauphin, at the hands of the cobbler, Simon,[6] set out on the road to martyrdom that would unite him two years later with his father and mother. There was a momentary lull while the volcano of the Mountain[7] lay dormant before erupting and devouring the Girondins.

Maurice felt the weight of this lull, the way you feel how heavy the atmosphere is before a storm, and he did not know what to do with the spare time that delivered him over entirely to passionate feelings which, if not love, certainly bore all the hallmarks. He reread the woman's letter, kissed the beautiful sapphire she had given him, and resolved that, though he had sworn not to, he would try one last time to find her.

The young man had of course thought of one thing, which was to go to the Jardin des Plantes section to gather information there from his colleague the secretary. But his initial thought, indeed, we might say his only thought, that his beautiful stranger might be involved in some kind of political intrigue, held him back. The idea that some indiscretion on his part might lead such a lovely woman to the place de la Révolution[8] and cause her angelic head to fall on the guillotine made his blood run cold.

And so he opted to go it alone, blindly. His plan, in any case, was very simple. The lists posted on every door should provide him with a few basic pointers; he could then question the concierges and thereby have light shed on the mystery. As secretary of the Lepelletier section, he had every right to conduct inquiries of the sort.

In any case, Maurice had no idea of the woman's name and would have to be guided by analogy. It was impossible that such a charming creature would not have a name in keeping with her appearance: the name of some sylph, fairy, or angel; for when she arrived on earth, her advent had to have been greeted as that of a superior and supernatural being. The name would thus, infallibly, guide him in his groping.

Maurice donned a carmagnole of coarse brown cloth, clapped a red cap on his head, and set off on his exploration without telling a soul what he was up to. In his hand, he held the gnarled cudgel known as a *constitution;* tucked into his manly wrist, this weapon was as good as Hercules' club. In his pocket, he carried his commission as secretary of the Lepelletier section, which was meant to ensure his physical safety and vouch for his moral stature at once.

So once more he found himself walking up and down the rue Saint-Victor and the old rue Saint-Jacques, trying to decipher in the dwindling daylight the names scrawled more or less legibly on the panel of each door.

He was up to his hundredth house, and, of course, his hundredth list, without in any way feeling he was getting any closer to tracking down his mystery woman, whom he would be unable to recognize in any case unless his eyes were to light on some fancy name of the kind he'd been dreaming about, when a brave cobbler read frustration writ large across his face and so opened his door and came out, leather thong and bodkin in hand, to peer over his glasses at Maurice.

"Do you need information about any of the tenants of this house? If so, speak, I'm prepared to tell you."

"Thank you, citizen," Maurice stammered, "but I'm looking for the name of a friend of mine."

"Tell me his name, citizen; I know everyone on the block. Where does this friend live?"

"He used to live in the old rue Saint-Jacques, I think; but I fear he may have moved."

"But what's his name? I need to know his name."

Maurice was stumped; he hesitated for a moment then said the first name that came into his head. "René."

"And what's he do, this René?"

Maurice was surrounded by tanneries. "He's a tanner's assistant."

"In that case," said a burgher who had stopped and was looking at Maurice with a friendly expression that did not exclude a certain mistrust, "you should address yourself to the master."

"That's right," said the doorman, "good advice. The masters know the names of their workers, and here's citizen Dixmer. Hang on, he's the manager of a tannery with more than fifty men working for him; he's your man if it's information you need."

Maurice turned and saw a fairly tall, decent-looking bourgeois gent with a placid face and the snazzy getup of the wealthy industrialist.

"But as the citizen doorman was saying," said the burgher, "we need to know the man's last name."

"Like I said: René."

"René's just a Christian name. I'm asking you for the family name. All the workers on my payroll are listed according to their last names."

"Heck," said Maurice, getting tired of this line of questioning, "I just can't remember his last name."

"Really?" said the burgher with a smile in which Maurice felt he could sense more irony than the man cared to reveal. "Really, citizen, you don't know your friend's last name?"

"No."

"In that case, you probably won't find him."

With that, the burgher graciously bowed to Maurice and disappeared into a decrepit-looking house in the old rue Saint-Jacques.

"The fact is, if you don't know his last name . . . ," said the doorman.

"No, I don't," snapped Maurice, spoiling for a fight as one way to give vent to his lousy mood. "What've you got to say about that?"

"Nothing, citizen, nothing at all; only, if you don't know your friend's last name, it's probable, as citizen Dixmer says, it's very probable that you won't find him."

With that, the citizen doorman went back inside his lodge, shrugging his shoulders. Maurice would have liked to give the citizen doorman a good thump, but the man was old and his very feebleness saved him. If he'd been twenty years younger, Maurice would have provided the scandalous spectacle of equality before the law but inequality before brute strength. Night was about to fall, in any case, and he only had a few minutes of daylight left.

He made use of them by taking the first alleyway, then the second; he examined every door in both, poked into every corner and crevice, peered over every fence, hoisted himself up on every wall, whipped his head inside every gate, peeked through every keyhole in every lock and even hammered on the doors of a few deserted shops without getting any reply. In the end, two solid hours went down the drain in this futile search.

Nine o'clock sounded. Night had fallen: there was no other sound to be heard, no movement to be detected in this deserted neighborhood, where life seemed to have fled with the light.

Maurice was about to turn back in despair when suddenly he saw a light shining in a narrow alleyway. He ventured down the dark passage without noticing that the very moment he did so a curious head, which had been following his every move for a quarter of an hour or so from behind a stand of trees, popped up over the wall and then swiftly ducked down behind it again.

A few seconds later, three men raced out of a tiny door in this same wall and threw themselves down the alley in which Maurice had just been swallowed up, while a fourth man closed the lane door in the interests of precaution.

At the end of the alley, Maurice located the light, shining on the far side of a courtyard. He knocked on the door of a lone, run-down house, but the light went out as soon as he knocked. He knocked harder but no one answered his knock, and Maurice realized it was deliberate policy not to answer around here and that he was stupidly wasting his time, so he crossed the courtyard and came back out into the alley.

At the same time, the door to the house turned silently on its hinges; three men came out and a whistle was heard. Maurice turned and saw three shadows five or six feet away. In the semidarkness, by the light of that sort of illumination you get when your eyes have become used to the dark for quite a while, three blades of steel glinted, throwing off silvery reflections.

Maurice knew he was surrounded. He tried to swing his cudgel, but the alley was so narrow it hit the walls on both sides. At the same moment, a violent blow to the head stunned him. It was an attack he hadn't foreseen, carried out by the four men who'd come out of the wall. Seven men at once threw themselves on Maurice and, despite the desperate resistance he put up, they got him to the ground, tied his hands behind his back, and blindfolded him.

Maurice had not uttered a single shout, not once called out for help. Strength and courage are always keen to be enough in themselves, and those who possess both seem to be ashamed of calling on outside help. Besides, Maurice could have called out all he liked in this deserted neighborhood; no one would have come.

So, there he was, noiselessly trussed and muzzled. At least, he thought, they didn't intend to kill him, not right away, or they would not have bothered with the blindfold. At Maurice's age hope springs eternal, and this seemed a hopeful reprieve, so he gathered his wits about him and waited.

"Who are you?" asked a voice still roused by the struggle.

"I'm the man you're assassinating," Maurice spat out.

"And you're a dead man if you make any noise."

"If I was going to make a noise I would have done so by now."

"Are you ready to answer my questions?"

"Ask me first, I'll see if I feel like answering."

"Who sent you here?"

"No one."

"So you came on your own initiative?"

"Yes."

"You're lying."

Maurice made a mighty move to disengage his bound hands, but it couldn't be done.

"I never lie!" he barked.

"In any case, whether you came on your own initiative or you've been sent, you're a spy."

"And you are cowards!"

"Cowards, eh?"

"Yes, you're seven or eight to one bound man and yet you insult that man. Cowards! Cowards! Cowards!"

Maurice's violence, instead of provoking his adversaries, seemed to calm them down, this very violence being proof that the young man was not what they accused him of being, for a true spy would have been quaking in his boots and begging for mercy.

"No insult intended," said a voice that was gentler yet at the same time more imperious than any of the others that had spoken so far. "In these troubled times, one can be a spy without being a criminal: only one risks one's life."

"Welcome, whoever spoke those words: I'll answer you in all honesty."

"What brought you to this neighborhood, monsieur?"

"I'm looking for a woman."

A murmur of incredulity greeted this excuse. The murmur grew to a howl of derision.

"You're lying!" the same voice said. "There is no woman and we know what we're talking about when it comes to women; there is no woman to pursue in this neighborhood. Tell us your plans or die."

"You're joking," said Maurice. "You won't kill me for the sheer pleasure of killing me—not unless you're proper crooks."

So saying, Maurice made an even more violent and sudden effort to free his hands from the rope that bound them; but a sharp and painful chill ripped through his chest and he lurched backward, unable to stop himself.

"Ah! You felt that all right!" said one of the men. "Well, there are another eight blades like the one you've just tasted."

"Get on with it then," said Maurice, resigned now to his fate. "At least it will be over and done with."

"Who are you? Let's have it!" said the soft yet imperious voice.

"You want to know my name?"

"Your name, yes!"

"I am Maurice Lindey."

"What!" someone shouted. "Maurice Lindey, the revolutionary . . . the patriot? Maurice Lindey, the secretary of the Lepelletier section?"

These words were said so heatedly that Maurice could tell they were decisive. To reply would be inexorably to seal his fate. Maurice was incapable of cowardice. He bolted upright like a true Spartan and spoke firmly and clearly:

"Yes, Maurice Lindey. Yes, Maurice Lindey, the secretary of the Lepelletier section. Yes, Maurice Lindey, the patriot, the revolutionary, the Jacobin. Maurice Lindey, in short, whose greatest day will be the day he dies for liberty."

His answer was greeted by a deathly silence.

Maurice Lindey presented his chest, waiting for the blade whose point he had already felt to plunge to the hilt at any moment into his heart.

After a few seconds, a voice betraying some emotion said, "Is that really true? Come on, young man; don't lie."

"Look in my pocket," said Maurice. "You'll find my commission. Look at my shirt. If my blood hasn't covered them up, you'll find my initials, an 'M' and an 'L,' embroidered on the front."

Maurice immediately felt himself lifted up by powerful arms and carried a short distance. He heard a first door open, then a second. But the second was narrower than the first and the men carrying him could barely squeeze in with him. The murmuring and whispering continued.

"I'm sunk," he said to himself. "They'll put a stone around my neck and throw me into some hole in the Bièvre River."

But after a short while he could feel that the men carrying him were going up some steps. A milder air struck his face and he was placed on a chair. Then he heard a door being shut and locked and footsteps receding and he sensed that he had been left on his own. He strained his ears the way a man does when his life hangs on a word, and he thought he heard the same voice that had already struck him with its mixture of hardness and softness say to the others:

"Let's deliberate and take a vote."

8

Geneviève

A quarter of an hour went by. It seemed like a century to Maurice. Which was only natural: young, handsome, vigorous, supported in his strength by a hundred devoted friends with whom he someday dreamed of doing great things, he suddenly felt himself, without warning, reduced to losing his life in a shameful ambush.

He knew he'd been locked up in some kind of room, but was the room being watched? As he made another attempt to get his hands free, his steely muscles pumped up and stiffened, but the rope cut into his flesh without breaking.

The worst of it was that his hands were tied behind his back, so he could not tear the blindfold off his eyes. If he could only see, perhaps he could get away. Yet his various efforts were being made without anyone objecting, without any movement near him. He deduced that he was alone.

He trod on something soft and yielding, sand or clay soil, perhaps. A penetrating acrid odor hit his nose, announcing the presence of vegetable matter. Maurice thought he might be in a greenhouse or something of that sort. He took a few steps, struck a wall, turned around to feel with his hands, felt plowing tools, and had to stifle a murmur of joy.

With stupendous effort, he managed to explore each instrument, one by one. His escape then became merely a matter of time: if only lady luck were to grant him five minutes and if among the tools he were to find some instrument with a cutting edge, he would be saved.

He found a spade.

The way Maurice was tied up, it was quite a struggle to turn the spade upside down so that the metal blade was uppermost. Along the edge of the metal, which he held against the wall with his back, he cut or rather sawed through the rope that bound his wrists. The operation took some little time; the metal edge of the blade cut slowly. Sweat ran down his brow. He could hear someone coming. He gave one last violent, supreme, superhuman tug and the rope, already half worn through, snapped.

This time he could not suppress a cry of joy, sure as he now was of at least dying while defending himself.

Maurice tore the blindfold from his eyes and saw that he had not been mistaken. It wasn't so much a hothouse he was in as a kind of pavilion where waxy plants too fragile to spend the winter out of doors were kept. In one corner were the gardening implements one of which had rendered him so great a service. Facing him was a window, which he dashed toward, but it had bars and there was a man armed with a rifle keeping guard outside.

On the far side of the garden, about thirty feet away, was a small pavilion matching the one Maurice was in. The shutters had been closed but a light shone through the slats.

He tiptoed to the door and listened; another watchman was pacing back and forth in front of the door. It was his steps he had heard.

But at the end of the hallway a jumble of voices sounded. The deliberations had clearly degenerated into an argument. Maurice couldn't hear all of what was being said. But a few words did reach him, and among these words, as though for those words only the distance was not so great, he heard the words *spy, dagger, death.*

Maurice became doubly alert. A door opened and he could hear more clearly.

"Yes," said a voice. "Yes, he's a spy; he's onto something and he has definitely been sent to ferret out our secrets. If we let him go, we run the risk of his denouncing us. But what about his word?"

"Naturally he'll give us his word and then he'll go back on it. Is he a gentleman that we should trust in his word?"

Maurice ground his teeth at the notion, still held by some, that you had to be a gentleman to keep your word.

"But does he know who we are to denounce us?"

"No, certainly not, he doesn't know who we are, he doesn't know what we're up to. But he knows this address and he'll come back with plenty of reinforcements."

The argument seemed pretty peremptory.

"Well, then," said the voice that had already struck Maurice several times as being the voice of the leader. "So it's decided!"

"Well, yes; a hundred times yes. I don't understand you and your magnanimity, my dear fellow; if the Committee of Public Safety got hold of us, you'd soon see whether they'd bother with all these niceties."

"And so you persist in your decision, gentlemen?"

"Of course we do, and I hope you're not going to oppose us."

"I have only one vote, gentlemen, and it was in favor of giving him back his liberty. You have six votes, all six in favor of death. So death wins."

The sweat pouring down Maurice's forehead suddenly turned to ice.

"He'll cry out, scream," said the voice. "I hope you've at least taken Madame Dixmer out of hearing?"

"She knows nothing, she's in the pavilion across the way."

"Madame Dixmer," murmured Maurice. "I'm beginning to see the light. I'm at that master tanner's place, the one who spoke to me in the old rue Saint-Jacques, who sneered at me when I couldn't tell him what my friend's name was. But why on earth does a master tanner want to assassinate me? In any case, before they assassinate me, I'll dispatch more than one of them."

And with that, Maurice bounded toward the inoffensive implement that would soon become a terrible weapon in his hands. Then he stood behind the door so that he would be shielded by it when it opened. His heart was beating fit to burst, and in the silence his heartbeat thundered out. Suddenly a chill ran down his spine as a voice said:

"If you take my advice, you'll just smash in a window and shoot him through the bars with a rifle."

"No, no, no; no explosions," said another voice. "An explosion could give us away. Ah! There you are, Dixmer. What about your wife?"

"I've just had a look through the shutters. She has no idea what's happening, she's reading."

"Dixmer, you decide. Are you for a rifle or a dagger?"

"I say the dagger. Let's go!"

"Let's go," the five or six other voices chorused.

Maurice was a child of the Revolution, with a heart of gold and a soul given to atheism, like so many young men at the time. But when he heard the words "Let's go" from behind the door that alone stood between him and death, he remembered the sign of the cross that his mother had taught him when he was just a little boy made to say his prayers on his knees at bedtime.

Footsteps drew near, then stopped; the key ground in the lock and the door slowly opened. In the minute it took, Maurice had said to himself: "If I waste time lashing out, I'll be killed. By rushing at my assassins, I'll take them by surprise; I'll reach the garden, the alleyway, I may just get away."

Immediately he sprang like a lion, giving a wild yell in which he managed to pack more menace than fear. He felled the first two men, who thought he was tied up blindfolded and so were far from expecting an onslaught; he then drove through the rest and covered thirty feet in one second flat, thanks to his calves of steel. He could see a door to the garden standing wide open at the end of a hallway and he flew at it, vaulted ten steps, and landed in the garden; getting his bearings as best he could, he ran to the outside door.

But this door was well and truly locked. Maurice tugged at the twin locks, tried to wrench the door open, but there was no key. Meanwhile, his pursuers had reached the back steps and spotted him.

"There he is. Shoot, Dixmer, shoot! Kill him! Kill him!"

Maurice let out a roar: he was trapped in the garden. At a glance he estimated that the surrounding walls were ten feet high.

All this happened in a flash as his assassins flew after him. Maurice was about thirty feet ahead of them. He looked around with the eyes of a doomed man who asks only to be able to slip through a crack in the ground.

He spotted the pavilion, the shutters, the light behind the shutters. It took only one bound, a leap of ten feet, for him to grab one of the shutters, rip it off, smash his way through the window, and fall into the illuminated room where a woman sat reading by the fire.

The woman shot to her feet in fright and screamed for help.

"Out of the way, Geneviève, out of the way," cried the voice of Dixmer. "Out of the way so I can kill the man!"

Maurice saw the barrel of the rifle level at him about ten feet away. But as soon as the woman laid eyes on him, she let out a terrible cry, and instead of getting out of the way as her husband had ordered she threw herself between Maurice and the barrel of the gun. That gesture focused Maurice's attention squarely on the generous creature whose first impulse was to protect him.

It was his turn to let out a cry, for it was none other than the mysterious woman he'd been trying so hard to find.

"You! . . . You! . . ." he cried.

"Quiet!" she said; turning to the assassins who had gathered at the window, with different weapons in their hands, she cried, "Oh, no you don't! You will not kill this man!"

"He's a spy!" cried Dixmer, whose soft placid face had taken on an expression of implacable determination. "He's a spy and he has to die."

"Him? A spy?" said Geneviève. "A spy, him? Come here, Dixmer, I have something to say to you that will prove you are peculiarly mistaken."

Dixmer approached the window and Geneviève went over to him, bent down, and whispered a few words in his ear. The master tanner shot his head up.

"Him?" he said.

"The very one," Geneviève replied.

"Are you sure?"

This time the young woman did not reply but turned to Maurice and held out her hand, smiling. Dixmer's features settled into a bizarre mix of kindly indulgence and disdain. He brought the butt of the rifle down hard against the ground.

"Well, then, that's a different matter," he said.

Then he signaled to his cohorts to follow him and they moved off into the dark.

"Hide the ring," Geneviève murmured meanwhile. "Everyone here knows it."

Maurice swiftly slipped the ring from his finger and into his vest pocket. An instant later, the door of the pavilion opened and Dixmer, unarmed, came toward him.

"Forgive me, citizen," he said, "for not acknowledging earlier the debt I owe you! My wife remembered the service you did for her the night of the tenth of March, but she'd forgotten your name. So we had no idea who we were dealing with. If we had, believe me, we would never for a moment have doubted your honor or suspected your intentions. And so forgive me, once again!"

Maurice was stupefied. He remained on his feet only by some miracle as he felt his head spin and sensed he was about to fall. He leaned against the mantelpiece for support.

"But what did you want to kill me for, anyway?" he said.

"I'll let you in on the secret, citizen," said Dixmer. "I trust your loyalty. I am, as you already know, the master tanner and manager of this tannery. Most of the acids I use in the preparation of my skins are prohibited goods. Now, the smugglers I employ got wind of a delegation made to the general council of the Commune. When I saw you taking down information, I panicked. My smugglers panicked even more than I did when they saw your red cap and how businesslike you looked, and I won't pretend we didn't vote to kill you."

"I'm well aware of that, thank you," Maurice said. "You're not telling me anything I don't know. I heard the debate, I saw your gun."

"I've already asked your forgiveness," Dixmer continued with an air of touching bonhomie. "You must understand that, thanks to these turbulent times, we—my associate, Monsieur Morand, and I—are sitting on a gold mine. We have been commissioned to supply bags for the army; every day we have fifteen hundred to two thousand of them made. Thanks to the happy state of affairs in which we live, the Council, which has its hands full, doesn't have the time to check our accounts thoroughly, so that, I must admit, we are sort of fishing in troubled waters; all the more so since, as I've told you, the preparatory stuff we smuggle in allows us to make two hundred percent."[1]

"Well!" said Maurice. "That seems to me to be an honest enough profit, and now I understand why you were afraid it would dry up if I denounced you. But now you know who I am, surely you are reassured?"

"Now," said Dixmer, "I wouldn't even ask you for your word of honor." He put his hand on Maurice's shoulder and beamed at him. "Come. Now we've had a bit of a talk and are among friends, tell me what you're really here for, young man. Of course," the master tanner added, "if you don't want to say, you're perfectly at liberty not to."

"But I think I told you," stammered Maurice.

"Yes, something about a woman," said the burgher. "I know there was talk of a woman."

"My God! Forgive me, citizen," said Maurice. "I'm only too well aware that I owe you an explanation. So, I was looking for a woman who told me, the other night—she was wearing a mask at the time—that she lived somewhere in this neighborhood. I don't know her name or her social standing or which house she lives in. I only know that I'm madly in love with her and that she was short."

Geneviève was tall.

"She was blond and pert. . . ."

Geneviève was dark with great soulful eyes.

"A working-class lass, I'd say. . . . That's why I'm decked out like a real man of the people like this—I thought she'd approve."

"So that explains everything," said Dixmer with an angelic naïveté not belied by even the slightest sly glimmer in his eye. Geneviève, though, had blushed and, feeling herself blush, turned away.

"Poor citizen Lindey," said Dixmer, laughing. "What a nasty hour we put you through, and you're the last person I'd have wanted to harm. Such a good patriot, such a brother! . . . But I truly thought someone with evil intentions had usurped your name."

"Let's say no more about it," said Maurice, who realized it was time to get cracking. "Point me in the right direction and we'll forget it ever happened...."

"Point you in the right direction?" cried Dixmer. "Send you packing? Not on your life! This evening I, or rather my partner and I, are hosting a supper for the brave boys who wanted to cut your throat a moment ago. I'm counting on you to eat with them so that you can see they're not quite as diabolical as they seem."

"But," protested Maurice, full of joy at the prospect of spending a few hours close to Geneviève, "I don't know if I really ought to accept."

"Why not! I think you really ought to accept," said Dixmer. "They're all good solid patriots like you; besides, I won't believe you've forgiven me until we've broken bread together."

Geneviève didn't say a word. Maurice was in agony.

"If the truth be known," he stammered, "I'm afraid of imposing on you, citizen.... In this getup, I look ... pretty rough...."

Geneviève gave him a timid glance.

"Our invitation is sincere," she said.

"I accept then, citizeness," Maurice said with a bow.

"Well then, I'll go and reassure our companions," said the master tanner. "Warm up a bit, meanwhile, dear friend."

He left. Maurice and Geneviève were alone.

"Ah, monsieur!" said the young woman with a woeful attempt at a rebuke. "You didn't keep your word, you've been indiscreet."

"What!" cried Maurice. "Oh, madame, have I compromised you? Please forgive me if I have; you won't see me again...."

"My God!" she cried, getting to her feet. "You've been wounded in the chest! Your shirt is stained with blood!"

Indeed, on Maurice's amazingly fine and amazingly white cambric shirt, a shirt that contrasted oddly with the rest of his coarse clothes, a large red blotch had spread and dried.

"Oh! Don't worry, madame. One of the smugglers scratched me with his dagger."

Geneviève went pale as she took his hand.

"Forgive me," she murmured, "for the wrong they have done you; you saved my life and I nearly brought about your death."

"Don't I have my reward in finding you again? You didn't think for a moment that I was looking for anyone else, did you?"

"Come with me," Geneviève broke in. "I'll get you some linen. . . . Our guests must not see you in this state. It would be too terrible a reproach to them."

"I really am imposing on you, aren't I?" Maurice replied with a sigh.

"Not at all; I'm just doing my duty." She added: "And doing it with great pleasure."

Geneviève led Maurice to a great linen cupboard of an elegance and distinction he wasn't expecting to find in the house of a master tanner. True, this particular master tanner seemed to be a millionaire. She flung open the cupboard doors. "Help yourself," she said. "Make yourself at home."

And with that, she withdrew.

When Maurice reappeared, he found Dixmer back on deck.

"Let's go," he said. "Dinner's ready! We're only waiting for you."

9

SUPPER

When Maurice entered the dining room along with Dixmer and Geneviève, the table had been set and dinner laid out, but the room, which was in the main building, where he had first been conducted, was still empty.

He watched each guest file in one by one; there were six of them. They all looked nice enough on the outside, most of them young and dressed in the fashion of the day. Two or three even sported the carmagnole and red cap. Dixmer introduced Maurice around, grandly announcing his title and credentials. Then he turned to Maurice.

"You see before you, citizen Lindey, all the men who help me in my business. Thanks to the times in which we live, thanks to the revolutionary principles that have eliminated distance, we all live on a footing of the most sacred equality. The same table brings us together and

I'm glad you agreed to share our family meal with us. So please sit down, citizen, and eat!"

"What about . . . Monsieur Morand," Geneviève timidly ventured. "Aren't we waiting for him?"

"Oh yes, right," replied Dixmer. "Citizen Morand, of whom I've already spoken to you, citizen Lindey, is my partner. He is the one charged with the moral side of the business, if I may use that term. He does all the bookkeeping, does the accounts, pays the bills, doles out and receives the money. Of all of us, he definitely has the most to do. The result is that he is sometimes late. I'll go and alert him."

At that very moment, the door opened and in came citizen Morand.

He was a short man with dark hair and bushy eyebrows; green glasses, the sort worn by people who work so hard their eyes get tired, screened his black eyes but did not obscure their twinkle. At his first words, Maurice recognized the voice, at once gentle and imperious, that had consistently urged clemency in the terrible deliberations of which he had been the victim. Morand was dressed in a brown suit with great big buttons and a vest of white silk. His rather fine jabot was often agitated over dinner, tormented by a hand whose whiteness and delicacy Maurice was impressed by, no doubt because it belonged to a merchant tanner.

Everyone took their place. Citizen Morand was seated on Geneviève's right, Maurice on her left; Dixmer sat down opposite his wife and the other guests sat anywhere they liked around the rectangular table.

The supper was refined. Dixmer had the appetite of an industrialist and did the honors of his table with a heavy dose of jollity. The workers, or those who passed for workers, made him good cheery company as such. Citizen Morand spoke little, ate even less, scarcely drank a drop, and laughed rarely. Maurice, perhaps because of the memories his voice recalled to mind, soon felt a strong liking for him. But he couldn't figure out the man's age and this gnawed at him. At times, Morand looked to him to be in his early forties; at other times, he seemed very young.

Dixmer, sitting down to dinner, felt obliged to offer his guests some kind of reason for admitting a stranger into their little circle. He did so in the guise of a naïve man little given to lying; but the guests weren't too demanding as far as explanations went, it seemed, for, despite the awkwardness with which the manufacturer of skins introduced the young man, his little opening speech seemed to satisfy everyone.

Maurice looked at him in amazement.

"Upon my word," he said to himself, "I must have got it wrong. Can this be the same man who, steely-eyed, voice threatening, pursued me with a rifle in hand, absolutely determined to kill me, three quarters of an hour ago? Then I'd have taken him for a hero or a killer. Good Lord! Looks like a love of skins can do something to a man!"

While he was busy making these observations, his heart was filled with such a profound mix of pain and joy that the young man would have been hard-pressed to tell the state of his soul. Here he was, finally, next to the beautiful stranger he'd sought so desperately. Just as he had dreamed, she had a soft and lovely name, and Maurice was intoxicated with happiness to feel her by his side; he drank in her every word, and the sound of her voice, every time it rang out, made his heart sing. But his heart broke at what he saw.

Geneviève was indeed everything he'd glimpsed: the reality had not destroyed that dream of a stormy night. She was indeed the same woman—elegant, sad-eyed, high-minded. It was a case of what so often happened in those years before the notorious year of '93 in which they found themselves: she was the perfect young woman of distinction obliged, because of the ruin into which the nobility was sinking deeper and deeper, to ally herself with the bourgeoisie, with mercantile interests. Dixmer seemed like a good sort of fellow. He was incontestably rich; his manners toward Geneviève seemed to be those of a man who makes it his job to make his wife happy. But this bonhomie, this wealth, these excellent intentions, could they really bridge the immense gap between the wife and the husband, between the poetic young girl, distinguished and charming, and the man of material occupations and such common appearance? With what feelings did Geneviève bridge the gulf?... Alas! As luck would have it, the answer was now clear to Maurice: with love. And he was forced to revise the initial opinion he'd had of the woman, that is, that she was returning home from a lovers' tryst the night he'd met her.

The idea that Geneviève loved another man sickened Maurice to his soul. So he sighed and regretted having come only to let himself in for an even stronger dose of that poison they call love.

Yet at other moments, listening to that soft, pure, melodious voice, questioning those beautifully limpid eyes that didn't seem to mind revealing her innermost soul, Maurice could not believe that such a creature could possibly lie or deceive; he then experienced a bitter joy in thinking that this beautiful soul made flesh belonged to the good burgher with the open smile and the vulgar jokes—and never would belong to him.

Politics was the topic—how could it be otherwise? What else did you talk about in an era in which politics cropped up everywhere, looked up at you from the bottom of dinner plates, papered the walls, was proclaimed at every hour in the street?

All of a sudden, one of the party who had maintained silence till that moment asked for the news of the prisoners in the Temple. Maurice shivered in spite of himself at the sound of that voice. He recognized the devotee of extreme action who had first struck him with his knife and then voted for his death.

And yet this man, an honest tanner, head of the workshop, or so Dixmer said, soon aroused Maurice's good humor by expressing the most patriotic ideas and the most impeccable revolutionary principles. In certain circumstances, the young man was not averse to the vigorous measures so fashionable at the time and whose apostle and hero was Danton. If he had been in this man's shoes, though the man's voice and weapon still caused his heart to lurch, he would not have opted to assassinate someone he took for a spy but would have released him in the garden, and there, equally armed, with a sword in hand like his enemy, he'd have done battle with him mercilessly, without pity or compassion. That is what Maurice would have done. But he soon realized it was too much to ask an assistant tanner to do what he himself would have done.

This extremist, who seemed to hold violent political notions as befit his private conduct, was talking about the Temple; he expressed amazement that the guarding of the prisoners was left to permanent Council personnel, so easy to corrupt, and to municipal officers whose loyalty had already been tempted more than once.

"Yes," said citizen Morand. "But you have to admit that, on every occasion, up till now, the conduct of the municipal officers has merited the confidence that the nation placed in them. History will show that it isn't just Robespierre[1] who deserves the name 'Incorruptible.'"

"No doubt, no doubt," the first man went on. "But just because something hasn't yet happened, it'd be absurd to conclude that it never will. Same thing for the National Guard. The companies of the different sections are all called upon to take their turn at Temple duty, come what may. Well, don't you accept that in a company of twenty to twenty-five men, there might be a handful of eight or ten perfectly determined thugs ready to cut the sentries' throats one fine night and carry off the prisoners?"

"Nonsense!" said Maurice. "You realize, citizen, that's not the way to go about it! They tried it three or four weeks ago and it didn't work."

"Right," Morand went on. "But only because one of the aristocrats in the patrol was silly enough to let the word *monsieur* escape his lips when talking to someone or other."

"And that," said Maurice, keen to prove that the police of the Republic were well-chosen, "is because they'd already noted that the Knight of Maison-Rouge had slipped back into Paris."

"Rubbish!" cried Dixmer.

"They knew that Maison-Rouge had slipped back into Paris?" Morand asked frostily. "And did they know how he got in?"

"Perfectly."

"Hell!" said Morand, leaning forward to peer at Maurice. "I'd be curious to know how; until now, they haven't been able to tell us anything definite about it. But, citizen, as secretary of one of the main sections of Paris, you must be better informed?"

"Naturally," said Maurice. "And what I'm about to tell you is nothing but the truth."

The whole table, including Geneviève, seemed suddenly to give Maurice their utmost attention.

"Well," said Maurice, "the Knight of Maison-Rouge was coming from the Vendée,[2] it seems. He crossed the whole of France with his usual ease and made it to the Roule checkpoint in daylight but waited till nine o'clock at night to get through. At nine o'clock at night, a woman disguised as a commoner exited by this checkpoint, taking the Knight the uniform of a chasseur of the National Guard. Ten minutes later, she came back—with him. The sentry, who'd seen her go through the first time alone, had his suspicions when he saw her coming back in with a man: he alerted the post, the post came running. But the guilty parties, having realized they were the target, darted into a hotel that opened a back door for them on the Champs Elysées. It appears that a patrol entirely devoted to the tyrants was waiting for the Knight on the corner of the rue Barre-du-Bec. You know the rest."

"Ah!" said Morand. "That's curious, what you're telling us there...."

"And particularly promising."

"Yes, it would seem so; but the woman, do they know what happened to her?"

"No, the lady vanished and we don't know who or what she is."

Dixmer's partner, and Dixmer himself, seemed to breathe easier. Geneviève had listened to the whole story, pale and silent and very, very still.

"But," said citizen Morand in his usual frosty fashion, "who can say the Knight of Maison-Rouge was part of the patrol that alarmed the Temple?"

"A municipal officer friend of mine who was on Temple duty that night recognized him."

"Did he have his description?"

"He'd seen him before."

"And what sort of man is he, physically, this Knight of Maison-Rouge?" Morand asked.

"A man of twenty-five or twenty-six, small, blond, with a pleasant face, magnificent eyes, and superb teeth."

Not a sound was heard; no one moved a muscle.

"So," said Morand, "if your municipal officer friend recognized this so-called Knight of Maison-Rouge, why didn't he stop him?"

"First because he didn't know the Knight was back in Paris and so he was afraid he was being fooled by a resemblance; then too, my friend is a little lukewarm; he did what wise men and the lukewarm do: when in doubt, he refrained from acting."

"You would have behaved differently, wouldn't you, citizen?" Dixmer asked Maurice with a sudden laugh.

"Yes," said Maurice, "I admit I'd have preferred to get it wrong than to let a man as dangerous as this Knight of Maison-Rouge get away."

"And what would you have done, monsieur?" Geneviève asked.

"What would I have done, citizeness?" said Maurice. "God knows it wouldn't have taken much. I'd have had all the Temple doors sealed. I'd have gone straight to the phony patrol and collared the Knight and I'd have told him: 'Knight of Maison-Rouge, I arrest you as a traitor to the nation!' And once I'd collared him, I would not have let him go, I can tell you."

"But what would have happened to him?" Geneviève asked.

"What would have happened is that he'd have been put on trial, he and his accomplices, and in this day and age he'd have been guillotined, it's as simple as that."

Geneviève shuddered and cast a glance of terror at her neighbor. But citizen Morand appeared not to notice. Emptying his glass phlegmatically he said, "Citizen Lindey is right. That was the thing to do. But, unfortunately, it wasn't done."

"And do they know where he got to, this Knight of Maison-Rouge?" asked Geneviève.

"Oof!" said Dixmer. "He didn't hang around to see what happened. Since the attempt failed, he would've immediately left Paris."

"Not at all," said Maurice.

"What! He was foolish enough to stay in Paris?" asked Geneviève.

"He hasn't budged."

A general ripple of amazement greeted this opinion, put forth by Maurice with such assurance.

"That is merely an assumption, what you're saying there, citizen," said Morand, "just an assumption, nothing more."

"No, it isn't, it's a fact."

"Oh!" said Geneviève, "I must say, for myself, I can't believe what you're saying, citizen; it would be unpardonably reckless of him."

"You are a woman, citizeness, so you'll understand that there is one thing that must have won out, with the sort of man the Knight of Maison-Rouge obviously is, over all possible considerations of personal safety."

"And what could win out over fear of losing your life in such a ghastly way?"

"Good God, citizeness!" said Maurice. "Love."

"Love?" repeated Geneviève.

"Without a doubt. Don't you know the Knight of Maison-Rouge is in love with Antoinette?"

Two or three hoots of fairly feeble forced laughter burst forth. Dixmer's eyes bored through Maurice as though trying to see into his soul. Geneviève felt her eyes mist with tears, and a shiver that did not escape Maurice ran the length of her body. Citizen Morand spilled the wine he was bringing to his lips and his marble pallor would have frightened Maurice if that young man's entire attention had not been riveted on Geneviève.

"You are moved, citizeness," Maurice murmured.

"Didn't you say I would understand because I'm a woman? Well, we women are always moved by such devotion, even if it is against our principles."

"And the devotion of the Knight of Maison-Rouge is all the greater for his never having spoken to the Queen, they say."

"Ah, there, citizen Lindey," said the extremist, "it seems to me you're being rather indulgent toward this Knight. . . ."

"Monsieur," Maurice returned, perhaps deliberately using the term that was no longer in use, "I admire all proud and courageous natures, but that doesn't stop me from taking them on when I encounter them among the ranks of my enemies. I don't despair of one day meeting the Knight of Maison-Rouge."

"And?" said Geneviève.

"And, if I do meet him . . . well, I'll take him on."

Supper was over. Geneviève declared it was time to go by herself getting up from the table. At that moment the clock chimed.

"Midnight," said Morand coldly.

"Midnight!" cried Maurice. "Midnight already!"

"Now there's an exclamation that makes me happy," said Dixmer. "It proves you weren't bored and gives me the hope we'll see you again. This is the house of a good patriot that is now open to you, and I hope you'll soon see, citizen, that it's the house of a friend."

Maurice bowed and turned to Geneviève:

"Does the citizeness also permit me to return?" he asked.

"I'll do better than permit it, I beg you to come back and see us," said Geneviève with real verve. "Adieu, citizen." With that, she headed back to her quarters.

Maurice took his leave of all the guests, paying particular attention to Morand, who had pleased him greatly; he shook Dixmer's hand and left, dazed, but a lot more happy than sad about the various events that had rocked his evening.

"Extremely annoying encounter!" said the young woman after Maurice had gone, bursting into tears in front of her husband, who had walked her to her room.

"Nonsense! Citizen Lindey, known patriot, secretary of a section, incorruptible, adored, popular, is, on the contrary, a most precious acquisition for a poor tanner housing contraband goods," Dixmer smirked.

"Do you really think so, my friend?" Geneviève asked.

"I think it's a patent of patriotism, a seal of absolution placed on our house. And I think that from tonight the Knight of Maison-Rouge himself would be safe here."

With that, Dixmer planted a kiss on his wife's forehead, with an affection far more paternal than conjugal, and left her in the little pavilion that was hers alone to rejoin the guests we've already met around his table in the main building, where he himself slept.

10

SIMON THE COBBLER

It was the beginning of the month of May. Lungs tired of taking in the freezing cold mists of winter expanded in the pure air and gentle rays of a mild, tonic sun as it shone down on the great black walls of the Temple.

At the inside wicket that cut the tower off from the gardens, the soldiers on duty laughed and smoked.

But despite the lovely day, despite the offer that was made to the prisoners to come down and take a stroll around the gardens, the three women refused: since the execution of her husband, the Queen kept obstinately to her room so she didn't have to pass the door to the second-floor apartment the King had occupied. Whenever she chanced to take the air since that fatal episode of the twenty-first of January, it was at the top of the tower, where the crenellations had been blocked off with shutters.

The National Guards on duty, who had been notified that the three women were authorized to go outside, thus waited in vain all day for them to avail themselves of the privilege. Toward five o'clock a man came down from the tower and approached the sergeant in command of the post.

"Ah! It's you, Tison, old boy!" said the sergeant, who appeared to be a particularly cheery National Guard.

"It's me all right, citizen. Your friend upstairs, citizen municipal officer Maurice Lindey, asked me to give you this permit granted by the Council of the Temple to my daughter to come and pay her mother a short visit this evening."

"And what do you mean by leaving the very moment your daughter's about to arrive, you unnatural father?" said the sergeant.

"Ah! It certainly costs me to have to leave, citizen sergeant. Of course I'd hoped to see my poor girl, too—I haven't seen her for two months—and give her a kiss and a cuddle—what you call it, gallantly—the way any father does his daughter. Don't think I don't! Might as well piss in the wind. Duty, blasted duty, forces me to leave. I have to go to the Commune and make my report. A hackney carriage is waiting for me at the door with a couple of gendarmes, right when my poor Héloïse is about to show."

"You poor unfortunate man!" said the sergeant.

> "And so love of the Nation alone
> Smothers in you the voice of blood.
> One man prays, the other moans:
> Duty calls just the same. . . .

"Tison, old boy, if you think of a word that rhymes with 'blood,' let me know. Damned if I can think of one for the moment."

"And you, citizen sergeant, when my daughter comes to see her poor mother who's missing her like mad, you'll let her through, won't you?"

"The order is in order," quipped the sergeant, whom the reader will already have recognized, no doubt, as our friend Lorin. "So I have nothing to say. When your daughter comes, your daughter will go through."

"Thank you, brave Thermopyle, thank you," said Tison. And off he went to make his report to the Commune, muttering, "Ah! My poor wife, won't she be happy!"

"You know, Sergeant," said one of the National Guards, watching Tison disappear and hearing him muttering as he did so, "you know it makes you tremble inside, that sort of thing!"

"What sort of thing, citizen Devaux?" asked Lorin.

"What do you think?" said the compassionate National Guard. "Seeing that man, with his hard face, that man with his heart of steel, that merciless guardian of the Queen, go off with a tear in his eye, half out of joy and half out of sorrow, thinking that his wife will see her daughter and he won't! Doesn't do to think about it too much, Sergeant, because, truth to tell, it makes you sad. . . ."

"No doubt, which is why he himself doesn't think about it, this man who is going off with a tear in his eye, as you say."

"And what should he think about, then?"

"Well, that it's also three months since the woman he brutalizes without pity has seen her child. Does he ever think of her sorrow? He thinks only of his own. That's all. It's true the woman was once the Queen," the sergeant went on in the same ironic tone, whose meaning would have been difficult to interpret, "and one isn't forced to have the same regard for a queen as for the wife of the odd-jobs man."

"Say what you like, it's all still pretty sad," said Devaux.

"Sad, but necessary," said Lorin. "So the best thing, as you say, is not to think about it. . . ."

And Lorin began to hum:

"Yesterday Nicette
Walked alone-ette
In the deep
Dark woods."

Lorin had only gotten that far in his bucolic ditty when, all of a sudden, a great clamor was heard coming from the left side of the post. It was composed of swearing, threats, and sobs.

"What the hell's that?" asked Devaux.

"Sounds like a child's voice," Lorin replied, listening intently.

"Right," said the National Guard. "Some poor kid having the daylights thrashed out of him. Honestly, they should only send guards here who don't have children."

"Are you going to sing now?" came a raucous, drunken voice, which then began to sing, as though setting an example:

Madame Veto[1] *promised*
To cut the throats of all Paris. . . .

"No," said the child. "I will not sing."

"Are you going to sing?" And the voice began again: "Madame Veto promised. . ."

"No," wailed the child. "No, no, no."

"Oh! You little bastard!" cried the raucous voice.

And the noise of a whistling strap rent the air. The child uttered a cry of pain.

"Good grief!" said Lorin. "It's that odious Simon thrashing little Capet."

Some of the National Guards merely shrugged their shoulders; two or three tried to smile. Devaux got up and moved away.

"As I was saying," he muttered, "they should never send us fathers here."

Suddenly a low door opened and the royal infant, chased by his guardian's whip, took several steps into the courtyard in a bid to get away. But something heavy crashed onto the cobblestones behind him and struck his leg.

"Ahhh!" the child shrieked as he stumbled and fell on his knees.

"Bring me my cobbler's last, you little monster, or I'll . . ."

The child picked himself up and shook his head in refusal.

"Ah! It's like that, is it?" cried the same voice. "Just you wait, just you wait, I'll show you. . . ."

And with that Simon the cobbler came out of his lodge like a wild beast out of its lair.

"Hold it right there!" said Lorin, frowning furiously. "Where do you think you're going like that, Master Simon?"

"To chastise that little demon," said the cobbler.

"Chastise him? What for?" said Lorin.

"What for?"

"You heard me."

"Because the little bastard won't sing like a good patriot should or work like a good citizen."

"Well, what's it to you?" said Lorin. "Did the nation entrust you with teaching Capet to sing?"

"Hey!" said Simon. "What business is it of yours, citizen sergeant, eh?"

"What business is it of mine? Anything that concerns any man with a heart is my business. It is unworthy of a man of feeling to see a child being beaten and do nothing about it."

"Poppycock. The son of the tyrant."

"—is a child, a child who had no hand in the crimes of his father, a child who is not guilty and who, as a consequence, should not be punished."

"And I'm telling you they gave him to me to do what I like with him. I'd like him to sing the song 'Madame Veto' and he's going to sing it."

"You miserable cur!" said Lorin. "Madame Veto is the child's mother—his own mother! How would you like it if they forced your son to sing that you were scum?"

"Me?" screamed Simon. "You lousy aristocrat of a sergeant!"

"No insults, thank you," said Lorin. "I'm not Capet—you won't get me to sing by force."

"I'll get you arrested, but, you rotten royalist."

"You!" said Lorin. "You will get me arrested? Just you try and get a Thermopyle arrested!"

"Right! Well, he who laughs last laughs loudest. Meanwhile, Capet, pick up my last and come and make your shoe or there'll be trouble. . . ."

"And I'm telling you," said Lorin, stepping forward, the blood drained from his face, putting up his fists and gritting his teeth, "I'm telling you he will not pick up your last; I'm telling you he will not make any shoes, do you hear me, you pathetic buffoon? Oh, yes! You've got your big long sword but it doesn't frighten me any more than you do. Just try and take it out!"

"Help! Murder!" screamed Simon, blanching with rage.

At that moment, two women entered the courtyard. One of them held a piece of paper in her hand. She addressed the sentry.

"Sergeant!" cried the sentry. "It's the Tison girl asking to see her mother."

"Let her through, the Council of the Temple has granted her permission," said Lorin, without turning his back for an instant on Simon, for fear the man would take advantage of the distraction to bash the child again.

The sentry let the two women through, but they had scarcely started up the dimly lit stairs when they encountered Maurice Lindey, who was coming down to the courtyard for a moment.

Night was beginning to fall, so that the women's facial features could hardly be distinguished. Maurice stopped them.

"Who are you, citizenesses?" he asked. "And what do you want?"

"I'm Héloïse Tison," said one of the women. "I've obtained permission to see my mother and so I've come to see her."

"Yes," said Maurice. "But the permission is only for you, citizeness."

"I've brought my friend along so that there are at least two of us women among all these soldiers."

"That's all very well, but your friend will not be able to go up."

"As you wish, citizen," said Héloïse Tison, squeezing the hand of her friend, who backed against the wall, seemingly stricken with shock and fright.

"Citizen sentries," cried Maurice, lifting his head and calling to the sentries standing guard on each landing. "Let citizeness Tison pass.

But her friend can't go up. She will wait on the stairs and you will see to it that she is shown respect."

"Yes, citizen," the sentries called down.

"Up you go, then," said Maurice.

The two women passed.

As for Maurice, he leapt the four or five bottom steps in a single bound and rushed into the courtyard.

"What's going on here, then? What was all the racket about?" he asked the National Guards. "You can hear a child crying all the way up in the prisoners' antechamber."

"What's going on," said Simon, who was used to the ways of the municipal officers and thought when he saw Maurice that he'd found reinforcements, "what's going on is that this traitor, this aristocrat, this royalist, is trying to stop me from giving Capet a good hiding."

He pointed to Lorin with his fist.

"I'll stop you all right," said Lorin, unsheathing his sword. "And if you call me a royalist, an aristocrat, or a traitor one more time, I'll run my sword right through your rickety body."

"He's threatening me!" cried Simon. "Guards! Guards!"

"I am the guard," said Lorin. "So I wouldn't call me if I were you, because if I come any closer to you, I'll exterminate you!"

"Over here, citizen municipal officer, over here!" cried Simon, feeling seriously threatened this time by Lorin.

"The sergeant is right," came the cold reply of the municipal officer Simon had called to his aid. "You dishonor the nation. Let go! Imagine beating a child!"

"And do you know why he's beating him, Maurice? Because the child doesn't want to sing 'Madame Veto,' because the son doesn't want to insult his mother."

"You miserable abortion!" said Maurice.

"You too?" said Simon. "So I'm surrounded by traitors?"

"You mongrel!" said the municipal officer, seizing Simon by the throat and tearing his strap out of his hands. "Just you try and prove that Maurice Lindey is a traitor."

With that, Maurice brought the strap down hard on the cobbler's shoulders.

"Thank you, monsieur," said the child, who was stoically watching the scene. "But he'll only take it out on me."

"Come, Capet," said Lorin, "come, child; if he hits you again, call for help and we'll come and chastise him, the butcher. Come, young Capet, let's go back to the tower."

"Why do you call me Capet, you who protect me?" said the child. "You know very well that Capet is not my name."

"Really? How so? It isn't your name?" said Lorin. "What is your name?"

"I am called Louis-Charles de Bourbon. Capet is the name of one of my ancestors. I know the history of France, my father taught me."

"And you want to teach cobbling to a child to whom a king has taught the history of France?" cried Lorin. "For crying out loud!"

"Don't you worry," said Maurice to the child. "I'll report him."

"And I'll report you," said Simon. "Among other things, I'll say that instead of one woman who had the right to enter the courtyard, you let in two."

At that moment, in fact, the two women were coming out of the dungeon. Maurice ran over to them.

"So, citizeness," he said, addressing the woman nearest to him. "Did you see your mother?"

Héloïse Tison immediately slipped between the municipal officer and her companion.

"Yes, thank you, citizen," she said.

Maurice would have liked to see the young woman's friend or at least hear her voice, but she was swaddled in her mantle and seemed determined not to utter a sound. It seemed to him that she was even trembling.

Smelling a rat, he swiftly ran up the stairs and, reaching the first room, saw through the glass the Queen hide in her pocket something he assumed to be a note.

"Oh, no!" he said to himself. "Have I been had?"

He called his colleague.

"Citizen Agricola," he said, "go to Marie Antoinette and don't let her out of your sight."

"Right!" said the municipal officer. "Is the . . ."

"In you go, I say, and don't lose a minute, an instant, a second."

The officer entered the Queen's chamber.

"Call Mother Tison," he said to a National Guard.

Five minutes later, Mother Tison arrived, beaming.

"I saw my daughter," she said.

"Where?" Maurice asked.

"Here, in this very room."

"Very well. And your daughter didn't ask to see the Austrian woman?"

"No."

"She didn't go into her room?"

"No."

"While you were talking to your daughter, no one came out of the prisoners' room?"

"How do I know? I was looking at my daughter—I hadn't seen her for three months after all."

"Think carefully."

"Ah, yes! I remember now, I think."

"What?"

"The girl came out."

"Marie Thérèse, the Queen's daughter?"

"Yes."

"Did she speak to your daughter?"

"No."

"Your daughter didn't hand her anything?"

"No."

"She didn't pick anything up off the floor?"

"My daughter?"

"No, Marie Antoinette's!"

"Yes, she did, she picked up her hanky."

"Ah! You sorry woman!" Maurice cried.

And he hurled himself at a bell-pull and gave it a good tug.

It was the alarm bell.

11

The Note

The other two officers of the Guard swiftly mounted the stairs, accompanied by a detachment from the post on duty. The doors were locked and two sentries came and stood at the entrance to each room.

"What do you want, monsieur?" the Queen asked Maurice when he stepped into the room. "I was about to go to bed five minutes ago, when the citizen municipal officer," here the Queen indicated Agricola, "burst into the room suddenly without stating what he wanted."

"Madame," said Maurice bowing, "it is not my colleague who wants something from you, it is I."

"You, monsieur?" asked Marie Antoinette, gazing at Maurice, whose good manners had inspired in her a certain gratitude. "And what is it you want?"

"I want you to kindly hand me the note that you were hiding a moment ago when I arrived."

Madame Royale and Madame Elisabeth both gave a start. The Queen went very pale.

"You are seeing things, monsieur," she said. "I hid nothing."

"You're lying, Austrian woman!" shouted Agricola.

Maurice promptly brought his hand down on his colleague's arm.

"One moment, my dear colleague," he said. "Let me speak to the citizeness. I'm a bit of a prosecutor."

"Go ahead! But don't be so nice to her, for pity's sake!"

"You were hiding a note, citizeness," Maurice said with severity. "You must hand over the note."

"But what note?"

"The one the Tison girl brought you and that the citizeness, your daughter," and here Maurice nodded toward the young princess, "picked up with her handkerchief."

The three women looked at one another in horror.

"But, monsieur, this is more than mere tyranny," said the Queen. "We are women! Women!"

"Let's be clear," said Maurice firmly. "We are neither judges nor executioners. We are prison supervisors, that is, citizens whose duty it is to keep watch over you. We have our orders; to violate them would be treason. Citizeness, please, give me the note you hid."

"Messieurs," said the Queen loftily, "since you are supervisors, perhaps you would care to have a look around and deprive us of sleep tonight as always."

"God keep us from manhandling women. I am going to notify the Commune and we will await orders. But you will not be going to bed. You will sleep sitting up in these chairs, thank you, and we will keep watch over you. . . . If need be, the search will begin."

"What's the matter now?" asked Mother Tison, showing her frazzled head at the door.

"The matter, citizeness, is that you have just deprived yourself of ever seeing your daughter again by lending a hand to her bout of treason."

"Ever seeing my daughter! . . . What are you saying, citizen?" asked Mother Tison, unable to grasp why she would not be seeing her daughter ever again.

"I'm telling you, your daughter did not come here to see you but to bring a letter to citizeness Capet; and she will not be coming back again."

"But if she doesn't come back again, I won't be able to see her, since we're not allowed to leave."

"This time you've only yourself to blame; it's your fault," said Maurice.

"Oh!" howled the poor mother, "My fault! What are you saying? My fault? But nothing happened, I'm sure of it. Oh! If I thought something had happened, you'd be in for it, Antoinette, you'd really catch it then!"

With that, the distraught woman shook her fist at the Queen.

"Don't you threaten anyone," said Maurice. "Try and use a little kindness instead to get us what we want. You're a woman, after all; citizeness Antoinette, who is also a mother, will no doubt take pity on a mother such as herself. Tomorrow your daughter will be arrested, tomorrow she will be locked up. . . . Then, if they find anything, and you know very well that when they want to find something they always do, she will be finished, and her friend with her."

Mother Tison, who had listened to Maurice with growing terror, turned on the Queen her almost deranged gaze.

"You hear that, Antoinette? . . . My daughter! . . . It's you who will have sunk my daughter!"

The Queen appeared horrified in turn, not of the threat that glinted in the mad eyes of her jailer but of the despair that she read there.

"Come, Madame Tison, I have something to say to you."

"Wait a minute! No huddling over there," yelled Maurice's colleague. "We're not here for nothing, for pity's sake! Everything has to be out in the open, in front of the municipality! Out in the open, I say!"

"Let her alone, citizen Agricola," Maurice whispered in the man's ear. "As long as we learn the truth, who cares how it comes to us."

"You're right, citizen Maurice, but still . . ."

"Let's go behind the glass, citizen Agricola, and turn our backs, if you'll just bear with me; I am sure that the woman for whom we show such indulgence will not cause us to regret it."

The Queen heard these words as she was meant to do. She threw the young man a grateful look. Maurice casually turned his head away and went through to the other side of the glass partition, followed by Agricola.

"You see that woman," he said to Agricola. "As Queen, she's more than guilty; as a woman, she is a most worthy and noble soul. It's a good thing to smash crowns; unhappiness purifies."

"Good grief, you talk beautiful, citizen Maurice! I could listen to you all day, you and your friend Lorin. Is that also poetry, what you just said?"

Maurice smiled.

During this conversation, the scene Maurice had anticipated was taking place on the other side of the glass. Mother Tison had approached the Queen.

"Madame," said the Queen, "your despair breaks my heart. I do not want to deprive you of your child, it hurts too much. Just think for a moment: if you do what these men are asking you to do, perhaps your daughter will also be lost."

"Do what they say!" shrieked Mother Tison. "Do what they say!"

"But first, I want you to think what you're doing."

"What am I doing?" asked the jailer with an almost crazed curiosity.

"Your daughter brought a friend with her."

"Yes, a working lass like herself. She didn't want to come alone because of the soldiers."

"This friend had given your daughter a note; your daughter dropped it. Marie went and picked it up. It's a perfectly insignificant piece of paper, but people with bad intentions could misconstrue it. Didn't the municipal officer say that when they want to find something they always do?"

"So? So? Go on!"

"Well, that's all; you want me to hand over this piece of paper. Do you want me to sacrifice a friend without necessarily getting you your daughter back for all that?"

"Do what they say!" cried the woman. "Do what they say!"

"But this piece of paper compromises your daughter," said the Queen. "Please understand!"

"My daughter is a good patriot, like me," shrieked the shrew. "Thank God! The Tisons are well known! Do what they say!"

"My God!" cried the Queen. "What can I do to convince you!"

"My daughter! I want my daughter back!" resumed Mother Tison, staggering. "Give me the note, Antoinette, give it to me."

"Here it is, madame."

With that, the Queen handed the unfortunate creature a piece of paper that the latter waved above her head, shouting, "Come back, come back, citizen municipal officers. I've got the note. Take it and give me back my child."

"You are sacrificing our friends, sister," said Madame Elisabeth.

"No, sister," the Queen replied, with sadness. "I'm only sacrificing ourselves. The note compromises no one."

At Mother Tison's eruption, Maurice and his colleague returned and stood before her; she handed over the note and they read: "In the Orient, a friend still keeps watch."

Maurice had barely glanced at the note when he began to tremble, for the writing seemed to him not unfamiliar.

"Oh, my God!" he intoned silently. "Surely this can't be Geneviève's writing! No, it's not possible! I'm mad. It looks like her writing, no doubt about that; but what connection could Geneviève possibly have with the Queen?"

He spun round and saw that Marie Antoinette was watching him. As for Mother Tison, she was devouring him with her eyes, waiting to hear her fate.

"You've done a good deed," he said to Mother Tison. "And you, citizen, a fine deed," he said to the Queen.

"Well then, monsieur," the Queen returned. "Let it be an example to you; burn this note and you will have done a charitable deed."

"You're kidding, Austrian woman," said Agricola. "Burn a piece of paper that'll help us catch a whole coven of aristocrats, maybe? Good grief, no! That'd be too silly for words."

"Yes, burn it," said Mother Tison, "it might compromise my daughter."

"I think it might—your daughter and all the rest of them," said Agricola, ripping out of Maurice's hands the note Maurice would gladly have burned if only he'd been on his own. Ten minutes later, the note was placed on the desk of the members of the Commune. There it was opened instantly and commented upon from every possible angle.

" 'In the Orient, a friend still keeps watch,' " someone read aloud. "What the hell does that mean?"

"Hell!" answered a geographer. "In the Orient—Lorient, that much is clear: Lorient[1] is a small town in Brittany, on the coast between Vannes and Quimper. Good grief! We should burn the town down if it's true they're harboring aristocrats that are still keeping watch over the Austrian woman."

"It's all the more dangerous," someone else piped up, "since Lorient is a seaport, so they could establish intelligence with the English."

"I propose," said a third, "we send a commission to Lorient and set up an inquiry there."

Maurice had been informed of the deliberations.

"I very much doubt," he said to himself, "Lorient can be the Orient in question; we're not talking about a place in Brittany, that's for sure."

The very next day the Queen, who, as we have said, no longer went down to the gardens so as not to have to pass the room her husband had been locked up in, asked to go up to the top of the tower to get a little fresh air with her daughter and Madame Elisabeth. The request was instantly granted. But unbeknownst to the ladies, Maurice went up too beforehand and, hiding behind a kind of compact sentry box housed at the top of the stairs, awaited the outcome of the note of the day before.

At first, the Queen sauntered casually about with her daughter and Madame Elisabeth, then she stood still while the two princesses continued to circle the tower platform. She turned to the east and looked intently at a nearby house in that direction, at whose windows several figures appeared. One of these figures was holding a white handkerchief.

Maurice meanwhile pulled a lorgnette from his pocket, and while he was adjusting it the Queen clearly waved her hand, as though to invite the curious souls at the window of the house to get back inside. But not before Maurice noticed the head of a man with blond hair and a pale complexion whose low bow had been respectful to the point of humility.

Behind this young man, for the curious fellow looked as if he was no more than twenty-five or twenty-six years old, a woman was half hidden. Maurice trained his lorgnette on her and, feeling he'd recognized Geneviève, gave himself away with a sudden jerk. Immediately the woman, who herself held a lorgnette in her hands, jumped back, dragging the young man with her. Was it really Geneviève? Did she in turn recognize Maurice? Or did the strange couple withdraw simply at the Queen's invitation?

Maurice waited a while, scarcely breathing, to see whether the man and the woman would reappear. But the window remained deserted; so he counseled his colleague Agricola to show the greatest possible vigilance and rushed back downstairs and out to the corner of the rue Porte-Foin, to lie in wait for the curious couple in the house to come out. But he waited in vain, for no one came.

Unable to resist the suspicion that had been gnawing at his heart from the moment the Tison girl's companion had deliberately kept herself covered up and mute, Maurice wended his way to the old rue Saint-Jacques, his mind in a turmoil of doubt.

When he entered the house, Geneviève was sitting in a white dressing gown by a big pot of jasmine, where she was in the habit of being served lunch. She gave Maurice the usual warm welcome and invited him to have a cup of hot chocolate with her.

Dixmer, too, arrived at that very moment, and appeared tickled pink at seeing Maurice at this unexpected hour of the day. But before Maurice was served the cup of chocolate he had accepted, Dixmer, ever enthusiastic when it came to his commercial enterprise, insisted that his friend the secretary of the Lepelletier section tour the workshops with him. Maurice could only go along.

"My dear Maurice," said Dixmer, taking the young man's arm and steering him along, "I have news of the utmost importance to tell you."

"To do with politics?" asked Maurice, preoccupied as he continued to be with his notion.

"Ha!" Dixmer barked, smiling. "You know we don't take much notice of politics here, my friend. No, no, it's a bit of industrial news, I'm glad to say! My honorable friend Morand, who, as you know, is a most distinguished chemist, has just discovered the secret of a red morocco leather never before seen till now. It's fade-resistant! It's this dye I want to show you. And you'll get to see Morand at work; he's a true artist, that one."

Maurice didn't quite see how you could be an artist in red morocco, but he accepted the invitation anyway and trailed after Dixmer through the workshops. In a sort of special dispensary, he saw citizen Morand at work. Morand was wearing his blue glasses this time, along with his work gear, and he seemed incredibly busy indeed, turning a dirty white sheepskin purple. His hands and arms, visible below rolled-up sleeves, were red to the elbow. As Dixmer said, he seemed to have given himself over heart and soul to the joys of cochineal—so much so that he merely nodded to Maurice without stopping what he was doing.

"So, citizen Morand," said Dixmer, "where were we?"

"We stand to gain a hundred thousand livres a year with this process alone," said Morand. "But I haven't slept for a week and the acids are burning my eyes."

Maurice quickly left Dixmer with Morand and went back to join Geneviève once more, murmuring very softly to himself, "I have to admit the job of municipal officer will turn even a hero into a hardened brute. At the end of a week at the Temple, you'd think you were an aristocrat yourself and turn yourself in. Dixmer's not a bad bloke and Morand's the real thing; as for Geneviève, she's as sweet as they come. To think I could suspect them even for a moment!"

Geneviève was waiting for Maurice with a smile so sweet as to dispel the suspicions he had, after all, entertained. She was all that she always was: gentle, warm and friendly, charming. The hours Maurice spent with Geneviève were those when he really felt alive. The rest of the time he suffered from the fever we might well call "the fever of '93," which split Paris into two camps and turned existence into an eternal struggle—every minute of the day.

At midday, nonetheless, he had to leave Geneviève and return to the Temple. At the far end of the rue Saint-Avoye, he met Lorin coming off duty. He was bringing up the rear, but broke rank and went over to Maurice, whose whole face still glowed with the bliss that seeing Geneviève always made him feel.

"Ah!" said Lorin giving his friend's hand a hearty shake:

> "In vain you seek to stifle your sighs
> I know what you desire.
> You say nothing; but you're on fire.
> Love is in your heart, love is in your eyes."

Maurice fumbled in his pocket for his whistle, which was his way of putting a damper on his friend's poetic verve. But Lorin saw what was coming and ran off laughing.

"By the way," said Lorin, turning to face Maurice again, "you've still got three days at the Temple, Maurice. I commend little Capet to you."

12

LOVE

After a while, Maurice was very happy and very unhappy at the same time. That is how it always is at the beginning of grand passions. He worked in the day within the Lepelletier section; at night, he visited the old rue Saint-Jacques and occasionally put in an appearance at the Thermopylae club. These things filled his days and nights.

He did not fool himself into thinking that seeing Geneviève every night was anything more than drinking long drafts of a love without hope. Geneviève was one of those apparently easygoing yet shy women who gladly hold out their hand to a friend, who innocently bend their forehead to receive his kiss with all the confidence of a sister or the ignorance of a virgin; to such women, words of love are blasphemy, physical desires sacrilegious.

If in the purest of dreams that the young Raphael managed to put down on canvas there is a Madonna with smiling lips, chaste eyes, and a celestial expression, she is the model we should borrow from Perugia's student of the divine to serve as the portrait of Geneviève.

Perched among her flowers, whose freshness and perfume she shared, sheltered from her husband's industry and from her husband himself, Geneviève appeared to Maurice, each time he saw her, like a living enigma whose meaning he could not divine and whose secret he dared not ask.

One night, as usual, they were left alone together, sitting at the casement window he had entered that first night with such a desperate din. The perfume of the lilies in flower floated on the gentle breeze that follows a radiant sunset. After a long silence during which Maurice tracked the intelligent and ecstatic eye of Geneviève as she watched a silver star hatch in the azure sky, he suddenly broke the silence and ventured to ask her how it was that she was so young when her husband was already past his prime; so distinguished, when all the signs were that her husband's education and upbringing were lower class; so poetic, finally, when her husband was so concerned merely to weigh, stretch, and dye the skins his factory produced.

"How come, in a master tanner's place, there are a harp and a piano and all these pastels that you admitted to me were your doing? How come—I have to say it!—all this aristocracy, which I loathe in other people and adore in you?"

Geneviève turned candid eyes on Maurice.

"Thank you," she said, "for asking me that question: it proves you are a man of delicacy and that you've never tried to find out about me from anyone else."

"Never, madame," said Maurice. "I have a devoted friend who would die for me, I have a hundred pals who are ready to go wherever I lead them; but of all these, there's only one heart I confide in when it comes to a woman, a woman like you, and that's my own."

"Thank you, Maurice. I'll tell you myself all you want to know."

"Let's start with your maiden name. I only know your married name."

Geneviève saw the amorous egoism of the question and smiled.

"Geneviève du Treilly," she said.

Maurice repeated it: "Geneviève du Treilly!"

"My family was ruined in the American War, in which my father and my elder brother took part."

"Both gentlemen?" asked Maurice.

"No, no," said Geneviève, going red.

"But you told me your maiden name was Geneviève du Treilly."

"Without the 'de,'[1] Monsieur Maurice; my family was rich, but there was nothing at all noble about them."

"You don't trust me," said the young man, smiling.

"No, no, I do," Geneviève went on. "In America my father became friends with Monsieur Morand's father. Monsieur Dixmer was Monsieur Morand's business agent. Seeing us ruined and knowing that Monsieur Dixmer had an independent fortune, Monsieur Morand introduced him to my father, who then introduced him to me. I could see that a marriage had already been settled on and arranged and that it was what my family wanted. I didn't love anyone and never had. I accepted. I've been Dixmer's wife now for three years, and I must say that for three years my husband has been so good, so wonderful to me, that I've never had a single moment of regret, despite the difference in age and outlook you've noticed."

"But when you married Monsieur Dixmer, he wasn't yet the head of this factory?"

"No. We lived in Blois.[2] After the tenth of August, Monsieur Dixmer bought this house and the workshops that go with it. So I would not be forced to mingle with the workers, to spare me even the sight of things that I might find upsetting given my inclinations, which are, as you said, Maurice, a little on the aristocratic side, he gave me this pavilion, where I live alone and out of the way, just the way I like it; or, if you prefer, according to my tastes, according to my desires, and I'm happy here, especially when a friend such as you comes and distracts me or shares my reveries with me."

With that, Geneviève gave Maurice her hand, which he kissed fervently, bringing the color back to her face.

"Now, my friend," she said, withdrawing her hand, "you know how I became Monsieur Dixmer's wife."

"Yes," said Maurice, not taking his eyes off her. "But you haven't told me how Monsieur Morand became Monsieur Dixmer's partner."

"Oh! That's simple enough.... As I told you, Monsieur Dixmer had something of a fortune, yet not enough of one to take on a factory this size all by himself. The son of Monsieur Morand, his protector, as I said, my father's friend, as you'll recall, put up half the money. As he had studied chemistry, he devoted himself to the development of the activity you've witnessed and thanks to which Monsieur Dixmer's business, of which he's in charge of the material side, has expanded enormously."

"Tell me, Monsieur Morand is also one of your close friends, is he not, madame?"

"Monsieur Morand is a noble soul, one of the purest hearts you will find under heaven." Geneviève spoke gravely.

"If the only proof he's given you of that," said Maurice, more than a little piqued at her high regard for her husband's partner, "is in sharing your husband's business and inventing a new leather dye, permit me to observe that your praise of him is extremely overdone."

"He has given me other proof, monsieur," said Geneviève.

"But he's still young, isn't he?" asked Maurice. "Although it is hard to tell with those green goggles exactly how old he is."

"He's thirty-five."

"Have you known each other long?"

"Since childhood."

Maurice bit his lip. He had from the first suspected Morand of being in love with Geneviève.

"Ah!" Maurice exclaimed. "That explains his familiarity with you."

"Restrained as it is within the limits you've always seen, monsieur," replied Geneviève, smiling, "it seems to me this familiarity, which is scarcely that of a friend, needs no explaining."

"Oh, forgive me, madame," said Maurice, "you know how jealous all strong affection is. As a friend I'm jealous of the friendship you seem to have with Monsieur Morand."

He shut up. Geneviève, too, remained silent. There was no more talk of Morand that day, and Maurice left Geneviève more in love than ever. For now he was jealous.

Love is blind, they say, and our young man certainly was, but whatever blindfold lay over his eyes, however troubled at heart his passion left him, there were many gaps in Geneviève's story, many hesitations, many things glossed over, which he hadn't really noticed at the time but which came back to haunt him strangely afterward, when he was out of her orbit. All the freedom Dixmer gave him to talk to Geneviève as often as he liked and as long as he liked, in the kind of solitude they both enjoyed every evening, could not do much to reassure him. There was something else: having become the regular dinner guest of the house, Maurice was not only left on his own with Geneviève in all confidence—it seemed to him that she was, after all, safely protected against his desires by her angelic purity—he also got to escort her on the little expeditions she was obliged to carry out in the neighborhood from time to time.

The better his standing with the household, the more one thing amazed him, and that was that the more he sought to be in a position, you could say, to police the feelings he believed Morand to have for Geneviève; the more he sought, let's say, to get acquainted with Morand, whose mind, despite his reservations, seduced him and whose refined manners captivated him increasingly every day; the more the bizarre man seemed keen to elude him. Maurice complained bitterly about this to Geneviève, for he had no doubt Morand felt him to be a rival and that jealousy on Morand's side drove him to keep his distance.

"Citizen Morand hates me," he complained to Geneviève one day.

"You?" said Geneviève gazing at him with her great round eyes. "You? Monsieur Morand hates you?"

"Yes, I'm sure of it."

"Why would he hate you?"

"Do you really want me to tell you?" cried Maurice.

"Of course."

"Well then, because . . ."

Maurice bit off his words. He was going to say: "because I love you."

"I can't tell you why," said Maurice, blushing to the roots of his hair. Around Geneviève, the staunch republican was as bashful and hesitant as a girl. Geneviève smiled.

"If you said there was no sympathy between you, I might believe you. You have an ardent, impetuous nature, a brilliant mind, you're very much sought after. Morand is a merchant grafted onto a chemist. He's shy, modest . . . and it's this shyness and this modesty that prevent him from making the first move toward you."

"So who's asking him to make the first move? I've made fifty moves toward him; he's never responded. No," Maurice continued, shaking his head, "no, it can't be that."

"Well then, what can it be?"

Maurice preferred not to say.

The day after Geneviève had offered him this explanation, he got to her place at two in the afternoon and found her dressed to go out.

"Ah, welcome," she said. "You can be my knight in shining armor."

"And where are you off to?"

"To Auteuil.[3] The weather's so delicious, I'd like to have a little walk. Our carriage will take us just past the city barrier, then we'll proceed to Auteuil on foot, and when I've finished what I have to do there, we'll walk back and pick it up again."

Maurice was enchanted. "Oh, what a gorgeous prospect—how can I resist!"

The two young people took off in the carriage, which dropped them off just past Passy. They sprang down to the side of the road and continued their promenade on foot. When they reached Auteuil, Geneviève stopped.

"Wait for me at the edge of the park," she said. "I'll come and join you when I've finished."

"Who are you going to see, then?" asked Maurice.

"A woman I know."

"And I can't go with you?"

Geneviève shook her head, smiling.

"No, you can't," she said.

Maurice bit his lip.

"Fine," he said. "I'll wait."

"What's wrong?" asked Geneviève.

"Nothing," Maurice answered. "Will you be long?"

"If I'd realized I was putting you out, Maurice, if I'd known your day was full, I would not have asked you to do me the small service of accompanying me. I'd have asked . . ."

"Morand?" Maurice promptly cut in.

"No. You know Monsieur Morand is at the factory in Rambouillet and won't be back till tonight."

"So that's why you asked me instead."

"Maurice," Geneviève said gently, "I can't keep the person who's expecting me waiting. If it's a nuisance taking me back to Paris, you go; just send the carriage back for me."

"No, no, madame," said Maurice sharply, "I'm at your service."

With that he bowed to Geneviève, who gave out a gentle sigh and set off into Auteuil. Maurice went to the meeting point and wandered around like Tarquin,[4] whipping the heads off the grasses and all the flowers and thistles in his path. This path was restricted to a pretty small space; like anyone lost in thought, Maurice paced back and forth relentlessly.

What was troubling Maurice was the weighty question of whether Geneviève loved him or not. She treated him the way a sister or close friend would; but for him, this was no longer enough. He loved her with all his heart. She had become the idea that occupied his every waking hour and that appeared to him in his dreams each and every night. Once he had asked only to be able to see her again. Now that was no longer enough: Geneviève had to love him back.

Geneviève was gone for a good hour, which seemed like a century to Maurice. When he saw her coming toward him with a smile on her lips, he strode toward her, frowning. Our poor hearts are so made that they seek to draw pain from happiness itself.

Still smiling, Geneviève took Maurice's arm.

"Here I am," she said. "Sorry to keep you waiting. . . ."

Maurice managed a nod by way of reply and they both turned down a sumptuous path, damp and shady and soft underfoot, which would take them back to the main road by a detour.

It was one of those lovely spring evenings when each plant sends its scent heavenward and each bird, sitting still on its branch or flitting among the bushes, sings its hymn of love to God, one of those evenings that seem destined to live on in memory.

Maurice was silent, Geneviève distracted and thoughtful; she was fingering the flowers in a bouquet she held in her other hand, the one resting on Maurice's arm.

"What's the matter?" Maurice suddenly asked. "What's making you so sad today?"

Geneviève might have said: "my happiness."

She turned her soft, poetic gaze upon him.

"But what about you? Aren't you sadder than usual?"

"I have every reason to be sad, I am unhappy; but you?"

"You, unhappy?"

"Of course. Can't you tell by the way my voice sometimes trembles that I'm suffering? Don't you notice that sometimes when I'm talking to you or your husband I'm suddenly forced to get up and go outside for air because it feels like my chest will burst?"

"But to what do you attribute this suffering?" asked Geneviève, at a loss.

"If I were some kind of neurasthenic," said Maurice, laughing a painful little laugh, "I'd say I had a case of nerves."

"Are you suffering at this moment?"

"Very much," said Maurice.

"Then we'll go back."

"So soon, madame?"

"Of course."

"Oh, yes, of course," the young man muttered. "I'd forgotten Monsieur Morand will be back from Rambouillet at nightfall, and night is beginning to fall."

Geneviève cast him a reproachful glance.

"Again!" she said.

"Just why did you praise him so pompously the other day?" asked Maurice. "It's your fault."

"Since when can one not say what one thinks of someone admirable to someone one admires?"

"That's some admiration that makes you race the way you're doing at the moment for fear of being a few minutes late."

"You are royally unjust today, Maurice. Haven't I spent a good part of the day with you?"

"You're right; I am too demanding," said Maurice, giving in to his impetuous nature. "Let's go and see Monsieur Morand!"

Geneviève felt a stab of bitter disappointment in the region of her heart.

"Yes," she said, "by all means let's go and see Monsieur Morand; he is one friend, at least, who has never caused me pain."

"Friends like that are precious," said Maurice, choking with jealousy. "I wish I had some."

They were now on the main road. The horizon was turning red as the sun disappeared, sending its dying rays dancing over the molten gold moldings of the dome of the Invalides.[5] A star, the first, the one that on another evening had attracted Geneviève's gaze, twinkled in the limpid azure sky.

Geneviève let go of Maurice's arm in sad resignation.

"Why do you make me suffer like this?" she said.

"Ah, well, it's because I'm not as clever as other people I know; I don't know how to make myself loved."

"Maurice!" cried Geneviève.

"Oh, madame! If he's always on his best behavior, always even-tempered, it's because he doesn't care."

Geneviève placed her white hand back on Maurice's powerful, manly arm.

"Please," she whispered in a changed voice, "let's not talk anymore, let's not!"

"Why not?"

"Because your voice hurts me."

"So there's nothing about me you like, not even my voice?"

"Be quiet, I beseech you."

"Your wish is my command, madame."

And the impetuous young man wiped his hand across his forehead, which was damp with sweat. Geneviève could see that he really was suffering. Men like Maurice feel pain others can't imagine.

"You are my friend, Maurice," said Geneviève, gazing at him with a heavenly expression. "A very precious friend. Please, Maurice, don't let me lose you."

"Oh! You won't miss me for long!" cried Maurice.

"You're wrong," said Geneviève. "I would miss you for a very long time—always."

"Geneviève! Geneviève! Have pity on me!" cried Maurice.

Geneviève shivered. It was the first time Maurice had pronounced her name with such deep longing.

"All right," Maurice continued, "since you've finally understood, let me get it off my chest, once and for all. For even if you were to kill me with a look, I've kept silent for too long. I will speak, Geneviève."

"Monsieur, I've already begged you to be quiet, in the name of our friendship, monsieur, I beg you once more, for my sake if not for yours—not another word, for heaven's sake, not another word!"

"Our friendship! Friendship! Ha! If this is the kind of friendship you feel for Monsieur Morand, I don't want any more of your friendship, Geneviève. I need more than what you give to other people."

"That's enough," said Madame Dixmer with a queenly flap of the hand. "Enough, Monsieur Lindey. Here is our carriage, please take me home to my husband."

Maurice was quivering with chills and fever. When Geneviève placed her hand on his arm again to hoist herself up into the carriage, which was indeed waiting only a few feet away, it seemed to the young man that her hand was on fire. They both climbed up into the carriage, Geneviève sitting at the back, Maurice at the front, and crossed the whole of Paris without either one saying a word. Yet Geneviève held her handkerchief to her eyes the entire trip.

When they reached the factory, Dixmer was busy in his office and Morand had returned from Rambouillet and was changing his clothes. Geneviève gave Maurice her hand as she moved off toward her room:

"Adieu, Maurice, farewell, since that is what you want."

Maurice did not reply. He went straight to the mantelpiece, where a miniature of Geneviève hung. He kissed it ardently, pressed it to his heart, put it back in its place, and left.

Maurice had no idea how he got home. He traversed Paris without seeing or hearing a thing. All he saw was a replay in his head of what had just happened, as in a dream, without being able to fathom his actions or his words or the feelings that inspired them. There are moments when the most serene, the most self-controlled person lets himself go with a violence demanded by the underhanded powers of the imagination that were previously subdued.

Maurice, as we have said, raced home rather than walked. He got undressed without the help of his manservant, did not answer his cook when she showed him supper was all ready; then he took the day's letters from his table and read them all, one after the other, without understanding a single word. The fog of jealousy, sending reason reeling, had not yet lifted.

At ten o'clock, Maurice got into bed as mechanically as he had done everything else since leaving Geneviève. If you'd told Maurice when he was cool and collected that someone else had behaved the way he had, he would have been baffled, would have regarded as a madman any man who indulged in such desperate action, not justified either by any great reserve or any great abandon on Geneviève's part. All that he registered was a terrible blow to hopes he hadn't been aware till then that he entertained and upon which, vague as they were, rested all his dreams of happiness, floating amorphous, like barely discernible wisps of smoke, toward the horizon.

What then happened to Maurice was what almost always happens in such cases: stunned by the blow received, he fell asleep as soon as his head hit the pillow. Or, rather, he lay there senseless until the next day. A noise awoke him, however, the noise his officieux made whenever he opened the door. He was coming, as was his wont, to open Maurice's bedroom windows, which looked over a great big garden, and to bring flowers.

They grew a lot of flowers in '93 and Maurice loved them, but he didn't even glance at this lot, half sitting up as he was, with his heavy head propped on his hand, trying for the life of him to remember what had happened the day before.

Maurice wondered why he felt so glum, but he couldn't quite hit on it. The sole thing he could come up with was his jealousy of Morand. But it was hardly the moment to play at being jealous of a man when that man was out of the way in Rambouillet and when he himself was alone with the woman he loved, enjoying such splendid isolation with all the sweetness laid out for them by nature, awakening on one of the first lovely days of spring.

It was not mistrust of what might have taken place in the house in Auteuil to which he'd taken Geneviève and where she had spent more than an hour. No, the constant torment of his life was this idea that Morand was in love with Geneviève; yet such were the tricks played by the mind, by caprice, that never had a gesture, a look, a word from Dixmer's partner ever lent any semblance of reality to such a supposition.

The manservant's voice snapped him out of his reverie.

"Citizen," he said, indicating the letters open on the table, "have you decided which ones you want to keep or should I burn the lot?"

"Burn what?" asked Maurice.

"The letters the citizen read last night before going to bed."

Maurice could not remember reading one.

"Burn the lot," he said.

"Here are today's, citizen," said the officieux, handing Maurice a bundle of letters and throwing the others into the fireplace.

Maurice took the bundle of letters, felt a thick seal beneath his fingers, and sensed vaguely a familiar perfume. Flipping through the pile he saw a stamp and handwriting that made him jump. This man, so unflinching in the face of danger, no matter how great, paled at the mere sight of a letter.

The officieux went over to see what was the matter, but Maurice waved him out of the room. When he was gone, he turned the letter over and over with the foreboding that it sealed his own doom. He felt the chill of the unknown slow down his blood.

Mustering all his courage, Maurice ripped the letter open and read the following:

CITIZEN MAURICE,

We must break ties that, on your side, threaten to exceed the bounds of friendship. You are a man of honor, citizen, and now that a night has passed since what happened between us yesterday evening, you will surely see that your presence in our house has become impossible. I am counting on you to provide my husband with whatever excuse you like. If I see a letter from you for Monsieur Dixmer arrive this very day, I will know I can regret a friend who has unfortunately gone astray, but whom all socially accepted standards of behavior prevent me from seeing again.

Adieu, now and forever.

GENEVIÈVE

P.S. My courier will wait for your answer.

Maurice called and the officieux reappeared.

"Who brought this letter?"

"A citizen delivery boy."

"Is he still here?"

"Yes."

Without a sigh, without a moment's hesitation, Maurice leapt out of bed, pulled on a pair of trousers, plunked down at his desk, grabbed the first sheet of paper he could find—it just so happened that this was a sheet of paper with the section letterhead printed at the top—and wrote:

CITIZEN DIXMER,

I was fond of you, I am still fond of you, but I cannot see you again.

Maurice tried to think of a reason for not being able to see citizen Dixmer again, but only one sprang to mind and it was simply the one that would have occurred to anyone in those times. He thus continued:

Certain rumors are making the rounds that you are lukewarm when it comes to politics. I do not want to accuse you, nor have I been given the mission of defending you. Please accept my regrets and rest assured that your secrets remain buried in my heart.

Maurice did not even reread this letter, which he tossed off, as you've seen, just like that, off the top of his head. He had no doubt of the effect it would have on Dixmer, who was a good patriot, as far as Maurice could tell—from what he said, at least. Dixmer would be annoyed when he got it; no doubt his wife and citizen Morand would press him to persevere, but he wouldn't even bother answering and would soon forget, oblivion like a black veil blanketing the past and transforming it into a gloomy future. Maurice signed and sealed the letter and handed it to his officieux, and the delivery boy went on his way.

Then a small sigh escaped from the republican's heart. He grabbed his hat and gloves and headed for the section, hoping, poor Brutus, to regain his stoicism when faced with public affairs.

Public affairs were terrible: the thirty-first of May[6] was gearing up. The Terror came rushing down from the top of the Mountain like a torrent, smashing into the dike with which the Girondins were trying to hold it back, audacious moderates that they were, they who had dared to demand revenge for the September massacres and to fight briefly to save the King's life.

While Maurice worked so assiduously, and the fever he was trying to work off racked his brain instead of his heart, the messenger had returned to the old rue Saint-Jacques and sent the place into a horrified spin. Geneviève gave the handwriting the once-over before handing it to Dixmer, who at first read the note without comprehending; he then communicated its message to citizen Morand, who smacked his alabaster white forehead with both hands.

In the situation in which Dixmer, Morand, and company found themselves, a situation Maurice knew absolutely nothing about but which our readers have been able to penetrate, the letter was, of course, a bolt from the blue.

"Can this man mean what he says?" Dixmer wondered anxiously.

"Yes," said Morand without hesitation.

"What does it matter!" said the extremist. "You see now we were wrong not to kill him."

"My friend," said Morand, "we are fighting against violence; we condemn it as a crime. We did the right thing not to kill a man, whatever happens. But then, as I've said before, I believe Maurice's to be a noble and honest heart."

"Yes, but if this noble and honest heart is that of a republican fanatic, perhaps he himself would think it was a crime, if he has stumbled on something, not to sacrifice his honor on the altar of the nation, as they say."

"But," said Morand, "do you really think he knows something?"

"Ha! Just listen to him! He talks about secrets that will remain buried in his heart."

"Those secrets are obviously those I confided in him about our contraband. He doesn't know about any others."

"Still," said Morand, "that meeting in Auteuil, you don't suppose he suspected something? You know he accompanied your wife?"

"I'm the one who told Geneviève to take him with her, to look after her."

"Listen," said Morand, "we'll soon see if these suspicions are well founded. Our battalion's on patrol at the Temple on the second of June—that is, in a week. You are the captain, Dixmer, and I'm the lieutenant. If your battalion or even our company receives a counterorder, like the Butte-de-Moulins battalion received the other day, when Santerre switched it with the Gravilliers battalion, it will mean they are onto us, and all that will be left for us to do will be to get out of Paris or die in combat. But if things go as planned . . ."

"We're sunk just as surely," replied Dixmer.

"How so?"

"Good Lord! Didn't everything depend on the cooperation of this particular municipal officer? Wasn't it he that was supposed to lead us straight to the Queen, albeit unwittingly?"

"That's true," said Morand, crushed.

"So you see," Dixmer continued gruffly, "we must get this young man back on board at any cost."

"But what if he refuses, what if he fears he's compromising himself?" said Morand.

"Listen," said Dixmer. "I'll have a word with Geneviève; she saw him last, she may know something."

"Dixmer," said Morand, "I can't see you getting Geneviève involved in our plots; not that I fear any indiscretion on her part, good Lord, no! But the game we're playing is a matter of life and death, and I would feel shame and pity, putting a woman's head on the line here."

"A woman's head," said Dixmer, "weighs as much as a man's wherever cunning, candor, or beauty can do as much and sometimes more than brute force, power, and courage; Geneviève shares our convictions and our sympathies, Geneviève will share our fate."

"Go ahead then, my friend," said Morand. "I've said all I have to say. Go ahead: Geneviève is in all respects up to the mission you intend to give her, or rather that she has given herself. Martyrs are made of saints."

And he held out his effeminate white hand to Dixmer, who pressed it between his own big hairy hands. Then Dixmer, cautioning Morand and company to be more vigilant than ever, went off to see Geneviève.

She was sitting at a table with her head down and her eye on her embroidery. She turned around at the sound of the door opening and acknowledged Dixmer.

"Ah, it's you, my friend," she said.

"Yes," said Dixmer with a placid, beaming face. "I've just had a letter from our friend Maurice that I can't make head or tail of. Here, you read it and tell me what you think."

Geneviève reached out for the letter; despite her best efforts at self-control, she couldn't stop from trembling as she took the letter and read.

Dixmer watched her, and sure enough, she scanned every line.

"Well?" he asked when she was done.

"Well, I think citizen Monsieur Maurice Lindey is an honest man," answered Geneviève with the greatest possible composure, "and that there is nothing to fear from him."

"Do you think he knows about the people you went to see in Auteuil?"

"I'm sure he doesn't."

"So why this sudden break? Did he seem to you colder or more emotional yesterday than usual?"

"No," said Geneviève. "I think he was much the same."

"Think carefully what you're saying there, Geneviève, because, as you know, your answer will have serious consequences for all our plans."

"Just a moment," said Geneviève with an emotion that broke through all her efforts at maintaining a cool demeanor. "Just a moment . . ."

"All right!" said Dixmer with a slight contraction of the muscles of his face. "All right, try to remember everything, Geneviève."

"Oh, yes," the young woman collected herself. "Yes, I remember now: yesterday he was most morose. Monsieur Maurice is a bit of a tyrant when it comes to his friendships . . . and he sometimes sulks and stays away from us days on end."

"So he's just sulking?" asked Dixmer.

"Probably."

"Geneviève, in our position, you understand, we can't be content with probabilities. We need certainties."

"Well then, my friend . . . I'm certain."

"So this letter is just a pretext for not coming to the house anymore?"

"My friend, how can you expect me to tell you such things?"

"Tell me, Geneviève," Dixmer went on. "I wouldn't ask any other woman."

"It is a pretext," said Geneviève, eyes downcast.

"Ah!" said Dixmer.

Then, after a moment's silence in which he frantically tried to suppress the beating of his heart with his hand, he pulled his hand out from his vest and placed it on the back of his wife's chair.

"Do something for me, dear friend," Dixmer said.

"What?" asked Geneviève, looking up, astonished.

"I don't want there to be even the shadow of a doubt. Perhaps Maurice knows more about our secrets than we realize. What you think is a pretext may be more than that. Drop him a line."

"Me?" gasped Geneviève, flinching.

"Yes, you; tell him it was you who opened the letter and that you'd like an explanation. He will come, you will question him, and that way you'll be able to make an informed guess as to what it's all about."

"Oh, no, never!" cried Geneviève. "I can't do what you ask of me and I won't."

"Dear Geneviève, when interests as powerful as those which rest on us are at stake, how can you recoil before puny considerations of pride?"

"I've given you my opinion of Maurice, monsieur," Geneviève replied. "He is honest, he is chivalrous, but he is changeable, and I do not wish to suffer any other servitude than that imposed upon me by my husband."

This statement was made so calmly and so firmly that Dixmer realized it would be useless to insist, at least for the moment. He did not say another word, looked at Geneviève without seeming to see her, wiped his hand across his clammy brow, and left.

Morand was waiting impatiently for him, and Dixmer gave him a blow-by-blow description of what had just been said.

"Fine," said Morand, "let's be content with that and put it out of our minds. Rather than cause the slightest hint of worry to your wife, rather than wound Geneviève's pride in any way, I would renounce . . ."

Dixmer laid his hand on his shoulder.

"You are mad, monsieur," he said staring straight into his eyes. "Either that or you don't mean a word you say."

"Dixmer! Do you think . . ."

"I think, Knight, that you are no freer than I am to allow yourself to get carried away by your feelings. Neither you nor I nor Geneviève belong to ourselves, Morand. We are objects called upon to defend a principle, and principles rest on objects, which they crush."

Morand shuddered and kept his silence, a silence that was pensive and painful. They circled the garden a few times without exchanging a single word before Dixmer took his leave.

"I have a few orders to give," he said in a perfectly calm voice. "I'll be off, Monsieur Morand."

Morand gave Dixmer his hand and watched him recede.

"Poor Dixmer," he said to himself. "I'm afraid that out of all of us, he is the one who stands to lose the most."

Dixmer did in fact go back to his workshop, issue a few orders, go over his newspapers again, order a distribution of bread and slops to the poor in that section of Paris, and then return home, get out of his work gear, and put on his Sunday best.

An hour later, Maurice was interrupted in the middle of his reading and public speaking practice by the voice of his officieux, who leaned toward his ear and whispered, "Citizen Lindey, there is someone with something very important to say to you, or so he says at least, waiting for you at your place."

Maurice swiftly returned home and was flabbergasted to find Dixmer settled in comfortably, leafing through the papers. On the way back he had questioned his servant the whole time, but the man had never met the master tanner and could hardly offer any enlightenment.

On seeing Dixmer, Maurice stopped dead in the doorway, coloring uncontrollably. Dixmer shot up and held out his hand, smiling.

"What's gotten into you? Why did you write me that nonsense?" he asked the young man. "In all truth, it was a bit below the belt, my dear Maurice. Me, lukewarm—a false patriot, you say? Come, come. You can't repeat such accusations to my face, can you? Why don't you just admit that you were trying to pick a fight with me."

"I'll admit whatever you like, my dear Dixmer, for you've always treated me like a gentleman; but that doesn't mean my mind is not made up. My decision is irrevocable. . . ."

"But why?" asked Dixmer. "On your own admission you have nothing to reproach us with, yet you're still determined to turn your back on us?"

"Dear Dixmer, please believe that to act as I do, to deprive myself of a friend like you, I must have pretty good reasons."

"Yes, but whatever they are," Dixmer continued, affecting a smile, "these reasons are not the ones you wrote to me. The ones you wrote to me are just an excuse."

Maurice reflected for a moment.

"Listen, Dixmer," he said, "we are living in an age when any letter expressing doubt can and should worry you. I realize it does not behoove a man of honor to leave you laboring under the weight of such anxiety. So, yes, Dixmer, the reasons I gave you were just an excuse."

This admission, which should have cleared the businessman's brow, on the contrary seemed to darken it.

"Well then, what's the real motive?" said Dixmer.

"I can't tell you. But if you knew what it was, you'd approve, I'm sure."

Dixmer pressed him.

"Do you really want to know?" asked Maurice.

"Yes," Dixmer replied.

"All right," said Maurice, who felt a certain relief in approximating the truth. "The reason is that you have a wife who is young and beautiful, and the chastity of this young and beautiful woman, however well established it is, has not stopped people from misinterpreting my visits to your home."

Dixmer paled slightly.

"Really?" he said. "Well then, my dear Maurice, the husband should thank you for the wrong you do the friend."

"You realize that I'm not silly enough to think my presence could possibly be dangerous for your peace of mind or that of your wife, but it could set malicious tongues wagging, and you know very well the more absurd calumny is the more readily it is believed."

"You child!" scoffed Dixmer, shrugging his shoulders.

"Scoff at me as much as you like," Maurice replied, "but from afar we won't be any less good friends, for we won't have anything to hold against each other; whereas close up, on the other hand . . ."

"Go on, close up?"

"Things could have ended up going sour."

"Maurice, do you really think that I could think . . . ?"

"Oh, for God's sake!" said the young man.

"But why did you write to me, Maurice, instead of telling me in person?"

"Well, precisely to avoid what is happening between us right now."

"So are you annoyed, Maurice, that I think enough of you to come and ask for an explanation?"

"No! Just the opposite," cried Maurice, "and I'm more than happy, I can tell you, to have seen you again one last time before giving up ever seeing you again."

"Ever seeing you again, citizen! But we are so very fond of you," said Dixmer, seizing the young man's hand and giving it a squeeze.

Maurice flinched.

"Morand," continued Dixmer, well aware Maurice was trying to disguise a tremor, "Morand said to me again this morning: 'Do everything you can to bring back our dear Maurice.'"

"Ah, monsieur!" said the young man, scowling and pulling back his hand, "I wouldn't have thought I was so high up on citizen Morand's list of friends."

"You doubt it?" asked Dixmer.

"I neither believe it or doubt it, I have no reason to question myself on the subject at all; whenever I went to your place, Dixmer, I went only for you and your wife, not for citizen Morand."

"You don't know him, Maurice," said Dixmer. "Morand is a beautiful soul."

"I'm sure he is," said Maurice with a bitter little smile.

"Now, let's get back to the purpose of my visit."

Maurice inclined his head to signal that Dixmer could go ahead; he himself had nothing further to say.

"So you're saying tongues have been wagging?"

"Yes, citizen," said Maurice.

"All right, then let's speak frankly. Why would you take any notice of the idle gossip of busybodies who have nothing better to do? Come, Maurice, don't you have a clear conscience and doesn't Geneviève have her honesty?"

"I'm younger than you," said Maurice, who was starting to marvel at the man's insistence. "And perhaps I'm a little more thin-skinned. This is why I say that the reputation of a woman like Geneviève should not be the subject of even the idle gossip of busybodies who have nothing better to do. Allow me therefore, dear Dixmer, to persist in my initial resolution."

"Come," said Dixmer, "since we seem to be going in for confessions, confess something else."

"What?" asked Maurice, going red. "What do you want me to confess?"

"That it is neither politics nor talk about how often you're at my place that has made you decide to drop us."

"What is it, then?"

"The secret you've discovered."

"What secret?" Maurice asked with a naïve curiosity that reassured the tanner.

"That contraband business you stumbled onto the very night we met in such a memorable way. You've never forgiven me for being involved in fraud, and you accuse me of being a bad republican because I use English products in my tannery."

"My dear Dixmer," said Maurice, "I swear to you that I completely forgot, whenever I went to your place, that I was in the home of a black marketeer."

"Really?"

"Really."

"You don't have any other motive, then, for abandoning the place other than what you've said?"

"On my honor."

"Well then, Maurice," said Dixmer, getting up and shaking the young man's hand, "I hope you'll think it over and go back on this resolution of yours that hurts us all so much."

Maurice inclined his head without answering—which amounted to a final rejection. Dixmer left in despair at having failed in his bid to win back a man whom certain circumstances rendered not only useful but quite indispensable.

It was high time he left, for Maurice was torn by a thousand contradictory emotions. Since Dixmer begged him to come back, Geneviève might be able to forgive him. So why did he feel despair? In his place

Lorin would most certainly have a host of aphorisms to pluck from his favorite authors. But there was Geneviève's letter, that formal dismissal which he'd carried with him to the section and learned by heart along with the note he'd received from her the day after he'd rescued her from the hands of those brutes who were roughing her up. But more than anything else, there was the young man's stubborn jealousy over the detested Morand, the initial cause of his break with Geneviève.

And so Maurice remained intransigent in his resolution. But it must be said that being deprived of his daily visit to the old rue Saint-Jacques left a huge hole in his life. And when first the hour struck when he would normally have set off toward the Saint-Victor neighborhood, he fell into a profound melancholy, and from that moment went through all the stages of waiting in vain and regret.

Every morning he woke expecting to find a letter from Dixmer, and he finally admitted to himself that although he had resisted the man's insistence face-to-face he would yield to a letter; every day he went out in the hope of running into Geneviève, his head full of opening lines he'd rehearsed in case it happened. Every evening, he came home in the hope of finding the messenger who had unwittingly one morning brought him pain, pain that had since become his eternal companion.

Often enough, too, in his hours of despair, this force of nature flared up and raged at the idea of suffering such torture without inflicting any back on the man responsible, since the primary cause of all his woes was Morand. Then he thought about going and picking a fight with Morand. But Dixmer's partner was so frail, so inoffensive, that to insult or provoke him would be an act of cowardice coming from a colossus like Maurice.

Naturally Lorin had come to pull his friend out of the doldrums, though Maurice was stubbornly remaining mum, without, however, denying that he was down. Lorin had done everything he could, in practice and in theory, to bring back to the fold of the nation a heart aching all over with another love. But though the situation was serious, though in any other frame of mind Maurice would have thrown himself body and soul into the political whirlwind, even the crisis in public life was unable to goad our young republican into resuming the original activism that had made him a hero of the fourteenth of July and the tenth of August.

In effect, the two political factions, which had been operating in tandem for close to ten months, only grazing each other slightly in that time and sparking only small skirmishes, were gearing up to tackle each other head-on. It was clear that the struggle, once begun, would be mortal for one side or the other. Both systems sprang from the Revolution itself, but one promoted moderation, as represented by the Girondins—that is, by Brissot, Pétion, Vergniaud, Valazé, Lanjuinais, Barbaroux, and so on; the other, the Terror or the Mountain, as represented by Danton, Robespierre, Chénier, Fabre, Marat, Collot d'Herbois, Hébert, and the rest, promoted terror and death.

After the tenth of August the moderate party seemed to gain the upper hand, as happens after any bout of action. A ministry had been cobbled together out of the rubble of the former ministry, with a few extras added. The former ministers Roland, Servan, and Clavières were recalled; Danton, Monge, and Le Brun were freshly appointed. With the exception of one man, who represented the energetic element among his colleagues, all the other ministers belonged to the moderate party.

When I say *moderate,* you understand I mean relatively speaking.

But the tenth of August created waves abroad as well, and the coalition hastened to move, to rescue not Louis XVI personally but the principle of royalty, which had been shaken to its foundations. That is when Brunswick's threatening words[7] rang out, and like a terrible embodiment of these words Longwy and Verdun[8] fell to the enemy. This was followed by the terrorist reaction and Danton's terrible September dream, which he made real with real blood, revealing to the enemy that all of France was complicit in an immense massacre and ready to fight for its compromised existence with all the energy of despair. That September saved France but placed it outside the law in doing so.

With France saved, activism became pointless, and so the moderate party regrouped and recovered. Recriminations over those terrible days of September then began; the words "murderer" and "assassin" were bandied about. A new word was even added to the nation's vocabulary, and that was *septembriseur*—Septembasher!

Danton bravely accepted the term. Like Clovis, he had for a moment dunked his head in this baptism of blood, only to raise it higher and more menacingly than before. A further occasion to resort to past terror presented itself with the trial of the King. Violence and moderation entered not yet into a battle of persons, but into a battle of principles. Relative strengths were tested on the royal prisoner. Moderation was vanquished and the head of Louis XVI fell on the scaffold.

As the tenth of August had done, the twenty-first of January gave the coalition back all its energy. The same man was still set up to oppose them, but the outcome was not the same. Dumouriez, halted in his military progress by the reigning chaos within the government, which ensured that the needed manpower and money never reached him, declared himself against the Jacobins, whom he blamed for all the chaos, adopted the party of the Girondins, and then promptly sank them by declaring himself their friend—the kiss of death.

The Vendée then rose up and the departments[9] threatened to follow suit; reversals led to betrayals and betrayals to reversals. The Jacobins accused the moderates of trying to polish them off on the tenth of March—that is, on the night on which our story opened. But too much haste on the part of their adversaries saved them, along with, perhaps, the rain that had caused Pétion, that profound anatomist of the *esprit de Paris,* to say: "It's raining, nothing will happen tonight."

But since the tenth of March everything had gone against the Girondins, spelling ruin: Marat[10] was accused and acquitted; Robespierre and Danton were now freshly reconciled, at least as far as a tiger and a lion can be reconciled for the purpose of bringing down a bull they're both keen to devour; Hanriot,[11] the Septembasher, was appointed commander-in-chief of the National Guard. Everything presaged the terrible day when the last dike that the Revolution had flung up to stem the stormy tide of the Terror would be smashed and swept away.

Those were the momentous events in which, in any other circumstances, Maurice would have taken an active part—which his powerful nature and his passionate patriotism naturally inclined him toward.

But, happily or unhappily for Maurice, neither Lorin's exhortations nor the terrible preoccupations of the street had been able to chase from his mind the single idea that obsessed him. When the thirty-first of May arrived, the fearsome assailant of the Bastille and the Tuileries was lying flat on his back in bed, racked by the fever that kills the strongest, and yet which a mere glance can dispel, a mere word heal.

13

THE THIRTY-FIRST OF MAY

On the infamous thirty-first of May, when the tocsins sounded the call to arms from the break of day on, the battalion of the faubourg Saint-Victor entered the Temple. When all the customary formalities had been completed and the posts distributed, the municipal officers on duty were seen to arrive and four units of cannoneer reinforcements joined those already in place in the artillery at the entrance to the Temple.

At the same time as the cannon, Santerre arrived with his yellow woolen epaulets and his usual getup, in which his patriotism could be read in great fat stains. He reviewed the battalion, which he found to be in a fit state, and counted the municipal officers, who numbered only three.

"Why only three municipals?" he asked. "Who's the bad citizen who's missing?"

"The one missing, citizen general, is nevertheless no wimp," answered our former acquaintance Agricola, "for it is the secretary of the Lepelletier section, the leader of the brave Thermopylae, citizen Maurice Lindey."

"Good, good," said Santerre. "Like you, I acknowledge the patriotism of citizen Maurice Lindey, but that won't stop him from being entered in the list of absentees if he doesn't turn up in the next ten minutes."

With that Santerre moved on to other things. A few feet away from the general, a captain of the chasseurs and a soldier were standing apart but within earshot, the first leaning on his rifle, the second sitting on top of a cannon.

"Did you hear that?" the captain half-whispered to the soldier. "Maurice hasn't turned up yet."

"Yes, but he'll come, don't worry, unless there's a riot."

"If he can't make it," said the captain, "I'll put you on sentry duty on the stairs, and as she is likely to go up the tower, you can have a word with her there."

At that moment, a man recognizable as a municipal by his tricolor scarf[1] entered, but this man was unknown to the captain and the chasseur, and they stared hard at him.

"Citizen general," said the newcomer, addressing Santerre, "please accept me in place of citizen Maurice Lindey, who is sick; here is the doctor's certificate. My tour of duty was to arrive in a week, so I'll do a swap with him; in a week he'll do my duty, and I'll do his today."

"If the Capets and Capettes are still alive in a week, of course," jeered one of the municipal officers.

Santerre responded with a faint smile to the zealot's joke. Then, turning to Maurice's replacement, he said, "That's fine. Go and sign the register in place of Maurice Lindey and write down the reasons for the swap in the comments column."

The captain and the chasseur looked at each other in joyful surprise. "One week," they chorused.

"Captain Dixmer," cried Santerre, "take up position in the garden with your company."

"Come, Morand," said the captain to his companion, the chasseur.

The drum rolled and the company, led by the master tanner, marched off in the prescribed direction. Arms were stacked and the company split into groups that began to pace up and down and all around, as the fancy took them.

Their patrol ground was the very garden where, in the days of Louis XVI, the royal family used to come sometimes to take the air. This garden was now barren, arid, and desolate, completely bare of flowers, trees, and greenery of any kind.

At approximately twenty-five paces from the section of the wall that lined the rue Porte-Foin stood a sort of shack, which the municipality in its foresight had allowed to be built for the greater convenience of the National Guards stationed at the Temple, who could get something to eat and drink there when the riots were on and no one was allowed out. There was stiff competition for the running of this little internal canteen, the concession finally being granted to an excellent patriot, the widow of a local killed on the tenth of August who answered to the name of Plumeau.

The little cabin, built out of wood and cob, a compact mixture of clay and straw, sat in the middle of a flower bed whose outer rim was defined by a hedge of dwarf boxwood. It comprised a single room about twelve foot square, with a cellar beneath. Access to the cellar was down a set of stairs roughly hacked out of the ground itself. That was where the widow Plumeau stored her liquids and comestibles, over which she and her daughter, a girl aged somewhere between twelve and fifteen, took turns keeping watch.

The National Guards had only just set up when, as we've said, they began to disperse, some strolling about the garden, others chatting to the concierges, others examining drawings traced on the wall, all representing some patriotic aim, such as the King strung up, with the inscription "Monsieur Veto air-bathing," or the King guillotined with "Monsieur Veto coughing up in the sack"; still others making overtures to Madame Plumeau regarding the gastronomic ideas suggested to them by their more or less compelling appetites.

Among the latter were the captain and the chasseur already noted.

"Ah! Captain Dixmer!" said the canteen lady. "I've got some marvelous Saumur wine today, come!"

"Lovely, citizeness Plumeau; but in my opinion, at least, a Saumur is nothing without a bit of Brie," replied the captain, who, before uttering this statement, had carefully looked around and noted the absence of this particular cheese, one of his favorites, from among the various comestibles proudly displayed on the shelves of the canteen.

"Ah, Captain! You wouldn't credit it, but the last slice has just been taken."

"Well, then," said the captain, "no Brie, no Saumur. Pity, I was going to treat the whole company—that would have been worth your while."

"My dear Captain, if you'll just give me five minutes, I'll run and get some from the citizen concierge who is in competition with me—he always has some. I'll pay more for it, but you're too good a patriot not to reimburse me."

"Yes, yes, off you go," Dixmer replied. "Meanwhile, we'll go downstairs and select our wine ourselves."

"Make yourself at home, Captain, please."

With that the widow Plumeau began to run in ungainly haste to the concierge's lodge, while the captain and the chasseur, armed with a candle, lifted the trapdoor and went down into the cellar.

"Perfect!" said Morand after a cursory inspection. "The cellar extends toward the rue Porte-Foin, it's nine to ten feet deep, and there is no masonry."

"What's the soil like?" asked Dixmer.

"Chalky tufa. It's all made ground; all these gardens have been turned over at different times, there are no rocks anywhere."

"Quick," cried Dixmer, "I can hear our *vivandière's* clogs; grab a couple of bottles of wine and we'll go back up."

They both popped up at the mouth of the trapdoor just as Mother Plumeau returned, carrying the famous Brie demanded with such insistence. Behind her traipsed several chasseurs, lured by the fine appearance of the cheese.

Dixmer did the honors, treating his company to a good twenty bottles of wine, while citizen Morand told of the devotion of Curtius, the disinterestedness of Fabricius, and the patriotism of Brutus and Cassius,[2] all stories almost as much appreciated as the cheese from Brie and the wine from Anjou Dixmer provided—which is saying a lot.

Eleven o'clock struck. It was at eleven-thirty that the sentries were due to be relieved.

"Doesn't the Austrian woman normally take a stroll between twelve and one?" Dixmer asked Tison, who was trotting past the hut.

"Between twelve and one, quite right." And the man began to sing:

> *"Madame mounts her tower,*
> *Uncle, beef, and onion stew . . ."*

This facetiousness was greeted with chuckles all round from the National Guards.

Dixmer immediately called the roll of the men of his company who were to mount the guard from eleven-thirty to one-thirty, recommended that lunch be hurried up, and got Morand to take up his arms in order to place him, as agreed, on the last floor of the tower, in that same sentry box in which Maurice had hidden the day he intercepted signals intended for the Queen from a window in the rue Porte-Foin.

If you could have seen Morand when he received these instructions, simple and expected as they were, you'd have seen him turn as white as a ghost beneath his long black locks.

All of a sudden a dull roar shook the courtyards of the Temple and a great tornado of shouts and growls could be heard in the distance.

"What's that?" Dixmer asked Tison.

"Hmmph! That's nothing!" said the jailer. "Brissotin[3] and his wretched cohorts, the Girondins, are just kicking up a bit of a stink before they're carted off to the guillotine."

The noise became more and more alarming; artillery could be heard rolling along and a throng of people passed close by the Temple, screaming: "Long live the sections! Long live Hanriot! Down with the Brissotins! Down with the Rolandists![4] Down with Madame Veto!"

"Great!" said Tison, rubbing his hands. "Think I'll go and open up for Madame Veto so she can enjoy unimpeded the love her people bear her."

With that he approached the dungeon wicket.

"Hey! Tison!" boomed a formidable voice.

"My general?" Tison replied, stopping in his tracks.

"No outing today," said Santerre. "The prisoners will not leave their room."

The order was without appeal.

"Suits me!" said Tison. "That's one thing less to worry about."

Dixmer and Morand exchanged a bleak glance. Then, while waiting for the changeover to the next shift to sound, pointless as that now was, they both strode off to stroll between the canteen and the wall lining the rue Porte-Foin. There Morand began pacing the distance using geometric steps, that is, steps three feet long.

"What's the distance?" said Dixmer.

"Sixty to sixty-one feet," replied Morand.

"How many days do we need?"

Morand thought for a moment and traced a few geometric figures in the sand with a stick before promptly rubbing them out.

"We'll need six or seven days, at least," he said.

"Maurice is on duty in a week," murmured Dixmer. "So we must be reconciled with Maurice a week from now—no matter what."

The half-hour sounded. Morand grabbed his rifle and sighed, then, led by the corporal, went to relieve the sentry who was pacing about the tower platform.

14

DEVOTION

The day after the day on which the scenes we have just recounted took place, that is, the first of June, at ten o'clock in the morning, Geneviève was sitting in her usual place by the window wondering why, for the last three weeks, the days always began so sadly for her, why they passed so slowly, and why, finally, instead of madly looking forward to the evening, she now dreaded its approach.

Her nights especially were sad; the nights of yore were so beautiful, those nights spent dreaming of the day before and the day to come. At a certain point her eyes fell on a magnificent tub of carnations, some striped and some solid red, which, since winter, she had taken out of the greenhouse where Maurice had been held captive to let them blossom in her room.

Maurice had taught her how to cultivate them in the mahogany tub they were now in; she had watered, pruned, and trained them herself when Maurice was around. For whenever he came in the evening, she liked to show him how the gorgeous flowers had grown overnight, thanks to their fraternal care. But since Maurice had stopped coming around the poor carnations had been neglected, and now, thanks to lack of tender loving care, the listless buds remained unopened and drooped, yellowing, over the edge of the tub only to fall on the ground, like half-withered peas.

Geneviève knew at the mere sight of them the reason they were so forlorn. She told herself it was the same for flowers as for certain friendships that you nourish and cultivate with passion and that cause your heart to blossom. But one day, a caprice or some misfortune cuts this friendship off at the roots and the heart revived closes up again, listless and shriveled.

The young woman felt a dreadful anxiety clutch at her heart; the feeling she had tried to fight and had hoped to conquer struggled more than ever for breathing space, screaming that it would only die along with her heart. She then had a moment of true despair, for she knew that it was a losing battle for her. She gently bent down and kissed one of the shriveled buds and sobbed.

Her husband entered just as she was wiping her eyes, but Dixmer was so preoccupied with his own thoughts that he didn't sense the painful crisis his wife had just endured and paid no attention to the telltale redness of her eyes. It is true that, when she saw her husband, Geneviève leapt up and ran to him, carefully turning her back to the window so that her face was in darkness. "Well?" she said.

"Well, nothing new; impossible to get near *her*, impossible to get anything to her; impossible even to get a glimpse of her."

"What!" cried Geneviève. "With all the mayhem in Paris?"

"It's precisely the mayhem that made the wardens so nervous. They were worried the general agitation would provide a cover for a fresh assault on the Temple, so just when Her Majesty was supposed to go up to the top of the tower, Santerre gave the order not to let out the Queen, Madame Elisabeth, or Madame Royale."

"The poor Knight, he must have felt horribly vexed."

"He was in despair when he saw the opportunity slip through our fingers. He went so white, I dragged him off for fear he'd give himself away."

"But," ventured Geneviève timidly, "weren't there any municipal officers at the Temple you knew?"

"Someone was supposed to be there but he didn't show."

"Who?"

"Citizen Maurice Lindey," said Dixmer in a tone he forced himself to keep neutral.

"And why didn't he show?" asked Geneviève, making the same effort at self-control.

"He was sick."

"Him, sick?"

"Yes, and pretty seriously, too. Patriot as you know him to be, he was forced to let someone else take his place."

Dixmer paused, then went on: "God knows, Geneviève, even if he'd been there, it would have amounted to the same thing. Since we're supposed to have fallen out, he might have avoided speaking to me."

"My friend," said Geneviève, "I think you're exaggerating the gravity of the situation. Monsieur Maurice may have given us the cold shoulder for some silly reason, but that does not make him our enemy. He may have cooled, but that would not stop him from being polite, and if he'd seen you coming toward him, I'm certain he'd have met you halfway."

"Geneviève," said Dixmer, "for what we were hoping to get out of Maurice, you need more than politeness—though that wasn't too much to hope for from a true and deep friendship. Our so-called friendship is in tatters. So there's nothing more to hope for from that quarter."

With that Dixmer let out a deep sigh, while his forehead, usually so untroubled, furrowed sadly.

"But," said Geneviève timidly, "if you feel Monsieur Maurice is so essential to your plans . . ."

"Let's just say that I despair of seeing them succeed without him."

"Well then, why don't you try a new tack with citizen Lindey?"

It seemed to her that in calling him by his last name, her voice sounded less tender than when she called him by his first name.

"No," said Dixmer, shaking his head. "No, I've done all I could: a new tack would seem strange—he'd smell a rat. No, and you know, Geneviève, I see further than you in all this business: there's a wound at the bottom of Maurice's heart: Maurice is hurting."

"A wound?" asked Geneviève, genuinely moved. "My God! What are you saying? Tell me, my friend."

"I'm saying that there's more to our break with citizen Lindey than a mere caprice, and you know it as well as I do, Geneviève."

"And to what do you thereby attribute such a break?"

"To pride!" said Dixmer with verve.

"Pride?"

"Yes, he was honoring us, or so he felt at least, this fine upstanding burgher of Paris, this strutting demiaristocrat fashion plate, preserving his susceptibilities beneath his patriotism; he was honoring us, this republican who is so high and mighty in his section, in his club, in his municipal council, by bestowing his friendship upon mere manufacturers of skins. Perhaps we didn't make enough of a fuss over him, perhaps we forgot our place."

"But," protested Geneviève, "if we didn't make enough of a fuss, if we did forget our place, it seems to me what you've done since should make up for that."

"Yes, supposing that the wrong comes from me; but what if, on the contrary, it comes from you?"

"From me! How do you imagine I've wronged Monsieur Maurice?" Geneviève cried in amazement.

"Well, who knows, with someone like that? Didn't you yourself say he was impetuous before anyone else did? Look, I've come back to my first idea, Geneviève: you were wrong not to write to Maurice."

"Me!" cried Geneviève. "Do you really think so?"

"Not only do I think so, but I have thought so for the three weeks since the break."

"And?" Geneviève timidly asked.

"And I regard such a measure as indispensable."

"Oh, no, no, Dixmer! Don't ask that of me."

"You know perfectly well, Geneviève, that I never ask anything of you; I'm not asking you, I'm begging you, it's as simple as that. Do you hear me? I beg you to write to citizen Maurice."

"But . . ." stammered Geneviève.

"Listen," Dixmer interrupted. "Either there are serious reasons why you and Maurice are fighting—for, as far as I'm concerned, there's never been any complaint about my conduct; or your tiff is part of some childish game."

Geneviève did not reply.

"If your little tiff is a childish game, you'd be mad to let it go on. If the cause is serious, we've come so far—let's be perfectly clear about this—we must not stand on our dignity, or even on our pride. We cannot let some puerile spat jeopardize immense interests. Do you hear me? Pull yourself together, drop citizen Maurice Lindey a line, and he'll be back in a flash."

Geneviève reflected for a moment.

"But," she said, "can't we find a less compromising means to restore the good understanding between you and Monsieur Maurice?"

"Compromising, you say? On the contrary, it seems a perfectly natural way to do it to me."

"Not to me, my friend."

"You really are stubborn as an ox, Geneviève."

"Allow me to observe that this is the first time you've noticed, at least."

Dixmer, who had been twisting his handkerchief for some little time, used it to wipe his forehead, which was covered in sweat.

"Yes," he said, "which is why I'm all the more astounded."

"My God!" said Geneviève. "Is it possible, Dixmer, that you really don't know why I'm resisting? Must you force me to speak?"

With that she hung her head and dropped her arms to her sides, exhausted, enfeebled, pushed to the limits. Dixmer appeared to be making a violent effort at self-control; he took Geneviève's hand, forced her to lift her head, and, focusing on a point between her eyes, burst out laughing in a way that would have seemed particularly forced to Geneviève if she herself had been any less agitated at that moment.

"I know what it is!" said Dixmer. "In truth, you're right. I was blind. For all your wit, my dear Geneviève, for all your distinction, you let yourself fall for a cliché: you were frightened Maurice might be in love with you."

Geneviève felt something like a mortal chill pierce her heart. This irony of her husband's about the love Maurice felt for her, a love of which, from what she knew of his nature, she could imagine all the violence, a love, in a word, that, without admitting it to herself other than by the nagging tug of remorse, she herself shared in her heart of hearts—this irony turned her to stone. She didn't have the strength to look up. She knew she couldn't possibly reply.

"I guessed right, didn't I?" crowed Dixmer. "Well, rest assured, Geneviève, I know Maurice. He's a fierce republican with no other love in his heart than love of his homeland."

"Monsieur," cried Geneviève. "Are you sure of what you're saying?"

"There's no doubt about it," Dixmer said. "If Maurice loved you, instead of falling out with me he would have turned himself inside out showing how much he cared about me as the man he needed to deceive. If Maurice loved you, he would not so easily have given up his position as firm friend of the family, by means of which this kind of betrayal is usually cloaked."

"For the sake of honor," said Geneviève, "please don't joke about such things!"

"I'm not joking, madame; I'm telling you Maurice doesn't love you, that's all."

"And I'm telling you," cried Geneviève, flushing wildly, "I'm telling you you're wrong."

"In that case," said Dixmer, "Maurice has had the strength to clear out rather than betray the confidence of his host; he is a good man. Now, good men are rare, Geneviève; you can't do too much to bring them back when they stay away. Geneviève, you will write to Maurice, won't you?"

"Oh, God!" said the young woman.

With that she dropped her head into both hands, for the one she was about to lean on at such a dangerous juncture suddenly wasn't there, and her head fell. Dixmer looked at her for a second, then forced himself to smile.

"Come, dear friend," he said, "no feminine pride. If Maurice makes some great declaration to you again, just laugh it off as you did the first time. I know you, Geneviève, you are a worthy and noble soul. I'm sure of you."

"Oh!" cried Geneviève, losing her footing so that one of her knees slipped and hit the ground. "Oh, God! Who can be sure of anyone else when no one can be sure of themselves?"

Dixmer went pale as though all his blood had rushed to his heart.

"Geneviève," he said. "I was wrong to put you through all the anguish you've been through. I ought to have said to you straightaway: Geneviève, we are in an age of great devotion; Geneviève, I have devoted to the Queen, our benefactress, not only my arm, not only my head, but also my happiness. Others will give their lives for her. I would do more than give my life for her; I would risk my honor. And my honor, if it were to perish, will be just one more drop in the ocean of pain welling up ready to flood France. But my honor is not at risk when it is in the hands of a woman like my Geneviève."

This was the first time Dixmer had ever wholly revealed himself.

Geneviève lifted up her head, fixed on him her beautiful eyes brimming with admiration; then she slowly rose and gave him her forehead to kiss.

"It's what you want?" she said.

Dixmer nodded.

"Tell me what to say, then."

And she picked up a quill.

"No," said Dixmer. "It's bad enough to use, perhaps abuse, this worthy young man. Since he'll be reconciled with you the moment he receives a letter from you, Geneviève, let the letter be from you and not from Monsieur Dixmer."

With that, Dixmer planted a second kiss on his wife's forehead, thanked her, and left.

So Geneviève wrote, trembling all the while:

CITIZEN MAURICE,

You knew how much my husband loved you. Three weeks' separation have seemed a century to us; have they made you forget? Come, we'll be waiting for you. Your return will be a real celebration.

GENEVIÈVE

15

THE GODDESS OF REASON[1]

As Maurice had sent word to General Santerre the day before, he was seriously ill. Since he'd kept to his room, Lorin had come regularly to see him and had done everything in his power to persuade his friend to find some distraction. But Maurice hadn't budged. There are some sicknesses you don't want to recover from.

On the first of June, Lorin arrived at one o'clock.

"What's so special today?" asked Maurice. "You're done up to the nines."

In fact, Lorin was wearing the compulsory getup: red bonnet, carmagnole, and red, white, and blue belt, decorated with the two implements then known as abbé Maury's cruets[2] but which, before that and ever since, have been known quite simply as pistols.

"The first thing," said Lorin, "is the general collapse of the Girondins, which is happening even as we speak—and faster than you can imagine, at that. Right now, for example, they're laying into them with cannonballs in the place du Carrousel. Then, speaking more precisely, there is a most solemn event to which I invite you the day after to-morrow."

"But what's on today, then? You say you've come to get me?"

"Yes. Today's the rehearsal."

"What rehearsal?"

"The rehearsal for the most solemn event."

"My dear friend," said Maurice, "you know I haven't been able to go out for a week, so I'm no longer up on anything and I really do need to be kept informed."

"Didn't I tell you?"

"You haven't told me a thing."

"To start with, my dear friend, you already knew that we'd gotten rid of God some time ago now and that we'd replaced him with the Supreme Being."[3]

"Yes, I know that."

"Well, it seems they realized something—which is that the Supreme Being was a moderate, a Rolandist, a Girondin."

"Lorin, please don't joke about sacred things; you know I don't like it."

"What's a person to do, my friend! You have to keep up with the times. I was pretty fond of the old God myself, first and foremost because I was used to Him. As for the Supreme Being, it appears he really does have some serious defects and that, since he's been up there, everything's been going to the dogs. In the end our legislators have decreed him deposed. . . ."

Maurice shrugged his shoulders.

"Shrug your shoulders all you like," said Lorin.

> "Thanks to philosophy
> We, great henchmen of Momus,
> Decree that madness
> Will have its cult *in partibus*.

" 'Without real functions'—so much so, in fact," Lorin continued, "that we've decided to worship the Goddess of Reason."

"And you're mixed up in all these masquerades?" asked Maurice.

"Ah, my friend! If you knew the Goddess of Reason like I know the Goddess of Reason, you'd be one of her hottest followers. Listen, I want you to meet her, let me introduce you."

"Leave me out of all your lunatic shenanigans. I'm sad, you know very well."

"All the more reason, for heaven's sake! She'll cheer you up, she's a good sort. . . . Oh! But you know her, the austere goddess that the people of Paris are going to crown with laurel and parade about on a chariot covered in gold leaf! It is . . . guess!"

"How do you expect me to guess?"

"Artemisia."[4]

"Artemisia?" said Maurice, trying to put a face to the name, without any such face popping into his head.

"Yes. A tall brunette I met last year . . . at the Opera ball. You came and had supper with us and got her drunk."

"Ah, yes! That's right," replied Maurice. "I remember now. So she's it?"

"She's got the best chance. I presented her at the competition: all the Thermopylae club promised me their votes. The general election's in three days. Today is the preview feast; we'll be spilling a bit of champagne. Maybe the day after tomorrow we'll be spilling blood! But whatever gets spilled, Artemisia will be goddess or the devil take me! So on your feet. We'll get her to try on her tunic for us."

"Thanks, but I don't think so. I've always hated that kind of thing."

"Dressing up goddesses? Christ, you're hard to please! All right, then, if it will amuse you, I'll put her tunic on for her and you can take it off."

"Lorin, I'm sick; not only do I not have an ounce of gaiety left in me, but the gaiety of other people makes me even sicker."

"Now you're beginning to scare me, Maurice. You've given up the fight, you've lost your sense of humor; you're not involved in some conspiracy by any chance, are you?"

"Me! Good God!"

"You mean: Good Goddess of Reason!"

"Leave me, Lorin; I can't, I won't go out. I'm in bed and I'm going to stay there."

Lorin scratched his ear.

"All right!" he said. "I see what it is."

"What do you see?"

"I see you're waiting for the Goddess of Reason."

"Hell's bells!" cried Maurice. "Witty friends are such a pain in the neck. Get lost or I'll heap curses upon you, you and your goddess. . . ."

"Heap away. . . ."

Maurice raised his hand to deliver a curse when he was interrupted by his officieux, who entered at that moment holding a letter for the citizen, his brother.

"Citizen Agesilaus," said Lorin, "you come at a bad time; your master was about to enjoy a moment of glory."

Maurice dropped his hand and reached out nonchalantly for the letter. But at the mere touch he shuddered; avidly bringing it closer to his eyes, he devoured the writing and the seal with a glance and, going pale all the while as though he were about to be sick, he broke the seal.

"Aha!" murmured Lorin. "Our curiosity's finally been aroused, it would seem."

Maurice was no longer listening. He was reading with all his soul Geneviève's few lines. After reading them once, he read them again, twice, thrice, four times, then he wiped his forehead and dropped his hands, gazing at Lorin like a man in a daze.

"Cripes!" said Lorin. "Now there's a letter that must bear interesting tidings!"

Maurice reread the letter for the fifth time and a new shade of scarlet colored his face. His dry eyes became moist and his chest rose in a profound sigh. Then, suddenly forgetting all about his illness and the weakness that had ensued, he leapt out of bed.

"My clothes!" he shouted to the stupefied officieux. "My clothes, my dear Agesilaus! Ah! My poor Lorin, my good Lorin! I was waiting for it every day but in all honesty I didn't expect it. This, white pants, a shirt with a ruffle, and I'll need my hair done and a shave right away!"

The officieux hastened to execute Maurice's orders and managed to do his hair and shave him at once in a remarkable sleight of hand.

"Oh! To think I'm going to see her again! I'm going to see her again!" cried the young man. "Lorin, in all honesty, I have never known what happiness was till this moment."

"My poor Maurice," said Lorin, "I think you're in need of that visit I advised."

"Oh, my dear friend," cried Maurice, "forgive me, but I've honestly lost my reason."

"Well then, let me offer you mine," said Lorin, laughing at this appalling play on words.

What was most amazing was that Maurice laughed too. Happiness had made him facile when it came to matters of wit. And that was not all.

"Here," he said, cutting off a branch of an orange tree covered in blossom. "My compliments to Artemisia, worthy widow of Mausolus."[5]

"About time!" cried Lorin. "We could use a bit of chivalry! Looks like I'll have to forgive you. And then it seems to me you really are in love, and I've always had the greatest respect for terrible misfortune."

"Yes! I am in love!" cried Maurice, whose heart was bursting with joy. "I am in love and now I can admit it, because she loves me; for she's asking me to come back—that means she loves me, doesn't it, Lorin?"

"No doubt," answered the worshiper of the Goddess of Reason rather casually. "But watch out, Maurice. The way you're going about it worries me. . . .

> "Often love of a Muse
> Leads you to choose
> Her over tyrant Cupid.
> Next to the best, you lose your head
> So love as I do Reason
> And you won't do anything stupid."

"Bravo! Bravo!" cried Maurice, clapping his hands.

On that note, he bolted down the stairs four at a time with his knees up around his neck, ran to the quay, and flew off in the oh-so-familiar direction of the old rue Saint-Jacques.

"I think he applauded me, didn't he, Agesilaus?" said Lorin.

"He certainly did, citizen, and there's nothing surprising about that: that was very nice, what you said just then."

"He's sicker than I thought," said Lorin.

And he descended the stairs too, though a little more calmly. Artemisia was not Geneviève, after all.

Scarcely had Lorin reached the rue Saint-Honoré, he and his orange blossom with him, than a mob of young citizens, to whom he was in the habit of distributing either centimes or kicks from under his carmagnole according to his frame of mind, trotted along respectfully behind him, no doubt taking him for one of those virtuous men Saint-Just[6] recommended be offered white apparel and bouquets of orange blossom.

The cortege grew and grew, so rare was it to see a virtuous man, even in those days, till there were at least several thousand young citizens by the time the bouquet was offered to Artemisia—a tribute that made several other Reasons, who had lined up, so sick they came down with migraines.

It was that very evening that the famous cantata spread throughout Paris:

> *Long live the Goddess of Reason!*
> *Pure flame, gentle light.*

And since it has come down to us without the name of its author, something that has certainly taxed revolutionary archaeologists, we might be so bold as to assert that it was written for the beautiful Artemisia by our friend Hyacinthe Lorin.

16

THE PRODIGAL SON

Maurice could not have gone any faster if he'd had wings. The streets were full of people, but Maurice only noticed the crowd at all because it hampered his progress. People were saying that the Convention was under siege, that the sovereignty of the people had been attacked along with its representatives, that no one was allowed to leave.... And all this was more than likely, for you could hear the clamoring of tocsins and the thundering of cannon fire sounding the alarm.

But what did cannon fire and tocsins matter to Maurice at this point in time? What was it to him whether the deputies could or could not leave the Convention, since the prohibition didn't extend to him? He just ran.

And as he ran, he imagined Geneviève waiting for him at her little window, gazing across the garden, ready to flash him her most charming smile the second she laid eyes on him in the distance.

Dixmer, too, had no doubt been alerted about this happy return and he would hold out his good old fat hand, so frank and so loyal in its handshake. He loved Dixmer that day; he loved everyone, even Morand, with his black hair and his green goggles behind which, till now, he'd always felt he could see a sly eye gleaming.

Maurice loved creation in its entirety, for he was happy; he would gladly have showered everyone with flowers so they could be as happy as he. Yet what he so hoped for was not to be. Poor Maurice got it wrong—which happens nine times out of ten when a man thinks with his heart and not his head.

Instead of the sweet smile awaiting Maurice, which was supposed to greet him from afar the moment he appeared, Geneviève had promised herself to show him only a frosty politeness—a weak rampart she busily erected to stem the torrent that threatened to swamp her heart. She had retired to her room on the first floor and intended to come down to the ground floor only when called.

Alas! Geneviève got it wrong, too.

Only Dixmer got it right. He was watching out for Maurice through a wire fence and smiling with a smirk of irony. Meanwhile, citizen Morand was phlegmatically applying black dye to little tails that were to be stuck on white catskins to turn them into ermine.

Maurice pushed open the little alley door and entered the garden the old familiar way. The doorbell rang the way it used to do to indicate that it was Maurice who had opened the door.

Geneviève, who was standing by her closed window, gave a start. She dropped the curtain she had parted.

The first thing Maurice felt on returning to his host's was therefore disappointment; not only was Geneviève not waiting for him at her ground-floor window, but even when he entered the small salon where he had taken his leave of her she wasn't there, and he was forced to have himself announced as though these three weeks of absence had turned him into a stranger.

His heart sank.

It was Dixmer Maurice saw first, Dixmer who ran up bleating for joy and gave Maurice a hug. Only then did Geneviève come down. She had whipped her cheeks with her mother-of-pearl spatula to bring the blood back, but by the time she'd descended the twenty steps, the artificially induced red had disappeared as the blood rushed back to her heart.

Maurice saw Geneviève appear in the doorway; with a smile on his face, he went toward her to kiss her hand. It was only then that he registered how much she had changed. On her side, she remarked with fright how thin Maurice had become, and the alarmingly feverish light in his eyes.

"So you are here, monsieur?" she said to him in a voice whose emotion she could not control. She'd promised to toss him an indifferent, "Hello, citizen Maurice. Why have you made yourself so scarce?" The variant still sounded frosty to Maurice, and yet, what a difference between the two!

Dixmer cut short the mutual prolonged examinations and recriminations. He saw to it that dinner was served, for it was close to two o'clock. Passing into the dining room, Maurice saw that his place had been set. Citizen Morand then arrived, dressed in the same brown outfit and the same jacket and still wearing his green glasses, his long limp strands of black hair, and his white ruffle. Maurice felt something like affection for the whole getup now—close up, it was infinitely less threatening than at a distance.

Indeed, what was the likelihood that Geneviève loved this little chemist? You'd have to be head over heels in love, and therefore completely mad, to dream up such poppycock. Besides, this was not the moment to be jealous. Maurice was carrying Geneviève's letter in the pocket of his jacket and his heart was beating beneath it, pounding fit to rupture with sheer joy.

Geneviève had regained her composure. Women are built in such a peculiar way as to be almost always able to wipe out all traces of the past and all threats of the future in favor of the present. Finding herself feeling happy, Geneviève regained her self-control, which meant she returned to being calm and collected, though affectionate—another nuance that Maurice wasn't quite strong enough to understand. Lorin would have found the explanation in Parny, the poet, or Bertin or Gentil-Bernard.

The conversation turned to the Goddess of Reason. The fall of the Girondins and the new cult of worship that caused the inheritance of the heavens to pass into female hands were the two main events of the day. Dixmer claimed he wouldn't have minded seeing this inestimable honor fall to Geneviève. Maurice nearly laughed out loud at the suggestion, but Geneviève sided with her husband and Maurice looked at them both, amazed that a mind as reasonable as Dixmer's and a nature as poetic as Geneviève's could be so led astray by patriotism.

Morand elaborated a theory about women in politics, starting with Théroigne de Méricourt,[1] the heroine of the tenth of August, and ending with Madame Roland,[2] that soul of the Gironde. In passing, he said what he thought of the tricoteuses—those bloodthirsty crones who did their knitting at the foot of the guillotine. His words made Maurice smile despite the cruel derision of these female patriots, later given the hideous name of guillotine-lickers.

"Ah! Citizen Morand," said Dixmer, "let's show a little respect for patriotism, even when it errs."

"As for me," said Maurice, "when it comes to patriotism, I find women are always patriotic enough as long as they're not too aristocratic."

"You're right there," said Morand. "Me, I frankly admit that I find a woman rather despicable when she puts on masculine airs and that a man is a coward when he insults a woman, even if that woman is his bitterest enemy."

Morand had just lured Maurice onto delicate ground. Maurice in turn gave a nod: the contenders had entered the lists. Like a herald ringing the bell, Dixmer then added, "One moment, one moment, citizen Morand. You except, I hope, women who are enemies of the nation."

A silence of several seconds followed this riposte to Morand's remark and Maurice's signal. It was Maurice who broke the silence.

"Let's not except anyone," he said sadly. "Alas! the women who have been enemies of the nation have been thoroughly punished by now, it seems to me."

"Do you mean the prisoners in the Temple, the Austrian woman and Capet's sister and daughter?" asked Dixmer so loudly his words came out devoid of all expression.

Morand went pale as he waited for the young municipal officer to reply. If you could have seen how deeply he dug his nails into his chest, you would have said they'd leave a scar.

"That's precisely who I mean," said Maurice.

"What!" said Morand in a strangled voice. "Is what they're saying true, citizen Maurice?"

"What are they saying?" asked the young man.

"That the prisoners are badly mistreated, at times, by those whose duty it is to protect them."

"There are men," said Maurice, "who aren't worthy of the name. There are cowards who did not fight and who need to torture the vanquished to persuade themselves they are the conquerors."

"Oh! You're not of those men, not you, Maurice, I'm certain of that," cried Geneviève.

"Madame," Maurice replied, "I who am speaking to you now, I mounted the guard on the scaffold on which the late King died. I had my sword in hand and I was there to kill with my own hands anyone who tried to save him. Yet when he came near me, in spite of myself, I took off my hat and turned to my men and I said to them: 'Citizens, I warn you, I'll run my sword through the body of the first person who insults this man who once was king.' Oh! I defy anyone to say a single cry was heard from my company. And it was I who wrote with my own hand the first of the thousands of notices that went up around Paris when the King came back from Varennes:[3] 'Whoever salutes the king will be mowed down; whoever insults him will be hanged.'

"Well," Maurice continued, without registering the terrible effect his words were having on the assembled company, "well, I've proved I'm a good and honest patriot, that I hate kings and their followers. And yet I declare, in spite of my opinions, which are nothing less than profound convictions, in spite of the certainty I have that the Austrian woman has had a hand in the calamities that are devastating France— in spite of all this, I say no man, not even Santerre himself, will ever, ever insult the former Queen in my presence."

"Citizen," Dixmer interrupted, shaking his head as though disapproving of such recklessness, "you know you have to be pretty sure of us to say such things in front of us?"

"In front of you as in front of anyone who'll listen, Dixmer; and I'll add this: she may perhaps perish on the same scaffold as her husband, but I'm not among those who are frightened of a woman, and I will always respect whoever is weaker than I am."

"And the Queen," Geneviève timidly asked, "has she at times shown you, Monsieur Maurice, that she was sensitive to this tact, to which she is far from accustomed?"

"The prisoner has thanked me several times for my consideration for her, madame."

"Then she must see your tour of duty come around with pleasure?"

"I think so," said Maurice.

"Then," said Morand, trembling like a girl, "since you're admitting what no one admits anymore these days—that is, to having a generous heart—you don't persecute children, either, I suppose?"

"Me?" said Maurice. "Ask that scoundrel Simon what it's like to be on the receiving end of the fist of a municipal officer in whose presence he's had the audacity to beat little Capet."

This response sent a spontaneous ripple around Dixmer's table. The whole company rose respectfully, Maurice alone remaining seated, without having any idea that he had caused such an outburst of admiration.

"What's the matter?" he asked, baffled.

"I thought someone was calling from the workshop," said Dixmer.

"No, no," said Geneviève. "I thought so too at first, but we're mistaken."

And everyone resumed their seats.

"Ah! So it's you, citizen Maurice!" said Morand with a quiver in his voice. "You're the municipal officer everyone's been talking about, the man who so nobly defended a child?"

"People have been talking about it?" said Maurice with almost sublime naïveté.

"Oh, there's a noble soul for you," said Morand, getting up from the table so as not to burst a blood vessel and withdrawing to the workshop as though some pressing project was claiming him.

"Yes, citizen," said Dixmer, "yes, everyone's talking about it, and I should say that anyone who has a heart and a modicum of courage has sung your praises without knowing who you are."

"And let's leave him anonymous," said Geneviève, "the glory we would crown him with would be too dangerous a glory."

And so in this odd conversation everyone, unwittingly, had said their bit about heroism, devotion, and sensitivity.

There had even been a cry of love.

17

The Miners

As they were leaving the table, Dixmer was informed that his notary was waiting for him in his office. He excused himself to Maurice, whom he was in the habit of quitting at this point in any case, and went to meet his legal worthy.

At issue was the purchase of a small house in the rue de la Corderie, opposite the Temple gardens. In fact it was more a position than a house Dixmer was buying, for the actual structure was falling in ruins, though he intended to have it rebuilt.

So negotiations with the owner can hardly be said to have dragged on. The very same morning, the notary had seen the vendor and negotiated a figure of 19,500 livres. He had now come to Dixmer's to have the contract signed and get the money in exchange for the building. The vendor was to clear the house out completely that same day and the workers were to be installed the following day.

With the contract signed, Dixmer and Morand accompanied the notary to the rue de la Corderie to see the new acquisition without wasting a moment, for it had been bought sight unseen.

The house was located more or less where number twenty stands today; it was three stories high and surmounted by a mansard. The lower part had once been rented by a wine merchant and possessed magnificent cellars. These cellars were the special boast of the vendor, for they were the truly noteworthy part of the house, though Dixmer and Morand showed only mild interest in them. Yet both went down into what the owner called his underground tunnel, though seemingly only out of politeness.

Unlike most proprietors, this one had not lied: the cellars were superb; one of them extended right under the rue de la Corderie, and when you were down there you could hear carriages rolling along overhead.

Dixmer and Morand appeared to appreciate this advantage only mildly and even spoke of having the cellars filled in, for, although all very well for a wine merchant, they were useless for good burghers intent on occupying the whole house.

After the cellars they visited the ground floor, the second floor, the third. From the third the view looked straight down on the Temple garden; as usual it was invaded by the National Guard, who had had it to themselves since the Queen stopped taking walks there.

Dixmer and Morand recognized their friend the widow Plumeau, going about her usual business doing the honors of her canteen. But doubtless their desire to be recognized by her was not great, for they stood hidden behind the owner as he pointed out to them the advantages of such a varied and pleasant view.

The buyer then asked to see the mansard, but the owner was obviously not expecting such a request, for he didn't have the key on him. Prompted by the wad of assignats[1] he was shown, though, he quickly ran down to get it.

"I was not mistaken," said Morand. "This house is perfect for our purposes."

"And what do you think of the cellar?"

"That it's a godsend that will save us days of work."

"Do you think it goes all the way to the canteen?"

"It runs a bit to the left, but that won't matter."

"But," asked Dixmer, "how can you follow your line underground and be sure of ending up where you want to?"

"Don't worry, my friend, that's my concern."

"What if we always give the signal from here that we're keeping watch?"

"But the Queen wouldn't be able to see it from the top of the tower; I think only the mansard is on the same level as the tower platform— and I'm not even sure of that."

"Never mind," said Dixmer. "Either Toulan or Turgy will see it from some opening somewhere, and they'll tell Her Majesty."

With that Dixmer tied knots at the bottom of a white calico curtain and threaded the curtain out the window as if it had been blown out by the wind. Then both men, pretending to be impatient to visit the mansard, went to wait for the proprietor on the stairs, after closing the door to the third floor behind them so the good man would not get the idea of pulling in his floating curtain.

The mansards, as Morand had anticipated, was not quite as high as the top of the tower. This was both a problem and an advantage: a problem because it meant not being able to communicate by signals with the Queen; an advantage because this impossibility would remove any suspicion. Tall houses were naturally the most carefully monitored.

"We'll have to find a way of telling her to be on the lookout—through Turgy or Toulan or the Tison girl," murmured Dixmer.

"I'll work on it," said Morand.

They went back down. The notary was waiting in the salon with the contract all signed.

"Wonderful," said Dixmer. "The house suits me. Count out the 19,500 livres agreed on for the citizen and get him to sign."

The proprietor carefully counted out the money and signed.

"You know, citizen," said Dixmer, "the principal clause stipulates that the house will be handed over to me this very evening so that I can put my workers to work first thing tomorrow morning."

"And I'll stick to that, citizen; you can take the keys away with you. This evening at eight o'clock sharp it will be perfectly free."

"One moment!" said Dixmer. "Didn't you tell me, citizen notary, that there was a way out onto the rue Porte-Foin?"

"There is, citizen," answered the proprietor, "but I had it blocked off, since I have only one officieux and the poor devil was run off his feet trying to keep his eye on two doors. In any case, the exit is constructed in such a way that you can easily open it up again with a couple of hours' work, if that. Do you want to see for yourselves, citizens?"

"Thank you, but there's no need," said Dixmer. "I doubt if I'll ever be needing that particular exit."

With that both men withdrew, after having for the third time gotten the proprietor to promise to leave the apartment empty by eight that night.

At nine both men were back, followed at a discreet distance by five or six men to whom no one paid any attention in the midst of all the pandemonium then reigning in Paris.

The two men entered first and saw that the owner had kept his word: the house was completely empty. They closed the shutters with the greatest care, killed the light, and lit candles that Morand had brought in his pocket. Then the other men filed in, one after the other. They were the master tanner's usual dinner guests, the same black marketeers who had tried to dispatch Maurice one night and had since become his friends.

They closed all the doors and went down into the cellar. This cellar, though virtually disregarded earlier that day, had come into its own that evening as the focal point of the house. They first set to work blocking all openings through which any inquisitive eyes could peer inside. Then Morand swiftly upended an empty barrel and began tracing geometric figures on a piece of paper.

While Morand was drawing, his cohorts, led by Dixmer, left the house and followed the rue de la Corderie to the corner of the rue de la Beauce, where they came to a halt by the side of a covered carriage.

In this carriage was a man who quietly handed each of them a pioneer's tool not to be found in a tanner's kit: one got a spade, the next a pick; the third a lever, the fourth a hoe. Each of the men hid the implement he had been given under his coat, then the miners retraced their steps back to the little house and the car disappeared.

Morand had finished his work. He went straight to one corner of the cellar.

"Here," he said, "start digging."

And the workers of deliverance immediately set to work.

The situation for the prisoners of the Temple had become more and more serious and, especially, more and more painful. For a moment, the Queen, Madame Elisabeth, and Madame Royale had had their hopes raised again. The municipal officers Toulan and Lepître, moved by compassion for the august prisoners, had shown them care and kindness. At first, unused to such marks of sympathy, the poor women were mistrustful. But you can't be mistrustful when you have hope. Besides, what more could happen to the Queen, separated as she was from her son by prison, separated from her husband by death? To go to the scaffold as he had done? That was a fate she had stared in the face for so long now that she had wound up growing used to it.

When Toulan and Lepître's tour of duty came around, the Queen asked them to tell her the details of the King's death, if it was true that they were concerned for her fate. This was a sad test of their sympathy. Lepître had been present at the execution and he obeyed the Queen's command. The Queen next asked for the newspaper reports of the execution and Lepître promised to bring them next time he was on duty—guard duty came up every three weeks.

In the King's day, there had been four municipal officers at the Temple. Once the King was dead, these were reduced to three: one who kept watch in the day and two who kept watch at night. Toulan and Lepître managed to rig it so that they were always on night duty together.

The guard duty roster was determined by drawing ballots from a hat. On one ballot you had to write "day" and on two other ballots "night." Each man drew his ballot from a hat so that luck sorted out the night guards. Every time Toulan and Lepître were on duty, they would write "day" on all three ballots before presenting the hat to the municipal officer they wanted to oust. The latter would plunge his hand into the improvised urn and would, of course, pull out a ballot with the word "day" on it. Toulan and Lepître would then destroy the other two ballots, muttering about Providence always handing them the most boring chore—that is, night duty.

When the Queen was sure of the two guards, she put them in contact with the Knight of Maison-Rouge. But then an escape plan was nipped in the bud. The Queen and Madame Elisabeth were supposed to flee disguised as municipal officers, with identity cards that would be procured for them. As for the two children, that is, Madame Royale and the young Dauphin, it had been remarked that the man who lit the oil lamps in the Temple always brought two children with him roughly the same age as the princess and the prince. It was agreed that Turgy, of whom we've already spoken, would don the lamplighter's clothes and cart off Madame Royale and the Dauphin.

Let's have a quick look at what sort of man this Turgy was.

Turgy was a former serving-man at the King's table, brought to the Temple along with a part of the household of the Tuileries, for the King at first enjoyed a pretty well organized table service. For the first month alone, this service set the nation back thirty to forty thousand francs.

But, as you can well understand, such prodigality could not last—the Commune saw to it that that was an order. The chefs were sent packing, along with kitchen hands and assistant kitchen hands. Only a single serving-man was retained, and that man was Turgy.

Turgy was thus a natural intermediary between the two prisoners and their followers, for Turgy could come and go, and so carry notes with him and carry back replies. In general these notes were rolled as stoppers in the carafes of almond milk the Queen and Madame Elisabeth were brought. They were written in lemon juice and remained invisible until held up to a flame.

Everything had been ready for the escape when one day Tison lit his pipe with the stopper from one of the carafes. As the paper burned he saw letters appear. He put out the half-burned piece of paper and took the fragment to the Temple Council. There it was held up to a flame, but only a few random words could be deciphered. The rest had been reduced to ashes.

But the Queen's handwriting was recognizable. Under interrogation, Tison told how he'd noticed Lepître and Toulan treating the prisoners indulgently now and then. The two agents were denounced to the municipal council and could no longer enter the Temple.

Turgy remained.

But wariness had been aroused to the highest degree. Turgy was never left alone with the princesses, and so all communication with the outside world became impossible.

Still, one day Madame Elisabeth had handed Turgy a small knife with a gold blade she used for cutting fruit and asked him to clean it. Turgy suspected something, and while wiping the knife he had tugged at the handle. It contained a note.

This note consisted of a whole alphabet of signs.

Turgy gave Madame Elisabeth back the knife, but a municipal officer who happened to be on the scene whipped the knife out of her hands and inspected it closely; he too pulled the blade out of the handle, but luckily the note was no longer there. Though that didn't stop the municipal officer from confiscating the knife.

It was at that point that the indefatigable Knight of Maison-Rouge dreamed up this second attempt, which would be carried out by means of the house Dixmer had just bought.

Yet, little by little, the prisoners had lost all hope. That day the Queen had been sickened by the cries from the street that reached her, informing her that the Girondins—the last bastion of moderation— were to be put on trial. She had been mortally sad when she heard the news. With the Girondins dead, the royal family had no one to defend them at the Convention.

At seven o'clock, supper was served. The municipal officers examined each dish as they normally did; they unfolded all the napkins one after the other; poked at the bread, one with a fork, the other with his fingers; smashed the macaroons and the nuts—all this for fear that a note might somehow reach the prisoners. Once these precautions had been taken, they invited the Queen and the princesses to sit at the table using this simple formula: "Widow Capet, you can eat."

The Queen shook her head to say she was not hungry. But at that moment Madame Royale came over as though to kiss her mother and whispered in her ear:

"Sit down at the table, madame, I think Turgy is signaling to you."

The Queen started and looked up. Turgy was standing opposite her, his napkin placed over his left hand and his right hand touching his eye.

She stood without further ado and went to take her usual place at the table. The two municipal officers were present throughout the meal, since they were forbidden to leave the princesses alone with Turgy even for a moment. Under the table, the Queen and Madame Elisabeth pressed each other's feet. As the Queen was seated opposite Turgy, none of the serving-man's gestures escaped her. Yet all his movements were so natural they could not and did not arouse any mistrust on the part of the municipal officers.

After supper, the table was cleared with the same precautions as it had been set; the tiniest bits of bread were collected and inspected;

and after that Turgy left first, followed by the officers. Only Mother Tison stayed behind.

This woman had become ferocious since she had been separated from her daughter, of whose fate she was completely in the dark. Every time the Queen embraced Madame Royale she flew into fits of rage that showed all the signs of madness. And so the Queen, whose maternal heart empathized with the mother's suffering, often stopped at the point of offering herself the consolation, the only one that remained to her, of hugging her daughter to her heart.

Tison came for his wife. But the woman first declared that she would retire only when the Widow Capet had gone to bed. Madame Elisabeth then said good night to the Queen and went into her room. The Queen undressed and hopped into bed, and so did Madame Royale. It was then that Mother Tison took the candle and left.

The municipal officers had already lain down on their camp beds in the hallway when the moon, the lodgers' sole, wan visitor, slipped an oblique ray of light through the opening in the canopy; it lay in a stripe from the window to the foot of the Queen's bed.

For a moment all remained calm and quiet in the room. Then a door squeaked softly on its hinges and a shadow passed between the ray of light and the foot of the bed. It was Madame Elisabeth.

"Did you see?" she asked in a low voice.

"Yes," said the Queen.

"So you understood?"

"So clearly that I can hardly believe it."

"Come, let's go over the signals."

"First, he touched his eye to indicate to us that something new was afoot."

"Then he passed his napkin from his left arm to his right arm, which means they are busying themselves with our deliverance."

"Then he brought his hand to his forehead as a sign that the help he announced was coming to us from inside France and not from abroad."

"Then, when you asked him not to forget your almond milk tomorrow, he made two knots in his handkerchief."

"So it is the Knight of Maison-Rouge once more. Noble heart!"

"It is he," said Madame Elisabeth.

"Are you asleep, my daughter?" the Queen asked.

"No, my mother," replied Madame Royale.

"Well then, pray for you-know-who."

Madame Elisabeth crept back to her room without a sound; for five minutes the voice of the young princess could be heard speaking to God in the silence of the night.

This was at the very moment that, under Morand's direction, the first blows of the pick were delivered in the little house in the rue de la Corderie.

18

CLOUDS

Apart from the intoxication of their first glances, Maurice found the reception Geneviève had given him well below his expectations, and he was counting on being alone with her to win back the ground he had lost—or seemed to have lost, at least—on the way to her heart.

But Geneviève had other plans and was counting equally strongly on not giving him the opportunity of being alone with her—all the more so as she remembered how dangerously sweet such tête-à-têtes could be.

Maurice was about to strike the following day, but a relative, no doubt alerted beforehand, popped up on a visit and Geneviève clung to her visitor for dear life. There was nothing Maurice could say this time, for it might well not have been Geneviève's fault.

When he was leaving, Geneviève asked Maurice to escort the relative home, as she lived in the rue des Fossés-Saint-Victor. Maurice walked away rather sullenly with his burden, but Geneviève flashed him a smile and he chose to interpret the smile as a promise.

Alas! Maurice was wrong again! The next day was the second of June, the terrible day that saw the Girondins fall. But Maurice sent his friend Lorin packing when Lorin had done his utmost to cart Maurice off to the Convention, putting everything else aside to go off and see the woman he loved. The Goddess of Liberty had a formidable rival in Geneviève.

Maurice found Geneviève in her little salon, and she was gracious and full of consideration. But by her side was a young chambermaid, sporting a red, white, and blue cockade, and busy marking handkerchiefs by the windowsill without any apparent intention of budging.

Maurice scowled; Geneviève could see the Olympian was in a bad mood and she laid her attentions on with a trowel. But as she didn't push amiability as far as getting rid of the young officieuse, Maurice decided he'd had enough and flounced off an hour earlier than usual.

Yet, since all this could have been sheer bad luck, Maurice decided to be patient. That evening, in any case, the situation was so terrible that, although Maurice had lived beyond the reach of politics for some time now, the news floored even him. It required nothing less than the fall of a party that had ruled France for ten months to distract him for a second or two from his love.

The next day saw the same caper on Geneviève's part, but Maurice had his own plan ready in anticipation: ten minutes into his visit, Maurice noticed that, after marking a dozen handkerchiefs, the chambermaid was starting on six dozen napkins, and so he pulled out his watch, saluted Geneviève, and left without a word. Better than that: as he left, he did not turn round once.

Geneviève, who'd gotten up to watch him cross the garden, remained momentarily blank, faint, and nervous; she fell back down onto her chair, completely distraught over the outcome of her little diplomatic exercise.

Right then, Dixmer strode in.

"Has Maurice gone?" he cried, astounded.

"Yes," stammered Geneviève.

"But he only just got here, didn't he?"

"About a quarter of an hour ago."

"So he's coming back?"

"I doubt it."

"Leave us, Peony," said Dixmer.

The chambermaid had taken the flower's name out of hatred of the name Marie, which she had the misfortune to share with the Austrian woman. On her master's invitation, she rose and left the room.

"Well, then, dear Geneviève," Dixmer coaxed, "have you made peace with Maurice?"

"Quiet the opposite, my friend. I believe we are on worse terms than ever at this moment."

"This time who's in the wrong?" asked Dixmer.

"Maurice, without a shadow of a doubt."

"Let me be the judge of that."

"What!" said Geneviève, flushing. "Can't you guess?"

"Why he's angry? No, I can't."

"He's allergic to Peony, it would seem."

"Oof! Really? Well then, we'll have to get rid of the girl. I'm not about to deprive myself of a friend like Maurice for the sake of some chambermaid."

"Oh!" said Geneviève. "I don't think he'll go as far as demanding we banish her from the house. I think he'll be satisfied with . . ."

"What?"

"With her being banished from my room."

"And Maurice is right," said Dixmer. "He comes to see you—not Peony; so there's no point in Peony's being there all the time when he comes."

Geneviève looked at her husband with amazement.

"But, my friend . . ." she said.

"Geneviève," Dixmer continued, "I thought you were an ally who would make the task I've imposed on myself easier; yet I find, on the contrary, that your fears are making our problems twice as bad. I thought we'd reached an agreement four days ago and now we're back at square one. Geneviève, didn't I tell you I trust in you, in your honor? Didn't I say to you that it was essential that Maurice be our friend again—a closer, more trusting friend than ever? God! Women are always getting in the way of our plans!"

"But, my friend, isn't there some other way? It would be better for all of us, as I've said, if Maurice stayed away."

"Yes, for all of us, perhaps; but for she who is above all of us, for she for whom we have sworn to sacrifice our fortunes and our lives and even our honor, this young man has to return to the fold. Did you know they suspect Turgy and that they're talking about providing the princesses with another servant?"

"All right; I'll send Peony away."

"My God, Geneviève!" said Dixmer, with a (rare) gesture of impatience. "Why are you bothering me with all this? Why fan the fire of my distress with yours? Why create difficulties for me in the midst of difficulty itself? Do what you have to do as an honest, devoted wife, Geneviève; that's what I'm saying to you. Tomorrow I won't be here; tomorrow I'll be replacing Morand in the engineering works. I won't be dining with you, but he will be; there's something he wants to ask Maurice—he'll explain to you what it is. What Morand asks Maurice, remember, Geneviève, that is the important thing. It may not be the end toward which we are working, but it is the means; it is the last hope of this good, noble, devoted man, your protector and mine, for whom we should lay down our lives."

"And for whom I would gladly lay down mine!" cried Geneviève with glee.

"Well then, this man, Geneviève, I don't know how it's happened, but you haven't managed to make Maurice love him, and it was especially important that he do so. So that now, in the lousy state you've left Maurice in, he will perhaps refuse what Morand asks him to do— and which he must at all costs do. Do you want me to spell out where all your delicacy and sentimentality have landed Morand, Geneviève?"

"Oh, monsieur!" cried Geneviève, joining her hands together in entreaty and blanching. "Monsieur, let's not broach that subject again, ever."

"Well then," Dixmer went on, bringing his lips to his wife's brow, "be strong and use your head."

With that, he spun on his heels and left.

"Oh, my God! My God!" murmured Geneviève in anguish. "Look how they're hammering me to get me to accept a love to which my whole soul soars!"

The next day, as we have already said, was a décadi[1]—the tenth day of the new ten-day division of time. There was a practice in the Dixmer family, as in all bourgeois families of the time, to have a longer and more ceremonious lunch on Sunday than on the other days of the week. Since Maurice had become a close friend of the family with a standing invitation to Sunday lunch, he had never missed one. That particular day, he arrived at twelve—even though the meal was never served before two o'clock—but hung back well out of sight without dismounting and waited.

The way he had stomped off last time, Geneviève almost despaired of seeing him. Indeed, it struck twelve without any sign of Maurice; then twelve-thirty, then one o'clock.

Words cannot tell what passed through Geneviève's heart while she waited. At first she had dressed as simply as possible; then, seeing he was dragging his feet, she had pinned a flower to her bodice and tucked another in her hair with the coquetry that comes so naturally to a woman, and she had gone on waiting, feeling her heart getting tighter and tighter. Finally it was almost time to eat, and still Maurice hadn't shown.

At ten to two, Geneviève heard the clip-clop of Maurice's horse, that sound she knew so well.

"Oh! Here he is," she cried silently. "His pride could not win out over his love. He loves me! He loves me!"

Maurice jumped down from his horse and handed it over to the assistant gardener, though ordering him to stay where he was. Geneviève watched him dismount and saw with anxiety that the gardener was not leading the horse off to the stables.

Maurice entered. That particular day he was resplendent in his big checked coat with wide lapels, his white vest and white cambric shirt, and suede pants that hugged his legs in the Apollo mold; his beautiful hair was brushed back, revealing a broad, polished brow. All in all, he looked the picture of elegant virility.

He entered and his presence filled Geneviève's heart with joy: she welcomed him, beaming radiantly.

"Ah! Here you are," she said, holding out her hand. "You will be eating with us, won't you?"

"On the contrary, citizeness," said Maurice frostily. "I came to ask your permission to absent myself."

"Absent yourself?"

"Yes, I'm needed on business at the section. I have come because I was afraid you might wait for me and that you would accuse me of being impolite otherwise."

Geneviève felt her heart clutch again after a momentary respite.

"Oh, my God!" she said, a little strongly. "But Dixmer's not here. . . . He was counting on finding you when he got back and so asked me to keep you here!"

"Ah! Now I understand your insistence, madame. Your husband gave you an order. I might have known! Really, I'll never get over my conceit."

"Maurice!"

"But it's up to me, madame, to take note of what you do, rather than what you say. It's up to me to figure out that if Dixmer isn't here that's all the more reason for me not to stay. His absence would be an added embarrassment for you."

"How so?" Geneviève asked gingerly.

"Well, because since my return you seem to be at pains to avoid me; because I came back for you, you alone—as you know very well, for God's sake!—yet since I came back, I've only ever found other people buzzing around you."

"Come now," said Geneviève, "you're annoyed again, my friend, yet I'm doing my best."

"No, you're not, Geneviève; you can do better than that: you can see me like you used to do or chase me away for good."

"Please, Maurice," said Geneviève tenderly, "you must understand my situation, guess at my anguish; stop playing the tyrant with me."

With that, the young woman strode over to him and looked at him with big, sad eyes. Maurice remained silent.

"What do you want, then?" she continued.

"I want to love you, Geneviève, for I feel now that I can't live without loving you."

"Maurice, for pity's sake!"

"If that's how you feel, madame," cried Maurice, "you should have let me die."

"Die?"

"Yes, die or forget."

"So you could forget, could you?" cried Geneviève, tears stinging her eyes.

"Oh, no, no!" murmured Maurice, falling to his knees. "No, Geneviève, die maybe, but forget—never!"

"And yet," Geneviève went on firmly, "it would be for the best, Maurice, for your love is a crime."

"Have you told Monsieur Morand that?" said Maurice, brought back to his senses by her sudden coldness.

"Monsieur Morand is not mad like you, Maurice, and I have never needed to point out to him how he should conduct himself in a friend's house."

"What do you bet," replied Maurice with a nasty smile, "what do you bet that if Dixmer's dining elsewhere, Morand hasn't absented himself, eh? Ha! That's what you need to hit me with, Geneviève, if you want to stop me from loving you. For as long as Morand is there by your side, not leaving you for a second," he spat out with contempt, "oh, then, no, no! I won't love you, or at least I won't admit to myself that I love you."

"And I," cried Geneviève, pushed to the limit by this everlasting suspicion, and squeezing the young man's arm in a sort of frenzy, "I swear to you, listen to me, Maurice, and let it be said once and for all time, let it be said so we never return to the subject again, I swear to you that Morand has never addressed a single word of love to me, that Morand has never loved me, that Morand will never love me; I swear to you on my honor, I swear to you on my mother's soul."

"Alas! Alas!" cried Maurice. "I'd like nothing better than to believe you!"

"Oh! Believe me, you poor lunatic!" she said with a smile that for anyone other than a jealous man would have been a thrilling confession. "Believe me; besides, do you want to know more? Well then, Morand loves a woman before whom all women on earth pale into insignificance—just as the flowers in the field are eclipsed by the stars in the heavens."

"What woman," asked Maurice, "could eclipse all others when you are numbered among them?"

"The one a man loves," Geneviève said smiling, "tell me, isn't she always the masterpiece of all creation?"

"But," said Maurice, "if you don't love me, Geneviève . . ."

The young woman waited anxiously for the rest of the sentence.

"If you don't love me," Maurice resumed, "can you at least swear to me that you'll never love another?"

"Oh! If that's all, Maurice, I swear to you and with all my heart," cried Geneviève, delighted that Maurice was himself offering her this trade-off with her conscience.

Maurice seized both hands Geneviève had raised heavenward and covered them with hot kisses.

"Well then, now I'll be good, docile, confident," he said. "Now I'll be generous. I want to laugh with you, I want to be happy."

"And you won't ask for anything more?"

"I'll try not to."

"Now," said Geneviève, "I think it's pointless having your horse held for you like this. The section can wait."

"Oh, Geneviève! I wish the whole world could wait and that I could make it wait for you."

Steps were heard in the courtyard.

"Someone's coming to tell us lunch is served," said Geneviève.

They squeezed each other's hand furtively.

It was Morand who'd come to tell them that everyone was waiting only for them to sit down at the table.

He, too, had dressed up for the occasion.

19

THE REQUEST

Maurice was most interested to see Morand decked out so luxuriously. The most refined young fop of a muscadin would have found nothing to reproach him with in the knot of his tie, the fold of his boots, the fineness of his linen. It has to be admitted, though: it was the same old hair and the same old glasses. But Maurice was so reassured by Geneviève's vow that it seemed to him he was seeing this hair and these glasses for the first time as they really were.

"Damn me," said Maurice to himself as he went to meet him, "and the devil take me if I'm ever jealous of you again, excellent citizen

Morand! You can put on your décadi-best dove-grey frock coat every day of the week if you like, and get yourself a décadi frock coat of spun gold. Starting from today, I promise to see only your lank hair and your goggles, and in particular never to accuse you of loving Geneviève again." You can imagine how much more frank and cheerful than usual was the handshake he gave to citizen Morand.

For once, there was only a small gathering for lunch. Only three places were set at a small table. Maurice realized that he could touch Geneviève's foot under the table and that their feet would be able to carry on the quietly amorous conversation their hands had begun.

They sat down. Maurice watched Geneviève out of the corner of his eye. She sat with her back to the light, between him and the window, her black hair gleaming with a blue reflection like a crow's wing, her complexion sparkling, her eyes moist with love.

When Maurice sought and found Geneviève's foot, he watched her face for a reflection of the first contact and saw her at once blush and turn white; but her tiny foot remained peacefully under the table, happily wedged between both of his.

With his dove-grey frock coat, Morand seemed to have resumed his décadi-best wit, that brilliant rapier wit Maurice had previously seen spurt from the lips of this strange man and which would no doubt have been beautifully accompanied by the flame in his eyes if those dreadful green spectacles hadn't extinguished any such fire.

He said heaps of hilarious things without once laughing: what gave Morand's jokes their punch, what lent a strange charm to his sallies, was his imperturbable cool. This merchant who had traveled so widely in the skin trade, seeking out all kinds of skins, from the coats of panthers to rabbit fur; this chemist with arms stained red with dye; he knew Egypt as well as Herodotus did, Africa as well as Levaillant and the opera and the boudoir[1] as well as any young blade of a muscadin.

"But I'll be damned, citizen Morand," said Maurice, "you not only know everything, you're wise with it."

"Oh! I've seen a lot, all right—or I've read a lot, more to the point," said Morand. "But then, shouldn't I prepare myself a bit for the life of leisure I count on throwing myself into as soon as I've made my fortune? It's time, citizen Maurice, it's high time."

"Bah!" said Maurice. "You talk like an old man! How old are you, anyway?"

Morand gave a start at the question, innocent as it was.

"I'm thirty-eight years old," he said. "Ah! That is what it is to be a savant,[2] as you call it: you are no longer any age in particular, you are ageless."

Geneviève giggled and Maurice chimed in; Morand made do with a small smile.

"So you've traveled a lot?" Maurice asked, trapping Geneviève's foot between his own, as it was tending imperceptibly to disengage.

"Part of my youth," replied Morand, "was spent abroad."

"You've seen so much! Pardon me, I should say *observed* so much," Maurice went on, "for a man like you can't see without observing."

"Good gracious, yes, I've seen a lot," Morand agreed. "I'd almost say I've seen it all."

"All, citizen, is a lot, indeed," Maurice went on, laughing. "And, if you think about it . . ."

"Ah, yes! You're right. There are two things I've never seen. It's true that, nowadays, these two things are harder and harder to see."

"And what are they?" said Maurice.

"The first," Morand answered gravely, "is a god."

"Ah!" said Maurice. "I don't have a god, citizen Morand, but I could show you a goddess."

"How do you mean?" Geneviève broke in.

"Yes, a goddess of a quite modern creation: the Goddess of Reason. I have a friend you've sometimes heard me speak of, the great Lorin, who has a heart of gold and only one fault, which is to speak in doggerel and puns."

"And so?"

"And so, he has just bestowed on the city of Paris a Goddess of Reason, in perfect mint, and with whom no one can find fault. She is the citizeness Artemisia, a former dancer with the Opera and now a perfumer in the rue Martin. As soon as she's officially crowned a goddess, I can take you to see her."

Morand thanked Maurice gravely with a nod and took up where he left off.

"The other thing I haven't seen," he said, "is a king."

"Oh! That, that's more difficult," said Geneviève, forcing herself to smile. "There aren't any anymore."

"You should have seen the last one," said Maurice. "That would have been prudent."

"The result is," said Morand, "that I haven't a clue what a crowned head looks like: it must be extremely sad?"

"Extremely sad, yes," said Maurice. "I can tell you, since I see one every month, just about."

"A crowned head?" asked Geneviève.

"Or at least," said Maurice, "one that has borne the heavy and painful burden of a crown."

"Ah, yes! The Queen!" said Morand. "You're right, Monsieur Maurice, it must be a gloomy sight. . . ."

"Is she as beautiful and as haughty as they say?" asked Geneviève.

"Haven't you ever seen her, then, madame?" Maurice asked in turn, amazed.

"Me? Never! . . ." replied the young woman.

"Really," said Maurice, "that's strange!"

"Why strange?" said Geneviève. "We lived in the country till '91; since then I've lived here in the old rue Saint-Jacques, which is like living in the country, except that you never see the sun and there's not as much air and very few flowers. You know what my life is like, citizen Maurice: it has always been the same. So how do you expect me to have seen the Queen? The occasion has never presented itself."

"And I don't think you will take advantage of the occasion that probably will present itself, unfortunately, fairly soon," said Maurice.

"What do you mean?" asked Geneviève.

"Citizen Maurice," said Morand, "is alluding to something that is no longer a secret."

"What?" asked Geneviève.

"The probable condemnation of Marie Antoinette and her death on the same scaffold where her husband died. The citizen is saying, I think, that in order to see her, you are not likely to take advantage of the day she leaves the Temple to go to the place de la Révolution."

"Oh, I certainly won't do that, no!" cried Geneviève to these words uttered by Morand with glacial sangfroid.

"Well then, say your good-byes now," continued the impassive chemist, "for the Austrian woman is heavily guarded, and the Republic is a fairy whose magic wand can make anyone it likes disappear."

"I must admit," said Geneviève, "I really would have liked to have seen that poor woman, though."

"Listen," said Maurice, anxious to fulfill all of Geneviève's dreams, "are you really so keen to see her? Just say the word: the Republic is a fairy, I grant citizen Morand that; but as a municipal officer, I'm something of a wizard."

"You could get me in to see the Queen, monsieur?" cried Geneviève.

"I certainly could."

"How so?" asked Morand, exchanging a rapid look with Geneviève that passed unnoticed by the young man.

"Nothing easier," said Maurice. "Of course, there are municipal officers who are considered a bit on the nose and not entirely to be trusted. But I've given enough proof of my devotion to the cause of liberty not to be counted among them. In any case, entry into the Temple depends jointly on the municipal officers and the post commanders. Now, the particular day I'm on duty again, the post commander is my friend Lorin, who I reckon will be appointed to replace General Santerre in a few months' time—he's shot up from the grade of corporal to that of adjutant-major in no time....[3] So come and get me at the Temple the day I'm on duty, which is next Thursday."

"Well," said Morand, "I hope they look after you. Do you know how to get there?"

"Oh, no!" said Geneviève. "No, I can't go."

"Why not?" cried Maurice, who could only view this visit to the Temple as a means of seeing Geneviève on a day when he thought he'd be deprived of such bliss.

"Because," said Geneviève, "it might mean exposing you, dear Maurice, to some kind of nasty conflict ... and if anything happens to you, our friend, any strife caused by satisfying one of my whims, I would never forgive myself—not as long as I live."

"You're absolutely right, Geneviève," said Morand. "Believe me, there is so much mistrust that the best patriots are suspect these days; you're better off giving up the whole idea, which, as you say, is just a simple whim of curiosity."

"Anyone would think you were jealous, Morand—as though, not having seen a king or a queen yourself, you don't want anyone else to see one. Come, enough talk. Why don't you join us?"

"Me? Good grief, no."

"It's no longer a matter of citizeness Dixmer's wanting to come to the Temple; it's I who am entreating her, along with you, to come and distract a poor prisoner. For once the main door is shut on me, I am just as much a prisoner for the next twenty-four hours as any king or prince of the blood."

Squeezing Geneviève's foot with both of his, he went on, "Please come, I beseech you."

"Go on, Morand," said Geneviève. "Come with me."

"It would mean losing a whole day," said Morand, "which means delaying by as much the day I retire from commerce."

"Well then, I won't go," said Geneviève.

"Why not?" asked Morand.

"Lord knows it's simple enough," said Geneviève. "I can't count on my husband to accompany me, so if you won't, as a decent man, a man of thirty-eight, I would never be so reckless as to go and confront on my own all those artillerymen, grenadiers, and chasseurs, asking for a municipal officer only three or four years my senior."

"Well," said Morand, "if you really think my presence is indispensable, citizeness . . ."

"Come on, citizen savant, be gallant, as if you were actually just an ordinary man," said Maurice. "Sacrifice half of your day to the wife of your friend."

"So be it!" said Morand.

"Now," said Maurice, "I ask only one thing of you and that is discretion. Any visit to the Temple is suspect conduct, and any mishap that might occur as a result of this visit will get us all guillotined. The Jacobins don't joke, damn them! You've seen how they treated the Girondins."

"Good Lord!" said Morand. "That's something to think about, what citizen Maurice is saying: such a way of retiring from commerce wouldn't suit me at all."

"Didn't you hear?" Geneviève said, smiling. "The citizen said *us all*?"

"So, us all?"

"All together."

"Yes, well, no doubt the company is perfectly pleasant," said Morand, "but I'd prefer to live in your company than to die in it, my sentimental beauty."

"Hear that! What was I thinking," Maurice said to himself, "when I thought this man was in love with Geneviève?"

"So it's agreed," said Geneviève. "Morand, it's you I'm talking to, you the absentminded professor, you the dreamer. We are set for next Thursday—so see that you don't go and start some chemical experiment Wednesday night that will keep you busy for twenty-four hours, as sometimes happens."

"Don't worry," said Morand. "You can always remind me, between now and then."

Geneviève rose from the table and Maurice followed suit. Morand was just about to rise too, and perhaps follow them, when one of the workers brought the chemist a small vial of liquid that absorbed all his attention.

"Quick," said Maurice, dragging Geneviève off.

"Oh! Don't worry," she said. "He'll be at it for a good hour at least."

With that, the young woman abandoned her hand in his and he squeezed it tenderly. She felt remorse for her treachery and so was rewarding him for her remorse by making him happy.

"You see," she said as they walked across the garden, pointing out the carnations that had been moved into the open air in their mahogany box to revive them if possible. "You see, my flowers died."

"And who killed them? You did, you neglected them," said Maurice. "Poor carnations!"

"It wasn't me who neglected them, it was you who abandoned them."

"But they asked for so very little, Geneviève, a bit of water, that's all. And my not being around must have left you plenty of time."

"Ah!" said Geneviève. "If flowers were watered with tears, these *poor* carnations, as you call them, would not have died."

Maurice wrapped his arms around her and pulled her fiercely toward him. Before she had time to defend herself, he pressed his lips to her half-smiling, half-swooning eyes as they gazed at the ravaged carnations.

Geneviève had so many things with which to reproach herself, she let him have his way without a struggle.

Dixmer came home late, and when he did he found Morand, Geneviève, and Maurice chatting about botany in the garden.

20

THE FLOWER GIRL

At last the big day arrived, the Thursday when Maurice was standing guard in the Temple.

The month of June had just begun. The sky was a deep blue, and against this backdrop of indigo the flat white of the new houses that had been built stood out. You could just feel the arrival of that terrible dog that the ancients represented as parched with an insatiable thirst and which, according to the commoners of Paris, licks the pavement clean. You could have eaten your dinner off the cobblestones of Paris they were so pristine, and a host of scents rained down from above, where they wafted from the trees and flowers in bloom, swirling around, intoxicating, as though to make the inhabitants of the capital forget for a while the vapor of blood fuming incessantly on the cobblestones of Paris's squares.

Maurice was to clock in at the Temple at nine. His two colleagues were to be Mercerault and Agricola. At eight o'clock he was at the old rue Saint-Jacques, all decked out in the full regalia of a citizen municipal officer, which included a red, white, and blue scarf tied tightly around his strong and supple waist. He had come as usual to Geneviève's on horseback and en route had attracted the unabashed praise and drooling approbation of the good female patriots who watched him ride by.

Geneviève was ready and waiting, wearing a simple muslin frock, a kind of mantilla in light taffeta, and a small bonnet decorated with the red, white, and blue cockade, and in such simple apparel she was dazzlingly beautiful.

Morand, who had had to be begged, as we have seen, had donned his everyday garb, this half-bourgeois, half-artisanal combination, no doubt out of fear of being suspected as an aristocrat otherwise. He had just gotten home and his face showed signs of exhaustion.

He claimed to have been up working half the night finishing an urgent job.

Dixmer had gone out as soon as his friend Morand had returned.

"Well then," said Geneviève, "what have you decided, Maurice? How are we to see the Queen?"

"Listen," said Maurice. "I have a plan. I'll arrive with you at the Temple; I'll hand you over to Lorin, my friend who's chief of the guard. I'll take up my post, and when there's a favorable moment I'll come and get you."

"But where will we see the prisoners and how will we see them?" asked Morand.

"While they're having dinner or supper, if that's all right with you, through the glass partition where the municipal officers are."

"Perfect!" said Morand.

Maurice then saw Morand go to the cupboard at the back of the kitchen and swiftly down a glass of strong wine. This surprised him. Morand was a most sober man and usually only drank water with a drop of red in it.

Geneviève noticed that Maurice was watching Morand drink in amazement.

"Imagine," she said, "he's killing himself with work, poor old Morand, so much so that he's capable of not having had anything to eat or drink since yesterday morning."

"So he didn't dine here last night?" asked Maurice.

"No, he's conducting experiments in town."

Geneviève's precaution was pointless, for Maurice, like a true lover, that is, like an egoist, had only remarked Morand's action with the superficial attention a man in love accords anything that is not his beloved.

To the glass of wine Morand added a slice of bread, which he gulped down.

"And now," he said with his mouth full, "I am ready, dear citizen Maurice. Whenever you are."

Maurice, who brushed the withered pistils off one of the dead carnations he had picked in passing, offered Geneviève his arm, saying, "Off we go."

And off they went. Maurice was so happy that his chest could barely contain his happiness; he would have cried for joy if he hadn't held himself in check. Indeed, what more could he desire? Not only was Morand not loved, he was sure of that now, but he himself, he hoped, was loved. God had sent beautiful sunshine raining down over the earth, Geneviève's arm trembled beneath his own, and the town criers, screaming their heads off about the triumph of the Jacobins and the fall of Brissot and his accomplices, announced that the nation was saved.

There truly are moments in life when a man's heart is too small to hold the joy or pain that builds there.

"Oh, what a beautiful day!" cried Morand.

Maurice turned round with amazement; this was the first such outburst to issue forth to his knowledge from this eternally buttoned-up man, who always seemed to be elsewhere.

"Oh, yes! Yes, it really is beautiful," said Geneviève, leaning on Maurice's arm. "Let's hope it remains clear and without a cloud until tonight, just as it is at this moment!"

Maurice thought her words were meant for him, and his happiness redoubled.

Morand looked at Geneviève through his green glasses, with a special expression of gratitude. Perhaps he, too, thought her words were meant for him.

And so they crossed the Petit-Pont, the rue de la Juiverie and the pont Notre-Dame, before crossing the place de l'Hôtel-de-Ville and following the rue Barre-du-Bec and the rue Sainte-Avoye. As they went along Maurice's step became lighter, whereas, on the contrary, his partner and her companion slowed more and more perceptibly.

They had reached the rue des Vieilles-Audriettes when, all of a sudden, a flower girl blocked their way, presenting them with her tray of flowers.

"Oh! Look at the magnificent carnations!" cried Maurice.

"Oh! Yes, aren't they gorgeous!" cried Geneviève. "Whoever grew them can't have had anything else to do, for they are not dead, not these."

This remark was music to the young man's ears.

"Ah! My handsome municipal officer," said the flower girl. "Buy a bouquet for the citizeness. She's all in white, and here are some superb red carnations. Red and white go well together—and when she holds the bouquet to her heart, since her heart is very close to your blue uniform, between you you'll have the national colors."

The flower girl was young and pretty. She delivered her little compliment with a special kind of grace, and besides, her compliment was admirably apt and she couldn't have done better in the circumstances if she'd been working at it. Furthermore, the flowers were almost symbolic. They were carnations similar to the ones that had died in the mahogany planter.

"Yes," said Maurice, "I'll buy you some, but only because they are carnations, you understand? I won't even look at other flowers."

"Oh, Maurice!" said Geneviève. "There's no point: we have so many in the garden!"

But despite this token rejection of the offer, Geneviève's glittering eyes told Maurice she was dying for a bunch. He chose the biggest and best of the bouquets, which just happened to be the one the pretty flower girl had held out to him.

It was composed of about twenty poppy carnations with a scent at once acrid and suave. Smack-dab in the middle of them all, dominating the others like a king, one enormous carnation stood out.

"Here," said Maurice to the flower girl, tossing an assignat of five livres onto her tray. "That's for you."

"Thanks, my handsome municipal officer," said the flower girl. "Many thanks!"

With that, she steered toward another couple of citizens in the hope that a day that had started so magnificently would turn out to be a good day. While this scene was taking place, apparently straightforwardly and lasting only a matter of seconds, Morand tottered on his pins and wiped his forehead and Geneviève paled and trembled. She gripped the bouquet Maurice presented to her with a clenched hand and brought it to her face, not so much to breathe in the scent as to hide her emotion.

They went the rest of the way gaily, or Maurice at least did. As for Geneviève, her gaiety was fairly restrained. Morand was gay in his own bizarre way, stifling sighs, bursting out laughing suddenly, and cracking outrageous jokes that rained down upon passersby like rounds of ammunition.

The party arrived at the Temple at nine o'clock, just as Santerre was calling the roll of municipal officers.

"Present!" shouted Maurice, leaving Geneviève under Morand's protection.

"Welcome back!" said Santerre, holding out his hand to the young man.

Maurice was careful to shake the hand that was offered him most warmly. Santerre's friendship was certainly one of the most precious you could enjoy in those days. At the mere sight of the man who had commanded the famous drumroll when the King was killed, Geneviève shivered and Morand turned white as a sheet.

"So who's the beautiful citizeness?" Santerre asked Maurice. "And what's she doing here?"

"That's the wife of good citizen Dixmer; you must have heard of that brave patriot, citizen general?"

"Yes, yes," said Santerre. "The head of a tannery, captain of the chasseurs of the Victor legion."

"That's the one."

"Good! Good! Cripes, she's easy on the eye. And who's that ape hanging on her arm?"

"That's citizen Morand, her husband's partner, a chasseur in Dixmer's company."

Santerre went over to Geneviève.

"Good day, citizeness," he said.

Geneviève made an effort. "Good day, citizen general," she replied with a bright smile.

Santerre was flattered by both the smile and the title.

"And what are you doing here, my lovely patriot?" Santerre went on.

Maurice leapt in. "The citizeness has never seen the Widow Capet and she'd like to see her."

"Yes," said Santerre, "before . . ." And he made an atrocious gesture.

"Exactly," Maurice replied, stiffly.

"All right," said Santerre. "Just make sure no one sees her going into the dungeon. It would set a bad example. Anyway, I have total confidence in you."

Santerre shook Maurice's hand once again, gave Geneviève a protective, avuncular nod, and went off to tend to his other duties.

After many movements of grenadiers and chasseurs and after a few cannon maneuvers, which produced the dull thuds thought to be good for spraying a bit of salutary intimidation around the neighborhood, Maurice took Geneviève's arm once more and, with Morand in tow, walked toward the command post at whose gate Lorin was madly yelling commands, directing his battalion in a maneuver.

"Well, I'll be!" he said to himself. "Here's Maurice, damn it! With a woman who looks a bit all right. Is the sly dog trying to give my Goddess of Reason a bit of competition? If he is, that's it for Artemisia!"

"What now, citizen chief?" asked the captain.

"Ah! That's right. Attention!" barked Lorin. "Left, left . . . Hello, Maurice. Quick march . . . March!"

The drums rolled, the companies went to take up their posts, and when everyone was in position, Lorin came running.

Initial compliments were exchanged all around as Maurice introduced Lorin to Geneviève and Morand before embarking on a few explanations.

"Yes, yes, I get you," said Lorin. "You want the citizen and the citizeness to go into the dungeon: that's easy, I'll put the sentries in place and tell them to let you and your party pass."

Ten minutes later, Geneviève and Morand entered the dungeon in the wake of three municipal officers and took their place behind the glass partition.

21

THE RED CARNATION

The Queen had only just arisen. Ill for two or three days, she had stayed in bed longer than usual. But having learned from her sister that the sun was up, magnificent, she had made an effort and had asked to take a walk on the terrace so that her daughter could get some air. The request was granted without any problems.

Then again, there was another reason that decided her. Once—just once, it is true—she had seen the Dauphin in the garden from the top of the tower. But at the first gesture exchanged between mother and son, Simon had intervened and whisked the child back inside.

But that didn't matter; she had seen him and that meant so much. It's true the poor little prisoner was very pale and wan and looked much the worse for wear. And then he was dressed like a child of the people, with a carmagnole and big baggy pants. But they'd left his beautiful curly blond hair, which gave him a halo that God no doubt wished the child martyr to take with him into heaven.

If only she could see him again one more time, what a sight for his mother's sore eyes.

Then again, there was a further reason.

"My sister," Madame Elisabeth had said to her, "you know we found a wisp of straw in the corridor, propped up in a corner against the wall. In our sign language that means to be alert to what is going on around us and that a friend is drawing near."

"That's right," the Queen had answered, looking with pity at her sister and daughter and reminding herself not to despair of their salvation.

The requirements of duty were completed and Maurice was all the more master of the Temple dungeon, as chance had singled him out for day duty and put the municipal officers Agricola and Mercerault on the night watch. The outgoing officers had left after dropping off their report to the Temple Council.

"So then, citizen municipal officer," said Mother Tison as she came to greet Maurice, "you've brought some company to have a peek at our pigeons? I'm the only one condemned not to see my poor Héloïse."

"They are friends of mine," said Maurice, "who've never seen the wife of Capet."

"Well then, they'd be in a perfect spot behind the glass partition."

"Indeed they would," said Maurice.

"Only," said Geneviève, "we'll look like cruel gawkers who have come to enjoy a prisoner's torment from the other side of the bars."

"Well then, why don't you put your friends on the stairs leading up to the top of the tower; since the Widow Capet is taking a walk there today with her sister and her daughter. They let her keep her daughter, all right! But I, who am not guilty, they took mine away from me. Oh, bloody aristocrats! Whatever happens, there'll always be perks for them, citizen Maurice."

"But they took her son away from her," Maurice replied.

"Ah! If only I had a son," muttered the jailer, "I reckon I wouldn't miss my daughter so much."

Geneviève meanwhile had exchanged a few looks with Morand.

"My friend," the young woman said to Maurice, "the citizeness is right. If you don't mind placing me somehow along Marie Antoinette's passage, that would be less awful for me than peering at her from here. It seems to me that this way of ogling people is humiliating both for them and for us."

"Good old Geneviève," said Maurice, "you really are thoughtfulness itself."

"Oh, for crying out loud, citizeness!" cried one of Maurice's two colleagues, who was having a breakfast of bread and sausage in the antechamber. "If you were a prisoner and the Widow Capet was curious to have a look at you, she wouldn't be so nice about satisfying her whim, the bitch."

Geneviève flashed a lightning glance at Morand to see what effect this insult had on him. Morand did, in fact, wince; his eyes glinted with a strange kind of phosphorescence and he clenched his fists for a second. But all these telltale signs were so rapid they went unnoticed.

"What's that officer's name?" Geneviève asked Maurice.

"That's citizen Mercerault," the young man replied. Then he added, as though to excuse the man's crassness: "A stonecutter."[1]

Mercerault heard him and gave him a sidelong look.

"Come, come," said Mother Tison, "finish your sausage and your half-bottle and let me clear the table."

"It's not the Austrian woman's fault if I'm eating at this hour," grumbled the municipal officer. "If she could've had me killed on the tenth of August, she wouldn't have given it a second thought; so the day she sneezes in the sack,[2] I'll be in the first row, hale and hearty and happy as a lark."

Morand turned deathly white.

"Let's go, citizen Maurice," said Geneviève. "Come and put us where you promised to put us. I feel like a prisoner here; I can't breathe."

Maurice whisked Morand and Geneviève away; the sentries, alerted by Lorin, let them pass without a protest. He set them up in a small hallway on the top floor, so that when the Queen, Madame Elisabeth, and Madame Royale went up to the gallery, the august prisoners had no choice but to go past them.

As the promenade was set for ten o'clock and there were still a few minutes to go, Maurice not only did not leave his friends but further, so that not even a whiff of suspicion should fall on this ever so slightly illegal initiative, having encountered citizen Agricola, he brought him along with them.

Ten o'clock sounded.

"Open!" cried a voice from the base of the tower that Maurice recognized as belonging to Santerre.

Immediately the guards took up arms, the gates were shut, the sentries primed their guns. Throughout the courtyard a great clatter of iron and stones and marching feet could be heard. It seemed to have made a vivid impression on Morand and Geneviève, for Maurice saw them both turn pale.

"So many precautions just to guard three women!" Geneviève murmured.

"Yes," said Morand, trying to laugh. "If the people trying to rescue them were in our shoes now and could see what we see, they'd think twice."

"Indeed," said Geneviève, "I'm beginning to think they won't get away."

"And me, I hope not," said Maurice. Leaning over the ramp at those words, he added: "Stand back. Here come the prisoners."

"Tell me who's who," said Geneviève, "I don't know them."

"The two in front are the sister and daughter of Capet. The one bringing up the rear, preceded by a little dog, is Marie Antoinette."

Geneviève took a step forward. But Morand, on the contrary, instead of peering down, pressed up against the wall. His lips were more livid and chalky than the stone of the dungeon.

With her white dress and her beautiful clear eyes, Geneviève looked like an angel in attendance on the prisoners, waiting to light the hard road they had to tread and put a little love in their hearts as they passed.

Madame Elisabeth and Madame Royale passed after glancing in amazement at the strangers, no doubt the first of them imagining that these were the friends announced by the signs, for she turned around sharply toward Madame Royale and squeezed her hand, while dropping her handkerchief as though to alert the Queen.

"Be careful, my sister," she said. "I seem to have dropped my handkerchief."

With that, she continued to mount the stairs with the young princess.

The Queen, whose panting breath and small dry cough indicated her malady, bent down to pick up the handkerchief that had fallen at her feet. But her little dog beat her to it; he snatched it and ran to give it to Madame Elisabeth. And so the Queen continued to climb the stairs. After a few steps she, too, found herself before Geneviève, Morand, and the young municipal officer.

"Oh! Flowers!" she cried. "It's such a long time since I've seen any. How good they smell and how lucky you are to have flowers, madame!"

As fast as the thought that had just found expression in these searing words, Geneviève held out her hand to offer her bouquet to the

Queen. At that point Marie Antoinette looked up and stared at her and an almost imperceptible blush appeared on her colorless brow.

With a sort of automatic movement, out of habit of passive obedience to the rules, Maurice put his hand out to stop Geneviève. The Queen stood hesistant; she looked at Maurice and recognized the young municipal officer who was in the habit of speaking to her firmly but, at the same time, with respect.

"Are flowers out of bounds, monsieur?" she asked.

"No, no, madame," said Maurice. "Geneviève, you may offer your bouquet."

"Oh, thank you, thank you, monsieur!" cried the Queen with real gratitude.

And acknowledging Geneviève with gracious affability, Marie Antoinette put out an emaciated hand and selected a carnation at random from among the mass of flowers.

"But take all of them, madame, take them," Geneviève said timidly.

"No," said the Queen with a charming smile. "This bouquet perhaps comes from someone you love and I wouldn't want to deprive you of it."

Geneviève blushed deeply and her high color made the Queen smile once more.

"Come on, citizeness Capet," said Agricola. "You must keep moving."

The Queen nodded and continued on her way. But before disappearing, she looked back and murmured:

"How good this carnation smells and how lovely that woman is!"

"She didn't see me," groaned Morand. Practically on his knees in the darkness of the hallway, he had, in fact, failed to come to the Queen's notice.

"But you saw her, didn't you, Morand? Geneviève?" asked Maurice, doubly delighted, first because of the show he had been able to put on for his friends, and then because of the pleasure he had just given at so little cost to the unhappy prisoner.

"Oh, yes, yes!" said Geneviève, "I saw her all right, and now, if I live to be a hundred, I'll go on seeing her."

"And how did you find her?"

"Very beautiful."

"What about you, Morand?"

Morand joined his hands together without answering.

"Tell me, then," Maurice said to Geneviève in a low voice, laughing all the while, "it wouldn't be the Queen Morand's in love with, would it?"

Geneviève gave a start but swiftly recovered.

"Heavens," she said, also laughing, "it certainly looks like it."

"Well then, you didn't tell me how you found her, Morand," Maurice insisted.

"I found her very pale," Morand replied.

Maurice took Geneviève's arm again and led her back down toward the courtyard. In the dark stairwell, it felt to him as though Geneviève kissed his hand.

"So," said Maurice, "what does that mean, Geneviève?"

"That means, Maurice, that I will never forget that, for a whim of mine, you risked your head."

"Oh!" said Maurice. "Let's not exaggerate, Geneviève. You know very well it's not gratitude I want from you."

Geneviève gently squeezed his arm.

Morand staggered after them.

When they reached the courtyard Lorin came to greet the two visitors and lead them out of the Temple. But before leaving him, Geneviève made Maurice promise to come and dine at the old rue Saint-Jacques the following day.

22

SIMON THE CENSOR

Maurice returned to his post, his heart full of an almost celestial joy, but he found Mother Tison there sobbing.

"Now what's the matter, Mother Tison?" he said.

"I'm furious, that's what's the matter!" the jailer shot back.

"Why's that?"

"Because everything is unjust for the poor of this world."

"Yes, but . . . ?"

"You're rich, you are; you're bourgeois; you come here for one day only and you're allowed to be visited by pretty women who give the Austrian woman flowers. And me, I practically nest in the dovecote all year round and I'm not allowed to see my poor daughter Héloïse."

Maurice took her hand and slipped her an assignat of ten livres.

"Here you go, good Mother Tison," he said. "Take that and have courage, eh? Heaven knows the Austrian woman won't last forever."

"An assignat for ten livres," said the jailer, "that's all very well; but I'd rather have a lock of my daughter's hair."

As she spoke, Simon, who was coming up the stairs, overheard her and saw the jailer pocket the assignat Maurice had given her.

We had better describe the mood Simon was in.

Simon had come from the courtyard, where he had met Lorin. There was definite dislike between the two men, and this dislike was not so much motivated by the violent scene we have already set before the eyes of our readers as by the genetic differences between them, that eternal source of the animosities or attractions we say are a mystery but which are actually so easily explained.

Simon was ugly, Lorin handsome; Simon was on the nose, Lorin smelled like a rose; Simon was a braggart of a republican, Lorin was one of those genuinely fervent patriots who had made nothing but sacrifices for the Revolution; and then, if it were ever to come to blows, Simon knew instinctively that the fist of the muscadin would have dealt him a thoroughly plebeian punishment, no less elegantly than Maurice would have done.

Simon had stopped short on seeing Lorin and gone pale.

"Not that battalion standing guard again, is it?" he groaned.

"What if it is?" replied a grenadier who was put off by the remark. "Seems to me they're as good as any other."

Simon pulled a pencil from the pocket of his carmagnole and pretended to be making a note on a piece of paper that was as black as his hands.

"Hey!" said Lorin. "So you've learned to write, Simon, now you're Capet's tutor? Look, citizens; my word of honor, he's taking notes: we give you Simon the Censor."

A universal burst of laughter broke out, beginning with the ranks of young National Guards, nearly all of whom were educated young men. It dazed, so to speak, the miserable cobbler.

"You'll get yours," he said, grinding his teeth and seething with rage. "They're saying you let strangers into the dungeon without the permission of the Commune. I'll show you: I'm going to get the municipal officer to file a report."

"At least he can write," Lorin retorted. "It's Maurice, Maurice, the Iron Fist, you know him?"

Just at that precise moment, Maurice happened to be giving Mother Tison the ten-livre assignat as a consolation and he paid no heed to the presence of this miserable wretch, whom he instinctively avoided whenever he came across him, as you avoid a poisonous or hideously repulsive snake.

"Ah, look at that!" said Simon to Mother Tison, who was wiping her eyes on her apron. "So you really are keen to get yourself guillotined, citizeness?"

"Me!" said Mother Tison. "Why do you say that?"

"What! You take money from municipal officers to let aristocrats in to see the Austrian woman!"

"Me?" said Mother Tison. "Shut your mouth, you're mad."

"This will be put down in the report," said Simon, with emphasis.

"What are you talking about? They're friends of municipal officer Maurice, one of the greatest patriots in existence."

"Conspirators, I tell you; and the Commune will be informed. Let them be the judge."

"Right, so you're going to denounce me, you police spy?"

"Exactly, unless you want to denounce yourself."

"But denounce what? What am I supposed to denounce?"

"What happened."

"But nothing happened."

"Where were they, the aristocrats?"

"There, on the stairs."

"When Widow Capet went up to the top of the tower?"

"Yes."

"And did they speak to each other?"

"Just a few words."

"A few words: you see! Anyway, it reeks of aristocrats here."

"You mean it reeks of carnations."

"Carnations! What have carnations got to do with it?"

"But the citizeness was carrying a bunch that filled the air with perfume."

"What citizeness?"

"The one watching the Queen go up the tower."

"You see what I mean: you say *the Queen*, Mother Tison. Hanging out with aristocrats will be the death of you. Right, well . . . Hang on, what have I stepped on here?" Simon bent down.

"Ha! That's one!" said Mother Tison. "It's a flower . . . a carnation. It must have fallen out of citizeness Dixmer's hands, when Marie Antoinette took one out of her bouquet."

"Mother Capet took a flower from citizeness Dixmer's bouquet?" asked Simon.

"Yes, and it was I who gave it to her, do you hear?" Maurice said in a menacing voice; he had been listening to this little conference for some minutes and he'd had enough.

"Well, well, well: three holes in the ground! A fellow sees what he sees and knows what he knows," muttered Simon, still holding the carnation he'd crushed with his great big boot.

"I know something too," retorted Maurice, "and I'll tell you what it is: it is that you have no business being in the dungeon; your job as a butcher is over there with little Capet, who you will not, however, beat today because I'm here and I forbid you to."

"Ha! You dare threaten me and call me a butcher!" cried Simon, squashing the flower between his fingers. "Ha! We'll see if aristocrats are allowed to . . . Hey, what's that?"

"What?" asked Maurice.

"What I can feel in the carnation, that's what! Aha!"

And to Maurice's stupefaction, Simon pulled a tiny piece of paper out of the calyx of the flower before his very eyes. It had been rolled with exquisite care and introduced artfully into the center of the flower's thick plume.

"Oh!" cried Maurice. "What the hell is it, for pity's sake?"

"We'll soon find out, we'll soon find out," chirped Simon, moving over to the window. "Ha! Your pal Lorin reckons I can't read? Well, I'll show you."

Lorin had defamed Simon; the man could read all the letters of the alphabet when they were printed, and even handwriting when it was big enough. But the note was written in such a fine hand that Simon was forced to resort to his spectacles. And so he put the note on the window-ledge while he foraged through his pockets looking for them. But as he was going through this laborious operation, citizen Agricola opened the door of the antechamber, which was right opposite the little window, and the current of air lifted aloft the piece of paper, which was as light as a feather. When Simon finally located his glasses and put them on his nose and turned round, he looked for the note in vain. It had disappeared.[1]

Simon let out a roar.

"There was a piece of paper here," he shrieked. "There was a piece of paper. You just watch it, citizen municipal officer, because it had better be found."

With that he swiftly descended the stairs, leaving Maurice flabbergasted.

Ten minutes later, three members of the Commune entered the dungeon. The Queen was still on the terrace, and the order was given to leave her there in a state of total ignorance of what had just occurred. The members of the Commune asked to be taken to her.

The first object that struck their gaze was the red carnation that she was still holding in her hand. They looked at one another in surprise and approached the Queen.

"Give us that flower," said the president of the delegation.

The Queen, who was not expecting this sudden eruption, gave a start and hesitated.

"Hand over the flower, madame," cried Maurice in a sort of terror, "I beg you."

The Queen held out the carnation; the president took it and withdrew, followed by his colleagues, into an adjacent room to complete the inspection and make a report.

When they opened the flower, it was empty.

Maurice breathed deeply.

"One moment, one moment," said one of the commissioners. "The heart of the carnation has been removed. It's true, the alveolus is empty; but a note was most certainly stuck in this alveolus."

"I am ready," said Maurice, "to provide any necessary explanation; but first and foremost, before anything further, I demand to be arrested."

"We take note of your proposition," said the president, "but we will not grant it. You are known as a good patriot, citizen Lindey."

"And I will answer with my life for the friends I was foolish enough to bring here with me."

"Don't answer for anyone," said the prosecutor.

A great racket was heard in the courtyard.

It was Simon who, having searched in vain for the tiny note that was gone with the wind, had run to get Santerre and had told him about the attempt to break out the Queen, adding all the props his wild imagination could come up with for such a bid at abduction. Santerre had come running. The Temple was sealed off and the guard changed, which greatly annoyed Lorin, who protested loudly against this offense given to his battalion.

"Ah! You lousy cobbler," he said to Simon, menacing him with his sword. "It's to you that I owe this little joke; but, never fear, I'll pay you back."

"I reckon it's you who'll be paying back the whole nation," gloated the cobbler, rubbing his grubby black hands together.

"Citizen Maurice," said Santerre, "keep yourself at the disposal of the Commune—they'll need to question you."

"I am at your orders, commandant; but I've already asked to be arrested and I'll ask again."

"Wait, wait," Simon muttered slyly, "since you're so keen, we'll see what we can do."

With that, he went off to find Mother Tison.

23

THE GODDESS OF REASON

All day they scoured the courtyard, the garden, and the surroundings for the tiny piece of paper that was causing all the commotion and which, no one doubted any longer, must contain a whole plot.

The Queen was separated from her sister and her daughter and interrogated; but she did not answer except to say that on the stairs she had met a young woman carrying a bouquet and that she had been happy just to pick one flower. And that she had only picked that flower with the consent of municipal officer Maurice. She had nothing else to say, it was the truth in all its simplicity and in all its force.

All of this was reported to Maurice when his turn came, and he confirmed that the Queen's deposition was frank and exact.

"But," said the president, "there was a plot, then?"

"That's not possible," said Maurice. "It was I who offered over dinner at Madame Dixmer's place to take her to see the prisoner, since she had never seen her. But nothing was arranged either as to the day or how we would do it."

"But she came equipped with flowers," said the president. "That bouquet was made up in advance, wasn't it?"

"Not at all. I was the one who bought the flowers, from a flower girl who came and offered them to us at the corner of the rue des Vieilles-Audriettes."

"But at least this flower girl presented you with the bouquet?"

"No, citizen, I chose it myself from among ten or twelve of them; it's true that I chose the most beautiful one."

"But the note could have been slipped in on the way?"

"It couldn't possibly have been, citizen. I didn't leave Madame Dixmer for a minute, and to perform the operation you're suggesting in each one of the flowers—for you know Simon claims each one of the flowers would have held a similar note—you'd need at least half a day."

"But in the end, couldn't someone have slipped a couple of notes all ready to go among the flowers?"

"But it was before my very eyes that the prisoner selected one at random, after having refused to take the whole bouquet."

"So then, in your opinion, citizen Lindey, there is no conspiracy?"

"There most certainly is a conspiracy," Maurice countered, "and I'm not the first not only to believe that but to confirm it; but this conspiracy does not originate with my friends. However, as the nation must not be exposed to any fear whatever, I'm standing security and turning myself in as a prisoner."

"No, you're not!" Santerre replied. "Do you think this is how we treat tried-and-true patriots like you? If you turned yourself in to answer for your friends, I'd turn myself in to answer for you. So it's all pretty straightforward. There is no positive denunciation, isn't that right? No one knows what happened. Let's be doubly vigilant, you especially, and we'll manage to get to the bottom of this without going public."

"Thank you, commandant," said Maurice. "But I'll say to you what you would say to me in my place. We can't let it rest there; we have to find the flower girl."

"The flower girl is long gone by now; but don't worry, we'll look for her. You, you keep a close eye on your friends; I'll check all prison correspondence."

Simon had been forgotten. But Simon had his little scheme. He popped up at the end of the session we have just recounted to ask the latest, and so learned of the Commune's decision.

"Ha! All that's needed is a formal denunciation to do the job," he said. "Hang about for a few minutes and I'll bring it."

"What's going on, then?" asked the president.

"What's going on," said the cobbler, "is that the brave citizeness Tison is about to denounce the underhanded machinations of this partisan of the aristocracy, this Maurice, and the ramifications involving another false patriot among his pals who answers to the name of Lorin."

"Go steady, Simon! Your zeal for the nation may well be leading you astray," said the president. "Maurice Lindey and Hyacinthe Lorin are true-blue patriots."

"We'll see about that in court," replied Simon.

"Think about it, Simon, the trial will be scandalous for all good patriots."

"Scandalous or not, what's that to me? Do you think I'm frightened of a bit of a scandal, me? At least we'll know the whole truth about those who are traitors."

"So you persist with this denunciation on behalf of Mother Tison?"

"I'll make the denunciation myself tonight at the Cordeliers' club, you make it with the others, citizen president, if you don't want to declare the arrest of the traitor Maurice."

"Well then, so be it," said the president, who, as was usually the case in those unhappy times, cowered before whoever yelled the loudest. "Well then, so be it; we'll arrest him."

While the decision was being delivered against him, Maurice had returned to the Temple, where the following note was waiting for him:

Our watch being violently interrupted, I probably won't see you again until tomorrow morning: come and have breakfast with me. While we're eating you can bring me up to date about the intrigues and conspiracies uncovered by master Simon.

> They say that Simon claims
> That a carnation is to blame;
> For my part, heaven knows,
> I'd lay bets on a rose.

Tomorrow, too, I'll tell you what Artemisia told me.

Your friend
LORIN

Maurice dashed off his reply:

Nothing new this end; sleep in peace tonight and eat without me in the morning; in view of today's incidents, I probably won't be up and about before midday.

I wish I were a zephyr to have the right to send a kiss to the rose of whom you speak.

I'll allow you to boo my prose as I boo your poetry.

Your friend
MAURICE

P.S. I think the conspiracy was just a false alarm, anyway.

Lorin had in fact left at eleven ahead of the rest of his battalion, thanks to the abrupt motion of the cobbler. He'd consoled himself for this humiliation with a quatrain and, as announced in this quatrain, he went straight to Artemisia's.

Artemisia was delighted to see Lorin. The weather was wonderful, as we noted earlier, and so she suggested a stroll along the banks of the Seine, and Lorin gladly agreed.

They ambled along the coal port chatting about politics, Lorin recounting his expulsion from the Temple and trying to figure out the circumstances that might have provoked it, when, having gotten as far as the rue des Barres, they spotted a flower girl who, like them, was following the right bank of the Seine upstream.

"Ah! Citizen Lorin," said Artemisia. "You will, I hope, offer me a bouquet."

"Why stop at one!" said Lorin. "You can have two if that's what your heart desires."

And they both picked up the pace to catch up to the flower girl, who was herself racing ahead as fast as she could go. When she reached the pont Marie, the girl stopped, leaned over the parapet, and emptied her basket into the river.

Single flowers spun for a moment in the air, while clusters fell more rapidly, dragged down by their weight; then both bouquets and individual flowers bobbed on the surface of the water and sped away with the current.

"Hey!" said Artemisia, looking at the flower girl who had such an original way of plying her trade. "It looks like . . . no, it can't be . . . yes, it can . . . no . . . yes, it is . . . Hmmm. How odd!"

The flower girl put a finger to her lips, as though entreating Artemisia to say nothing, and disappeared.

"What is it, then?" said Lorin. "Do you know that mortal, goddess?"

"No. I thought at first . . . But obviously I was mistaken."

"Yet she signaled to you," Lorin insisted.

"Why is she being a flower girl this morning?" Artemisia wondered out loud.

"So you admit you know her, Artemisia?" asked Lorin.

"Yes," said Artemisia. "She's just a flower girl I sometimes buy from."

"Whatever the case," said Lorin, "your flower girl has a strange way of getting rid of her goods."

They both took a last look at the flowers, which were already whirling past the wooden footbridge, propelled by a second arm of the river that passes under the arches there; then they continued walking toward La Rapée, where they were planning to dine tête-à-tête.

For the moment the incident rested there. But because it was strange and smacked of a certain mysteriousness, it burned itself into Lorin's poetic imagination.

Meanwhile, Mother Tison's denunciation, brought against Maurice and Lorin, caused a great stir at the Jacobin club. Maurice, at the Temple, received the advice of the Commune that his liberty was threatened by public indignation. This was an invitation to the young municipal officer to hide if he was guilty. But Maurice remained at the Temple, since he had nothing to hide, and when they came to arrest him they found him at his post.

Maurice was interrogated on the spot. While sticking to the firm resolution not to implicate friends of whom he was sure, Maurice was not a man to sacrifice himself ridiculously by remaining silent like some hero in a romantic novel, and so he demanded that the flower girl be called to account.

It was five o'clock in the evening when Lorin got home. He learned that instant of Maurice's arrest and the demand that the latter had made. The flower girl of the pont Marie, throwing her flowers into the Seine, immediately sprang to mind as sharply as a sudden revelation. This strange woman, the nearness of the neighborhoods in question, Artemisia's half-confession, everything screamed that there lay the explanation of the mystery Maurice demanded be clarified.

Lorin bolted from his room, flew down the four flights of stairs as though he had wings, and ran to the Goddess of Reason's, where he found her embroidering gold stars on a dress of blue gauze. This was to be her dress as a divinity.

"Enough stars, dear friend," said Lorin. "They arrested Maurice this morning and I'll probably be arrested tonight."

"Maurice, arrested?"

"Yes, by God! These days what could be more common than major calamities; no one pays any attention anymore because they now come in droves, that's just how it is. But nearly all these major events are brought about by totally trivial things. Let's not neglect the totally trivial. Who was that flower girl we saw this morning, dear friend?"

Artemisia jumped.

"What flower girl?"

"Oh, for crying out loud! The one who was tossing her flowers so extravagantly into the Seine."

"Oh, for heaven's sake!" said Artemisia. "Is that such a serious matter that you have to keep harping on it?"

"So serious, dear friend, that I beseech you to answer my question this very instant."

"My friend, I can't."

"Goddess, there's nothing you can't do."

"I'm honor-bound not to say."

"And I am honor-bound to make you say."

"But why are you so insistent?"

"Because . . . Christ! So Maurice doesn't get the chop!"

"Oh, my God! Maurice guillotined!" cried the young woman in fright.

"To say nothing of myself, though I'm not sure I can honestly say I've still got my head screwed on to begin with."

"Oh! No. No," said Artemisia. "It would mean losing your head, without fail."

At that moment, Lorin's officieux rushed into Artemisia's room.

"Ah, citizen!" he cried. "Run! Run!"

"Why would I do that?" asked Lorin.

"Because the gendarmes have come for you. While they were breaking down the door, I managed to get through to the house next door over the rooftops so I could come and warn you."

Artemisia gave out a terrible cry. She really loved Lorin, after all.

"Artemisia," said Lorin, facing her squarely, "are you saying the life of a flower girl is worth more than that of Maurice—and that of your lover? If that's how it is, I declare that I cease to take you for the Goddess of Reason and proclaim you the Goddess of Unreason."

"Poor Héloïse!" cried the erstwhile Opera dancer. "It's not my fault if I betray you."

"Good! Good! Dear friend," said Lorin, handing Artemisia a sheet of paper, "you've already gratified me with a Christian name; now how about giving me the surname and address."

"Oh, no. I can't write it down! Never!" cried Artemisia. "You win: I'll tell you."

"So tell me and don't worry, I won't forget."

Artemisia then gave Lorin the name and address of the phony flower girl in a voice that did not waver.

Her name was Héloïse Tison and she lived at 24, rue des Non-nandières.

At the name, Lorin gave a cry and darted off at full speed.

He hadn't gone as far as the end of the street when a letter arrived at Artemisia's. The letter contained only these three lines:

> Not a word about me, dear friend; the revelation of my name would finish me off without fail. . . . Wait till tomorrow to name me, for tonight I will have left Paris.
>
> YOUR HÉLOÏSE

"Oh, my God!" cried the future Goddess. "If only I'd realized, I'd have waited till tomorrow."

She dashed to the window to call Lorin back, if there was still time; but Lorin had vanished.

24

MOTHER AND DAUGHTER

We have already said that in a few hours the news of this event was all over Paris. Indeed, in those days, leaks and lapses in discretion were only too easy to understand on the part of a government whose policies were made and unmade in the street.

And so the rumor, terrible and threatening, reached the old rue Saint-Jacques, and two hours after Maurice's arrest they knew all about it there.

Thanks to Simon's industry, the details of the plot had promptly broken through the confines of the Temple. But as everyone had had their little embellishments to add to the basic story, the truth arrived at the master tanner's a little altered. It was a poisoned flower, they said, that had been handed to the Queen, with which the Austrian woman was to put the guards to sleep in order to make her escape from the Temple. . . . This version neatly dovetailed with certain suspicions about the loyalty of the battalion that had been sent packing the day before by Santerre. What it all came to was that a number of victims had already been identified for the people to hate.

But at the old rue Saint-Jacques, they were under no illusions about the real nature of events—and with good reason. Morand immediately dashed out one side of the house and Dixmer the other, leaving Geneviève in the grip of the most violent despair.

Indeed, if anything were to happen to Maurice, Geneviève would be to blame. It was she who had led the blind young man by the nose right up to the cell he would be locked up in, and which he would not be leaving except for a short trip to the scaffold.

But, whatever happened, Geneviève was determined that Maurice would not pay with his head for his determination to please her. If Maurice was condemned, Geneviève was going to accuse herself at the Tribunal; she would confess all. She would take the responsibility upon herself as a matter of course and she would save Maurice even if it meant losing her own life.

Instead of trembling at the thought of dying for Maurice, Geneviève, on the contrary, savored it with a kind of bittersweet relish. She loved him. She loved him more than was right for a woman who was not free. For her it was a way of remitting to God's care her pure and stainless soul just as she had received it from Him.

On leaving the house, Morand and Dixmer had gone their separate ways. Dixmer wended his way toward the rue de la Corderie and

Morand ran to the rue des Nonnandières. When he reached the far end of the pont Marie, Morand saw the usual horde of idlers and gawkers that flock to Paris during or after a major event and plunk themselves down wherever the event took place, the way crows flock to a battlefield.

The sight caused Morand to stop in his tracks. His legs turned to jelly and he was forced to lean against the parapet of the bridge. After a few seconds, though, he got back his energy, that fabulous power that he had over himself in momentous circumstances, and he began to mingle among various clusters of people, asking questions and getting answers. He learned, for example, that ten minutes previously they had nabbed a young woman from 24, rue des Nonnandières, and that this young woman was most certainly guilty of the crime of which she was accused, since she had been caught in the act of packing her bags.

Morand found out what club the poor girl was to be interrogated in and learned that she had been brought to the main section, the Jacobins' club. He set off without further ado.

The club was packed to the rafters by the time Morand got there, yet he managed to elbow and punch his way into one of the galleries. The first thing he saw was the tall and noble figure and disdainful countenance of Maurice, standing in the dock glaring witheringly at Simon as the cobbler held forth.

"Yes, citizens," cried Simon, "yes, citizeness Tison accuses citizen Lindey and citizen Lorin. Citizen Lindey talks of some flower girl whom he wants to blame for his crime. But I can tell you now, the flower girl won't be found. We're dealing with a conspiracy hatched by a ring of aristocrats who keep pointing fingers at one another like the cowards they are. You saw how citizen Lorin flew the coop as soon as he was called on. Well, you won't run into him now any more than you will the flower girl."

"You're lying, Simon," cried a voice full of fury. "You'll run into him all right, for here he is." With that, Lorin burst into the room. "Make way!" he cried, knocking spectators out of the way. "Move!"

He made his way to the front and took a seat next to Maurice. Lorin's entrance, made unaffectedly but with all the frankness and verve inherent in the young man's nature, produced the greatest effect on the gallery, who began to clap and cheer "Bravo!"

Maurice was content to smile and give his friend his hand, as a man who has said to himself, "I'm sure I won't be on my own in the dock for long."

The spectators gazed upon the two dashingly handsome young men with visible interest, accused as they were by the revolting Temple cobbler as though by a demon jealous of youth and beauty.

The latter couldn't help but notice that he was losing his audience thanks to the stark comparison. He resolved to strike a final blow.

"Citizens," he screeched, "I demand that the generous citizeness Tison be heard, I demand that she speak, I demand that she accuse."

"Citizens," said Lorin, "I ask that beforehand the young flower girl, who has just been arrested and who will no doubt be brought before you, be heard."

"No," said Simon, "it's just another false witness, some partisan of the aristocrats. Besides, citizeness Tison is just dying to enlighten the court."

Meanwhile, Lorin had a few enlightening things to whisper to Maurice.

"Yes," cried the gallery. "Yes, bring on the evidence of Mother Tison! Yes, yes, let her testify now!"

"Is citizeness Tison in the room?" asked the president.

"Of course she's here!" cried Simon. "Citizeness Tison, say you're here, then."

"Here I am, my president," said the jailer. "But if I give evidence, will they give me my daughter back?"

"Your daughter has nothing to do with the matter that concerns us," said the president. "Give your evidence first, and then address yourself to the Commune to ask for your daughter again."

"You hear that? The citizen president is ordering you to give your evidence," cried Simon. "So give it to him: what are you waiting for?"

"One moment," said the president, turning to Maurice. The calm of this man, ordinarily so fiery, amazed him. "One moment! Citizen municipal officer, don't you have anything to say first?"

"No, citizen president; except that before calling a man like me a coward and a traitor, Simon would have done better to wait till he was better informed."

"You reckon? You reckon?" repeated Simon in the sniggering tone of the man of the people peculiar to the plebs of Paris.

"I reckon, Simon," said Maurice more in sadness than in anger, "that you will be cruelly punished shortly, when you see what's about to happen."

"So what's about to happen, then?" asked Simon.

"Citizen president," said Maurice, without bothering further with his odious accuser, "I join my friend Lorin in asking you to let the young girl who has just been arrested be heard before they make that poor woman say what they've no doubt coached her to say in evidence."

"You hear that, citizeness?" shrieked Simon. "You hear that? They're saying over there that you're a false witness!"

"Me, a false witness?" said Mother Tison. "Ha! You'll see. Just you wait. Just you wait."

"Citizen," said Maurice, "please order this unfortunate woman to hold her tongue."

"Ha! You're frightened!" cried Simon. "You're frightened! Citizen president, I request the testimony of citizeness Tison."

"Yes, yes, the testimony!" shouted the galleries.

"Silence!" cried the president. "The deputies of the Commune are back."

At that moment, a carriage could be heard rolling up outside with a great clang of arms and the noise of shouting.

Simon wheeled around anxiously to the door.

"Leave the gallery," the president said to him. "You no longer have the floor."

Simon got down.

At that moment, gendarmes entered with a stream of curious on-lookers, who were swiftly shoved back as a woman was propelled toward the front of the courtroom.

"Is that her?" Lorin asked Maurice.

"Yes, yes, that's her," said Maurice. "Oh! The poor girl, she's finished!"

"The flower girl! The flower girl!" the gallery murmured, whipped up by curiosity. "It's the flower girl!"

"I demand Mother Tison be heard before anything else," screamed the cobbler. "You ordered her to give her evidence, president, and you can see she's not giving it."

Mother Tison was called and she began a terrible and detailed denunciation. According to her, the flower girl was certainly guilty; but Maurice and Lorin were her accomplices.

The denunciation had a visible effect on the public.

But Simon was gloating, triumphant.

"Gendarmes, bring on the flower girl!" cried the president.

"Oh! This is dreadful!" murmured Morand, hiding his head in his hands.

The flower girl was called and stood at the foot of the gallery, facing Mother Tison, whose testimony had just made the crime the girl was accused of a capital offense.

It was only then that she lifted her veil.

"Héloïse!" cried Mother Tison. "My daughter . . . You, here?"

"Yes, Mother," the young woman softly replied.

"But why are you standing there between two gendarmes?"

"Because I stand accused, Mother."

"You . . . accused?" cried Mother Tison in anguish. "But who by?"

"By you, Mother."

A fearful silence, the silence of death, suddenly descended on the noisy rabble, and the painfulness of this horrible scene clutched at everyone's heart.

"Her daughter!" voices whispered softly and as though far away. "Her daughter, that poor, poor woman!"

Maurice and Lorin looked at accuser and accused with a feeling of profound commiseration and respectful misery.

Simon, while wishing to see how the scene played out, still hoping Maurice and Lorin would remain compromised, tried to duck Mother Tison's gaze as she swiveled her eyes around dementedly.

"What is your name, citizeness?" said the president, himself moved, to the calm and resigned young woman.

"Héloïse Tison, citizen."

"How old are you?"

"Nineteen years old."

"Where do you live?"

"Number 24, rue des Nonnandières."

"Is it you who sold to citizen municipal officer Lindey, who is there in the dock, a bouquet of carnations this morning?"

The Tison girl turned toward Maurice and looked him full in the face.

"Yes, citizen. It was I," she said.

Mother Tison herself looked at her daughter with eyes huge with horror.

"Do you know that each of the carnations contained a note addressed to the Widow Capet?"

"I know," replied the accused.

A ripple of horror and admiration spread throughout the room.

"Why did you offer the carnations to citizen Maurice?"

"Because I saw his municipal scarf and thought he might be heading to the Temple."

"Who are your accomplices?"

"I have none."

"What! You mean you planned the conspiracy all by yourself?"

"If it is a conspiracy, I planned it all by myself."

"But did citizen Maurice know about it?"

"That the flowers contained notes?"

"Yes."

"Citizen Maurice is a municipal officer; citizen Maurice could see the Queen in private any hour of the day or night. If citizen Maurice had something to say to the Queen, he had no need to write, since he could speak."

"So you didn't know citizen Maurice?"

"I used to see him on duty at the Temple in the days when I was there with my poor mother; but I only knew him by sight!"

"You see, you murderous swine!" Lorin cried, showing Simon his fist. Crushed by the turn things were taking, Simon put his head down as he tried to slip out unnoticed. "You see what you've done?"

All eyes turned on Simon in outrage.

The president resumed his questions.

"Since it was you who handed over the bouquet, since you knew each flower contained a piece of paper, you must also know what was written on the paper?"

"Of course I know."

"Well then, in that case, tell us, what was on the paper?"

"Citizen," said the girl firmly, "I've said all I can say, and, more to the point, all I want to say."

"So you refuse to answer?"

"That's right."

"You know what you're exposing yourself to?"

"Yes."

"Perhaps you're pinning your hopes on your youth and your beauty?"

"I am pinning my hopes on God alone."

"Citizen Maurice Lindey," said the president, "citizen Hyacinthe Lorin, you are free. The Commune recognizes your innocence and acknowledges your community spirit. Gendarmes, conduct citizeness Héloïse to the section prison at the Conciergerie."[1]

At those words, Mother Tison seemed to snap out of her trance; she gave a terrible cry and rushed at her daughter to try to embrace her one more time. But the gendarmes stopped her.

"I forgive you, Mother," cried the young woman as she was dragged away.

Mother Tison uttered a bloodcurdling scream and dropped to the ground as though dead.

"Noble girl!" murmured Morand in grief.

25

THE NOTE

A final scene was added to the events that we have just recounted, as though to complete the tragedy that began to unfold with this somber episode.

Mother Tison, destroyed by what had just happened, abandoned by those who had escorted her, for there is something heinous even in an involuntary crime—and it is quite a crime for a mother to kill her own child, even if it be through excessive patriotic zeal—Mother Tison, after staying absolutely dead still for some little time, raised her head and looked around her, unhinged. Observing that she was on her own, she gave a cry and rushed to the door.

A few curious souls, more relentless than the rest, were still camped at the door, but they moved aside as soon as they saw her, pointing at her and saying to one another: "You see that woman? She's the one who denounced her own daughter."

Mother Tison uttered a cry of despair and dashed off in the direction of the Temple. But a third of the way down the rue Michel-le-Comte, a man came and blocked her path. With his face hidden in his coat, he said: "Are you happy now? Now that you've killed your child?"

"Killed my child? Killed my child?" shrieked the poor mother. "No, no, I can't have."

"And yet you have, for your daughter has been arrested."

"Where have they taken her?"

"To the Conciergerie; from there she'll go to the Revolutionary Tribunal, and you know what happens to people who go there."

"Get out of my way," said Mother Tison. "Let me pass."

"Where are you going?"

"To the Conciergerie."

"What are you going to do there?"

"See her again."

"They won't let you in."

"They'll let me bed down at the door, live there, sleep there. I won't budge until she comes out, and then I'll see her again one more time at least."

"What if someone promised to get you back your daughter?"

"What are you saying?"

"I'm asking you, suppose a man were to promise to get you back your daughter, would you do what this man told you to do?"

"Anything for my daughter! Anything for my Héloïse!" cried the woman, twisting her arms around each other in despair. "Anything! Anything! Anything!"

"Listen," the stranger went on. "It's God that's punishing you."

"But what for?"

"For the torture you've inflicted on a poor mother like yourself."

"Who are you talking about? What do you mean?"

"You've often led the prisoner to the brink of despair, that abyss where you find yourself at this moment, through your brutality and your constant spying. God is punishing you by leading this daughter you loved so much to death."

"You said there was a man who could save her. Where is this man? What does he want? What is he asking for?"

"This man wants you to cease persecuting the Queen, he wants you to ask her forgiveness for the outrages you have done to her, and he wants you, if you perceive that this woman—who is also a mother who suffers, who weeps, who despairs—by some impossible circumstance, by some miracle of the heavens, is about to escape, instead of opposing her flight to help her all you can."

"It's you, isn't it, citizen?" said Mother Tison. "You're this man?"

"What of it?"

"It's you who promises to save my daughter?"

The stranger remained silent.

"Do you promise me? Will you do it? Swear to me? Answer me!"

"Listen. All that a man can do to save a woman, I will do to save your daughter."

"He can't save her!" cried Mother Tison, howling. "He can't save her. He was lying when he promised to save her."

"You do what you can for the Queen, I'll do what I can for your daughter."

"What do I care about the Queen? She's just a woman who has a daughter, that's all. But if anyone's going to get her throat cut, it won't be her daughter, it'll be her. Let them cut my throat if they like, but let them save my daughter. Let them take me to the guillotine; as long as they don't touch a hair on her head, I'll go to the guillotine singing:

> *"Ah, things will all be better soon*
> *When we string the aristocrats from the lampposts. . . ."*[1]

With that Mother Tison began to sing in an alarming voice; then, suddenly, she stopped singing and burst into crazy laughter. The man in the coat appeared frightened himself by this onset of madness and took a step back.

"Oh! You won't get away that easily," said Mother Tison in despair, holding him by his coat. "You don't come and tell a mother 'Do this and I'll save your child' only to tell her afterward 'Maybe.' Will you save her?"

"Yes."

"When?"

"The day they take her from the Conciergerie to the scaffold."

"Why wait? Why not tonight, this evening, this very instant?"

"Because I can't."

"Ha! You see, you see," shrieked Mother Tison. "You see: you can't! Well, I can."

"What can you do?"

"I can persecute the prisoner, as you call her; I can keep an eye on the Queen, as you call her, aristocrat that you are! I can go into her cell anytime I like, day or night, and don't think I won't. As for her escaping, we'll see about that. Ha! We'll see about that all right, since you don't want to save my daughter, we'll see if she gets out, that one. A head for a head, is that what you want? Madame Veto was Queen, I know very well; Héloïse Tison is just a poor girl, I know very well. But on the guillotine we're all equal."

"Well then, so be it!" said the man in the coat. "You save her—and I will save her."

"Swear."

"I swear."

"On what?"

"On whatever you like."

"Do you have a daughter?"

"No."

"Well then," said Mother Tison, dropping both arms in defeat, "what are you going to swear on?"

"Listen, I swear to God."

"Bah!" replied Mother Tison. "You know very well they've taken down the old one and they haven't put the new one up yet."

"I swear to you on my father's grave."

"Don't swear on a grave, that'll bring her bad luck. . . . Oh! My God! My God! When I think that maybe in three days I'll be able to swear on my daughter's grave! My daughter! My poor Héloïse!" bellowed Mother Tison, so loudly—for a woman with a carrying voice to start with—that several windows flew open.

At the sight of the windows being opened, another man seemed to detach himself from the wall and come toward the first man.

"There's nothing to be done with this woman," said the first to the second. "She is mad."

"No, she's a mother," said the second, dragging his companion away.

Seeing them walking away, Mother Tison seemed to come to her senses.

"Where are you going?" she shouted. "Are you going to save Héloïse? Wait for me, then, I'm coming with you. Wait for me, wait for me, for heaven's sake!"

The poor woman rushed after them, screaming. But at the nearest street corner she lost sight of them, and, not knowing which way to turn, remained for a moment undecided, looking every which way; seeing herself all alone in the night and the heavy silence, that double symbol of death, she gave a shattering scream and fell unconscious to the ground.

Ten o'clock rang out.

Meanwhile, as that same hour was tolling from the Temple clock, the Queen was sitting by a smoky lamp in the room we have come to know, between her sister and her daughter. Hidden from the view of the municipal officers by Madame Royale, she pretended to hug her, while secretly rereading a tiny note written on the finest paper to be found, in a hand so fine that her eyes, scalded by tears, had scarcely enough strength left to decipher it. The note went as follows:

Tomorrow, Tuesday, ask to go down to the garden, which they'll allow you to do without any problems, since the order has been given to grant you this favor whenever you ask. After circling the garden three or four times, feign fatigue, go to the canteen, and ask Mother Plumeau for permission to sit down in the canteen. After you've been there a moment, pretend to feel much worse and faint. They will then shut the doors so that help can be gotten for you, and you will stay there with Madame Elisabeth and Madame Royale. The trapdoor of the cellar will immediately open; hurry down through it with your sister and your daughter and you will all three be saved.

"My God!" said Madame Royale. "Could our luckless destiny be changing?"

"Or could the note be a trap?" said Madame Elisabeth.

"No, no," said the Queen. "These characters have always spelled the presence of a friend—a mysterious but very brave and very faithful one."

"Is it from the Knight?" asked Madame Royale.

"The man himself," replied the Queen.

Madame Elisabeth joined her hands in an attitude of prayer.

"Let us each read the note again to ourselves," the Queen went on, "so that if one of us forgets something, the others will remember."

And the three of them scanned the note once more, but just as they had finished reading, they heard the door of their room creak on its hinges. The two princesses turned round: the Queen alone remained just as she was; but by an almost imperceptible movement she brought the tiny note to her hair and slipped it into her piled-up coiffure.

One of the municipal officers was at the door.

"What do you want, monsieur?" Madame Elisabeth and Madame Royale chorused.

"Hmmmn!" said the municipal officer. "It seems to me you're staying up pretty late tonight. . . ."

"So," said the Queen, turning round with her usual dignity, "is there a new decree of the Commune determining what time I go to bed?"

"No, citizeness," said the officer, "but if necessary, they'll make one."

"In the meantime, monsieur," said Marie Antoinette, "please respect, I won't say a queen's bedchamber, but that of a woman."

"Really," grumbled the officer, "these aristocrats always talk like they're somebody."

But just the same he was subjugated by the woman's dignity, once bordering on arrogance in prosperity but now quiet and touching after three years of suffering, and he withdrew.

A moment later the lamp went out, and as usual the three women got undressed in the dark, using obscurity as a veil for their modesty.

The next day, at nine o'clock in the morning, screened by the curtains around her bed, the Queen reread the note of the day before so as not to depart from the least of its instructions. She then tore it up into almost invisible pieces and threw on her clothes behind the curtains of the bed and went to wake her sister before going in to her daughter in the adjoining room. A moment later she reemerged and called the municipal officers.

"What do you want, citizeness?" asked one of them, popping his head in the door, while the other didn't even pause in scarfing his breakfast to answer the royal call.

"Monsieur," said Marie Antoinette, "I've just come from my daughter's room and the poor child truly is quite sick. Her legs are painfully swollen, for she takes too little exercise. As you know, monsieur, it is I who have condemned her to such inaction. I was authorized to go down into the garden whenever I liked; but as that meant going past the door of the room where my husband lived while he was still alive, the first time I went past his door my heart failed me; I didn't have the strength to proceed, so I went back up and have restricted myself ever since to taking the air on the terrace. That promenade is no longer enough for my poor daughter's health. So I beseech you, citizen municipal officer, to appeal to General Santerre in my name to reclaim the use of this liberty that was granted to me. I would be most grateful to you."

The Queen had spoken so sweetly and at the same time with such dignity, she had so carefully avoided any qualification that might wound the republican prudery of her interlocutor, that the latter, who had presented himself to her with his head covered, as most of these men were in the habit of doing, gradually removed his red cap from its perch on top of his skull and, when she had finished, nodded to her and said:

"Don't worry, madame, we'll ask the citizen general for the permission you desire."

He then withdrew and, as though to persuade himself that he was yielding to fairness and not to weakness, he muttered, "It is only right, when it all boils down to it, it is only right."

"What's right?" asked the other municipal officer.

"That the woman take her daughter out for a walk, since she's sick."

"So? . . . What does she want?"

"She wants to go down and walk around the garden for an hour."

"Bah!" said the other officer. "Let her walk from the Temple to the place de la Révolution, that's a decent walk."

The Queen heard these words and went pale, but they were also galvanizing, and she drew fresh courage from them to tackle the momentous event that was gearing up.

The municipal officer finished his breakfast and went downstairs. For her part, the Queen asked to have her breakfast in her daughter's room, which was granted. Madame Royale remained in bed to confirm the story about being ill, and Madame Elisabeth and the Queen stayed by her side.

At eleven o'clock, Santerre arrived. His arrival was, as usual, announced by the beating of drums in the neighboring fields and by the entrance of the new battalion and fresh municipal officers relieving the outgoing guard. When Santerre had reviewed both the outgoing battalion and the incoming battalion, when he had paraded his heavy horse with its squat legs around the Temple courtyard, he paused for a moment. This was the time when those who needed to speak to him delivered their claims, their denunciations, and their requests.

The municipal officer seized the moment to approach him.

"What do you want?" Santerre snapped.

"Citizen," said the officer, "I've come to say to you on behalf of the Queen . . ."

"What's that, the *Queen*?" asked Santerre.

"Ah, yes, golly," said the officer, himself astonished that he'd gotten so carried away. "What am I saying? Am I mad? I've come to say to you on behalf of Madame Veto . . ."

"That's better," said Santerre. "If you put it like that, I know what you're talking about. Well then, get on with it—what have you come to say to me?"

"I've come to say to you that the young Veto is sick, apparently, for lack of air and exercise."

"Is that the nation's fault? The nation gave her the right to walk in the garden; she turned it down, so that's the end of that!"

"But that's just it; she's sorry now and she wants to know if you'll let her come down."

"No worries. You hear that, the rest of you?" said Santerre, addressing the entire battalion. "The Widow Capet wants to come down and have a walk in the garden. She is allowed to, thanks to the nation; you just make sure she doesn't jump over the walls and run away. For if that happens, you'll all get the chop."

An outburst of Homeric laughter greeted this little joke of the citizen general's. "Don't say you weren't warned," said Santerre. "So long. I'm off to the Commune. It looks like Barbaroux's[2] caught up with Roland in the suicide stakes; they need to be issued a passport for the next world."

This was the news that had put the citizen general in such a good mood. Santerre galloped away. The outgoing battalion followed close behind, and finally the previous shift's municipal officers made way for the newcomers who had received Santerre's instructions regarding the Queen.

One of these went to see Marie Antoinette to tell her the general had granted her request.

"Oh!" she thought, gazing at the sky through her window. "Will your anger rest, Lord, are you tired of bearing down on us with your terrible might?"

"Thank you, monsieur," she said to the municipal officer with the same stunning smile that was the finish of Barnave and had made so many men lose their heads. "Thank you!"

Then she turned to her little dog, who was leaping at her as he stood on his two hind legs, for he understood from his mistress's expression that something extraordinary was going on.

"Let's go, Black," she said, "we're going for a walk."

The little dog began to yap and dance about; he cast a grateful look at the municipal officer, no doubt knowing that it was from this human source that the news that made his mistress so happy came; he crawled over to him groveling and wagging his long silky tail and even took the risk of licking him.

This man, who might well have remained unmoved by the Queen's entreaties, was quite overcome by the caresses of the dog.

"If only for this little fellow, citizeness Capet, you should have gone out more often," he said. "Humanity demands that we take care of all creatures."

"What time are we to go out, monsieur?" asked the Queen. "Don't you think the heat of the middle of the day will do us good?"

"You can please yourself," said the officer. "There is no specific recommendation on this point. But if you want to go out at midday, that's when we change shifts, so there'll be less of a bustle in the tower."

"Well then, let it be midday," said the Queen, pressing her hand to her heart to stop it from beating so hard.

She examined this man, who didn't seem as hard as his colleagues and who might well be about to lose his life in the struggle the conspirators were contemplating for deigning to accede to the Queen's wishes.

But just when a certain compassion was about to weaken the woman's heart, the soul of the Queen took over. She thought of the tenth of August and of the bodies of her friends strewn over the carpets of her palace; she thought of the second of September and the head of the Princesse Lamballe looming up on a pike[3] in front of the palace windows; she thought of the twenty-first of January and her husband dying on the scaffold to the sound of a drumroll that drowned out his voice; finally, she thought of her son, that poor little boy whose cries of pain she had more than once heard coming from his room without being able to help him—and her heart hardened.

"Alas!" she murmured. "Calamity is like the blood of the ancient Hydras: it is blood and bone fueling fresh new calamities."

26

BLACK

The municipal officer left to call his colleagues and read the outgoing officers' report. The Queen remained alone with her sister and her daughter. All three looked at one another. Madame Royale threw herself into the Queen's arms and held her tight. Madame Elisabeth went to her sister and gave her her hand.

"Let us pray to God," said the Queen. "But let's do it quietly so no one suspects we are praying."

There are fatal periods in history in which prayer, the natural hymn God has planted firmly in mankind's heart, becomes suspect in the eyes of men, for prayer is an act of hope or gratitude. Now, in the eyes of her guardians, hope or gratitude were a cause for concern, since the Queen could only hope for one thing—escape—and since the Queen could only thank God for one thing—giving her the means to achieve it.

This unspoken prayer finished, all three sat without saying a word. Eleven o'clock sounded, then midday. As soon as the last stroke rang out in all its bronze reverberations, a clatter of arms began to fill the spiral staircase, rising as far as the Queen.

"That's the sentry being relieved," she said. "They'll shortly come and get us."

She saw her sister and her daughter blanch.

"Courage!" she said, herself looking perfectly ashen.

"It's midday!" someone cried below. "Bring down the prisoners."

"Here we are, messieurs," said the Queen, who, with a feeling almost of regret, cast a final farewell glance over the blackened walls and the furniture that, if on the crude side, was at least nice and simple—companions of her captivity.

The first wicket opened: it gave onto the corridor. The corridor was dark, and in the darkness the three captives could hide their emotion. Black ran ahead, but when they reached the second wicket, which was the door Marie Antoinette dreaded, she tried to avert her gaze; but the faithful animal nuzzled the door studs with its muzzle and gave a few plaintive yaps before letting out a painful and prolonged howl. The Queen staggered past without having the strength to call her dog back, groping for the support of the wall.

After taking a few more steps, the Queen's legs failed her and she was forced to stop. Her sister and her daughter rushed over to her and, for a moment, the three women remained standing, still as statues in a sorrowful group study, the mother with her forehead propped against the head of Madame Royale.

Little Black ran and joined them.

"Well then," cried the same voice. "Is she coming down or isn't she?"

"We're coming," said the municipal officer, who had remained stationary out of respect for a suffering so great in its simplicity.

"Let's go!" said the Queen.

With that, she descended the remaining stairs.

When the prisoners had reached the bottom of the spiral staircase, opposite the last door, under which the sun flung broad bands of golden light, there was a drumroll to summon the guard; it was followed by an intense silence provoked by curiosity, and then the heavy door creaked slowly open on stiff hinges.

A woman was sitting on the ground, or rather sprawling in the corner created by the post adjoining the door. It was Mother Tison, whom the Queen had not laid eyes on for twenty-four hours, though several times that morning and the night before she had wondered with amazement where Mother Tison could be.

The Queen could already see the daylight, the trees, the garden, and beyond the barrier that enclosed the garden her avid eye scanned for the little canteen hut where her friends no doubt awaited her; then, at the sound of her footsteps, Mother Tison yanked her hands away from her face and the Queen saw a pale and broken mask beneath hair that had gone grey overnight.

The change was so great that the Queen stopped in her tracks, aghast.

With that slowness people acquire when they've lost their minds, the woman knelt before the door, blocking Marie Antoinette's path.

"What do you want, good woman?" asked the Queen.

"He said you had to forgive me."

"Who is that?" asked the Queen.

"The man in the coat," replied Mother Tison.

The Queen looked at Madame Elisabeth and at her daughter in amazement.

"Come on, move," said the municipal officer. "Let the Widow Capet past; she's got permission to take a walk in the garden."

"I'm well aware of that," said the old woman. "That's why I came here to wait. Since they wouldn't let me go up and I'm supposed to ask her pardon, I had to wait for her, didn't I?"

"Why wouldn't they let you come up?" the Queen asked.

Mother Tison began to laugh.

"Because they reckon I'm mad!" she said.

The Queen looked at the poor woman and saw in her deranged eyes that unmistakably weird gleam, that vague glint, that indicates that the mind has fled.

"Oh, my God!" she said. "Poor woman! What's happened to you?"

"What's happened to me is ... So you don't know?" asked the woman. "Yes, you do.... You know all right, since it's because of you that she's been condemned...."

"Who?"

"Héloïse."

"Your daughter?"

"Yes, who else! ... My poor daughter!"

"Condemned ... But by whom? How? Why?"

"Because she's the one who sold the bouquet...."

"What bouquet?"

"The bouquet of carnations ... but she isn't a flower girl," Mother Tison mused as though sifting through her memories, trying to recall something. "So how could she sell that bouquet?"

The Queen shivered. An invisible thread connected this scene to her present predicament; she knew she must not waste time in a pointless exchange.

"My good woman," she said, "please let me pass; you can tell me all about it later."

"No, right now; you have to forgive me. I have to help you escape so he'll save my daughter."

The Queen turned a deathly white.

"My God!" she murmured, raising her eyes to the skies before turning toward the municipal officer.

"Monsieur," she said, "please be so good as to remove this woman; you can see she is mad."

"All right, all right, let's go," said the officer. "Move it."

But Mother Tison clung to the wall.

"No!" she shrieked. "She has to forgive me so he'll save my daughter."

"But who are you talking about?"

"The man in the coat."

"My sister," whispered Madame Elisabeth, "offer her a few words of consolation."

"Oh, gladly!" said the Queen. "Indeed, I believe that would be the quickest way."

Turning to the madwoman, she said: "Good woman, what do you want? Tell me."

"I want you to forgive me for making you suffer all the insults I've heaped on you and for the denunciations I've made; and I want you, when you see the man in the coat, to order him to save my daughter, since he does anything you ask."

"I don't know who you mean by the man in the coat," the Queen replied, "but if all that's needed to salve your conscience is to obtain my forgiveness for the offenses you believe you have committed against me—oh! from the bottom of my heart, poor woman! I forgive you most sincerely; and may those I've trespassed against similarly forgive me!"

"Oh!" cried Mother Tison in an inexpressible note of joy. "So he'll save my daughter, since you've pardoned me. Your hand, madame, your hand."

The Queen was bewildered and, without understanding a word, held out her hand, which Mother Tison grabbed fervently and to which she frantically applied her lips.

At that moment, the hoarse voice of a town crier was heard in the rue du Temple.

"Here," the man cried, "is the judgment and arrest of the girl Héloïse Tison, condemning her to death for the crime of conspiracy!"

Scarcely had these words struck the ears of Mother Tison when her face disintegrated; she shot up onto one knee and spread her arms wide so that the Queen could not get past.

"Oh, my God!" murmured the Queen who hadn't missed a word of the terrible announcement.

"Condemned to death?" cried the mother. "My daughter condemned? My Héloïse finished? He didn't save her, then, he can't save her! So it's too late? . . . Ah!"

"Poor woman," said the Queen. "Believe me, I pity you."

"You?" the woman gasped, her eyes becoming bloodshot. "You? You pity me? Never! Never!"

"You're wrong. I pity you with all my heart. But you must let me pass."

"Let you pass!" Mother Tison burst out laughing. "Not on your life! I was going to let you get away because he told me that if I asked your pardon and let you get away, my daughter would be saved. But now that my daughter's going to die, you will not escape."

"Over here, messieurs! Come to my aid," cried the Queen. "My God! My God! Can't you see this woman's mad?"

"No, I'm not mad, not at all; I know what I'm saying," cried Mother Tison. "You see, it's true, there was a plot. It's Simon who caught on to it; it's my daughter, my poor daughter, who sold the bouquet. She admitted it at the Revolutionary Tribunal . . . a bouquet of carnations . . . There were bits of paper inside. . . ."

"Madame," said the Queen, "for heaven's sake!"

Once again the town crier's voice was heard, as he repeated: "Here is the judgment and arrest of the girl Héloïse Tison, condemning her to death for the crime of conspiracy!"

"Do you hear that?" screamed the madwoman, now surrounded by a group of National Guards. "You hear that? Condemned to death? It's for you, for you, that they're going to kill my daughter! You hear? For you, the Austrian woman!"

"Messieurs," said the Queen, "for heaven's sake! If you won't get rid of this poor madwoman for me, let me at least go back upstairs. I cannot bear this woman's blame: unjust as it is, it is breaking my heart."

The Queen turned her head away, letting a painful sob escape.

"That's right, weep, hypocrite!" jeered the madwoman. "Your bouquet has cost her dearly. . . . Besides, she should have known. It's the way all those who serve you end up. You bring bad luck, you Austrian witch: they've killed your friends, your husband, your defenders; finally they'll kill my daughter. When in hell are they going to kill you, so no one else dies for you anymore?"

The unhappy woman hurled these last words at the Queen, accompanying them with a threatening gesture.

"Wretched woman!" risked Madame Elisabeth. "Have you forgotten that the woman you are speaking to is the Queen?"

"The Queen? Her? . . . The Queen?" stammered Mother Tison, whose derangement was becoming more pronounced by the minute. "If she's the Queen, let her forbid the executioners to kill my daughter. . . . Let her grant my poor Héloïse pardon. . . . Kings let people off. . . . Until now, all you've ever been is a woman, and a woman who brings bad luck, a woman who kills!"

"Ah! For pity's sake, madame," cried Marie Antoinette. "See my pain, see my tears."

With that Marie Antoinette made an attempt to pass, no longer in the hope of escaping but instinctively, to get away from this woman with her alarming obsession.

"Oh, no, you don't!" screamed the old woman. "You want to escape, Madame Veto. . . . I know all about it, the man in the coat told me. You want to go and join the Prussians. . . . But you're not going to get away," she went on, clinging to the Queen's frock. "I'll stop you! I will! String her up, Madame Veto! *Aux armes, citoyens! Marchons . . . qu'un sang impur! . . .*"[1]

And, her arms twisted, her wild grey hair all over the place, her face purple with apoplexy, her eyes swimming in blood, the unhappy woman fell backward, ripping a strip off the frock to which she clung.

The Queen, dazed but at least free of the lunatic, was about to flee into the garden when, all of a sudden, a terrible cry erupted, mingled with barking and some other strange noise. The National Guards snapped out of the stupor they had fallen into as they stood around Marie Antoinette, lured by the scene we have just described.

"To arms! To arms! Treason!" cried a man the Queen recognized by his ugly voice as the cobbler Simon.

Next to this man, who, saber in hand, stood guard at the threshold of the canteen, little Black was barking like fury.

"To arms, all guards!" cried Simon. "We have been betrayed! Get the Austrian woman back inside! To arms! To arms!"

An officer came running over. Simon spoke to him, his eyes inflamed, pointing to the interior of the canteen. The officer in turn cried out:

"To arms!"

"Black! Black!" the Queen called, taking a few steps forward. But the dog did not respond and went on barking like fury.

The National Guards ran to take up arms and rushed toward the cabin, while the municipal officers grabbed hold of the Queen, her sister, and her daughter and forced the prisoners back through the wicket gate, which closed behind them.

"Arms at the ready!" cried the municipal officers to the sentries, and the sound of guns being loaded was heard.

"In there, in there, under the trapdoor," cried Simon. "I saw the trapdoor move. Nothing surer. Anyway, the Austrian woman's dog, and a good little fellow he is—he's not involved in the plot—he yapped at the conspirators, who are probably in the cellar. Listen; you hear? He's still yapping."

Indeed, goaded on by the song and dance Simon was making, Black barked twice as hard.

The officer grabbed the ring of the trapdoor. Two of the sturdiest grenadiers, seeing he couldn't budge it, rushed to his aid, though without any greater success.

"You can see they're holding the trapdoor down from the inside," said Simon. "Fire! Through the trapdoor, my friends, fire!"

"Hey!" cried Madame Plumeau. "You'll break my bottles!"

"Fire!" Simon repeated. "Fire!"

"Shut up, you loudmouth!" said the officer. "And you, bring an ax or two and start on the floorboards. Now, let there be a squad standing by. Watch out! And fire into the trapdoor as soon as it's open."

The groan of wooden boards and a sudden jolt told the National Guards that some kind of movement had just been accomplished down below. Soon afterward, an underground noise was heard that sounded like an iron portcullis clanging shut.

"Courage!" said the officer to the sappers who came running.

The man with the ax struck into the floorboards. Twenty rifle barrels were pointed downward in the direction of the hole he hacked out, which grew wider second by second. But no one was to be seen through it. The officer lit a torch and threw it into the cellar. But the cellar was empty. The trapdoor was whipped back and this time yielded without the slightest resistance.

"Follow me!" cried the officer, bravely rushing down the stairs.

"Forward! Forward!" cried the National Guards, hurling themselves after their officer.

"Ah! Mother Plumeau," said Tison, "you've been lending your cellar to aristocrats!"

A wall had been knocked down. Numerous feet had scuffed the damp soil, and a sort of ditch, three feet wide and five feet high, similar to a trench, had been carved out in the direction of the rue de la Corderie.

The officer ventured into the mouth of the ditch, determined to pursue the aristocrats to the center of the earth if he had to; but he had scarcely taken three or four steps when he was stopped by an iron grille.

"Halt!" he said to the men pushing him from the rear. "You can't go any further. It's blocked off."

"What's happened?" chirped the municipal officers, who had come running to hear the latest after locking up the prisoners again. "Let's have a look."

"Cripes!" said the officer, reemerging. "There is a conspiracy all right: the aristocrats were hoping to abduct the Queen during her promenade—probably with her connivance."

"Blast!" cried one of the municipal officers. "Someone go get citizen Santerre and alert the Commune."

"Soldiers," said the officer, "stay in the cellar and kill anyone who pops up."

Having given this order, the officer went back upstairs to write up his report.

"Aha!" blared Simon, rubbing his hands with glee. "Aha! Who's going to say I'm mad now? Good old Black! Black is a tremendous patriot, Black has saved the Republic. Come here, Black, here boy!"

The vile man made eyes at the poor dog, only to give him a swift kick in the backside as soon as he was within range, sending Black flying twenty feet away.

"Oh! How I love you, Black!" he crowed. "You'll cause your mistress's head to roll yet. Here boy, here Black, come on boy."

But this time Black did not oblige and opted instead for the way back to the dungeon, yelping.

27

THE MUSCADIN

The events we have just recounted were still roughly two hours old when Lorin was to be found pacing around Maurice's room, while Agesilaus polished his master's boots in the antechamber. To make conversation easier the door was left open, and in his travels Lorin would stop by the door and fire questions at the officieux.

"And you say, citizen Agesilaus, that your master went out this morning?"

"For God's sake! Yes!"

"At the usual time?"

"Ten minutes earlier, ten minutes later, I couldn't tell you."

"And you haven't seen him since?"

"No, citizen."

Lorin set off again and circled the room three or four times before perching once more by the door.

"Did he have his sword with him?" he asked.

"Oh! When he goes to the section, he always does."

"And you're sure that he was going to the section?"

"That's what he told me, anyway."

"In that case, I'll go and catch up with him there," said Lorin. "If we miss each other, tell him I called and that I'll be back."

"Wait," said Agesilaus.

"What?"

"I can hear him on the stairs."

"You think so?"

"I know so."

Indeed, almost at that same instant, the door to the stairs opened and Maurice came in. Lorin swiftly gave him the once-over and, seeing that nothing looked amiss, said, "Ah! Here you are at last! I've been waiting for you for two hours."

"Well, so much the better," said Maurice, smiling. "You would've had time to come up with a few good distichs and quatrains."

"Ah! My dear Maurice," said the improviser, "I've given up."

"Distichs and quatrains?"

"That's right."

"Good Lord! It must be the end of the world!"

"Maurice, my friend, I am sad."

"You, sad?"

"I am unhappy."

"You, unhappy?"

"Yes, what do you think? I feel rotten: it's called remorse."

"Remorse?"

"Remorse, yes! Christ!" said Lorin. "It was you or her, my friend. There was no middle ground. You or her. You understand I didn't hesitate—not for a second; but all the same, Artemisia is in despair, she was her friend."

"Poor girl!"

"And since she's the one who gave me her address . . ."

"You would have done a lot better to let things follow their course."

"Oh, yes, and it'd be you right now who'd be on the block in her place. Well thought out, dear friend. To think I came to ask your advice! I thought you were better at logic than that."

"Never mind. Ask me anyway."

"Well then, you know? The poor girl. I wanted to do something to try and save her. I feel like a bit of a punch-up on her behalf. It seems to me that'd do me some good."

"You are insane, Lorin," said Maurice, shrugging his shoulders.

"Come on, what if I tried something at the Revolutionary Tribunal?"

"It's too late, she's been condemned."

"I have to say it's horrible to watch that young woman perish like this."

"All the more horrible in that it's my salvation that's spelled her doom. But, after all, Lorin, we must take some consolation in the fact that she was conspiring."

"You're kidding! My God! Isn't everyone conspiring these days, more or less? She just did what everyone else does. Poor woman!"

"Don't feel too sorry for her, friend, and don't feel sorry for her too loudly, whatever you do," said Maurice, "for some of her taint has rubbed off on us. Believe me, we're not so free of the accusation of complicity that it hasn't left its mark. Today at the section I was called a Girondin by the captain of the Saint-Leu chasseurs, and just a moment ago I had to give him a jab of my sword to prove him wrong."

"So that's why you're so late getting back?"

"Precisely."

"Why didn't you tell me?"

"Because you can't control yourself when it comes to a showdown; it had to be nipped in the bud straightaway so that no one would get to hear about it. We both grabbed whoever happened to be there as our seconds and the duel was over in two passes."

"And that scumbag called you a Girondin, you, Maurice, a true believer?"

"For pity's sake, yes! Which goes to show you, my dear Lorin, that one more episode like that one and we'll become unpopular. And you know what the synonym of unpopular is, in these terrible times, don't you, Lorin: it's *suspect*."

"I know," said Lorin. "And that word causes even the bravest to quake in their boots. Never mind. . . . I just hate letting poor Héloïse go to the guillotine without asking her pardon."

"So what do you want to do about it?"

"I want you to stay here, Maurice, you have nothing to reproach yourself with in her regard. For me, you see, it's an entirely different story; but since I can't do anything for her anymore, I just want to put myself in her path; I want to be there, Maurice, my friend, you understand me, and if she would just give me her hand . . ."

"I'll go with you, then," said Maurice.

"No way, my friend, think about it: you are a municipal officer, you are the secretary of your section, you've been implicated, whereas I've merely defended you. They'll think you're guilty, so stay. It's entirely different for me. I risk nothing by going, and that's what I'm going to do."

Everything Lorin said was so just that there was nothing to say. If Maurice were merely to exchange a sign with the Tison girl as she walked to the scaffold, he would be announcing his complicity himself for all the world to see.

"Go on, then," he said to Lorin, "but be careful."

Lorin smiled, shook Maurice's hand, and left.

Maurice opened his window and bade him a sad farewell. But before Lorin had turned the corner of the street, Maurice ran back to the window more than once, and each time, as though attracted by a kind of sympathetic magnetism, Lorin turned round to smile at him.

Finally, when Lorin had disappeared around the corner of the quay, Maurice shut the window and lapsed into the kind of somnolence which, in strong natures and nervous dispositions like his, presages great turbulence, resembling as it does the calm before the storm.

He was only drawn out of his reverie, or rather trance, by the officieux, who had been on an errand in the outside world and had returned with that bristling air of a domestic servant bursting to tell his master the news he's just picked up.

But seeing Maurice preoccupied, he didn't dare distract him and contented himself with passing back and forth in front of his master, apparently innocently—and without letup.

"What is it, then?" said Maurice cavalierly. "Speak, if you have something to say."

"Ah, citizen! Another incredible plot, eh?"

Maurice shrugged his shoulders.

"A plot to make your hair stand on end," continued Agesilaus.

"Really!" said Maurice in the tone of a man perfectly accustomed to the thirty or so plots a day that then used to occur.

"Yes, citizen," said Agesilaus. "It makes you tremble in your bed, it does. Just thinking about it gives good patriots goose bumps."

"So what sort of plot was it?" asked Maurice.

"The Austrian woman nearly got away."

"Hmph!" Maurice snorted, starting to get interested.

"It seems," said Agesilaus, "that the Widow Capet was involved with the Tison girl they're going to guillotine today. She asked for it, poor thing."

"And how could the Queen be mixed up with that girl?" asked Maurice, who could feel himself breaking out in a sweat.

"It was all done with a carnation. Imagine, citizen, they passed her the instructions in a carnation!"

"In a carnation! . . . Who did?"

"Monsieur, the Knight of . . . wait a sec . . . You know the name as well as anything. . . . I never can remember names. . . . A Knight of Château . . . Strike! I'm a goose! There are no more châteaux. . . .[1] A Knight of Maison . . ."

"Maison-Rouge?"

"That's it!"

"It can't be."

"What do you mean, it can't be? I'm telling you they found a trap-door, an underground tunnel, coaches."

"Hold your horses—you haven't told me a thing yet."

"Oh, well then, I'll tell you all about it, then."

"Get on with it: if it's a tall tale, at least it's a good one."

"No, citizen, it's not a tall tale, not by a long shot, and the proof is I got it from the citizen porter. The aristocrats dug a mine; this mine started at the rue de la Corderie and went as far as the cellar of the citizeness Plumeau's canteen, and even she was nearly compromised for complicity, was citizeness Plumeau. You know her, I hope?"

"Yes, I do," said Maurice, "but go on."

"Well, the Widow Capet was supposed to get away through this underground tunnel. She already had one foot on the stairs going down, can you imagine! It was citizen Simon who yanked her back by her dress. Hold on, they're sounding the alarm in town and the summons in the sections. Can you hear the drums over there? They say the

Prussians are at Dammartin and that their reconnaissance is practically at the border."

In all this barrage of words—some true, some false; some possible, some absurd—Maurice more or less got ahold of the main thread. Everything began with that carnation given to the Queen under his own nose and bought by him from the unfortunate flower girl. That carnation contained the instructions of a plot that had just been dismantled, more or less precisely as elaborated by Agesilaus.

That moment the sound of the drums drew near and Maurice heard shouting in the street:

"Major plot uncovered in the Temple by citizen Simon! Major plot in support of the Widow Capet uncovered in the Temple!"

"Yes, yes," said Maurice, "it's just as I thought. There is some truth in all that. And Lorin's in the middle of these jubilant hordes. . . . He could very well hold out his hand to that girl and get himself hacked to pieces. . . ."

Maurice grabbed his hat, buckled on his sword, and was in the street in two bounds.

"Where is he?" Maurice wondered. "No doubt on the road to the Conciergerie."

And so he bolted off toward the quai de l'Horloge.

At the far end of the quai de la Mégisserie, pikes and bayonets caught his eye, spiking the air over a mob of people's heads. He thought he could make out the uniform of a National Guard in the middle of what was clearly a hostile crowd jostling around him. He ran, his heart lurching, toward the mob blocking the waterfront.

The National Guard pressed by the troop from Marseilles was Lorin . . . and he was pale, his mouth tight, eyes glowering menacingly, hand on the hilt of his sword, busy calculating where to place the blows he was preparing to strike. Two paces from Lorin was Simon, cackling away with a spine-chilling sound and pointing out Lorin to the Marseillais and the rabble at large.

"Hey! Hey! You see that guy there? He's one of the aristocrats I flushed out of the Temple yesterday! He's one of the ones who like to put mail in carnations. He's the accomplice of the Tison girl, who'll be coming by shortly. So, you see him? He's taking a quiet stroll along the Seine while his accomplice is about to walk to the guillotine. And maybe she was more than his accomplice, eh? Maybe she was his mistress and he came here to bid her farewell—or try and help her escape!"

Lorin was not a man to put up with this sort of talk for long. He drew his sword from its scabbard. At the same time, the crowd parted before a man barreling his way into them headfirst, knocking three or four onlookers aside with his broad shoulders, just as they were gearing up to have a go at Lorin.

"You'll be happy now, Simon," said Maurice. "I bet you were sorry I wasn't here before with my friend so you could do a proper job as the Great Denouncer. Denounce away, Simon, denounce! I'm here now."

"My word, yes," said Simon with his hideous sneer, "and you're here just in time. This one," he said to the mob, "is the handsome Maurice Lindey. He was accused at the same time as the Tison girl, but he managed to wriggle out of it because he's rich."

"String 'em up, string 'em up!" cried the imports from Marseilles.

"Go on, just you try it!" said Maurice.

With that he took a step forward and pricked one of the most savage of the cutthroats right in the middle of the forehead as though testing his aim; the man was immediately blinded by blood.

"Murder!" he screamed.

The Marseillais put down their pikes and took up their machetes or loaded their pistols. The crowd scattered in fear, leaving the two friends isolated and exposed, like a double target to be attacked by all comers.

They gave each other one last sublime smile, for they fully expected to be devoured by this storm of iron and flame threatening to break over them, when suddenly the door of the house they had backed into swung open and a swarm of young muscadins in fancy regalia, every one of them armed with a saber and every one of them sporting a pair of pistols at his belt, fell upon the Marseillais and began to wade into them.

"Hooray!" cried Lorin and Maurice as one, recharged by this shot in the arm, without reflecting for a moment that by fighting in the ranks of the muscadins they were proving Simon's accusations true. "Hooray!"

But if they weren't thinking of their salvation, someone else was doing it for them. A short young man of twenty-five or twenty-six, with blue eyes and the hands of a woman, began wielding a sapper's saber with great vigor, although he looked too fragile to be able to lift the thing. Seeing that Maurice and Lorin had failed to flee through the door he seemed to have left open deliberately and were fighting by his side, he turned to them and spoke in a lowered voice:

"Get away through the door; what we're doing here doesn't concern you—you are compromising yourselves for no reason."

The two friends hesitated.

"Get back!" he cried to Maurice. "No patriots with us. Municipal officer Lindey, only aristocrats here, please!"

At that name and at the incredible gall of a man who openly boasted of belonging to a caste that at the time spelled certain death, the crowd gave out a great roar.

But the young blond man and three or four of his foppish friends, far from being daunted by the mob, pushed Maurice and Lorin into the alley and shut the door on them before turning back to throw themselves into the fray with gusto once more. By then the numbers had swelled due to the approach of the cart.

Miraculously saved, Maurice and Lorin looked at each other in amazement. The exit they had been pushed through looked built for the purpose. It led to a courtyard with a small door hidden on the far side, giving onto the rue Saint-Germain-l'Auxerrois.

At that moment, a detachment of gendarmes appeared from the Pont-au-Change and would soon have swept through the quai, despite the fact that from the cross street where our friends were a fierce battle could be heard raging.

The gendarmes preceded the cart that was taking poor Héloïse to the guillotine.

"Faster!" cried a voice. "Faster!"

The cart bolted forward at a gallop. Lorin could see the poor girl, standing, a smile on her lips and a glimmer of pride in her eye. But he could not even exchange a wave with her; she passed without seeing him through a crazed storm of people, all shouting:

"Death to the aristocrat! Death!"

The noise grew more distant until it receded as far as the Tuileries. At the same time, the door Maurice and Lorin had initially taken opened again and three or four muscadins, their clothes torn and bloodstained, emerged. They were probably all that remained of the small troop.

The young man with blond hair emerged last.

"Alas!" he said. "It looks like our cause is doomed."

And throwing his chipped and bloody sword down on the ground, he rushed toward the rue des Lavandières.

28

THE KNIGHT OF MAISON-ROUGE

Maurice hurried back to the section to bring a complaint against Simon. It is true that before separating from Maurice Lorin had come up with a more effective plan, which was to assemble a few Thermopylae members, wait till Simon was due to leave the Temple, and kill him in an orderly battle. But Maurice put paid to the scheme.

"You're finished," he said to Lorin, "once you descend to battery. We'll crush that bastard Simon all right, but let's crush him legally. Lawyers would have a field day with him."

And so Maurice went off to the section next morning to make his official complaint. He was perfectly stunned when the president of the section turned a deaf ear, declaring himself unable to act and saying he could not take sides between two good citizens both motivated by love of the nation.

"Right!" said Maurice. "Now I know what you have to do to merit the reputation of being a good citizen. Ha! All you have to do is gather a bunch of thugs together to assassinate a man you don't like! You call that being motivated by love of the nation? I'm quickly coming round to Lorin's view, which I was silly enough to rule out. From today I'll practice patriotism as you understand it, and I'll start by experimenting on Simon."

"Citizen Maurice," replied the president, "Simon may well be less in the wrong than you in this matter. He uncovered a plot without being called upon to do so by the terms of his employment. Furthermore, you have either chance or deliberate dealings—which? That we don't know; we just know you have them—with the enemies of our nation."

"Me!" cried Maurice. "Ah, this is novel, I'll grant you that. And with whom then, citizen president?"

"With citizen Maison-Rouge."

"Me?" said Maurice, stunned. "Me? I have dealings with the Knight of Maison-Rouge? I don't even know him, I have never . . ."

"You were seen talking to him."

"Me?"

"Shaking his hand."

"Me?"

"Yes—you."

"Where? When? . . . Citizen president, you are making it up!" said Maurice, carried away by the conviction of his innocence.

"You're taking your zeal for the nation a bit far, citizen Maurice," said the president. "And you'll be sorry in a moment that you said what you just said, when I give you proof that I've spoken nothing but the truth. Here are three different reports accusing you."

"Well, you wouldn't credit it!" said Maurice. "Do you really think I'm naïve enough to believe in your Knight of Maison-Rouge?"

"And why wouldn't you believe in him?"

"Because he is a conspirator bogeyman you always keep up your sleeve, ready to overpower your enemies with talk of some dreadful plot or other."

"Read the denunciations."

"I won't read anything," said Maurice. "I protest that I have never seen the Knight of Maison-Rouge and that I have never spoken to him. Let anyone who doesn't believe my word of honor come forward and tell me to my face. I know what I'll say to him."

The president gave a shrug. Maurice, not wanting to be outdone by anyone, did the same.

There was something sinister and reserved about the rest of the session, and afterward the president, a brave and good patriot who had been elevated to the first rank of the district by the vote of his fellow citizens, approached Maurice:

"Come with me, Maurice, I've got something to say to you."

Maurice followed the president, who led him to a small cabinet adjacent to the room in which meetings were held. Once they were there, he looked him in the face and put his hand on his shoulder:

"Maurice, I knew and esteemed your father, which means that I esteem you and feel great fondness for you. Believe me, Maurice, you are running a grave danger if you let yourself lose faith—that's the first sign of decadence in a truly revolutionary mind. Maurice, my friend, once you lose faith, you lose faithfulness. You don't believe in the enemies of the nation: from that stems the fact that you brush past them without seeing them and you become the instrument of their plots without realizing it."

"What the devil!" said Maurice. "I know myself, I'm a man who acts from the heart, a zealous patriot. But my zeal doesn't make me a fanatic: there are twenty so-called plots that the Republic all attributes to the same man. I'd like to see the author of these plots, once and for all."

"You don't believe the conspirators exist, Maurice?" said the president. "Well, then, tell me, do you believe in the red carnation for which they guillotined the Tison girl yesterday?"

Maurice started.

"Do you believe in the underground tunnel dug under the Temple garden, running from citizeness Plumeau's cellar to a certain house in the rue de la Corderie?"

"No," said Maurice.

"Well, then, do as doubting Thomas did and go and see for yourself."

"I'm not on guard duty at the Temple and they probably won't let me in."

"Anyone can get into the Temple now."

"How come?"

"Read this report; since you're so incredulous, I'll only proceed further by showing you official documentation."

"What!" said Maurice, reading the report. "It's gone this far!"

"Keep reading."

"They're taking the Queen to the Conciergerie?"

"What of it?" said the president.

"Oh! Oh!" Maurice groaned.

"Do you think it's on the basis of some dream, what you call imagination, some nonsense, that the Committee of Public Safety has adopted such a serious measure?"

"This measure has been adopted, but it won't be carried out, like a whole host of measures I've seen taken, that's all. . . ."

"Read to the end," said the president.

And he handed Maurice one last report.

"The receipt of Richard, jailer of the Conciergerie!" cried Maurice.

"She was committed to prison there at two o'clock this morning."

This time Maurice remained thoughtful.

"The Commune, you know," the president continued, "acts on the bigger picture. It has carved out a broad and straight course for itself; its measures are not childish games, you know; it has put into practice Cromwell's[1] dictum *Kings should be hit only on the head*. Read this secret police memo."

Maurice read:

Given that we are certain that the former Knight of Maison-Rouge is in Paris; that he has been seen about town in sundry places; that he has left traces of his passage in several plots happily dismantled, I invite all the heads of sections to redouble their vigilance.

"What do you make of that?" said the president.

"I'm forced to believe you, citizen president," cried Maurice. He continued to read:

Profile of the Knight of Maison-Rouge: five foot three inches tall, blond hair, blue eyes, straight nose, chestnut-colored beard, round chin, softly spoken, hands of a woman. Thirty-five to thirty-six years old.

At this description a strange light traveled across Maurice's brain. He thought of the young man commanding the troop of muscadins who had saved Lorin's and his life the day before, and how resolutely he had struck out at the Marseillais with his sapper's sword.

"Good grief!" murmured Maurice. "Could that be him? In that case, the denunciation that says I've been seen talking to him would not be wrong. But I don't remember shaking his hand."

"Well then, Maurice," said the president, "what do you say to all that now, my friend?"

"I say I believe you," replied Maurice, slipping into a contemplative melancholy, for without knowing what evil influence was making his life so sad, he had felt gloom descending all around him for some little time now.

"Don't toy with your popularity like this, Maurice," the president advised. "Today popularity means life. Watch out: unpopularity means suspicion of treason, and citizen Lindey can't be suspected of being a traitor."

Maurice had nothing with which to counter a doctrine he recognized as his own. He thanked his old friend and left the section.

"Ah," he murmured, "I need to breathe for a bit. That's enough suspicion and combat for one day. Let's take the straight road to rest, innocence, and joy. Let's go directly to Geneviève."

And so Maurice opted for the way to the old rue Saint-Jacques. When he arrived at the master tanner's, Dixmer and Morand were supporting Geneviève, who had fallen victim to an attack of nerves. Instead of allowing him free passage as usual, a domestic servant barred his way.

"Announce me anyway," said Maurice anxiously. "If Dixmer can't see me, I'll leave."

The servant went into the little pavilion while Maurice stayed in the garden. It seemed to him that something strange was going on in the house. The tannery workers were not at their work, scurrying instead across the garden looking deeply anxious. Dixmer himself came to the door.

"Come in," he said, "dear Maurice, come in. You aren't one of those to whom the door is closed."

"But what's going on?" the young man asked.

"Geneviève is ill," said Dixmer. "Worse than ill, she's delirious."

"Oh, my God!" cried the young man, overcome at finding trouble and suffering even here. "What's ailing her?"

"You know, dear boy," said Dixmer, "no one knows much about women's troubles, especially not the husband."

Geneviève was recumbent on a sort of chaise longue. Near her stood Morand, getting her to sniff salts.

"Well?" asked Dixmer.

"The same," answered Morand.

"Héloïse! Héloïse!" murmured the young woman through white lips and clenched teeth.

"Héloïse!" Maurice repeated, stunned.

"Oh, God, yes!" Dixmer said vehemently. "Geneviève had the misfortune to go out yesterday and see that awful cart passing with some poor girl called Héloïse in it; they were taking her to the guillotine. From that moment, she has had five or six attacks of nerves and just repeats that name."

"What struck her especially was that she recognized the girl as the flower girl who sold her the carnations you know about."

"I certainly do know, since they nearly got my throat cut."

"Yes, we heard about that, dear Maurice, and please believe me we were horrified; but Morand was at the session and he saw you get off scot free."

"Shush," cried Maurice. "She's talking again, I think."

"Oh! Words here and there, unintelligible," said Dixmer.

"Maurice," murmured Geneviève, "they're going to kill Maurice. Go to him, Knight, go to him!"

A profound silence followed these words.

"Maison-Rouge," murmured Geneviève. "Maison-Rouge!"

Maurice felt a lightning flash of suspicion, but it was just a flash. In any case, he was too upset by Geneviève's suffering to comment on what she said.

"Did you call a doctor?" he asked.

"Oh! It's nothing," said Dixmer. "She's a bit delirious, that's all."

He squeezed his wife's arm so hard that Geneviève came to and, giving a small shriek, opened eyes that until then she had held tightly shut.

"Ah, here you all are," she said, "and Maurice with you. Oh! I'm so happy to see you, my friend; if you only knew how I . . ."

She recovered herself in time: "We've really been through a lot these last two days!"

"Yes," said Maurice, "we're all here; so you can stop worrying, stop scaring yourself with such terrors. There is one name in particular, you know, that you must get used to not saying anymore, given that it no longer has the slightest whiff of sanctity."

"What name is that?" Geneviève shot out.

"The name of the Knight of Maison-Rouge."

"I named the Knight of Maison-Rouge, did I?" asked Geneviève, horrified.

"Funnily enough," said Dixmer with a forced laugh. "But you understand, Maurice, there's nothing funny in that, really, since they're saying publicly that he was the accomplice of the Tison girl and that it was he who directed the escape attempt that, happily, came to grief yesterday."

"I'm not saying there's anything funny in it," replied Maurice. "I'm just saying he'd better keep himself hidden."

"Who?" asked Dixmer.

"The Knight of Maison-Rouge! Who do you think! The Commune is looking for him and its bloodhounds have pretty good noses."

"Let's hope they get him," said Morand, "before he comes up with some other scheme that he pulls off better than this last one."

"In any case," said Maurice, "it won't involve helping the Queen."

"Why not?" asked Morand.

"Because the Queen is now beyond help—even his."

"Where is she, then?" asked Dixmer.

"In the Conciergerie," said Maurice. "They took her there last night."

Dixmer, Morand, and Geneviève all gave a cry that Maurice took for an exclamation of surprise.

"So you see," he continued, "that's it for the plans of the Queen's chevalier! The Conciergerie is a bit more secure than the Temple."

Morand and Dixmer exchanged a look that Maurice missed.

"Oh, my God!" he cried. "Madame Dixmer's gone very pale again."

"Geneviève," Dixmer said to his wife, "you must get into bed, my child, you aren't well."

Maurice picked up that he was being dismissed; he kissed Geneviève's hand and left, accompanied by Morand as far as the old rue Saint-Jacques. There Morand left him to say a few words to a servant who was holding a horse all saddled. Maurice was so preoccupied he didn't even ask Morand, to whom he had not addressed a word since they'd left the house together, who the man was and what the horse was doing there.

He took the rue des Fossés-Saint-Victor and reached the embankment.

"It's strange," he said to himself as he walked along. "Is it my mind that's growing dim? Or are things getting weightier? Everything looks bigger to me, as though I'm seeing it all through a microscope."

To get back a bit of serenity, Maurice held his face up to the night breeze and leaned against the parapet of the bridge.

29

THE PATROL

Maurice was silently completing this reflection, leaning on the parapet of the bridge and watching the water flow past with that melancholy attention whose symptoms can be found in any Parisian born and bred, when he heard a small troop coming his way, in step like a patrol.

He turned round; it was a company of the National Guard, arriving from the far side of the river. Maurice thought he could make out Lorin in the darkness. It was Lorin, in fact, and as soon as he saw Maurice he ran to him with open arms.

"It's you!" cried Lorin. "At last! Heaven knows, you're not easy to find.

> "But since I've found my faithful friend
> My rotten luck will surely end.

"That's pure Racine,[1] not Lorin, so I hope you won't complain this time."

"What are you doing here, then, on patrol?" Maurice asked anxiously, now that everything made him jumpy.

"I'm heading a little expedition, my friend—in the interests of rebuilding our shattered reputation."

He turned to his company: "Shoulder arms! Present arms! Arms up!" he bellowed. "Right now, children, the night isn't dark enough. Chat among yourselves for a bit, we'll do likewise."

Turning back to Maurice, he said: "I learned two major items of news today at the section."

"What?"

"The first is that we've begun to be suspect, you and I."

"I know that. Next?"

"Ah! You know that!"

"Yes."

"The second is that the whole carnation plot was directed by the Knight of Maison-Rouge."

"I know that too."

"But what you don't know is that the carnation plot and the underground tunnel plot are one and the same."

"I know that too."

"Well, then, let's move on to a third bit of news. This you don't know—of that I'm sure. We are going to take the Knight of Maison-Rouge tonight."

"Take the Knight of Maison-Rouge?"

"Yes."

"So you've become a gendarme now?"

"No. But I am a patriot. A patriot dedicates himself to the nation. Now, the nation is abominably ravaged by this Knight of Maison-Rouge, who keeps heaping plot on plot. So the nation orders me, me, a patriot, to rid it of the said Knight of Maison-Rouge, who is embarrassing it horribly, and so I obey the nation."

"Say what you like," said Maurice, "it's still strange you're taking on such a commission."

"I'm not taking it on, it's been foisted on me. But anyway, I have to say, I'd have done anything to get the job. We need a masterstroke to rehabilitate ourselves, given that our rehabilitation means not only the safety of our existence but also the right to stick six inches of steel into the guts of the foul Simon at the first opportunity."

"But how do they know it was the Knight of Maison-Rouge who headed the underground plot?"

"It's still not entirely sure, but they're assuming it was him."

"Aha! You're proceeding by induction?"

"We are proceeding by certainty."

"How do you figure that? Eh? After all ..."

"Listen well."

"I'm listening."

"Scarcely had I heard the shout go up: 'Major conspiracy uncovered by Simon'—that turd Simon! He's everywhere, the lousy mongrel!—than I decided to judge the truth for myself. There was talk about an underground tunnel."

"Does it exist?"

"Oh, it exists! I've seen it.

> "Seen, seen with my own eyes, which is called seeing.

"Hey! Why aren't you booing?"

"Because that's Molière,[2] and because, I must confess, I find the circumstances a little too serious to joke."

"Well, but what does one joke about if not about what's serious?"

"You say you saw it. ..."

"The underground tunnel ... I repeat, I have seen the underground tunnel, I have been through it, and it ran from citizeness Plumeau's cellar to a house in the rue de la Corderie, the house at number 12 or 14, I can't quite remember which."

"Really! You went through it?"

"The whole way, and a very nicely cut passageway it is too, I can tell you. It was divided by three iron grilles, which we had to remove one by one, but if the buggers had succeeded those grilles would have given them all the time they needed—all they had to do was sacrifice a few of their men to whisk Madame Widow Capet away to a secure place. Luckily things didn't work out that way—and the foul Simon was also onto that."

"But surely the first thing they should have done is arrest the inhabitants of the house in the rue de la Corderie."

"And that's exactly what they would have done if they hadn't found the house completely devoid of occupants."

"But surely the house belongs to someone?"

"Yes, to a new owner, but no one knew who it was. It was known that the house had changed hands two or three weeks ago, that's all. The neighbors heard a bit of noise, of course, but they just thought it was repairs being carried out, as the house was old. As for the former owner, he'd left town. That's where I came in:

" 'Heck!' says I to Santerre, pulling him aside, 'you're all in a bit of a tight spot!'

" 'True enough,' he says, 'we are.'

" 'The house was sold, wasn't it?'

" 'Yes.'

" 'Two weeks ago?'

" 'Two or three weeks.'

" 'Sold in the presence of a notary?'

" 'Yes.'

" 'Well then, we have to go through all the notaries in Paris to find out which one sold the house and get ahold of the deed. The name and address of the buyer will be on it.'

" 'Marvelous! That's what I call good thinking,' says Santerre. 'And coming from a man they're accusing of being a bad patriot. Lorin, Lorin, old mate! I will rehabilitate you or the devil take me.'

"In a word," Lorin went on, "no sooner said than done. The notary was sought, the deed was found, and on the deed the name and address of the guilty party. So Santerre kept his word and appointed me to arrest him."

"And this man, it was the Knight of Maison-Rouge?"

"No, only his accomplice—that is, most likely."

"Well then, how come you said you were going to arrest the Knight of Maison-Rouge?"

"We're going to arrest both of them together."

"To start with, do you know the Knight of Maison-Rouge?"

"Very well."

"You have his description?"

"Of course I do! Santerre gave it to me. Five foot two or three inches tall, blond hair, blue eyes, straight nose, chestnut beard. Anyway, I've seen him."

"When?"

"This very day."

"You saw him?"

"You did too."

Maurice started.

"That young runt with the blond hair that freed us this morning—you know, the one who commanded the troop of muscadins, who fought so hard."

"So that really was him? I'd hoped it wasn't true...."

"The man himself. They followed him and lost him somewhere near the home of the owner of the rue de la Corderie, so they presume they share a house."

"That seems likely."

"It's certain."

"But Lorin," said Maurice, "aren't you lacking gratitude a little if you arrest tonight the man who saved us this morning?"

"For crying out loud!" said Lorin. "Do you really think he saved us in order to save us?"

"Why not?"

"Of course he didn't. They were hiding out at that spot to carry off poor Héloïse Tison when she passed. The thugs from Marseilles got in their way, so they fell upon the thugs. We were saved as an aftereffect. Now, since everything is in the intention and the intention wasn't in it, I don't have to reproach myself in the least with being ungrateful. Besides, you see, Maurice, the crucial thing is necessity, and there is a dire necessity for us to rehabilitate ourselves by pulling off a real coup. I vouched for you."

"To whom?"

"To Santerre. He knows you're in command of the raid."

"How so?"

" 'Are you sure of arresting the culprits?' he asked.

" 'Yes,' says I, 'as long as Maurice is in on it.'

" 'But are you sure of Maurice? He's been getting a little lukewarm for some time now.'

" 'Those who say that are wrong. Maurice is no more lukewarm than I am.'

" 'And you'll answer for him?'

" 'As I would for myself.'

"So I went to your place but didn't find you in; I then came this way, first because it's the way I always come, and then because it's the way you usually go. Finally I run into you, here you are: forward, march!

> Victory, singing,
> Opens the gate for us. . . ."

"My dear Lorin, it's driving me to despair, but I just can't work up any enthusiasm for this raid. Say you didn't see me."

"No, I can't—the men all saw you."

"Well then, say you saw me but I didn't want to join the party."

"I can't say that either."

"Why not?"

"Because this time you won't just be lukewarm, you'll be suspect. . . . And you know what they do with anyone suspect, don't you? They take you to the place de la Révolution and invite you to salute the statue of liberty; only instead of lifting your hat, you lift your head."

"Well then, Lorin, whatever will be, will be. But I suppose, when it comes down to it, that what I'm about to tell you will sound strange to you."

Lorin opened his eyes wide and gazed at Maurice.

"Well, the truth is, I am disgusted with life. . . ."

Lorin burst out laughing.

"Right!" he said. "We've had a little tiff with our true love and it's given us melancholy notions. Get off the grass, beautiful Amadis.[3] Be a man again and after that we'll work on the citizen. I, on the other hand, am never a better patriot than when I've had a row with Artemisia. Speaking of which, Her Divinity the Goddess of Reason sends you her warmest regards."

"Please thank her on my behalf. Adieu, Lorin."

"What do you mean, adieu?"

"Yes, I'm going."

"Where are you going?"

"Home, for heaven's sake!"

"Maurice, you're going to your doom."

"I couldn't care less."

"Maurice, think, friend, think."

"I have."

"I didn't tell you everything. . . ."

"Everything—what?"

"Everything Santerre said to me."

"What did he say to you?"

"When I asked for you to be head of the expedition he said: 'Watch out!'

" 'What for?' I said.

" 'For Maurice,' he said."

"Me?"

"Yes. 'Maurice,' he went on, 'often visits that neighborhood.' "

"What neighborhood?"

"Maison-Rouge's neighborhood."

"What!" cried Maurice. "This is where he hides out?"

"They assume he does, at least, since this is where his presumed accomplice lives, the man who bought the house in the rue de la Corderie."

"Faubourg Victor?" Maurice asked.

"Yes, faubourg Victor."

"And what street in the faubourg?"

"The old rue Saint-Jacques."

"Oh, my God!" murmured Maurice, stunned as though struck by

lightning, shading his eyes with his hand. After an instant, and as though in that instant he had summoned all his courage, he said:

"What's his job?"

"Master tanner."

"And his name?"

"Dixmer."

"You're right, Lorin," said Maurice, using all his willpower to suppress any sign of emotion. "I'll go with you."

"You're doing the right thing. Are you armed?"

"I have my sword, as always."

"Take these two pistols as well."

"What about you?"

"I have my rifle. Shoulder arms! Carry arms! Forward, march!"

The patrol started marching again, accompanied by Maurice, who stuck close to Lorin behind a man dressed in grey, who was directing the operation. This was the man from the police.

From time to time a shadow would slip out of a street corner or a doorway and come to exchange a few words with the man in grey: they were police surveillance.

The party reached the familiar alleyway. The grey man did not hesitate a single instant. He was well informed. He took the alley and only stopped when he came to the garden gate through which Maurice had been led, all trussed up, that first time.

"This is it," he said.

"This is what?" asked Lorin.

"This is where we'll find the two chiefs."

Maurice leaned against the wall, feeling like he was going to fall backward.

"Now," said the grey man, "there are three entrances: the main entrance, this one here, and one that leads to a pavilion. I'll take six to eight men and go in through the main entrance. You guard this entrance here with four or five men and put three solid fellows on the pavilion exit."

"And I'll go over the wall," said Maurice, "and keep watch in the garden."

"Good idea," said Lorin, "especially seeing as you'll be able to open the door for us from the inside."

"Gladly," said Maurice. "But don't clear the passage and come unless I call you. I'll see anything that happens inside from the garden."

"So you know this place?" asked Lorin.

"I wanted to buy it once."

Lorin hid his men in the hedges and doorways while the police agent moved off with eight or nine National Guards to force the main entrance as discussed. After a moment, the noise of their footfalls died away without having attracted the slightest notice in this desert.

Maurice's men were at their post, camouflaged as well as they could be. You would have sworn everything was as quiet and uneventful as usual in the old rue Saint-Jacques, so Maurice began his climb over the wall.

"Wait," said Lorin.

"What?"

"The watchword."

"Oh, that's right."

"*Carnation and underground tunnel.* Stop anyone who doesn't give you those four words. Let anyone past who does. Those are orders."

"Thanks," said Maurice, before promptly jumping from the top of the wall down into the garden.

30

CARNATION AND UNDERGROUND TUNNEL

The first blow had been terrible, and Maurice had needed all the self-control he could muster to hide from Lorin the shock that had shaken his whole body. But once he was in the garden, once he was alone, once he was in the silence of the night, his mind became calmer and his thoughts stopped roiling haphazardly in his brain, instead presenting themselves logically so his reason could analyze and comment on them.

He could not believe it. This house that Maurice had so often visited out of the sheerest pleasure, this house that had been for him paradise on Earth, was just a den of murderous intriguers! All the warm welcomes he had been given, all the protests of undying friendship—all that was nothing but hypocrisy; all Geneviève's love was nothing but fear!

We already know the layout of the garden, where our readers have followed our young protagonists more than once. Maurice darted from one dark mass to the next until he was sheltered from the moon's rays by the shadow of the hothouse in which he'd been locked up that first day.

The hothouse was opposite the pavilion where Geneviève lived. But this night, instead of there being a single light burning steadily in the young woman's bedroom alone, there were lights all over the house, moving from one window to the next. Maurice spotted Geneviève through a curtain that lifted accidentally; she was shoving things frantically into a portmanteau, and he saw with astonishment that a weapon gleamed in her hands.

He hoisted himself up on a ledge to get a better view. A great fire caught his eye, burning away in the fireplace. Geneviève was burning papers!

At that moment a door opened and a young man walked into Geneviève's room. Maurice's first idea was that this was Dixmer. The young woman ran to him and seized his hands and they stood looking at each other for a moment, seemingly in the grip of some intense emotion. What was this emotion? Maurice couldn't guess; their words did not reach him. But Maurice quickly sized the man up.

"That's not Dixmer," he muttered. Indeed, the man who had just walked in was thin and short; Dixmer was tall and stocky.

Jealousy is a powerful stimulant. In one second flat Maurice had estimated the height of the stranger to within a quarter of an inch and compared this with the husband's silhouette.

"That's not Dixmer," he muttered again, as though he had to repeat it to himself to be convinced of Geneviève's perfidy.

He drew closer to the window, but the closer he got the less he could see. His forehead was on fire, and he stumbled and knocked a ladder with his foot. The window was about seven or eight feet from the ground. He leaned the ladder against the wall, climbed up, and glued his eyes to the gap in the curtain.

The stranger in Geneviève's bedroom was a young man of twenty-seven or twenty-eight, with blue eyes and an elegant demeanor; he was holding the young woman's hands, talking to her and wiping the tears that veiled her beautiful eyes.

A slight noise that Maurice made caused the young man to wheel around to the window. Maurice bit off a cry of surprise: he recognized his savior from the place du Châtelet.

At that moment, Geneviève withdrew her hands from the stranger's and went to the fireplace to assure herself the papers had been consumed.

Maurice couldn't contain himself any longer. All the terrible passions that can torture a man—love, lust for vengeance, jealousy—tore at his heart with their teeth of fire. He seized his chance, violently pushed open the loose casement window, and sprang into the room.

At the same moment two pistols were aimed at at his chest. Geneviève had turned around at the noise and was absolutely dumbfounded at seeing Maurice.

"Monsieur," said the young republican coldly to the man who held his life twice over at the end of two barrels, "monsieur, so you are the Knight of Maison-Rouge?"

"And what if I were?" replied the Knight.

"Oh! If you were, you are a brave man and so a reasonable man, and I have a couple of things to say to you."

"Say away," said the Knight without lowering his guns.

"You can kill me, but not before I utter a cry, or rather I won't die without having uttered one. If I call out, a thousand men who are circling this house even as we speak will have reduced it to ashes in a matter of minutes. So put down your pistols and listen to what I have to say to madame."

"To Geneviève?" asked the Knight.

"To me?" murmured Geneviève.

"Yes, to you."

Geneviève, whiter than a marble statue, clutched at Maurice's arm. The young man pushed her away.

"You know what you told me, madame," said Maurice with profound contempt. "I see now that you told the truth. You do not, obviously, love Monsieur Morand."

"Maurice, listen to me!" cried Geneviève.

"I have nothing to listen to, madame," said Maurice. "You lied to me; you have broken in one blow all the bonds that bound my heart to yours. You told me you did not love Monsieur Morand but you did not tell me you loved another."

"Monsieur," the Knight interrupted, "why are you going on about Morand? Or rather, which Morand are you going on about?"

"Morand the chemist."

"Morand the chemist stands before you. Morand the chemist and the Knight of Maison-Rouge are one and the same."

And reaching to a nearby table he instantly grabbed and clapped on his head that old black wig that had for so long made him unrecognizable to the young republican.

The Knight made a threatening move.

"Monsieur," Maurice continued, "please let me have a word with madame; stay and listen to our little chat, if you like; it won't be long, I can assure you."

Geneviève signaled to Maison-Rouge to be patient.

"So," Maurice resumed, "so, Geneviève, you've made me a laughingstock among my friends! A thing of loathing to my own people! You used me, blind as I was, to serve your plots! You used me as though I were some handy implement! What you've done is base! But you'll be punished for it, madame; for this man is going to kill me before your very eyes! But he'll be lying lifeless at your feet too before five minutes are up. Or if he lives it will be to carry his head to the scaffold."

"Him, die!" cried Geneviève. "Him, carry his head to the scaffold! But don't you understand, Maurice, that he is my chevalier, my protector, that of my family; that I would give my life for his; that if he dies I will die; and that if you are my love, he is my religion?"

"Ah!" said Maurice. "So you are going to go on saying you love me, perhaps. Women truly are the most pathetic cowards."

Then he turned around: "Do it, monsieur," he said to the young royalist. "Kill me or die."

"Why?"

"Because if you don't kill me I'll arrest you."

Maurice lunged forward and grabbed the man by the collar.

"I won't fight you for my life," said the Knight of Maison-Rouge. "Here!"

And he threw his weapons on an armchair.

"Why won't you fight me for your life?"

"Because my life is not worth the remorse I would feel in killing a gallant man, and, more to the point, because Geneviève loves you."

"Ah!" cried the young woman, clasping her hands. "Ah! You are always so good, grand, loyal, and generous, Armand!"

Maurice watched them both in such amazement his mouth was gaping like an idiot's.

"Here," said the Knight. "I'm going back to my room. I give you my word of honor that it is not to escape but to hide a portrait."

Maurice swiftly glanced at Geneviève's portrait on the wall, but it was in its place. Either Maison-Rouge guessed Maurice's thoughts or he wished to push his generosity to the limit: "Come," he said, "I know you are a republican, but I also know you are a pure and loyal heart. I trust you to the end, you see! Have a look!"

And he drew from his breast pocket a miniature, which he showed to Maurice. It was a portrait of the Queen. Maurice looked askance and brought a hand to his forehead.

"I await your orders, monsieur," said Maison-Rouge. "If you still want to go ahead and arrest me, knock on this door when the time comes for me to hand myself over. Life has lost its meaning for me now that it is no longer sustained by the hope of saving the Queen."

The Knight left the room without Maurice making a single move to stop him. He was barely out of the room when Geneviève threw herself at Maurice's feet.

"Forgive me," she begged. "Forgive me, Maurice, for all the wrong I have done you. Forgive me for all my deceit, forgive me in the name of all my suffering and my tears, for, I swear to you, I've nearly drowned in my tears, I've nearly died of suffering. Ah! My husband left this morning; I don't know where he's gone and perhaps I'll never see him again. And now a single friend remains to me—no, not a friend, a brother—and you're about to have him killed. Forgive me, Maurice! Forgive me!"

Maurice pulled her up off the floor.

"What do you expect?" he said. "It's fate. Everyone is playing for their lives now. The Knight of Maison-Rouge has played like all the rest, but he has lost. Now he has to pay."

"That is to say he'll die, if I understand you correctly."

"Yes."

"He has to die and you're the one who is telling me that?"

"It's not me, Geneviève; it's destiny."

"Destiny hasn't had the last word yet in this affair, for you can save him."

"At the cost of my word and so of my honor. I see, Geneviève."

"Close your eyes, Maurice, that's all I'm asking you to do; I promise you, I'll be as grateful as it is possible for a woman to be."

"I would close my eyes in vain, madame; there is a watchword, a watchword without which no one can get out of here; for, I repeat, the house is surrounded."

"But you know what it is?"

"Of course I know what it is."

"Maurice?"

"Well?"

"My friend, my dear Maurice, tell me the watchword, I must have it."

"Geneviève!" cried Maurice. "Geneviève! Who are you to come to me and say: Maurice, in the name of the love I feel for you, forgo your word, forgo your honor, betray your cause, renounce your beliefs? What are you offering me, Geneviève, in exchange for all that, you who are thus tempting me?"

"Oh, Maurice! Save him first, and then you can ask for my life."

"Geneviève," said Maurice in a somber voice, "listen to me: I have one foot on the road to infamy; to go down that road completely I need a good reason at least to defeat my own purpose and sink myself. Swear to me, Geneviève, you don't love the Knight of Maison-Rouge. . . ."

"I do love the Knight of Maison-Rouge, but like a sister, like a friend, not otherwise, I swear to you!"

"Geneviève, do you love me?"

"Maurice, I love you, as surely as God can hear me."

"If I do what you ask me to do, will you abandon family, friends, your country, to flee with such a traitor?"

"Maurice! Maurice!"

"She's hesitating. . . . Ah! She's got to think about it!"

With that Maurice jerked back with all the violence of disdain. With his support suddenly removed, Geneviève fell to her knees.

"Maurice," she said wringing her hands. "Maurice, I'll do anything you want, I swear; just say the word and I will obey."

"You will be mine, Geneviève?"

"Whenever you ask."

"Swear to Christ!"

Geneviève stretched out her arm. "My God!" she said. "You forgave the woman taken in adultery, I hope you will forgive me."

Enormous tears rolled down her cheeks and fell on long wisps of hair floating over her breasts.

"Oh, not like that!" cried Maurice. "How can I accept your vow now?"

"My God!" she started again. "I swear to consecrate my life to Maurice, to die with him, and if need be for him, if he saves my friend, my protector, my brother, the Knight of Maison-Rouge."

"That's enough! He will be saved," said Maurice. And he called the Knight.

"Monsieur," he said, "put Morand the tanner's outfit back on. I'm giving you back your word, you are free."

"And you, madame," he said to Geneviève, "here are the words: *Carnation and Underground Tunnel.*"

Then, as though he could not bear to remain in the room where he had pronounced the words that made him a traitor, he flung the window open and jumped from the room to the garden.

31

THE SEARCH

Maurice had resumed his position in the garden opposite Geneviève's casement window; but the light was now out. Geneviève had gone back in to the Knight of Maison-Rouge.

Maurice had fled just in time, for he had scarcely reached the hothouse when the garden door opened and the man in grey appeared, followed by Lorin and a handful of grenadiers.

"Well?" asked Lorin.

"As you can see," Maurice answered, "I'm at my post."

"No one has tried to force their way out?" asked Lorin.

"No one," Maurice answered, happy to have avoided telling a lie by the manner in which the question had been posed. "No one! What about you? What have you been up to?"

"We have confirmed with certainty that the Knight of Maison-Rouge entered this house one hour ago and has not come out since," answered the man from the police.

"And you know which is his room?" asked Lorin.

"His room is separated from citizeness Dixmer's only by a hallway."

"Aha!" said Lorin.

"There was no need for any separation at all: apparently this Knight of Maison-Rouge is a horny dog."

Maurice felt the blood rush to his head; he closed his eyes and a blaze of light hit his eyeballs.

"I see! But . . . what about citizen Dixmer? What did he have to say about that cozy arrangement?" asked Lorin.

"He felt rather honored."

"Right!" said Maurice in a strangled voice. "What have we decided?"

"We have decided," said the man from the police, "that we'll go and take him in his room, maybe even in his bed."

"He doesn't suspect anything?"

"Absolutely nothing."

"What is the layout of the terrain?" asked Lorin.

"We have a perfectly exact floor plan," said the grey man. "A pavilion is situated in one corner of the garden—there it is; you go up four steps—see them here? You find yourself on a landing. To the right, the door of citizeness Dixmer's apartment; no doubt that's it, where we can see the window. Opposite the window, at the back, there's a door opening onto the hall, and off the hall, the door of the traitor's room."

"Good, well, that's some map," said Lorin. "With a plan like that you could get around blindfolded, or better still with your eyes open. So let's go."

"Are the streets well-guarded?" asked Maurice with a keenness that all those present naturally attributed to the fear that the Knight would escape.

"Streets, passageways, crossroads, the whole shebang," said the grey man. "I defy a mouse to get through without the watchword."

Maurice shivered; all these precautions made him fear that his treason would not be crowned with bliss.

"Now," said the grey man, "how many men do you need to arrest the Knight?"

"How many men?" asked Lorin. "I certainly hope Maurice and I can do the trick on our own, eh, Maurice?"

"Yes," stammered Maurice, "I would think the two of us would be enough."

"Listen," said the man from the police, "no pointless boasting. Are you determined to nab him?"

"For heaven's sake! Are we determined?" cried Lorin. "I should think so! Eh, Maurice? We have to get him, don't we?"

Lorin emphasized the verb. As he had said, the beginnings of suspicion were hovering over them, and suspicion had to be given no time to take hold, for in those days it took no time at all for it to firm up into fact. Lorin knew that no one would dare doubt the patriotism of the two men who had managed to bag the Knight of Maison-Rouge.

"Well then!" said the man from the police. "If you really are determined, let's take three men rather than two with us, four rather than three; the Knight always sleeps with a sword under his pillow and two pistols on his night table."

"Damn!" said one of the grenadiers from Lorin's company. "Let's all go in, no special treatment for anyone. If he gives himself up, we'll hold him for the guillotine; if he resists, we'll rip him to shreds."

"Well said!" said Lorin. "Forward! Do we go through the door or the window?"

"Through the door," said the man from the police. "Maybe, if we're lucky, the key will be in it, whereas if we go in by the window we have to break a few panes, and that'll make a noise."

"The door it is!" said Lorin. "As long as we enter, who cares how? Off we go, sword in hand, Maurice."

Maurice drew his sword from its sheath mechanically. The small troop advanced toward the pavilion. They found everything as the man in grey had indicated, encountering first the front steps before finding themselves on the landing and then in the hallway.

"Ah!" cried Lorin gleefully. "The key is in the door!"

He had reached out in the dark and, incredibly, felt the cold metal of the key.

"What are we waiting for! Open up, citizen lieutenant!" said the grey man.

Lorin turned the key in the lock with care; the door opened. Maurice wiped his forehead, dripping with sweat.

"Here we are," said Lorin.

"Not yet," said the grey man. "If our topographical information is correct, we are now in the apartment of citizeness Dixmer."

"We can check," said Lorin. "Light some candles, there's still a bit of a fire in the grate."

"Let's light the torches," said the grey man. "Torches don't go out like candles."

He took two torches from the hands of a grenadier and lit them by the dying fire. He stuck one in Maurice's hand and the other in Lorin's.

"You see," he said, "I was not mistaken: here's the door that leads to citizeness Dixmer's bedroom and here's the one that leads to the hallway."

"Forward!" said Lorin. "Into the hallway!"

They opened the door at the back, which was no more locked than the first had been, and found themselves opposite the door to the Knight's apartment. Maurice had seen this door twenty times and had never asked where it led. For him, the world was centered on the salon where Geneviève received him.

"Oh! Oh!" Lorin whispered. "Here we change our tune; there is no key and the door is locked."

"But," croaked Maurice, barely able to speak, "are you sure this is the one?"

"If the plan is correct, this must be it," replied the man from the police. "Anyway, we'll soon see. Grenadiers, break the door down. And you, citizens, stand ready; as soon as the door's down, run into the room."

Four men designated by the police envoy raised the butts of their rifles and, at a sign from the man directing the show, struck the door with a single blow each: the door splintered and fell apart.

"Give yourself up or you're dead!" shouted Lorin, hurling himself into the room.

No one replied: the curtains on the bed were closed.

"The alley! Watch the alley!" cried the man from the police. "Take aim at the bed, and at the first signs of movement from behind the curtains, fire."

"Wait!" said Maurice. "I'll draw them."

With that, apparently in the hope that Maison-Rouge was hiding behind the curtains and that the first thrust of a dagger or shot of a pistol would have done him in, Maurice rushed at the curtains and flung them back squealing on their rod.

The bed was empty.

"Damn!" cried Lorin. "No one!"

"He must have got away," stammered Maurice.

"He can't have, citizens! It's not possible!" cried the grey man. "I tell you he was seen entering an hour ago and no one saw him come out; all the exits are guarded."

Lorin opened cabinets and cupboards and poked around everywhere, even where it was plainly impossible for a man to hide.

"No one! You see for yourself: no one!"

"No one," repeated Maurice with an emotion easy to understand. "You can see for yourself, in fact, there is no one."

"Citizeness Dixmer's room!" said the man from the police. "Maybe he's there?"

"Oh!" Maurice protested. "Surely we should respect a woman's bedroom."

"What are you talking about?" said Lorin. "Certainly we'll respect it, and citizeness Dixmer too, but we'll enter all the same."

"Enter citizeness Dixmer?" snickered one of the grenadiers, delighted to crack a rude joke.

"No," said Lorin, "just the room."

"Well then," said Maurice, "let me go first."

"Go on," said Lorin, "you're the captain: honor where honor is due."

They left two men behind to guard the room and went back to the room where they had lit the torches. Maurice approached the door leading to Geneviève's bedroom.

It was the first time he would be entering it. His heart was beating like a hammer. The key was in the door. Maurice brought his hand to the key, but then hesitated.

"Well then," said Lorin, "open it!"

"But what if citizeness Dixmer is asleep in bed?"

"We'll look in her bed, under her bed, up her chimney, and in her cupboards," said Lorin. "After that, if there's no one but her, we'll wish her good night."

"No, we won't," said the man from the police. "We'll arrest her. Citizeness Geneviève Dixmer was an aristocrat who has been recognized as the accomplice of the Tison girl and the Knight of Maison-Rouge."

"You open up then," said Maurice, handing over the key. "I don't arrest women."

The man from the police gave Maurice a sidelong glance, and the grenadiers muttered among themselves.

"Oh! So you're whispering now?" said Lorin. "Whisper for the two of us, then, while you're at it. I share Maurice's view." And he took a step back.

The grey man grabbed the key and turned it sharply, and the door yielded. The soldiers rushed into the room. Two candles were burning on a small table, but Geneviève's room, like that of the Knight of Maison-Rouge, was uninhabited.

"Empty!" cried the man from the police.

"Empty!" cried Maurice, turning pale. "Where can she be?"

Lorin looked at Maurice in shock.

"Search!" said the man from the police. With the militia in tow, he began to turn the entire house upside down, from the cellars to the workshops.

Scarcely had they turned their backs when Maurice, who had watched them go with great impatience, also launched himself into the bedroom, opening cupboards he had already opened and calling in a voice full of anguish, "Geneviève! Geneviève!"

But Geneviève did not reply. Her room really was empty. Maurice also began to comb the entire house in a sort of frenzy. Hothouses, sheds, outhouses, he went through the lot, but in vain.

Suddenly a great commotion was heard: a troop of armed men presented themselves at the door, exchanged the password with the sentry, and immediately invaded the garden before spreading through the house. At the head of the reinforcements shone the plumed panache of Santerre.

"Well then!" he said to Lorin. "Where is the conspirator?"

"What do you mean, where is the conspirator?"

"I'm asking you what you've done with him!"

"I might ask you yourself: if your detachment had been guarding the exits properly they would surely have arrested him, since he was no longer in the house when we went in."

"What are you saying, there?" cried the furious general. "You mean you let him get away?"

"We couldn't let him get away, since we never had him to begin with."

"Then I don't get it," said Santerre.

"What?"

"What you said to me through your envoy."

"We sent you an envoy, did we?"

"Of course you did. That fellow with the brown coat and the black hair and green glasses who came to alert us on your behalf that you were on the point of nabbing Maison-Rouge but that he was defending himself like a lion. When I heard that, I came running."

"A fellow in a brown coat, black hair, and green glasses?" Lorin repeated.

"No doubt about it, with a woman on his arm."

"Young, pretty?" cried Maurice rushing over to the general.

"Young, pretty. Yes."

"It was the man himself and citizeness Dixmer."

"What man?"

"Maison-Rouge . . . Oh! Miserable wretch that I am not to have killed both of them!"

"Come, come, citizen Lindey," said Santerre. "We'll catch up with them."

"But how the hell did you let them pass?" said Lorin.

"Hell's bells!" said Santerre. "I let them pass because they had the password."

"They had the password!" cried Lorin. "But that means there's a traitor among us!"

"No, no, citizen," said Santerre. "Everyone knows who you are, and we know there are no traitors among you."

Lorin looked all around him as though searching for the traitor whose existence he had just proclaimed. He met the somber brow and vacillating gaze of Maurice.

"Oh!" he murmured to himself. "What can this this mean?"

"The man can't be far," said Santerre. "Turn the neighborhood inside out. Maybe he's fallen into the hands of some patrol cleverer than us who won't have let themselves be had."

"Yes, yes; we'll keep looking," said Lorin.

He grabbed Maurice by the arm and dragged him out of the garden on the pretext of continuing the search.

"Yes, we'll keep looking," chimed the soldiers, "but before we go . . ."

And with that, one of them chucked his torch under the shed where the chopped wood was piled along with stacks of kindling.

"Come away," said Lorin. "Come."

Maurice put up no resistance. He followed Lorin like a child; they both ran as far as the bridge without exchanging a single word further. There they stopped and Maurice turned around. The sky was red at the horizon of the faubourg, and thousands of sparks could be seen dancing over the houses.

32

Faith Sworn

Maurice shuddered from head to toe and pointed to the rue Saint-Jacques.

"Fire!" he cried. "Fire!"

"Well, yes," said Lorin. "Fire. So?"

"Oh, my God! My God! What if she came back?"

"If who came back?"

"Geneviève."

"Geneviève: that's Madame Dixmer, isn't it?"

"Yes, that's her."

"There's no danger of that, she didn't leave just to come back again."

"Lorin, I've got to find her, I've got to avenge myself."

"Oh, no!" said Lorin.

> "Love, tyrant of gods and mortals,
>   It's no longer incense you need on your altars."

"You'll help me find her, won't you, Lorin?"

"Good heavens! That won't be hard."

"How do you mean?"

"Obviously, if you're so interested in the fate of citizeness Dixmer, and it certainly looks like you are from where I'm standing, you must know her; and if you know her, you must know who her closest friends are. She won't have left Paris; they're all desperate to stay in town. She's taken refuge with some confidante, and tomorrow morning you'll receive via some Rose or some Chrysanthemum a little note more or less along these lines:

"If Mars wants to see Cythera again
Let him borrow Night's azured shawl.

And let him present himself at the concierge's office at such and such a number of such and such a street and ask for Madame Trois-Etoiles. Voilà."

Maurice shrugged his shoulders. He knew only too well that Geneviève had nowhere to go.

"We won't find her," he murmured.

"Allow me to tell you something, Maurice," said Lorin.

"What?"

"That it may not be such a bad thing if we don't find her."

"If we don't find her, Lorin," said Maurice bleakly, "I will die."

"Oh, Christ!" said the young man. "So this is the woman you nearly died of love for?"

"Yes," answered Maurice.

Lorin thought for a moment.

"Maurice," he said, "it must be about eleven o'clock, the place is deserted, there's a bench over there that looks as though it was made for a couple of pals like us to sit on. Grant me the favor of an intimate interview, as they used to say under the ancien régime. I give you my word I'll speak only in prose."

Maurice looked around him and finally plunked down next to his friend.

"Speak," said Maurice, dropping his heavy head into his hands.

"Listen, dear friend, without exordium, without periphrasis, without commentary, I'll tell you something: we are sinking, or rather you are sinking us."

"How do you mean?"

"There is, tenderhearted friend," Lorin went on, "a certain decree of the Committee of Public Safety that declares a traitor to the nation anyone who maintains relations with the enemies of said nation. Eh? You are familiar with this decree?"

"Naturally," said Maurice.

"You're sure you know the one?"

"Yes."

"Well then! It seems to me you're not a bad candidate as a traitor to your nation. What do you say to that, as Manlius Capitolinus would say?"

"Lorin!"

"Seems fairly cut and dried—unless you regard as idolizing the nation those who give bed and board to Monsieur the Knight of Maison-Rouge, who is not quite the zealous republican, it would seem; not actually accused, for the moment at least, of having carried out the September massacres."

"Ah, Lorin!" Maurice sighed.

"So it looks to me," the moralist continued, "like you have been, and still are, a little too chummy with the enemy of the nation. Wake up, Maurice, don't give up the fight, dear friend. You're like old Enceladus[1]—you'd move a mountain if you rolled over. So I repeat, don't give up the fight, just admit openly you're no longer a zealot."

Lorin had said these words with all the gentleness he was capable of, glossing over the whole thing with an artfulness worthy of Cicero. Maurice contented himself with a gesture of protest. But the gesture was declared null and void, and Lorin continued:

"Oh! If we lived in some controlled hothouse climate, a forthright, honest climate, where the barometer invariably sat on sixteen degrees Celsius according to the laws of botany, I'd say to you, my dear Maurice, how elegant, how just the ticket; let's be a bit aristocratic from time to time, it does you good and it smells so nice. But we're frying today in thirty-five to forty degree heat! The tablecloth is burning—next to it anyone is merely lukewarm; compared with that kind of heat anyone looks cold. And when one is cold, one is suspect. You know that as well as I do, Maurice. And when one is suspect—you have too much intelligence not to see, my dear Maurice, not to know what one is shortly after that. Or, rather, what one no longer is."

"Well then! So! Let them kill me and get it over with!" cried Maurice. "I'm tired of living anyway."

"For the last quarter of an hour!" said Lorin. "Actually, we don't have enough time left for me to let you have your way; then again, when a person dies these days, you understand, it has to be as a republican, whereas you would die an aristocrat."

"Oh! Christ!" Maurice exploded, his blood beginning to boil thanks to the agonizing pain caused by consciousness of his own guilt. "Christ! You're going too far, my friend."

"I'll go further still, for, I warn you, if you turn yourself into an aristocrat . . ."

"You'll denounce me?"

"Honestly! No! But I'll lock you in a cellar and make them search for you to the sound of drums, like some missing object. Then I'll declare that the aristocrats, knowing what you had in store for them, have sequestered you, starved you, martyred you; so that when they find you, you'll be crowned publicly with flowers, like the Provost de Beaumont, Monsieur Latude, et al., by the ladies of Les Halles[2] and the ragpickers of the Victor section. So hurry up and start acting like Aristides again or the outcome is a foregone conclusion."

"Lorin, Lorin, I know you're right, but I'm being dragged down, I'm sliding downhill. Do you hold it against me if fate is dragging me down?"

"I don't hold it against you, but I will pull you back up. Remember the trouble Pylades kicked up for Orestes on a daily basis? Proving triumphantly that friendship is nothing if not a paradox, since such model friends bicker and fight from morning to night."

"Forget me, Lorin, you'd be better off."

"Never!"

"Then let me love and go insane at my leisure; I may even be a criminal, for if I see her again I feel I might well murder her."

"Or fall at her feet . . . Ah, Maurice! Maurice in love with an aristocrat: who'd have thought it! You're like that pathetic Osselin, member of the Convention, who fell in love with the marquise de Charny."[3]

"That's enough, Lorin, please."

"Maurice, I'll get you over it or rot in hell. I don't want you to win Sainte Guillotine's lottery, that I do not, as the grocer of the rue des Lombards would say. Watch you don't push me too far, Maurice. You'll turn me into a blood drinker. Maurice, I feel the need to set fire to the île Saint Louis: a torch, a firebrand!

       "But no, I should just quiet down.
         Why demand a torch, a flambeau?

> Your fire's enough, Maurice, you beau
> To burn your soul, this place, the town."

Maurice couldn't help but smile in spite of himself.

"You know we agreed to speak only in prose?" he said.

"Yes, but you exasperate me with your madness," said Lorin. "And . . . here, come and have a drink, Maurice. Let's get sozzled, let's move motions, and study political economics. But for the love of Jupiter, don't let's be in love, let's love only liberty."

"Or Reason."

"Ah! Good point! By the way, the goddess sends you her greetings and finds you a charming mortal."

"And you're not jealous?"

"Maurice, to save a friend, I feel myself capable of any sacrifice."

"Thank you, my poor Lorin, I do appreciate your devotion. But the best way for me to console myself, you see, is to drown in my suffering. Adieu, Lorin, go and see Artemisia."

"What about you? Where are you going?"

"I'm going home."

Maurice did take a few steps toward the bridge.

"So you've moved to the old rue Saint-Jacques now, have you?"

"No, but that's the way I feel like going."

"To see where your inhuman friend used to live one more time?"

"To see if she's come back where she knows I'll be waiting for her. Oh, Geneviève! Geneviève! I would never have believed you capable of such betrayal!"

"Maurice, a tyrant who knew the fair sex well,[4] since he died from having loved too many of them, once said:

> "Woman is so apt to change
> Whoever trusts her is completely deranged."

Maurice gave a sigh and the two friends walked back toward the old rue Saint-Jacques. The closer they got, the louder the noise; they saw the light grow brighter, they heard the patriotic songs that, in daylight, in full sunshine, in the atmosphere of combat, came across as heroic hymns, but which at night, by the light of a raging inferno, took on the lugubrious tones of some cannibalistic intoxication rite.

"Oh, my God! My God!" cried Maurice, forgetting God had been abolished.

And he forged ahead, sweat streaming from his brow. Lorin watched him go and murmured between clenched teeth:

> "Love, Love, when you take hold of us:
> We might as well say adieu prudence."

All of Paris seemed to be flocking to the theater of the events we have just described. Maurice was forced to plow through a hedgerow of grenadiers, ranks of section members, and then the pushing and shoving throngs of a populace that, in those days, was always in a fury, always on the alert, hurtling, screaming, from one spectacle to the next.

As he got closer, Maurice sped up in his crazed anxiety, leaving Lorin to keep pace with him as best he could; but Lorin loved him too much to leave him on his own at such a moment.

The show was almost over when they got there. The fire had spread from the shed where the soldier had thrown his flaming torch to the workshops, built of weatherboard and so assembled as to leave decent air vents; all the stock and merchandise had burned to ash, and now the house itself was starting to go up.

"Oh, my God!" Maurice said to himself. "What if she came back, what if she was in one of the rooms, encircled by flames, waiting for me, calling out to me. . . ."

And, half out of his mind with misery, preferring to believe in the madness of the woman he loved rather than in her treachery, Maurice launched himself headfirst at the pavilion door, which he could just make out through the smoke.

Lorin was still following behind; he would have followed Maurice to hell.

The roof was ablaze; the fire was beginning to spread to the stairs.

Maurice, panting, combed the first floor, the salon, Geneviève's bedroom, the bedroom of the Knight of Maison-Rouge, the hallways, calling out in a choking voice:

"Geneviève! Geneviève!"

No one answered.

Going back to the first room, the two friends saw gusts of flames lapping around the door. Despite Lorin shouting directions to the window, Maurice passed through the flames.

Then he ran to the house and crossed the courtyard strewn with broken furniture, found the dining room, Dixmer's salon, the cabinet of Morand the chemist; all of it full of smoke, debris, shattered glass, but Maurice would stop for nothing. The fire had just reached this part of the house too, and swiftly began to devour it.

He did what he had done in the pavilion, searching every room, every hall and recess, and then went down to the cellars, imagining perhaps that Geneviève had taken refuge from the fire below ground.

But there was no one.

"Damn!" cried Lorin. "You can see for yourself that no one could hold out here, except perhaps for a few salamanders, and I don't think that's the fabulous creature you're looking for. Come on, let's get out of here. We'll ask around, we'll find out from all these gawkers whether anyone has seen her."

Wild horses could not have dragged Maurice away from the house. Only hope, to which he clung by a thread, was able to drag him out and back onto the street to begin investigations. They combed the whole area, stopping any women passing by, scouring the myriad alleyways, but to no avail. It was one o'clock in the morning. Despite his athletic vigor, Maurice was shattered with fatigue. He finally gave up running around, going up and down, endlessly battling the crowd. A fiacre came along; Lorin flagged it down.

"My dear Maurice," he said, "we've done all that is humanly possible to find your Geneviève. We've worn ourselves out; we've gotten ourselves scorched; we've gotten ourselves beaten up for her. Cupid may be demanding, but he can't demand any more than that from a man in love, and especially from one who's not. Let's get in the fiacre and let's both go home to bed."

Maurice did not reply, he just let himself go with it. They arrived at his door without exchanging another word. The moment Maurice got out of the cab, a window of his apartment could be heard shutting.

"Oh, good! They've waited up for you. I feel happier about that. Now knock."

Maurice knocked and the door opened.

"Good night!" said Lorin. "Wait for me in the morning before you go out."

"Good night," Maurice said, like a zombie. And the door closed behind him.

On the very first flight of steps he ran into his officieux.

"Oh, citizen Lindey!" the man cried. "We've been so worried about you!"

Maurice was struck by the word *we*.

"We?" he asked.

"Yes, me and the little lady who's waiting for you."

"The little lady!" Maurice repeated, thinking it was a bad moment for one of his old flames to turn up. "I'm glad you told me; I'll go sleep at Lorin's."

"Oh, no, you can't. She was at the window, she saw you get out of the cab, and she cried out: 'There he is!'"

"Hmmph. What's it to me if she knows it's me; I don't have the heart to make love! Go back up and tell this woman she was mistaken."

The officieux turned to obey, then stopped.

"Oh, citizen! This isn't right! The little lady is already so sad; if I tell her that, she'll despair."

"Who on earth is this woman?" Maurice asked.

"Citizen, I didn't see her face; she's all wrapped up in a cloak and she's in tears; that's all I know."

"In tears!" Maurice exclaimed.

"Yes, just quietly, putting on a brave show, trying to hold back her sobs."

"In tears," Maurice repeated. "So there is someone in the world who loves me enough to worry about my absence to the point of tears?"

He climbed the stairs slowly behind the officieux.

"Here he is, citizeness, here he is!" cried the officieux, rushing into the room.

Maurice came in behind him. He spotted a quivering heap in the corner with her face buried in cushions, a woman you'd have thought was dead if it weren't for the convulsive moans that racked her.

He signaled to his officieux to leave. The man obeyed, shutting the door behind him. Maurice ran to her and lifted up her head.

"Geneviève!" he cried. "Geneviève, you're here, at my place! Have I gone mad, God?"

"No, you haven't lost your mind, my friend," replied the young woman. "I promised you I'd be yours if you saved the Knight of Maison-Rouge. You saved him, so here I am! I've been waiting for you."

Maurice misunderstood. He stepped back and looked at her sadly.

"Geneviève," he said softly, "so you don't love me?"

Geneviève's gaze was clouded with tears. She turned her head away and, leaning against the back of the sofa, burst out crying again.

"Alas!" said Maurice. "You see for yourself you don't love me anymore; and not only don't you love me anymore, Geneviève, but you must feel something like hate for me to despair like this."

Maurice packed so much exhilaration and pain into these last words that Geneviève sat up and took his hand.

"My God!" she said. "Must the man I think of as the best of men always be such an egotist!"

"An egotist, Geneviève? What do you mean?"

"But don't you understand what I'm going through? My husband has flown the coop, my brother's been outlawed, my house is in flames—all that in one night—and then that horrible scene between you and the Knight!"

Maurice listened to her enraptured, for it was impossible, even under the influence of the maddest passion, not to accept that such accumulated griefs could lead to the state of pain Geneviève was in.

"So you have come, you are here, I'm holding you, you won't leave me again!"

Geneviève shivered.

"Where else could I have gone?" she replied with a flash of bitterness. "Do I have a refuge, a safe place, a protector other than a man who named a price for his protection? Oh, I was wild with rage, Maurice. I ran onto the Pont-Neuf and stopped to look at the black water swirling around the arches below; and I have to say it drew me, mesmerized me. The jig is up for you, you poor woman, I said to myself. There lies shelter, down there. There lies inviolable rest. There lies oblivion."

"Geneviève! Geneviève!" cried Maurice. "Is that what you thought? . . . So you don't love me?"

"I told you," Geneviève whispered. "I told you, and I came."

Maurice let out a breath and let himself slide to her feet.

"Geneviève," he murmured, "stop crying, Geneviève. Console yourself for all your misfortune, since you love me. In the name of heaven, Geneviève, tell me it's not the violence of my threats that brought you here. Tell me that even if you hadn't seen me tonight, finding yourself alone, on your own, without a refuge, you would have come to me; and accept the vow I'm making now to release you from the oath I made you swear."

Geneviève gazed down upon Maurice with an ineffable expression of gratitude in her eyes.

"So generous!" she said. "Thank you, God, for making him so generous!"

"Listen, Geneviève," said Maurice. "They may be hunting God out of the temples here, but they can't hunt Him out of our hearts, where he has put love; and it's God who has made tonight look so dark and gloomy on the surface, but underneath it's sparkling with joy and happiness. God has led you to me, Geneviève; He has placed you in my arms. He speaks to you through my breath. God, God Himself, finally wants to reward us for all the suffering we've endured, all the virtue we have shown in fighting a love that seemed illicit—as though a feeling so lastingly pure and deep could be a crime! So don't cry anymore, Geneviève, dry your eyes! Give me your hand. Do you want to feel like you're in a brother's house? Do you want this brother to kiss the hem of your dress and leave you alone? Do you want him to say a prayer for you and go out the door without so much as a backward glance? Well then! Just say the word, give me a sign and I'll go; you'll be alone, free and safe as a virgin in a church. But if, on the other hand, my adored Geneviève, you care to remember that I've loved you so much I nearly died of it, that because of this love, which you could make fatal or a source of bliss, I've betrayed my own people, I've made myself odious and vile even to myself—then think of all the happiness the future holds for us, of the strength and energy we have because we're young and in love and we can defend our dawning happiness against whoever and whatever tries to attack it! Oh, Geneviève! You, you who are an angel of goodness, tell me—is this what you want? Do you want to make one man so happy he'll stop regretting this life and looking forward to eternal happiness in the next? Well then, if you do, stop pushing me away. Give me a smile, my Geneviève, let me put your hand on my heart. Come to me. I long for you with all my strength, all my desire, all my soul. Geneviève, my love, my life; Geneviève, don't take back your vow!"

The young woman's heart soared at these words: the languor of love, combined with the fatigue of all her suffering, overcame all her resistance; the tears no longer sprang to her eyes, and yet her burning breast still heaved with stifled sobs.

Maurice sensed she no longer had the courage to resist; he seized her in his arms. She dropped her head on his shoulder and her long hair spilled down over the fiery cheeks of her lover.

At the same time Maurice felt her breast rise, heaving like waves after a storm.

"Oh! You're crying again, Geneviève," he said with deep sadness. "You're crying. Oh, don't worry! I will never force myself where I'm not wanted. My lips will never besmirch themselves with a kiss that a single tear of regret would poison."

With that he pulled his arms from around her, he unlocked his brow from hers and slowly turned away. But immediately, in one of those reactions that come so naturally to a woman who defends herself while feeling acute desire, Geneviève threw her trembling arms around Maurice's neck, pressed herself against him violently, and plastered her cheek, still cold and wet with tears, against his burning face.

"Oh!" she murmured. "Don't abandon me, Maurice, you're all I have left in the world!"

33

THE MORNING AFTER

Golden sunshine streamed through the green shutters, gilding the leaves of three tall rose trees standing in wooden boxes on Maurice's windowsill.

The roses were all the more precious since the season was almost over. Their perfume filled the air of a small, stone-floored, sparkling clean dining room where Geneviève and Maurice had just sat down to a table sparsely but elegantly laden.

The door was closed, for the table held everything the couple could want. And naturally they had both agreed to serve themselves.

Yet the officieux could be heard bustling about in the room next door, all in a flurry, like Phedra's Ardelio. The heat and vibrancy of the last lovely days of summer filtered through the shutters along with the light, making the sun-kissed rose leaves glimmer like gold and emeralds.

Geneviève dropped the fruit she was holding onto her plate and smiled dreamily, but with her mouth only, while her great big eyes drooped forlornly; she remained silent, numb, even though she was alive and happy and basking in the sunshine of love as the gorgeous roses were soaking up the sunshine from the sky above.

Her eyes soon sought those of Maurice, which she found fixed on her; he was gazing at her and dreaming. She stretched her arm, so soft, so luminously white, and draped it across the young man's shoulder, causing him to shudder with pleasure; then she leaned her head there with that confidence and abandon that are so much more than love.

Geneviève returned his gaze in silence and blushed. Maurice had only to incline his head slightly for his lips to press the open lips of his lover; he inclined his head. The color drained from Geneviève's face, and her eyes closed like the petals of a flower hiding its inner cup from the rays of the sun.

They were still in this half-asleep state, enjoying unaccustomed bliss, when the sharp noise of the doorbell made them jump. They leapt apart as the officieux entered and mysteriously shut the door.

"It's citizen Lorin," he said.

"Ah! Good old Lorin," said Maurice. "I'll go and get rid of him. Excuse me, Geneviève."

Geneviève stopped him.

"Get rid of your friend, Maurice!" she said. "A friend, a friend who has comforted you, helped you, supported you? No, I don't want to chase such a friend from your house any more than your heart. Let him in, Maurice, let him in."

"Really? You don't mind?"

"I want him to come in," said Geneviève.

"Oh! So you don't think I love you enough," cried Maurice, delighted by this delicacy. "You want to be idolized."

Geneviève flushed and gave Maurice a nod; Maurice opened the door and Lorin strode in, beautiful as the day in his foppish muscadin getup. Seeing Geneviève, he showed surprise but swiftly followed this with a respectful greeting.

"Come, Lorin, come," said Maurice, "you see madame. You've been dethroned, Lorin; there is now someone I prefer to you. I would have given my life for you. For her—I'm not telling you anything you don't already know, Lorin, I know—but for her I've given my honor."

"Madame," said Lorin with a gravity that betrayed profound emotion, "I'll try to love Maurice more than you do so he won't stop loving me completely."

"Please sit down, monsieur," said Geneviève, smiling.

"Yes, do sit down," said Maurice, who had just given his friend his right hand and Geneviève his left, and so was brimming with all the joy a man can hope for in this world.

"So you're not thinking about throwing in the towel and curling up your toes anymore? You no longer want to get yourself killed?"

"What do you mean?" asked Geneviève.

"Oh, God!" said Lorin. "What a versatile animal man is; philosophers are right to despise his flightiness! Here's a man, if you can believe it, madame, who only last night wanted to throw himself in the river and drown; who declared there was no happiness left on Earth for him. And here I find him this morning gay as a lark, jubilant, a smile on his lips, happiness on his brow, life in his heart, before a well-laden table. True, he's not eating, but that doesn't mean he's unhappy about it all."

"Really!" said Geneviève. "Was it that bad?"

"Worse. I'll tell you all about it later. Right now I'm starving. It's Maurice's fault, he had me running all over the quartier Saint-Jacques last night. Allow me to dig into your breakfast, which I see neither of you has touched."

"You know, he's right!" cried Maurice, with infantile joy. "Let's eat. I haven't had a thing and neither have you, Geneviève."

He glanced at Lorin when he said her name, but Lorin didn't bat an eye.

"So you guessed it was her? Really?" he asked Lorin.

"It wasn't exactly hard!" replied Lorin, cutting himself a thick slice of rosy ham.

"I'm hungry too," said Geneviève, holding out her plate.

"Lorin," said Maurice, "last night I was sick, you know."

"You were more than sick, you were out of your mind."

"So be it! But I think it's you who aren't feeling well this morning."

"How do you mean?"

"You haven't yet made up a rhyme."

"I was just getting around to it, this very instant," said Lorin.

> "When he sits among the Graces
>   Phoebus always strums his lyre;
> But when he follows Venus's traces
>   Phoebus of music can quickly tire."

"That's more like it! He's always got a quatrain up his sleeve!" laughed Maurice.

"But you'll have to make do with that one, since we're about to broach matters that aren't so gay."

"What is it now?" asked Maurice anxiously.

"What it is is that I'll soon be on guard duty at the Conciergerie."

"At the Conciergerie!" cried Geneviève. "Near the Queen?"

"Near the Queen . . . I think so, yes, madame."

Geneviève went pale. Maurice frowned and made a sign to Lorin, who cut himself another slice of ham, twice the size of the first.

The Queen had, in fact, been conducted to the Conciergerie, where we will now follow her.

34

The Conciergerie

At the corner of the pont-au-Change and the quai aux Fleurs, where the flower market is, sit the remains of the old palace of Saint Louis,[1] which was known as the Palace par excellence, just as Rome was once called the Capital; it continues to bear this sovereign name even though, for some time now, the only kings to inhabit it are clerks of the court, judges, and litigants.

It is a huge and somber palace, the Palais de Justice, promoting fear rather than love of that harsh goddess. On show there you'll find all the paraphernalia of human vengeance brought together in one compact space. Here are the rooms where they hold those charged and awaiting trial; further along are the rooms where they are judged; below that the cells where they are locked up when they have been condemned; at the door the small space where they are branded with an abominable branding iron that burns; and a hundred and fifty paces away from the main square lies that other, larger square where they are killed. This is the place de Grève,[2] where what is begun in the Palais de Justice is finished off.

Justice, as you can see, has everything to hand.

This whole pile of buildings heaped on top of one another, mournful, grey, pierced by tiny barred windows, where the cavernous vaults resemble the iron-barred caves along the quai des Lunettes—this is the Conciergerie.

The prison has dungeons that the waters of the Seine regularly slosh with black alluvium. It has mysterious exits that once ejected into the river victims it was in certain interests to make disappear.

From the perspective of 1793, as tireless purveyor of victims for the scaffold, the Conciergerie was, you might say, overflowing with prisoners who could be turned into the condemned in an hour at most. In those days, the old prison of Saint Louis really meant business—as the leader in the death trade.

Under the archway over the entrance, at night, a red lantern swung as sinister ensign of this house of horrors.

The day before the day when Maurice, Lorin, and Geneviève breakfasted together, a heavy sound of rolling wheels shook the cobblestones of the quai de l'Horloge and the prison windows. The rolling stopped in front of the ogival door. Gendarmes banged on the door with the scabbards of their sabers, the door opened, and the carriage rolled into the courtyard; with the door firmly shut behind her and the bolts shot home, a woman descended.

She was immediately swallowed up by the cavernous registration office. A few curious heads bobbed up, creeping forward to check out the prisoner by the light of their torches, and appeared in halftones before plunging back into darkness. Then a few vulgar guffaws could be heard, along with crude farewells batted about by men leaving the building who could be heard but not seen.

The woman brought in had remained penned inside the first wicket with the gendarmes. She could see that she had to go through a second wicket, but she did not realize that she needed to pick her feet up and lower her head at the same time, for suddenly a step comes up at you from ground level right where the ceiling descends.

Still unused to prison architecture, no doubt, despite the prolonged stay she had already enjoyed in one, the prisoner forgot to duck and banged her head violently against the iron beam.

"Did you hurt yourself, citizeness?" one of the gendarmes asked.

But the woman moved on without a murmur of complaint, even though her forehead clearly bore the mark of contact with the iron beam and looked about to bleed.

Soon the concierge's armchair could be made out, an armchair more venerable in the eyes of prisoners than a king's throne is in the eyes of courtesans, for the concierge of a prison is the dispenser of favors and every favor is vital for a prisoner, for often the slightest favor changes his or her gloomy sky into a luminous firmament.

Richard,[3] the concierge, was comfortably ensconced in his armchair, and though thoroughly convinced of his importance he had not budged an inch, despite the clanging of the gates and the rolling of the carriage, which announced the arrival of his new guest. Richard the concierge took up his tobacco, eyed the prisoner, opened a great walloping register, and hunted around for a quill on a small black wooden inkstand, where the ink, solidified around the edges, still preserved a bit of moist sludge in the middle, just as there is always a bit of molten matter in the middle of a volcano's crater.

"Citizen concierge," said the chief of the escort, "do the committal on this one for us and make it snappy—they're waiting impatiently for us in the Commune."

"Oh! It won't take long!" said the concierge, pouring into his inkpot a few drops of the dregs of the wine in his glass. "My hand's made for the job, thank the Lord! Your surname and Christian name, citizeness?"

Dipping his pen in the improvised ink, he prepared to squeeze in at the bottom of a page that was already practically full the committal details of the new inmate, while the benign-looking citizeness Richard stood behind him, gazing with open-mouthed amazement that bordered on respect at the woman her husband was questioning—a woman who looked so sad, so noble, and so proud at once.

"Marie Antoinette Jeanne Josèphe de Lorraine," the prisoner replied, "Archduchess of Austria and Queen of France."

"Queen of France," the concierge repeated, gripping the arms of his chair and hoisting himself up in amazement.

"Queen of France," repeated the prisoner in the same uninflected tone.

"In other words, Widow Capet,"[4] said the chief of the escort.

"Which of the names will I list her as?" asked the concierge.

"Whichever you like," said the chief escort, "as long as you list her pronto."

The concierge fell back into his chair and, with some trepidation, wrote in his register the Christian names, surname, and titles that the prisoner had given herself, listings whose reddish ink can still be seen today, though the rats of the revolutionary Conciergerie have gnawed the page at the most precious spot in all the register.

Mother Richard went on standing behind her husband's armchair; but a feeling of religious commiseration had caused her to join her hands in an attitude of prayer.

"Your age?" continued the concierge.

"Thirty-seven years and nine months," replied the Queen.

Richard began writing again, then listed the details of her physical features and ended with general formulae and personal notes.

"Right!" he said. "Done!"

"Where are we taking the prisoner?" asked the chief of the escort.

Richard took a second pinch of tobacco and looked at his wife.

"Blast!" said the woman. "We weren't notified, so heaven knows. . . ."

"Find somewhere!" said the brigadier.

"There's the Council Chamber," ventured Madame Richard.

"Hmmm. That's on the spacious side," muttered Richard.

"So much the better if it is! All the more room to lodge the guards there."

"The Council Chamber it is, then," said Richard. "But it's uninhabitable for the present, as it doesn't have a bed."

"True," said his wife, "I didn't think of that."

"Bah!" went one of the gendarmes. "We'll put a bed in there tomorrow, and tomorrow will soon be upon us."

"In any case, the citizeness can spend the night in our room," said Madame Richard.

"Oh, yes, and what about us?" asked her husband.

"We won't go to bed; like the citizen gendarme says, a night is soon over."

"Well, then," said Richard, "take the citizeness to my room."

"While we're doing that, you'll get the receipt ready for us, won't you?"

"It'll be here when you get back."

Madame Richard took a candle that was burning on the table and led the way. Marie Antoinette followed without a word, composed and pale as ever. Two wicket clerks to whom Madame Richard signaled closed off the stairs. The Queen was shown a bed, which Madame Richard promptly made up with fresh white sheets. The clerks stationed themselves at the exits, and then the door was locked with a double lock and Marie Antoinette found herself alone.

How she passed that night no one knows, for she passed it face-to-face with God.

It was only the next day that the Queen was taken to the Council Chamber, an extended rectangular box whose wicket gate opened onto a corridor of the Conciergerie and which was divided into two sections lengthwise by a half-curtain partition that did not come up to the ceiling.

The men on guard duty took over the outer section. The other became the Queen's bedroom.

A thickly barred window let light into each of the two sections. A screen was used as a door, separating the Queen from the guards and closing off the opening between the two cells. The entire chamber was tiled with clay bricks. The walls had once been decorated with gilt wood paneling and fleur-de-lys[5] wallpaper, and strips of paper still hung raggedly here and there.

A bed set up facing the window, a chair placed close to the screen— such was the furnishing of the royal prison cell.

On entering the room, the Queen asked to be brought her books and her needlework. She was brought *Les Révolutions d'Angleterre,* which she had begun at the Temple, as well as *Le Voyage du jeune Anarcharsis*[6] and her tapestry.

The gendarmes settled into the neighboring cell, for their part. History has preserved their names, as it does all the most insignificant beings whom Providence associates with great catastrophes and who see reflected on themselves a spark of that luminous energy that causes thunder as it smashes either the thrones of kings or the kings themselves.

The Commune had appointed these two men as brave patriots; they were supposed to remain at their fixed post in the cell until Marie Antoinette's judgment. It was hoped that this expedient would prevent the almost inevitable hitches of shift duty with guards changing several times a day. Thus the two guards had had a terrible responsibility thrust upon them.

The Queen learned of this arrangement the very day it came into play through the conversation between the two men, whose every word reached her unless they had some special reason for lowering their voices. She felt both anxiety and joy when she heard about it, for if, on the one hand, she was bound to realize that the two men must be rock solid if they had been selected from among so many men, she reflected that, on the other, it would be easier for her friends to corrupt two known guards at a fixed post than a hundred unknown men picked at random and coming into her orbit unexpectedly and for just a day at a time.

The first night, before getting into bed, one of the guards had a smoke, as was his habit. The tobacco smoke slid through the gaps in the partition and laid siege to the unhappy Queen, whose sufferings had exacerbated her sensitivities rather than blunting them. She soon found herself seized by the vapors and nausea; her head was heavy with lack of oxygen. But, faithful to her policy of indomitable pride, she did not complain.

As she lay awake, with an insomnia brought on by her physical ills, listening to the undisturbed silence of the night, she thought she heard a whine coming from outside. The whine was mournful and prolonged; it was eerie and piercing, like the noise of wind whistling through deserted passages when a tempest borrows a human voice to breathe life into the passions of the elements.

She soon recognized that this noise that had at first made her start, this painful and persistent cry, was the mournful lament of a dog howling on the quai. She immediately thought of her poor Black, whom she had forgotten while being shunted from the Temple and whose voice she felt she recognized. Indeed, the poor animal whose excessive vigilance had given his mistress away had followed behind her, out of sight, and pursued her carriage right to the Conciergerie gates; he had only run away momentarily when he was almost chopped in two by the double iron blade that shut on her.

But the poor creature had soon come back and, realizing that his mistress was locked away in this great stone tomb, was calling her, howling, as he waited for the caress of a reply, ten feet away from the sentry.

The Queen did reply—with a sigh that caused her guards to prick up their ears. But as this sigh was followed by complete silence, they were quickly reassured and dropped back off to sleep.

The next day, the Queen was up and dressed at the crack of dawn. Sitting by the barred window through which the filtered daylight descended, bluish, over her thin hands, she looked as though she was reading, but her thoughts were miles away.

The gendarme known as Gilbert pushed the screen back a little and watched her in silence. Marie Antoinette heard the noise the screen made as it folded in on itself and scraped the brick floor; but she did not look up.

She had positioned herself in such a way that the gendarmes could see her head entirely bathed in the morning light. The gendarme Gilbert signaled to his comrade to come and watch her with him through the opening. Duchesne went over.

"You see," said Gilbert in a lowered voice, "how pale she is; it's positively frightening! Her eyes are red, she's in pain; you'd have to say she's been bawling her eyes out."

"You know very well," said Duchesne, "the Widow Capet never cries; she's too proud for that."

"Well then, she must be sick." Raising his voice, Gilbert said: "Tell me then, citizeness Capet, are you sick?"

The Queen raised her eyes slowly and her gaze was level, clear, and quizzical as she studied the two men.

"Are you talking to me, messieurs?" she asked in a voice full of sweetness, for she felt she'd noticed a spark of interest in the tone of the man who had addressed her.

"Yes, citizeness, we were," Gilbert continued. "We asked you if you were sick."

"Why sick?"

"Because your eyes are very red."

"And you're very pale, too," Duchesne put in.

"Thank you, messieurs. No, I'm not ill; but I suffered a lot last night."

"Oh, yes, with all your worries."

"No, messieurs; my worries being always the same, and religion having taught me to lay them at the foot of the Cross, my worries don't make me suffer more one day than any other. No, I'm ill because I didn't sleep last night."

"Ah! You're not used to the new digs, the new bed," said Duchesne.

"And then again, the lodgings aren't the best," added Gilbert.

"It's not that either, messieurs," said the Queen, shaking her head. "Ugly or beautiful, where I live is a matter of indifference to me."

"What is it, then?"

"What is it?"

"Yes."

"Please forgive me for saying so, but I was most put out by the odor of the tobacco that monsieur is still exhaling as we speak."

Indeed, Gilbert was smoking again; it was, when it came down to it, his most common occupation.

"Oh, my God!" he cried, quite troubled by how sweetly the Queen had spoken to him. "So that's it! Why didn't you say so, citizeness?"

"Because I didn't think I had any right to disrupt your habits, monsieur."

"All right, you won't be inconvenienced any more, not by me at least," said Gilbert, throwing away his pipe, which smashed on the tiles. "I won't smoke again."

With that he turned and closed the screen again, dragging his companion with him.

"It's possible they'll cut her head off—that's the nation's business; but why make that woman suffer any more than she has to? We're soldiers, not torturers like bloody Simon."

"It's all a bit aristocratic, what you're doing there, mate," said Duchesne, shaking his head.

"What do you call aristocratic? Go on, tell me."

"I call aristocratic anything that vexes the nation and pleases our enemies."

"So in your books," said brave Gilbert, "I'm vexing the nation because I don't continue to smoke out the Widow Capet? Come off it! You see, me, I remember my oath to the nation and the orders of my brigadier, that's all. Now, I know my orders by heart: 'Do not let the prisoner escape, do not let anyone in to see her, remove any correspondence she tries to write or maintain, and die at your post.' That's what I promised to do and I'll keep my promise. Long live the nation!"

"All I've got to say to that is that it's not that I hold it against you—on the contrary; but it hurts me to see you compromise yourself."

"Quiet! Here comes someone."

The Queen hadn't missed a word of this conversation, even though the men had kept their voices down. Captivity certainly sharpens your senses. The noise that had attracted the attention of the two guards was that of feet approaching the door. It opened. Two municipal officers barged in, followed by the concierge and a host of clerks.

"Well, then," they asked, "what about the prisoner?"

"She's in there," the two gendarmes chimed.

"How is she lodged?"

"Have a look."

Gilbert pulled back the screen.

"What do you want?" asked the Queen.

"The Commune's come to visit, citizeness Capet."

"This man is a good man," Marie Antoinette thought to herself, "and if my friends really want to . . ."

"All right, all right," said the municipal officers, pushing Gilbert to one side and entering the Queen's room. "You don't have to make such a song and dance about it."

The Queen did not look up, and you would have been forgiven for thinking, at her impassiveness, that she had neither seen nor heard what had just occurred, imagining herself to still be alone.

The Commune delegates sniffed around every inch of the room with shameless curiosity, tapped the woodwork, the bed, the bars on the window that opened onto the Women's Courtyard, and then, after recommending the greatest vigilance to the guards, left without having addressed a single word to Marie Antoinette and without the latter appearing to have been remotely aware of their presence.

35

THE HALL OF LOST FOOTSTEPS

Toward the close of that same day that saw the commissioners inspect the Queen's cell with such minute attention, a man dressed in a grey carmagnole, his head covered with thick black hair and on this thick black hair one of those furry caps that at the time distinguished the lunatic fringe of the patriots from the common lot, strolled about the large room known so philosophically as the Hall of Lost Footsteps. He seemed to be extremely interested in all the people coming and going who made up the customary population of the room, a population strongly increased at the time, when trials had acquired a major importance and when cases were no longer pleaded much anymore, other than to argue about who, between the executioners and citizen Fouquier-Tinville,[1] their indefatigable supplier, finally got to have your head.

The attitude adopted by the man whose portrait we have just sketched was in the best of taste. Society at the time was split into two classes: the sheep and the wolves. One of them must have frightened the other, since half of society now devoured the other half.

Our ferocious stroller was short in stature; he brandished the cudgel known as a constitution from a dirty black hand. It is true that the hand that was swinging this terrible weapon so wildly would have looked pretty damn dainty to anyone who wanted to amuse themselves by playing the inquisitor to this strange character, a role he himself had arrogated in relation to others. But no one would have dared question a man who looked so terrible.

Indeed, with his getup and his attitude, the man with the cudgel sent shock waves of grave anxiety through certain groups of pencil-pushers in their cubbyholes who were holding forth about politics and the state—which, at the time, was starting to go from bad to worse, or from good to better, depending on whether you were a conservative or a revolutionary. From the corners of their eyes, these brave scribes were carefully scanning the man's long black beard and his greenish eyes, set deep beneath eyebrows as bushy as brushes; and they shuddered each time the terrible patriot came near them as he paced the entire length of the Hall of Lost Footsteps.

What they were especially terrified of was the fact that, each time they decided to approach him or even to look at him too closely, the man with the cudgel made the flagstones ring with his heavy weapon, which he brought down hard, crashing against stones in the process and dislodging them with a sound now dull and flat, now shrill and resonant.

But it was not only the fine fellows in the booths of whom we have spoken, who are generally known as the rats of the Palais, who experienced the thrill of fear. So did the various individuals coming into the Hall of Lost Footsteps through its wide main door or through one of its narrow *vomitoires,* who scuttled past as soon as they spotted the man with the cudgel. But he just continued to cross from one end of the room to the other, undeterred, finding at every moment an excuse to set his cudgel ringing against the flagstone floor.

If the scribes had been less frightened and the persons coming and going a bit sharper, they would no doubt have discovered that our patriot, capricious like all eccentric or extreme personalities, seemed to have a distinct preference for certain flagstones; those, for example, located a little way from the right-hand wall and more or less in the middle of the room, which gave out the purest and loudest sounds.

He even wound up concentrating his rage on a mere handful of flagstones, especially those in the center of the room. For a second he even forgot himself enough to stop and measure something like a distance. It is true that this lapse lasted only a second and that the man quickly put back on his face the ferocious scowl that a flash of joy had momentarily replaced.

Almost that same instant, another patriot—in those days everyone wore their political views emblazoned on their brows, or rather on their sleeves—almost at the same instant, as we were saying, another patriot entered by the gallery door and, without in any way seeming to share the general terror inspired by the original occupant, crossed his path with a step more or less the same as his, so that halfway across the room their paths met.

Like the first man, the newcomer sported a fur cap, a grey carmagnole, filthy hands, and a cudgel. In addition, he had a huge sword that kept battering his calves. But what made the second man much scarier than the first was that, just as much as the first man looked frightening, the second looked phony, hateful, and low.

And although the two men looked as though they belonged to the same cause and shared the same views, those present were prepared to risk losing an eye to see what would happen, not from their meeting, for they were not treading the exact same axis, but from their close encounter. Onlookers' expectations were dashed in the first round, for the two patriots made do with exchanging a look—but what a look! It made the smaller man pale; but by the involuntary twitch of his lips, it was clear that his pallor was occasioned not by fear but by disgust.

And yet the second time around the patriot's face, till then so surly and daunting, suddenly brightened, as though he had succeeded in mastering his feelings by some violent effort; something like a would-be gracious smile passed over his lips, and he inclined his path slightly to the left, with the evident aim of stopping the second patriot in his tracks.

They came together virtually in the center of the hall.

"I'll be damned! If it isn't citizen Simon!" said the first patriot.

"The man himself! But what do you want with him, old citizen Simon? And who are you, anyway?"

"You're not going to pretend you don't recognize me!"

"I don't recognize you, and for the good reason that I've never laid eyes on you before."

"Pull the other one! You don't recognize the man who had the honor of parading la Lamballe's head around on a pike?"

These words, delivered in a sort of quiet fury, shot hotly from the carmagnole-wearing patriot's mouth and crackled in the air. Simon started.

"You!" he said. "You?"

"That surprises you, does it? Ah, citizen! I thought you were a bit more discerning when it comes to friends, to the faithful! . . . You wound me."

"It's a good thing, what you did," said Simon, "but I never met you."

"It's a bit more of an advantage guarding the little Capet, you're more in the public eye—you see, I know you and I think highly of you."

"Oh! Thanks!"

"Think nothing of it. . . . So, having a bit of a wander?"

"Yes, I'm waiting for someone. . . . What about you?"

"Me, too."

"What's your name, then? I'll mention you at the club."

"The name's Théodore."

"Théodore what?"

"That's all: that not enough for you?"

"Oh, no, that's fine! . . . Who are you waiting for, citizen Théodore?"

"A friend I've got a good little denunciation ready for."

"Really! Tell me about it."

"A nest of aristocrats."

"What are their names?"

"No, truly; that's for my friend's ears alone."

"You're on the wrong tack, for here's my mate coming toward us, and I reckon this one knows enough about procedure to take care of your business straightaway, eh?"

"Fouquier-Tinville!" cried the first patriot.

"No less, my friend."

"Well, that's good."

"Of course it's good. . . . Hello, citizen Fouquier."

Fouquier-Tinville, pale, calm, alert as usual, with beady black eyes set deep below bushy eyebrows, had emerged from a side door and strode into the room, register in hand, bundles of papers under his arm.

"Hello, Simon," he said. "What's new?"

"Plenty. First, a denunciation by citizen Théodore here—he's the fellow who carried Lamballe's head around. Let me introduce you."

Fouquier fixed his intelligent gaze on the patriot, who was not exactly happy under the man's scrutiny, despite the courageous tension of his nerves.

"Théodore, eh?" said Fouquier. "Who's this Théodore?"

"I am," said the man in the carmagnole.

"You carried Lamballe's head, did you?" said the public prosecutor, with an expression of doubt he made no attempt to hide.

"I did, rue Saint-Antoine."

"But I know someone else who boasts he did," said Fouquier.

"Me, I know ten!" citizen Théodore bravely retorted. "But those fellows are all asking for something and I'm not, so I hope I get preference."

This joke made Simon laugh and even cheered up Fouquier.

"Right you are," he said, "and if you didn't do it, you should have. Leave us, please; Simon has something for me."

Théodore moved off, scarcely offended by the brusque manner of the citizen public prosecutor.

"Hang on!" cried Simon. "Don't send him packing just yet; let's hear his denunciation first."

"Ah!" Fouquier-Tinville said distractedly. "A denunciation?"

"Yes, a nest of 'em," said Simon.

"Marvelous! Tell me. What are we talking about here?"

"Oh, it's practically nothing! Only citizen Maison-Rouge and friends."

Fouquier leapt back; Simon raised his arms to the heavens.

"Really?" the two men chimed.

"Nothing but the truth. Do you want to nab them?"

"Immediately. Where are they?"

"I met Maison-Rouge on the rue de la Grande-Truanderie."

"You're mistaken, he's not in Paris," replied Fouquier.

"I saw him, I tell you."

"You can't have. We put a hundred men on his tail. He's the last person who'd show up in the street."

"It was him, as sure as there's a nose on your face," said the patriot. "A brute with brown hair, big, and hairy as a bear's ass."

Fouquier shrugged his shoulders with contempt.

"Another piece of garbage," he said. "Maison-Rouge is small and thin and hasn't a whisker of a beard."

The patriot dropped his arms to his sides with a disconcerted air.

"Never mind, good intentions are always appreciated. Well then, Simon, it's you and me; get on with it, they're waiting for me at the clerk's office; this is the time the carts go out."

"Well, nothing new; the kid's going well."

The patriot turned his back so as not to appear indiscreet—and so that he could eavesdrop undeterred.

"I'll be off if I'm in your way," he said.

"Adieu," said Simon.

"Good-bye," said Fouquier.

"Tell your friend you got it wrong," Simon added.

"All right, I'll wait for him."

With that, Théodore moved to a spot where he was still within earshot and leaned on his cudgel.

"Ah! The little fellow's going well," Fouquier said. "But what about his morale?"

"He's putty in my hands."

"So he's talking?"

"When I want him to."

"Do you think he could testify at Antoinette's trial?"

"I don't think so—I know so!"

Théodore leaned against a pillar, his eye on the doors. But that eye was sightless, while his ears suddenly pricked up under the vast fur cap. He may well have seen nothing—but he certainly caught an earful.

"Think carefully," said Fouquier. "We don't want to make the Committee look bad—no what they call clerks' bungles! Are you sure Capet will talk?"

"He'll say whatever I want him to."

"He talked to you about what we are going to ask him about?"

"He did."

"This is important, citizen Simon, what you are promising here. Such a confession on the part of the child will be fatal for the mother."

"I bloody well hope so!"

"Nothing like it has been seen since Nero's confession to Narcissus,"[2] muttered Fouquier in a somber voice. "Think again, Simon."

"You'd think you took me for an idiot, citizen. You keep repeating the same thing. Listen, here's a comparison for you: when I put the leather in water, does it become supple?"

"But . . . I have no idea," said Fouquier.

"It becomes supple. Well now, the little Capet becomes as supple in my hands as the softest leather. I've got ways and means, you see."

"So be it," stammered Fouquier. "That's all you wanted to tell me?"

"That's all. . . . Oh, I forgot! Here's a denunciation."

"Another one! You want to kill me with work?"

"A man's got to serve his country."

With that, Simon presented a piece of paper as black as one of the leather skins he'd just referred to, but decidedly less supple. Fouquier took it and read it.

"Your citizen Lorin again; you really hate that man, don't you?"

"I find he's always hostile to the law. He said 'Adieu, madame' to a woman who waved at him from her window last night. . . . Tomorrow I hope to give you something about another suspect: that Maurice, who was one of the municipal officers in the Temple at the time of the red carnation."

"Details! Details!" cried Fouquier, smiling at Simon. "It's all in the details!"

He held out his hand to Simon and turned on his heel with a haste that didn't augur well for the cobbler.

"What more bloody details do you want me to come up with? They've given people the chop for less."

"Patience! Patience!" Fouquier sang out serenely. "We can't do everything at once."

On that note, Fouquier went back through the wickets with a determined stride. Simon looked around for his citizen Théodore for a bit of commiseration. He couldn't see him anywhere in the room. Yet scarcely had Simon disappeared through the west gate than Théodore reappeared at the corner of a scribe's booth, the inhabitant of the booth by his side.

"What time do they shut the gates?" Théodore asked the man.

"Five o'clock."

"And then what happens here?"

"Nothing; the room's empty till the next day."

"No rounds, no visits?"

"No, monsieur, our booths are locked."

The term *monsieur* made Théodore frown, and he looked round with concern.

"The pliers and the pistols are in the booth?" he asked.

"Yes, under the rug."

"Go back to our place. . . . Speaking of which, show me again the courtroom that doesn't have bars on the window and that looks over a courtyard near the place Dauphine."

"It's on the left between the pillars, under the lantern."

"Good. Off you go and keep the horses at the appointed place!"

"Oh! Good luck, monsieur, good luck! . . . You can count on me!"

"This is the moment. . . . No one's looking. . . . Open your booth."

"Done, monsieur; I'll pray for you!"

"It's not for me that we need to pray! Adieu."

With a last eloquent look, citizen Théodore slipped so adroitly under the little roof of the booth that he simply dematerialized, like the shadow of the scribe shutting the door.

The worthy scribe pulled the key out of the lock, stuck some papers under his arm, and left the vast hall with its few remaining employees, flushed out of their offices by the clock striking five like a rear guard of late-returning bees.

36

CITIZEN THÉODORE

Night had enveloped in its greyish cloak this immense hall, whose unhappy echoes were doomed to repeat the sharp words of lawyers and litigants' supplications.

Here and there in the gloom, white columns stood straight and unmoving like sentinels keeping watch over the place, or like phantoms protecting some sacred site.

The only sound that could be heard in the darkness was the gnawing and four-legged galloping of rats, chewing away at all the pap locked away in the scribes' booths, after having first chewed their way through the wood.

At times the sound of a carriage could also be heard, penetrating as far as the sanctuary of Themis, the Goddess of Law, as an academic would say, along with the dim clinking of keys that seemed to come from below ground. All of this was just distant rustling, but nothing brings out the opacity of silence as much as remote noise, just as nothing brings out the darkness as much as the appearance of a light in the distance.

Certainly anyone who had risked being in the vast Palais hall at this hour would have been seized with a dizzying terror; the outside walls were still red with the blood of the victims of September, when the staircases had seen twenty-five dead men walking; and a thickness of only several feet separated the flagstones from the dungeons of the Conciergerie, peopled by the bleached bones of skeletons.

Yet in the middle of this fearful night, in the middle of this almost solemn silence, a faint grinding noise could be detected: the door of one of the scribes' booths was opening with a screech of hinges and a shadow, blacker than the shadow of night, slipped carefully out of the bunker.

Then the patriot *enragé*, who was called *monsieur* sotto voce and who claimed out loud to be one Théodore, trod lightly over the uneven flagstones.

He held a heavy pair of iron pliers in his right hand, and steadied with his left a pistol with two bullets that hung at his belt. Counting his steps as he went, he felt around with the tip of his toe for the crack that time wears between each stone join.

"Let's see," he murmured, pausing. "Did I get my measurements right? Will I be strong enough? Will she have enough courage? Oh, yes! I know how courageous she can be, I've seen it. Oh, God! When I take her hand, when I say to her: 'Madame, you are saved!' . . ."

He stopped dead as though crushed by the weight of such a hope.

"Oh!" he went on, "what a reckless, insane plan! That's what others would say as they burrowed under the covers or contented themselves with hanging around the Conciergerie dressed as lackeys. But that's because they don't have what it takes for such daring—and I do: it's not just the Queen in her I want to save, it's the woman.... So, to work! Let's go over it one more time. Taking up the flagstone is a piece of cake; leaving it open, a gaping hole—there's the danger, for a round could turn up.... But they never have rounds patrolling at night. No one suspects anything, for I have no accomplices, and then again, how much time do you need to run down a dark corridor when you feel as passionately as I do? I'll be underneath her room in three minutes; in five minutes, I'll take up the stone that serves as the hearthstone in the fireplace. She'll hear me at work, but she has so much courage and composure, she won't be afraid! On the contrary, she'll know it's her liberator coming.... She is guarded by two men; no doubt these two will come running.... Well, what are two men, after all?" said the patriot with a gloomy smile, glancing from the weapon he held in his hand to the one dangling at his waist. "Two men means two bullets— or two wallops of the iron bar. Poor blighters! ... But plenty of others have died—men no more guilty than they are. Let's go!"

With that, citizen Théodore resolutely applied his pliers to the join between the two flagstones.

At that very instant, a bright light slid like a streak of molten gold across the flagstones and a noise ricocheting around the echoing vaults made the conspirator's head whip around; in a single bound, he was crouching down again in the scribe's stall.

Voices, made faint by distance and by the emotions that all men feel at night in a cavernous building, soon reached Théodore's ears. He hunkered down further and peered through a slit; first he saw a man in military garb whose huge sword, ringing on the flagstones, was one of the noises that had first caught his attention. Then came a man in a pistachio green suit, holding a ruler in his hand and rolls of paper under his arm; then a third man, in a big ratiné jacket and fur cap; then, finally, a fourth man, wearing a carmagnole and sabots[1] on his feet.

The Haberdashers' Gate screeched on its noisy hinges and slammed against the iron chain that held the gate open in the day.

The four men entered.

"A round," Théodore murmured. "Praise be to God! Ten minutes later and I'd have been a goner."

Focusing intently, he tried to work out who the men were who thus composed the round. Indeed, he recognized three of them. The one in the lead, dressed as a general, was Santerre; the man in the ratiné jacket and fur cap was Richard, the concierge; the man with the carmagnole and clogs was probably the wicket clerk.

But he had never before seen the man decked out in pistachio green with a ruler in hand and scrolls under his arm. Who could this man be, and what were the general of the Commune, the warden of the Conciergerie, a wicket clerk, and this unknown man doing together at ten o'clock at night in the Hall of Lost Footsteps?

Citizen Théodore leaned on one knee, holding his pistol cocked with one hand and with the other arranging his cap on his hair, which in his haste he had messed up much too much for the wig to look natural.

Until then the four nocturnal visitors had remained silent, or at least the words they had spoken had not reached the ears of the conspirator other than as ambient noise. But suddenly Santerre spoke, only ten feet away from his cubbyhole, and the general's voice reached citizen Théodore distinctly.

"Let's see," said Santerre, "we're in the Hall of Lost Footsteps now. It's up to you to guide us after this, citizen architect, and make sure above all that your great revelation isn't a piece of poppycock. For, you see, the Revolution has been through all this nonsense before, and we don't believe in underground tunnels any more now than we believe in ghosts. What do you say, citizen Richard?" Santerre added as an afterthought, turning to the man in the fur cap and ratiné jacket.

"I've never said there is no underground passage under the Conciergerie," Richard replied. "Gracchus[2] here, he's been a wicket clerk for ten years, and so he knows the Conciergerie like the back of his hand, but he's never heard of this underground passage citizen Giraud's talking about. But, since citizen Giraud is a city architect, he'd have to know more about it than we do . . . since that's his job."

Théodore shivered from head to toe on hearing these words.

"Luckily," he murmured, "the hall is huge; they'll be looking for two days at least before they find what they're looking for."

But the architect unrolled his great scroll, put on his glasses, and knelt in front of a map, which he examined by the flickering light of the lantern Gracchus was holding.

"I'm afraid," said Santerre, "that citizen Giraud has been dreaming."

"You'll see, citizen general," the architect shot back, "you'll see if I'm a dreamer. Just wait."

"I am waiting," said Santerre.

"Fine," said the architect as he started measuring. "Twelve and four are sixteen," he said. "And eight is twenty-four, which, divided by six, is four; after that we still have half over; that's it, I've got my bearings, and if I'm off by a foot, tell me I'm an ignoramus."

The architect pronounced these words with such assurance that citizen Théodore froze in terror. Santerre looked at the map with a kind of respect; you could see he admired it all the more because it didn't make the slightest sense.

"Listen carefully to what I'm about to say."

"Where do we look?" asked Santerre.

"At the map I've made, for pity's sake! Are you with me? Thirteen feet from the wall, there's a loose flagstone. I've marked it. You see it?"

"I see an A, of course," said Santerre. "Do you think I can't read?"

"Underneath this flagstone there's a staircase," the architect continued unperturbed. "See, I've marked it with a B."

"B," Santerre repeated. "I can see a B, but I can't see the staircase." The general guffawed at his joke.

"Once we've taken up the flagstone, once we've got our feet on the last step," the architect went on, "count out fifty paces three feet long and look around; you'll find yourself right at the registrar's office, where the tunnel will come up after passing under the Queen's cell."

"The Widow Capet's, you mean, citizen Giraud," said Santerre, frowning sternly.

"Ah, yes! The Widow Capet's."

"It's just that you said the *Queen's*."

"Old habit."

"And you reckon we'll be under the office?" asked Richard.

"Not only under the office, but I can tell you what part of the office we'll be under: we'll be under the stove."

"Wait a minute, that's odd!" said Gracchus. "Every time I drop a log at that spot the stone reverberates!"

"In all honesty, if we find what you say we'll find, citizen architect, I'll have to admit that geometry is a beautiful thing."

"Well then, admit it, citizen Santerre, because I'm about to take you to the spot marked with the letter A."

Citizen Théodore dug his nails into his flesh.

"When I've seen it with my own eyes," said Santerre. "I'm a bit like Saint Thomas, a bit of a doubting Thomas, I am."

"Ha! Saint Thomas, you say?"

"Cripes, yes, just like you said the Queen, out of habit; but no one's going to accuse me of plotting to save Saint Thomas."

"Or me the Queen."

With that retort, the architect delicately took his ruler, did his sums, and, when he stopped, after having carefully measured all the distances, he tapped on a flagstone.

It was exactly the same flagstone citizen Théodore had tapped during his little performance of wild rage.

"This is it, citizen general!" said the architect.

"You think so, citizen Giraud?"

Still kneeling in the scribe's booth, the patriot forgot himself to the point of violently whacking his thigh with his closed fist and giving out a low groan.

"I'm sure of it," Giraud said. "With your expertise and my report, we'll prove to the Convention that I am not mistaken. Yes, citizen general," the architect said with heavy emphasis, "this flagstone opens onto a tunnel that ends in the office after passing under the cell of the Widow Capet. Let's take up the stone. Come down into the tunnel with me and I'll prove to you that two men, or even one man on his own, could lift the Queen out overnight without anyone suspecting a thing."

A murmur of fright and admiration excited by the architect's words rippled through the group and died in citizen Théodore's ear. He sat transfixed as though turned to stone.

"That is the risk we are running," Giraud went on. "So now, with a gate that I'll put inside the tunnel and which will cut it in half before it gets to the Widow Capet's cell, I will save our nation."

"Oh!" uttered Santerre. "Citizen Giraud, that's a stroke of genius you've had there."

"May you rot in hell, you moron," growled the patriot with a surge of rage.

"Now, lift up the flagstone," said the architect to citizen Gracchus, who was carrying pliers as well as his lantern.

Citizen Gracchus got to work and the stone was raised in no time. The tunnel appeared, a gaping hole with stairs that went down into its depths out of sight, and a cloud of moldy air escaped, thick as smoke.

"Yet another attempt thwarted!" murmured citizen Théodore. "Oh! Heaven can't want her to escape, then, and her cause is cursed!"

37

CITIZEN GRACCHUS

For a moment the men stood as though rooted to the spot at the mouth of the tunnel as the wicket clerk plunged his lantern into the opening; the light didn't go far, the tunnel was so deep and dark. The triumphant architect lorded it over his three companions from the height of his genius.

"Well then," he said after a while.

"I'll be buggered!" replied Santerre. "There really is a tunnel, it's incontestable. But it remains to be seen where it goes."

"Yes," echoed Richard, "that remains to be seen."

"Well then, down you go, citizen Richard, and see for yourself if what I said is true."

"I've got a better idea than going down there," said the concierge. "Why don't we go back with you and the general to the Conciergerie and then you can pull up the flagstone where the stove is and we'll see."

"Very good!" said Santerre. "Off we go."

"But take care," said the architect. "If we don't put the stone back properly, it might give someone ideas."

"Who the hell do you think's going to turn up here at this hour?" asked Santerre.

"Anyway," Richard added, "the hall's deserted; if we leave Gracchus here, that'll be good enough. Stay here, citizen Gracchus, and we'll come back to you from the other end of the tunnel."

"As you wish," said Gracchus.

"Are you armed?" asked Santerre.

"I have my sword and these pliers, citizen general."

"Marvelous! Keep your eyes peeled. We'll be back in ten minutes."

With that, all three shut the gate and went back to the Conciergerie through the Haberdashers' Gallery.

The wicket clerk watched them go and followed them with his eyes as far as he could see them; he listened to them as long as he could hear them; and when at last everything went silent and he was on his own, he put his lantern on the ground, sat at the edge of the hole with his legs dangling into the darkness of the tunnel, and began to dream.

Wicket clerks do dream sometimes like the rest of us. Only, usually no one goes to the trouble of finding out what they dream about.

Suddenly, and while he was in the depths of his daydream, he felt a heavy hand on his shoulder. He turned around, saw an unknown face, and made to cry out in alarm. But at that very instant a pistol pressed its cold muzzle into his forehead. His voice died in his throat, his arms fell inert, his eyes took on the most imploring expression they could muster.

"Not a word," said the newcomer, "or you're dead."

"What do you want, monsieur?" stuttered the wicket clerk.

Even in '93 there were, as you see, moments when people addressed each other formally and forgot to call each other *citizen*.

"I want you to let me down there," said citizen Théodore.

"What for?"

"What's it to you?"

The clerk looked at the man who had made this request with sheer astonishment. But there was a spark of real intelligence in that look as well, or so the object of his astonishment felt. He lowered his gun.

"Would you turn down the chance to make your fortune?"

"I don't know; no one's ever made me a proposition on the subject."

"Well then, let me be the first."

"You're offering to make my fortune?"

"Yes."

"What do you mean by fortune?"

"Fifty thousand livres in gold, say: money is thin on the ground, and fifty thousand livres in gold is worth a million today. So I'm offering you fifty thousand livres."

"To let you go down there?"

"Yes—but on condition that you come with me and help me do what I have to do there."

"But what will you do there? In five minutes, the tunnel will be packed with soldiers who'll arrest you."

Citizen Théodore was struck by the gravity of his words.

"Can you stop the soldiers from going down?"

"I don't know how; I can't think, I'm trying to think of a way, but I can't."

And it was clear the clerk was bringing all his perspicacity to bear on a problem that was worth fifty thousand livres to him to solve.

"What about tomorrow?" asked citizen Théodore. "Can we get down there then?"

"Yes, no doubt; but before that they're going to put an iron gate in the tunnel—one that'll go all the way across, and for greater security it's been decided that the gate will go all the way to the roof, and it will be solid and it won't have a door."

"Then we need to find some other way," said citizen Théodore.

"Yes, we need to find some other way," said the clerk. "Let's think."

As you can see from the collective pronoun with which citizen Gracchus expressed himself, there was already an alliance between him and citizen Théodore.

"That's my problem," said Théodore. "What is it you do at the Conciergerie?"

"I'm a wicket clerk."

"Which means?"

"That I open doors and shut them."

"Do you sleep there?"

"Yes, monsieur."

"You eat there?"

"Not always. I have time off."

"And then?"

"I make use of it."

"How?"

"To court the lady who runs the cabaret, the Puits-de-Noé—she's promised to marry me when I have twelve hundred francs."

"Where is this Puits-de-Noé located?"

"Near the rue de la Vieille-Draperie."

"Perfect."

"Quiet, monsieur!"

The patriot strained to hear.

"Ah! Ah!" he said.

"Do you hear?"

"Yes . . . footsteps."

"They're coming back. You can see we wouldn't have had time."

That *we* was becoming more and more conclusive.

"True. You're a brave lad, citizen; I've got the feeling you're pre-destined for great things."

"Like what?"

"Being rich one day."

"May God hear you!"

"So you believe in God?"

"Sometimes, now and again. Today, for instance . . ."

"Yes?"

"I'd gladly believe."

"Then believe," said citizen Théodore, popping ten louis in the clerk's hand.

"Christ!" said the clerk, staring at the gold by the light of his lantern. "So it's serious?"

"It doesn't get more serious."

"What do I have to do?"

"Be at the Puits-de-Noé tomorrow, I'll tell you what I need you to do then. What's your name?"

"Gracchus."

"Well then, citizen Gracchus, between now and tomorrow, get yourself fired by Richard the concierge."

"Fired? What about my job?"

"Do you count on remaining a clerk once you've got fifty thousand francs to yourself?"

"No, but at least as a clerk and a poor man, I'm pretty sure of not being guillotined."

"Sure?"

"As good as; whereas if I'm rich and free . . ."

"You'll hide your money and go and court a *tricoteuse* instead of the woman who runs the Puits-de-Noé."

"Well then, enough said."

"Tomorrow, at the cabaret."

"What time?"

"Six o'clock in the evening."

"You'd better fly, quick, here they come. . . . I say *fly*, since I suppose you came down from the roof."

"See you tomorrow," Théodore repeated before making good his escape.

It was, indeed, just in the nick of time. The sound of feet and voices was getting closer. You could see that the dark tunnel was already bright with the light of approaching lamps. Théodore ran to the door pointed out to him by the scribe whose hut he had borrowed. He popped the lock with his pliers, reached the window he'd been told about, opened it, slipped down to the ground, and found himself on the cobblestones of the republican street.

But before leaving the Hall of Lost Footsteps, he managed to catch citizen Gracchus questioning Richard and the concierge's answer:

"The citizen architect was perfectly right: the tunnel goes under Widow Capet's room; it was dangerous."

"I should think so!" said Gracchus, who was conscious of uttering the simple truth.

Santerre appeared at the mouth of the stairs.

"What about your workers, citizen architect?" he asked Giraud.

"They'll be here before the break of day and they'll put the gate in place without further ado," answered a voice that seemed to come from the bowels of the earth.

"And you will have saved our nation!" Santerre said, half mockingly, half seriously.

"You don't know how right you are, citizen general," muttered Gracchus.

38

THE ROYAL CHILD

Meanwhile, the case for the Queen's trial had begun to be prepared for judgment, as we saw in the preceding chapter.

Already it was anticipated that only the sacrifice of her illustrious head would satisfy the popular hate that had been so long brewing. Reasons for causing her head to fall were hardly lacking, and yet that deadly prosecutor, Fouquier-Tinville, determined to leave no stone unturned, decided to investigate the new avenue of accusation Simon had promised to open up for him.

The day after he and Simon had met in the Hall of Lost Footsteps, a great clamor of arms came to churn the stomachs of the royal prisoners still housed in the Temple. These royal prisoners were Madame Elisabeth, Madame Royale, and the infant, who, having been called Majesty from birth, was now no more than little Louis Capet.

General Hanriot, he of the red, white, and blue panache, the fat squat horse, and the great sword, strode into the dungeon where the royal infant languished, followed by several National Guards.

By the general's side was a mean-looking clerk of the court, equipped with a writing case and a roll of paper and struggling with an extravagantly long quill. Behind the scribe came the public prosecutor. We've already met the man and this is not the last we'll see of the dry, jaundiced, and chilling old stick, whose bloodshot eyes used to cause even the ferocious Santerre himself to quake in his boots.

A handful of National Guards and a lieutenant brought up the rear.

Simon, smiling a queerly artificial smile and holding his bear-cub cap in one hand and his cobbler's foot-pull in the other, went ahead to show the committee the way. They came to a room that was dark, spacious, and bare. At the back of the room was the young Louis, sitting on his bed in a state of perfect immobility.

When we last saw the poor child, fleeing from the brutal Simon, there was still a sort of vitality left in him, enough for him to react against the disgraceful treatment of the Temple cobbler. He ran away, he cried out, he sobbed—this meant he was afraid, which meant he was in pain, which meant he still had hope.

Now fear and hope had both vanished. No doubt he still suffered, but if he did, this child martyr who was made to pay so cruelly for the sins of his parents, he kept it buried in the darkest depths of his heart and veiled it under the appearance of complete insensibility.

He did not even raise his head when the commissioners marched up to him. They took their seats without preamble and settled in, with the public prosecutor at the head of the bed, Simon at the foot, the court clerk by the window, and the National Guards and their lieutenant to one side in the shadows.

Those among the men present who looked at the little prisoner with any interest or even curiosity remarked the child's appalling pallor, his peculiarly distended stomach, which was more than mere bloating, and the strange sagging of his legs, whose joints were beginning to swell.

"This child is very ill," said the lieutenant with an assurance that made Fouquier-Tinville sit up, ready and raring as he was to begin the interrogation.

Little Capet looked up and scanned the company for the man who had uttered these words in the semidarkness. He recognized the young man who had already once, in the Temple garden, prevented Simon from hitting him. A soft, intelligent light flashed in his dark blue eyes and then was gone.

"Well! If it isn't citizen Lorin!" cried Simon, thereby calling the attention of Fouquier-Tinville to Maurice Lindey's friend.

"In person, citizen Simon," replied Lorin with his imperturbable aplomb.

Furthermore, for although he was always ready to face danger Lorin was not the kind of man to seek it for no reason, he took advantage of the opportunity to greet Fouquier-Tinville, who politely returned his greeting.

"You have observed, I think, citizen," said the public prosecutor, "that the child is ill; are you a doctor?"

"I have at least studied medicine, even if I'm not a doctor."

"Well then, what do you think he has?"

"As symptoms of illness, you mean?" asked Lorin.

"Yes."

"I find he has puffy eyes and cheeks, pale, emaciated hands, swollen knees, and, if I felt his pulse, I'd say, I'm sure, that he had a high pulse rate—something like eighty-five to ninety."

The child seemed impervious to the listing of his ailments.

"And to what can science attribute the state of the prisoner?" asked the public prosecutor.

Lorin scratched the end of his nose, muttering:

> "Philis would like me now to discourse;
> But I have nothing to say, of course."

Out loud, he said: "Good grief, citizen, I'm not familiar enough with little Capet's daily routine to answer . . . but . . ."

Simon lent an attentive ear and cackled behind his hand to see his enemy so close to stepping in it and compromising himself.

"But," continued Lorin, "I believe he isn't getting enough exercise."

"Indeed he isn't, the little bastard!" said Simon. "He won't walk anymore."

The child remained insensible to the cobbler's outburst. Fouquier-Tinville stood up, went over to Lorin, and spoke to him in a low voice. No one could hear what the prosecutor was saying, but it was clear his words were in the form of questions.

"Oh! Really! Do you think so, citizen? That is a most serious matter . . . for a mother. . . ."

"In any case, we'll get to the bottom of it," said Fouquier. "Simon claims the boy told him himself, and Simon has taken measures to get him to confess."

"It would be hideous," said Lorin. "But I suppose it's possible: the Austrian woman is not exempt from sin, and, right or wrong, it doesn't concern me. . . . They've already made a Messalina out of her, but not to be happy with that, to want now to turn her into an Agrippina. . . .[1] It seems to me that's going a bit too far, I have to admit."

"That's what Simon has reported," said Fouquier, impassive.

"I don't doubt Simon said so. . . . There are those who balk at nothing, for whom no accusation is too vicious, none too improbable. . . . But don't you find," Lorin went on, staring hard at Fouquier, "you who are an intelligent and perceptive man, you who are a powerful man, let's not forget, don't you find that to ask a child for such details about the woman whom the most normal and sacred laws of nature command him to respect, is almost to insult humanity as a whole in the person of this child?"

The prosecutor didn't bat an eye; he took a note from his pocket and showed it to Lorin.

"The Convention orders me to inform; the rest is not my concern. I just inform."

"Fair enough," said Lorin, "and I have to admit that if the child really did confess . . ." The young man shook his head in disgust.

"In any case," Fouquier continued, "we are not going on Simon's denunciation alone; the accusation is in the public domain, you see." Fouquier pulled a second piece of printed matter from his pocket. This was an issue of the tabloid known as *Le Père Duchesne*, which, as we know, was edited by Hébert.[2] The accusation was spelled out in its pages most unambiguously.

"It's been written, it's even in print, but so what? Until I hear such an accusation from the mouth of the child himself—and I mean voluntarily, freely, without threats or under duress—well then . . ."

"Well then?"

"Well then, whatever Simon and Hébert say, I'd doubt it as much as you do yourself."

Simon awaited the outcome of this conversation impatiently. The miserable wretch had no inkling of the power exercised over the intelligent man by the gaze he makes out in the crowd when he is suddenly drawn to a complete stranger out of a feeling of sympathy, or repelled by instant hatred. But whether it is a force of repulsion or attraction, the man's thoughts and even his being suddenly flow to that stranger of equal or greater force that he recognizes in the crowd.

But Fouquier had felt the weight of Lorin's gaze on him and wanted to be understood by this particular observer.

"The interrogation will begin," said the public prosecutor. "Clerk of the court, take up your quill."

The clerk had just been jotting down preliminary notes toward a statement of offense and was waiting, like Simon, like Hanriot, like everyone else, for the confabulation between Fouquier-Tinville and Lorin to end.

Only the child seemed completely oblivious of the scene in which he was the star player; he had readopted the blank mask that had lit up for a moment with the fierce light of a supreme intelligence.

"Silence!" said Hanriot. "Citizen Fouquier-Tinville will now interrogate the infant."

"Capet," said the prosecutor, "do you know what has happened to your mother?"

Little Louis swiftly changed color, going from the pallor of marble to a burning red. But he did not reply.

"Did you hear me, Capet?" the prosecutor went on.

Same silence.

"Oh, he hears all right!" said Simon. "But he's a little monkey; he doesn't want to answer for fear he'll be taken for a man and made to work."

"Answer, Capet," said Hanriot. "It's the Committee of the Convention that is interrogating you, and you owe obedience to the law."

The child went pale again but did not reply.

Simon made a movement of rage; in such brutal and stupid natures, fury is a form of intoxication, accompanied by the same hideous symptoms as intoxication from wine.

"You answer, you little devil!" he shouted, showing his fist.

"Shut up, Simon," said Fouquier-Tinville, "you do not have the floor."

These words were out before he could stop himself, for he had formed the habit of so speaking at the Revolutionary Tribunal.

"You hear that, Simon," said Lorin. "You don't have the floor. That's the second time you've been told to shut up in my hearing; the first time was when you accused Mother Tison's daughter, whose head rolled, thanks to you."

Simon shut up.

"Did your mother love you, Capet?" asked Fouquier.

Same silence.

"They say she did not," the prosecutor went on.

Something like a faint smile passed over the child's lips.

"But I told you he told me she loved him a bit too much!" screamed Simon.

"Poor Simon! Isn't it annoying how little Capet is so chatty in his tête-à-têtes with you but clams up the moment anyone else is around?" said Lorin.

"Oh! If I had him alone!" said Simon.

"Yes, if you had him alone; but you don't, unfortunately. Oh! If you had him alone, brave Simon, excellent patriot, you'd beat the poor child to a pulp, eh? But you don't have him alone and you don't dare touch him in front of the rest of us, you loathsome thug! We are honest people who know that the ancients, on whom we're trying to model ourselves, respected all that was weak; you don't dare for you are not alone, and you are not so valiant, my worthy man, when you have children over five foot ten to deal with."

"You!" hissed Simon, grinding his teeth.

"Capet," Fouquier resumed, "did you confide in Simon?"

The child did not flinch but gazed directly at the prosecutor with an expression of irony impossible to describe.

"About your mother?" continued the prosecutor.

A flash of scorn fired the boy's gaze.

"Answer *yes* or *no!*" cried Hanriot.

"Answer *yes!*" shouted Simon, raising his lash over the child, who shivered but made no move to avoid being hit.

All those in attendance gave a cry of revulsion. Lorin went one better; he dashed forward and seized Simon's wrist before he had a chance to strike.

"Let go of me!" Simon hissed, purple with rage.

"You see," said Fouquier, "there's no harm in a mother loving her son. Tell us in what way your mother loved you, Capet. It could help her."

The young prisoner gave a start at the idea that he could help his mother.

"She loved me the way any mother loves her son, monsieur," he said. "There is only one way a mother loves her children or children love their mother."

"And I say, you little snake, that you told me your mother . . ."

"You must have dreamed it," said Lorin. "You must often have nightmares, Simon."

"Lorin! Lorin!" hissed Simon.

"Yes, Lorin . . . go on! You can't beat Lorin, you know: he's the one who beats others when they're horrible. There's no way you can denounce me, either, for what I did in stopping your arm I did in front of General Hanriot and citizen Fouquier-Tinville, who approved. And they aren't lukewarm, those two! So there's no way you can have me guillotined like Héloïse Tison. It is annoying, I agree, even infuriating, but that's how it is, my poor Simon!"

"You'll keep!" replied the cobbler, cackling, as usual, like a hyena.

"Yes, friend," said Lorin. "But I hope, with the help of the Supreme Being—ah! you were hoping I'd say 'God'!—I hope with the help of the Supreme Being and my trusty sword to rip your guts open beforehand. Now get out of the way, Simon, I can't see."

"Bastard."

"Shut your mouth. I can't hear."

Lorin crushed Simon with a look.

Simon balled his hands, whose ingrained dirt he was so proud of, into fists; but as Lorin said, he was forced to restrict himself to that gesture.

"Now that he has started to speak, no doubt he'll continue," said Hanriot. "Go on, citizen Fouquier."

The child withdrew into his silence.

"You see, citizen, you see!" said Simon.

"The obstinacy of this child is odd," said Hanriot, troubled in spite of himself by such perfectly royal steadfastness.

"He's been getting bad advice," said Lorin.

"From whom?" demanded Hanriot.

"His boss, of course!"

"You're accusing me?" cried Simon. "You think you can denounce me? Ha! That's funny. . . ."

"Let's try a little kindness, see if that wins him over," said Fouquier.

Turning back to the child who you'd have thought completely oblivious, he said:

"Come, my child, answer the National Commission; don't aggravate your situation by refusing to provide useful clarification. You told citizen Simon your mother used to stroke you, you described the way she used to stroke you, her way of loving you."

Louis gave each of the assembled company a look that filled with hate when it alighted on Simon. But he did not respond.

"Are you unhappy?" asked the prosecutor. "Are you badly lodged, badly fed, badly treated? Would you like more freedom, a different diet, a different prison, a different guardian? Would you like a horse to ride? Would you like us to grant you the company of children your own age?"

Louis sank into the profound silence which he had only broken to defend his mother. The Commission remained speechless with amazement. Such firmness, such intelligence were incredible in a child.

"Hmmph! These kings!" said Hanriot in a lowered voice. "What a race! They're like tigers: even when they're small, they're nasty."

"How do I write the report?" asked the embarrassed court clerk.

"The only thing for it is to get Simon to do it for you," said Lorin. "There's nothing to write, which will suit him to a tee."

Simon showed his fist to his implacable enemy; Lorin started to laugh.

"You won't laugh like that the day you sneeze in the sack," said Simon, beside himself with fury.

"I don't know if I'll go before or after you in the little ceremony you threaten me with," said Lorin. "But what I do know is that a lot of people will laugh the day it's your turn. Ye Gods! . . . I said 'Gods' in the plural. . . . *Gods!* You'll look ugly that day, Simon! You'll be hideous."

With that Lorin withdrew behind the Commission, laughing cheerfully. There was nothing further for them all to do but leave. As for the child, once freed from his interrogators, he began to softly sing a melancholy little song sitting on his bed: it was one of his father's favorites.

39

THE BOUQUET OF VIOLETS

Peace, as one might have foreseen, could not long inhabit the love nest where Maurice and Geneviève lived ensconced. When a tempest unleashes thunder and wind, the doves' nest is shaken along with the bough that holds it.

Geneviève lurched from one fright to the next; she no longer trembled for Maison-Rouge, she now trembled for Maurice. She knew her husband well enough to know that, from the moment he disappeared, he was safe; thus sure of his salvation, she trembled for herself.

She didn't dare confide her woes to the least timid man of an age in which everyone was fearless. But they were manifest in her red eyes and bloodless lips.

One day Maurice entered quietly while Geneviève was plunged into a deep reverie and didn't hear him come in. He stopped at the door and saw her sitting, not moving, her eyes staring, her arms hugging her knees, her face buried in her chest.

He watched her for a moment in deep distress; for all that went through the young woman's heart was revealed to him as though she were an open book and he could read to the bottom of her soul.

He took a step toward her and said: "You don't love France anymore, Geneviève. You can tell me. You don't even want to breathe the air here anymore—you don't go near the window without dread."

"Alas!" said Geneviève. "I'm well aware I can't hide my thoughts from you, Maurice. You guessed right."

"Yet it's a beautiful country!" said the young man. "Life here matters and is so rewarding. There's so much happening these days—all the bustle of the Tribunal, the clubs, the plots: it makes time off at home so blissful. You love all the more passionately when you come home at night not knowing if you'll be able to love the next day, because the next day you might not be alive!"

Geneviève shook her head. "An ungrateful country to serve!" she said.

"How so?"

"Yes, look at you—you who have done so much for liberty, aren't you half-suspect today?"

"But you, dear Geneviève," said Maurice, with a look drunk with love, "you, a sworn enemy of such liberty, you who have done so much against it, you sleep peaceful and inviolate beneath the roof of a republican. There is some compensation, as you see."

"Yes," said Geneviève, "yes. But it won't last long, for what is unjust can't last."

"What do you mean?"

"I mean that I, that is, an aristocrat, I who slyly dream of defeating your party and ruining your ideas, I who plot in your very house the return of the ancien régime, I who, as a known felon, condemn you to death and disgrace, according to your views at least, I, Maurice, will not stay here like the bad genie of the house. I will not drag you with me to the scaffold."

"And where will you go, Geneviève?"

"Where will I go? One day when you've gone out, Maurice, I'll go and denounce myself without saying where I've been."

"Oh!" cried Maurice pierced to the heart. "There's gratitude for you!"

"No," she said, throwing her arms around Maurice's neck. "No, my friend, it's love and the most devoted love, I swear to you. I didn't want my brother to be taken and killed as a rebel; I don't want my lover to be taken and killed as a traitor."

"Is that really what you're going to do, Geneviève?" cried Maurice.

"As sure as there's a God in heaven!" she cried. "Besides, fear is nothing, what I feel is remorse."

"Oh, Geneviève!" said Maurice.

"You know what I'm saying and what I'm going through, Maurice," Geneviève continued. "For you feel the same remorse. You know, Maurice, that I gave myself without being mine to give; that you took me without my having the right to give myself."

"That's enough," cried Maurice, "enough!"

He frowned and a grim determination shone in his eyes.

"I will show you, Geneviève, that I love only you; I will give you proof that no sacrifice is too great for my love. You hate France: well then, we'll leave France."

Geneviève clapped her hands together and looked at her lover with an expression of wild admiration.

"You're not putting me on, Maurice?"

"When have I ever put you on?" Maurice asked. "Was it the day I dishonored myself to have you with me?"

Geneviève brought her lips to Maurice's and remained suspended, so to speak, from her lover's neck.

"Yes, you're right, Maurice. I'm putting myself on. What I feel isn't remorse anymore; perhaps it's the degradation of my soul. But at least you'll understand, I love you too much to feel anything but fear of losing you. Let's go far away, my friend; let's go where no one can ever reach us."

"Oh, thank you!" said Maurice, over the moon.

"But how can we get away?" said Geneviève, shuddering at the bleak prospect. "These days you can't easily escape the daggers of the assassins of the second of September, or the axes of the executioners of the twenty-first of January."

"Geneviève!" cried Maurice. "God will protect us. Listen, a good act I tried to do apropos the second of September is going to bear fruit today. I wanted to save a poor priest who once studied with me. I sought out Danton and, at his request, the Committee of Public Safety signed a passport for the priest and his sister. This passport Danton gave to me; but the unhappy priest, instead of coming and getting it from me as I proposed, locked himself up in the Carmes[1]— and he died there."

"What happened to the passport?" asked Geneviève.

"I still have it. Today it's worth a million; it's worth more than that, Geneviève. It's worth life, it's worth happiness!"

"God be praised!" cried Geneviève.

"Now, as you know, my fortune consists in some land managed by an old family servant, a pure patriot and loyal soul we can trust completely. He'll send the revenues on to me wherever I am. When we get to Boulogne we can go and see him."

"Where does he live?"

"Near Abbeville."[2]

"When will we leave, Maurice?"

"In an hour."

"No one must know we are going."

"No one will know. I'll run over to Lorin's. He has a cabriolet without a horse, I have a horse without a carriage. We'll leave as soon as I get back. You stay here and get everything ready for our departure. We don't need much, we'll buy whatever we lack in England. I'll give Agesilaus a job that gets him out of here for quite a while and Lorin can explain to him what's happened tonight: by tonight we'll be long gone."

"But what if we're stopped en route?"

"Won't we have our passport? We're going to Hubert's place—Hubert is the intendant. He belongs to the municipality of Abbeville; he'll go with us and safeguard us from Abbeville to Boulogne; at Boulogne we'll buy or hire a boat. I can, in any case, drop in at the Committee and score myself some mission for Abbeville. But no—no tricks, right, Geneviève? Let's gain our happiness by merely risking our lives!"

"Yes, yes, my love: and we'll succeed. But you smell so delicious this morning!" said Geneviève, burying her face in Maurice's chest.

"True; I bought a bunch of violets for you this morning when I was passing Palais-Egalité. But when I got home and saw you looking so sad I forgot about everything else."

"Give them to me! I'll pay you back."

Geneviève breathed in the smell of the violets with the sort of fanatic pleasure nervous people almost always get from perfumes. Suddenly her eyes were swimming with tears.

"What's wrong?" Maurice asked.

"Poor Héloïse!" murmured Geneviève.

"Ah, yes," said Maurice with a sigh. "But we have to think of ourselves now and let the dead, whatever party they belonged to, rest in peace in the grave their devotion dug for them. Adieu. I'm off."

"Come back soon."

"I'll be back in less than thirty minutes."

"But what if Lorin's not at home?"

"It won't matter! His servant knows me; I can take whatever I like from his place even if he's not at home, just as he would do here."

"All right! All right!"

"You, my Geneviève, you get everything ready, and try not to pack more than is strictly necessary, as I said. We don't want it to look like we're moving out."

"Don't worry."

The young man took a step toward the door.

"Maurice!" cried Geneviève.

He turned back and saw her arms stretched toward him.

"Good-bye! Good-bye, my love!" he said. "Be brave! I'll be back before you know it."

Geneviève was alone in the house with the mission of packing for the journey. She threw herself into the task with a kind of frenzy. While she remained in Paris it seemed to her she was doubly guilty. Once they were out of France, once they were on foreign soil, it seemed to her that her crime, a crime that was more fate's than her own, would surely weigh less. She even went so far as to hope that in some future splendid isolation she would wind up forgetting that any man but Maurice ever existed.

They had to flee to England, that much was agreed. They would find a small house, a cottage somewhere, on its own, isolated, shut well away from the prying eyes of others. They would change their names, making a single shared name out of the two they bore.

Once there they would take on a couple of servants, who would know nothing whatever about their past. Providence evidently wanted both Maurice and Geneviève to speak English. Neither of them was leaving anything behind in France they would miss—but for the mother you can't help but miss even when she is wicked; the mother that goes by the name of motherland, nation. . . .

And so Geneviève began to sort out the objects that were indispensable for their voyage, or rather their flight. She felt ineffable pleasure in distinguishing among them the things for which Maurice had a predilection: the jacket that fitted most snugly into his waist, the cravat that best set off his ruddy coloring, the books he most often flicked through.

She had already made her choice; already, awaiting the chests that would safely contain them and bear them away, frocks, linen, and books covered the chairs, the sofas, and the piano. Suddenly she heard the key grind in the lock.

"Ah!" she thought. "That must be Agesilaus coming back. Maurice must have met up with him."

She continued at her task. The doors of the salon were open, so she could hear the officieux shifting about in the anteroom. At that precise moment she was holding a roll of sheet music and looking for something to tie it with.

"Agesilaus!" she called out.

Someone's tread, coming nearer, resounded in the neighboring room.

"Agesilaus!" Geneviève called out again. "Come here, would you?"

"Here I am!" said a voice.

At the sound of the voice, Geneviève turned around sharply and gave a terrible shriek.

"My husband!" she shrieked.

"In person," said Dixmer calmly.

Geneviève was standing on a chair; she had been reaching up to feel around for some sort of ribbon or string somewhere to tie the music. She felt her head spin, reached out her arms, and let herself fall backward, as though into an abyss below that she could plummet into. But Dixmer caught her and carried her to a sofa and sat her down.

"What could be the matter with you, dear heart?" he asked. "Is it my presence that produces such an unpleasant effect on you?"

"I'm dying!" cried Geneviève, lying back with both hands over her eyes so as not to see the terrible apparition.

"Right!" said Dixmer. "Did you think I had already passed away, my darling? Do you think I'm a ghost?"

Geneviève looked around her, dazed, and, seeing the portrait of Maurice, let herself slip off the sofa onto her knees, as though to beseech the help of this powerless and insensate image that continued to beam at her. The poor woman knew only too well all the menace that Dixmer hid under the affected calm.

"Yes, my dear child," the tanner continued, "it really is me. Perhaps you thought I was miles away from Paris, but I wasn't: I stayed here in town. The day after the day I left the house I went back and saw a lovely heap of ashes in its place. I asked after you but no one had seen you. I began to look for you and I had a devil of a job finding you. I confess I didn't think to look for you here; but I did have my suspicions, since as you see I came. The main thing is, here I am and there you are. . . . And how is Maurice? In all truth, I'm sure you have suffered greatly—you such a good little royalist, to be forced to live under the same roof as such a republican fundamentalist."

"My God!" murmured Geneviève. "My God! Have pity on me!"

"After that," Dixmer went on, looking around, "what consoles me, my dear, is that you are so well set up here—you don't look to me as though you've suffered too badly from being in hiding. Me, since the fire in which our home and our fortune went up in smoke, I wandered about willy-nilly, living in basements, the holds of boats, sometimes even the sewers that flow into the Seine."

"Monsieur!" said Geneviève.

"You've got some lovely-looking fruit there. . . . I often had to go without dessert, being forced to go without dinner."

Geneviève hid her head in her hands and sobbed.

"Not that I lacked for money," Dixmer went on. "Thank God, I carried about thirty thousand francs in gold on me, which is now worth five hundred thousand francs. But how can a coalman, a fisherman, or a rag and bone man pull louis[3] out of his pocket to buy a bit of cheese or sausage? Oh, God, yes, madame! I played each of those roles in turn. Today I'm a patriot, an extremist one, a Marseillais,[4] all the better to disguise myself. I roll my r's and I swear like a trooper. Heavens! What do you think! A middle-aged outlaw doesn't get around Paris as easily as a pretty young woman, and I wasn't lucky enough to know some fanatic republican woman who would stow me away."

"Monsieur, monsieur!" cried Geneviève. "Have mercy on me! Can't you see I'm dying?"

"Of worry, yes, I can imagine. You were so very worried about me.

But console yourself, madame, I'm back, and we won't leave each other's sight again."

"Oh! You're going to kill me!" cried Geneviève.

Dixmer looked at her with a terrifying smile.

"Kill an innocent woman! Oh, madame! What are you saying? You must have missed me so much you've gone out of your mind. . . ."

"Monsieur," cried Geneviève. "Monsieur, I beg you with joined hands to kill me rather than go on torturing me with such cruel gibes. No, I am not innocent. Yes, I am a criminal. Yes, I deserve death. Kill me, monsieur, kill me!"

"So you admit you deserve death?"

"Yes, yes."

"And that, to expiate I know not what crime you accuse yourself of, you would accept such a death without complaining?"

"Strike me, monsieur, smite me down; I won't utter a sound. Far from cursing the hand that strikes me, I will bless it."

"No, madame, I don't want to strike you. But you will die; that's more than likely. But instead of being ignominious, as you might well fear, your death will be glorious, on a par with the very finest deaths. Thank me, madame: in punishing you I will immortalize you."

"Monsieur, what will you do?"

"You will pursue the goal we were aiming at when we were so rudely interrupted. For your sake and for mine, you will be brought down, guilty; for everyone else's sake, you will die a martyr."

"Oh, my God! You'll make me lose my mind, talking like that. Where are you taking me? What are you dragging me into?"

"To your death, probably."

"Then let me say a prayer."

"Your prayer?"

"Yes."

"To whom?"

"None of your business! From the moment you kill me I'll have paid my debt, and when I've paid it I'll owe you nothing."

"That's only fair," said Dixmer, withdrawing to the other room. "I'll wait for you."

He left the salon.

Geneviève went to kneel before the portrait of Maurice, pressing both her hands to a heart that was breaking.

"Maurice," she said softly, "forgive me. I didn't expect to be happy myself, but I hoped to be able to make you happy. Now I am taking away from you a happiness that was your life, Maurice. Forgive me for your death, my beloved!"

She then cut a long lock of her hair and wound it around the bouquet of violets, which she laid at the base of the portrait. This inanimate, silent canvas seemed to take on a painful expression on seeing her depart. Or so it seemed to Geneviève through her tears.

"Well, then; are you ready, madame?" asked Dixmer.

"Already!" murmured Geneviève.

"Oh, take your time, madame!" replied Dixmer. "I'm in no hurry! Besides, Maurice probably won't be long getting back, and I'd be delighted to thank him for the hospitality he has shown you."

Geneviève gave a lurch of terror at the idea that her lover and her husband might meet. She shot up as though on a spring.

"It's over, monsieur," she said. "I'm ready."

Dixmer went out first; Geneviève followed him on unsteady legs, her eyes half shut, her head thrown back. They climbed into a fiacre that was waiting at the door and the car rolled away.

As Geneviève had said, it was over.

40

THE PUITS-DE-NOÉ BY NIGHT

The man dressed in a carmagnole whom we saw striding up and down the Hall of Lost Footsteps, and whom we heard exchanging a few words with the wicket clerk who had remained behind on guard duty at the mouth of the tunnel during the expedition of Giraud the architect, General Santerre, and old man Richard; this patriot *enragé*, with his furry bear-cub cap and thick mustache, who had tried to put himself over on Simon as having paraded the head of the Princesse de Lamballe, found himself the day after that night full of varied emotions at the Puits-de-Noé cabaret at around seven o'clock in the evening. The cabaret, as you'll recall, was on the corner of the rue de la Vieille-Draperie.

He was there at the house of the liquor licensee—who, in this case, was a woman—sitting at the back of a room made sooty and smoky by tobacco and candles, pretending to devour a dish of fish in black butter sauce.

The room he was eating in was just about deserted; only two or three regulars had stayed behind, enjoying the privilege their daily visit to the establishment gave them. Most of the tables were empty; but it must be said in honor of the Puits-de-Noé that the tablecloths, which were red going on purplish blue, revealed the passage of a gratifying number of satisfied customers.

The last three customers filed out one after the other, and at around a quarter to eight the patriot found himself on his own. At that point he pushed away, with the most aristocratic disgust, the coarse dish he had appeared to be so greatly relishing just a moment before and pulled from his pocket a bar of Spanish chocolate, which he consumed slowly and with a very different expression from the one we have tried to lend his physiognomy.

From time to time, as he continued munching his Spanish chocolate together with his black bread, he glanced anxiously and impatiently at the glass door, which was covered with a red and white checked curtain. At times he pricked up his ears, interrupting his frugal meal so absentmindedly that the mistress of the house, seated at her counter quite close to the door on which the patriot's gaze was riveted, began to think, without too much vanity, that she was the object of his interest.

At last the doorbell rang, and so loudly as to give our man quite a jolt. He went back to his fish without the mistress of the house noticing that he threw half of it to a poor skinny dog that had been staring at him with its tongue hanging out and the other half to a cat who aimed a delicate but deadly paw at the dog.

The door with the red and white checked curtain opened and a man came in dressed more or less like the patriot with the exception of the fur cap, for which he had substituted the ubiquitous red cap. An enormous bunch of keys hung from the man's belt, as did a large infantry sword with a copper scabbard.

"My soup! My booze!" the man called out, stepping into the common room without touching his red cap or doing more than giving a nod to the mistress of the establishment. Then, with a sigh of weariness, he plopped down at the table next to the one where our patriot was having his supper.

In deference to the priority she gave the newcomer, the mistress of the house got up and placed the order herself.

The two men turned their backs to each other, one of them looking out into the street, the other toward the back of the room. Not a word was spoken between them until the mistress of the cabaret had completely disappeared.

When the door was shut behind her and when, by the light of a single candle suspended by a length of wire in such a cunning way that the light could be shared by both tables, the man with the fur cap at last could see, thanks to the mirror facing him, that the room was perfectly deserted, he spoke.

"Good evening," he said to his companion without looking round.

"Good evening, monsieur," said the newcomer.

"Well then," the patriot asked, affecting the same indifference, "where are we?"

"Well then, we're done."

"What's done?"

"As we agreed, I picked a fight with old man Richard over my duties, I said I was hard of hearing and had my dizzy spells, and I keeled over in the middle of the office."

"Good stuff; and then?"

"And then old man Richard called his wife and his wife rubbed my temples with vinegar, which brought me around."

"Good! After that?"

"After that, as we agreed between ourselves, I said it was the lack of air that gave me these dizzy spells, given my sanguine temperament, and that the work at the Conciergerie, where there are four hundred inmates at the moment, was killing me."

"What did they say?"

"Mother Richard felt sorry for me."

"And old man Richard?"

"He showed me the door."

"But it's not enough that he showed you the door."

"Wait a second: then Mother Richard, who's a good woman, balled him out for having no heart, seeing as I've got a family to feed."

"And what did he say to that?"

"He said she was right, but that the first requirement for being a wicket clerk was to remain in the prison to which he was attached; that the Republic meant business; and that it cut the heads off anyone who had dizzy spells in the exercise of their duties."

"Lord!" exclaimed the patriot.

"And he was not wrong, old man Richard; since the Austrian woman's been there, surveillance has gotten out of hand. The fellows in there would look twice at their own fathers."

The patriot gave his plate to the dog to lick, and the dog got bitten by the cat.

"Get on with it," he said.

"To make a long story short, monsieur, I started moaning and groaning, which means I was really sick. I asked for the nurse and assured them my children would die of starvation if my pay was stopped."

"And old man Richard?"

"Old man Richard said that when you are a wicket clerk, you don't make babies."

"But Mother Richard was on your side, I suppose?"

"Luckily! She kicked up quite a stink and attacked him for having no heart, and old man Richard ended up saying to me: 'Well then, citizen Gracchus, see if you can make a deal with one of your pals who can give you something as a guarantee; send him to me as your replacement and I promise you I'll see he's accepted.' At that I left, saying: 'Say no more, old man Richard, I'll find someone.'"

"And did you find someone, my brave boy?"

At that moment the mistress of the establishment returned with citizen Gracchus's soup and pot of rotgut. Neither Gracchus nor the patriot took any notice; but they were not done yet.

"Citizeness," said the clerk, "I got a small bonus from old man

Richard today, so I can afford the pork chop with gherkins and the bottle of Burgundy. Send your servant out to the butcher's for the chop and go and get me the wine from your cellar, will you?"

The hostess immediately gave the command; a servant slipped out the door into the street, and the hostess through the door to the cellar.

"All right," said the patriot. "You're a smart boy."

"So smart that I'm not fooling myself what's in store for both of us, whatever you like to promise me. Do you have any idea what we're risking?"

"Yes, perfectly."

"Our necks are both on the block!"

"Don't you worry about mine."

"It's not your neck, monsieur, I have to admit, that's giving me the most worry."

"It's your own?"

"Yes."

"But if I'm paying twice what it's worth . . ."

"Steady on, monsieur! A neck is a very precious thing—and so's the head that's on it."

"Yours is not."

"What! Mine isn't precious?"

"Not at this point in time, at least."

"What are you trying to say?"

"I mean that your head isn't worth an *obole*.[1] If I were an agent of the Committee of Public Safety, for instance, you'd be guillotined tomorrow."

The clerk turned around so swifty the dog started barking at him. He was as pale as a corpse.

"Don't turn around and don't look as though you're going to pass out," said the patriot. "Just quietly finish your soup. I am not an agent provocateur, my friend. Get me into the Conciergerie, set me up as your replacement, give me the keys, and tomorrow I'll count you out fifty thousand livres in gold."

"You're for real at least?"

"Oh! You've got pretty good security! You're holding my head in your hands."

The clerk thought about it for a few seconds.

"Come," said the patriot, who could see him in the mirror. "Come, don't give in to bad thoughts; if you denounce me, you'll only have done your duty and the Republic won't give you a brass razoo. If, on the other hand, you work with me, you won't have done your duty, and because it's unjust to do something for nothing in this world, I'll give you the fifty thousand livres."

"Oh, I get it all right," said the clerk. "I stand to gain by doing what you want me to do; but I'm afraid of the consequences...."

"The consequences! . . . What is it you have to fear? Come on, it's not me who's going to denounce you, on the contrary."

"I guess so."

"The day after I'm in place, you do a round at the Conciergerie. I'll count you out twenty-five rolls of two thousand francs each; the twenty-five rolls will easily fit in your pocket. With the money, I'll give you a pass for getting out of France. Wherever you go, even if you're not rich, you'll be independent."

"Well then, you've got a deal, monsieur, come what may. I'm just a poor devil, I am, a nonentity; I don't get mixed up in politics. France has always done all right without me and it won't die if I'm not here. If you're up to no good, too bad for you."

"In any case," said the patriot, "I don't think I can do any worse than what they're doing now."

"Monsieur will permit me not to judge the politics of the National Convention."

"I admire your philosophical bent and your insouciance, my good man. Now, let's see, when will you introduce me to old man Richard?"

"Tonight, if you like."

"Yes, certainly. Who am I?"

"My cousin Mardoche."

"Mardoche, so be it; I like the name. What do I do for a living?"

"Tailor."

"From tanner to tailor, it's just a flick of the wrist."

"Are you a tanner?"

"I could be."

"True."

"What time tonight?"

"In half an hour, if you like."

"Nine o'clock, then."

"When will I get the money?"

"Tomorrow."

"Does that mean you're filthy rich?"

"I'm well off."

"An ex-aristo, right?"

"What do you care!"

"To have money and then give your money away running the risk of getting the chop, ex-aristos must be pretty thick!"

"You can't have everything! The sans culottes are so smart there's just not enough to go around!"

"Quiet! Here's my wine."

"See you later tonight, outside the Conciergerie."

"Yes."

The patriot paid his bill and left. You could hear him call out in a thundering voice from the doorway:

"Hurry it up, citizeness! The chops with gherkins! My cousin Gracchus is dying of hunger."

"Good old Mardoche!" said the clerk, sipping the glass of Burgundy the cabaret owner had just poured him, gazing upon him tenderly.

41

THE CLERK FROM THE WAR MINISTRY

The patriot had walked out, but he had not gone far. Through the smoky windows he watched the clerk to make sure he didn't enter into communication with any agents of the republican police, one of the most effective forces that ever existed, for half of society was spying on the other half, not so much for the greater glory of the government as for the greater security of one's own head.

But nothing the patriot feared occurred, and at a few minutes before nine the clerk got up, chucked the cabaret owner's chin, and left. The patriot joined him at the quai de la Conciergerie and they went into the prison together. That very night the deal was sealed: old man Richard accepted Mardoche as a replacement clerk, filling in for Gracchus.

But two hours before the deal was clinched in the jail, something happened in another part of the prison that, although without apparent interest, was no less crucial for the principal characters of this story.

The Conciergerie registrar, tired after a long day, was about to put his books away and go home when a man turned up at his office, led by citizeness Richard.

"Citizen registrar," she said, "this is your colleague from the War Ministry, who comes on behalf of the citizen minister to remove some nuts and bolts the army needs."

"Ah, citizen," said the registrar, "you're a bit late. I was just closing up shop."

"Dear colleague, forgive me," replied the newcomer, "but we have so much to do we can hardly get through all our chores except in our spare time, and our spare time, let me tell you, is almost always when others are eating or sleeping."

"If that's how it is, do what you have to, my dear colleague; but hurry it up, won't you, for as you say, it's time to eat and I'm hungry. Have you got your authorization?"

"Here it is," said the clerk from the War Ministry, flashing a wallet that his colleague, in a hurry though he was, nonetheless examined scrupulously.

"It all seems to be in order," said Mother Richard. "My husband has already given it a thorough going-over."

"Never mind that," said the registrar, continuing his inspection.

The clerk from the War Ministry waited patiently, like a man used to the strict accomplishment of formalities.

"Marvelous!" said the registrar of the Conciergerie. "You may now begin whenever you like. Do you have many nuts to take out?"

"About a hundred."

"Then you'll be at it for several days?"

"Yes, and so, dear colleague, I'd like to set myself up properly here, if you don't mind, of course."

"What do you mean?" asked the registrar of the Conciergerie.

"I'll explain it all to you when I take you to dine at my place this evening; you said you were hungry."

"And I won't unsay it."

"Well then, you can meet my wife—she's quite a good cook, and you'll get to know me—I'm not a bad sort."

"Indeed, yes, that's the way you strike me; but, dear colleague . . ."

"Oh, why don't you just accept without further ado! I'll buy the oysters at the place du Châtelet on the way and we'll pick up a chicken from our rôtisseur; we'll also have two or three little dishes Madame Durand makes to perfection."

"You're making my mouth water, dear colleague," said the registrar of the Conciergerie, dazzled by the kind of menu a registrar in the pay of the Revolutionary Tribunal at the rate of two livres in assignats was not accustomed to, those two livres being in reality scarcely worth two francs.

"So you accept?"

"I accept."

"In that case, the work can wait till tomorrow. That's enough for this evening; let's go."

"Right you are."

"Are you coming?"

"One second; just let me go and alert the gendarmes guarding the Austrian woman."

"Why do you need to alert them?"

"So they know I'm going out and therefore there is no one in the office; they can keep an ear out for any suspect noise."

"Ah, of course! Excellent precaution, I must say!"

"You understand, don't you?"

"Perfectly. Off you go."

The registrar of the Conciergerie did indeed go off and hammer at the wicket door, which one of the gendarmes opened.

"Who's there?" he asked.

"Me! The registrar, you know. I'm off. Good night, citizen Gilbert."

"Good night, citizen registrar."

And the wicket closed again.

The clerk from the War Ministry had followed the whole scene with the closest attention, and when the door to the Queen's cell was open, his gaze had rapidly plunged into the depths of the first compartment. He had seen the gendarme Duchesne at the table, and had assured himself that the Queen had, in fact, only two guards.

It goes without saying that when the registrar of the Conciergerie returned, his colleague once more looked as blank as he could possibly get his physiognomy to look.

As they were leaving the Conciergerie, two men were making their way in. These two men were citizen Gracchus and his cousin Mardoche. Cousin Mardoche and the clerk from the War Ministry, each with a movement that seemed to arise from a similar feeling, pushed their respective headgear down over their eyes the moment they saw each other—the one his fur cap, the other his broad-brimmed hat.

"Who are those men?" asked the clerk from the War Ministry.

"I only know one of them: he's a wicket clerk name of Gracchus."

"Ah!" said the other man with affected indifference. "So wicket clerks can leave the Conciergerie?"

"They have their day off."

The investigation was left there as the two new pals took the pont-au-Change. At the corner of the place du Châtelet the clerk from the War Ministry, as he had said he would, bought a bucket of twelve dozen oysters. Then they went on their merry way along the quai de Gesvres.

The War Ministry clerk's home was very simple: citizen Durand lived in a three-room apartment on the place de Grève in a house without a porter. Each tenant had a key to the alley, and it was agreed that they would alert one another if one of them accidentally locked themselves out by knocking once, twice, or three times with a hammer, according to which floor they lived on: whoever was expecting someone and recognized the signal would then come down and open the door. But citizen Durand had his key in his pocket and didn't need to knock.

The Palais registrar found Madame Durand very much to his liking. She was, in fact, a charming woman, whose face was made powerfully attractive at a glance by an expression of deep sadness that suffused her entire physiognomy. It is a known fact that sadness is one of the surest means of seduction available to good-looking women; sadness makes all men amorous, without exception—even registrars, for, whatever they say, registrars are men, and no matter how fiercely proud or hardhearted a man is, there isn't one who doesn't hope to console a pretty woman so afflicted and turn the white roses of a pallid complexion into gaily blushing roses, as the citizen poet Dorat would say.

The two clerks supped with gusto; only Madame Durand had no appetite. Yet questions were bandied back and forth in between mouthfuls. The war clerk asked his colleague, with a truly remarkable curiosity in these times of everyday tragedy, what went on in the Palais on days of judgment and what were the means of surveillance. The Palais registrar, delighted to have such an attentive audience, happily supplied answers, rabbiting on about the practices of the jailers, those of Fouquier-Tinville, and finally those of Sanson,[1] the star performer in the tragedy staged on a daily basis in the place de la Révolution.

Then, addressing himself to his colleague and host, he asked him in turn about his ministry.

"Oh!" said Durand. "I'm not as informed as you are, being a person infinitely less important. I'm just the secretary of the appointed clerk of the place; I do the hard work for the chief clerk. As an obscure employee, I get the pain, the illustrious get the gain: that's how it goes in all bureaucracies, even revolutionary ones. The earth and the sky may shift one day, but bureaucracies won't."

"Well then, I'll lend you a hand, citizen," said the Palais registrar, won over completely by his host's good wine and especially by the beautiful eyes of the host's wife.

"Oh, thank you!" cried the man to whom this gracious offer was made. "Any change of routine or location is a distraction for a poor employee, and I fear my work at the Conciergerie will end sooner rather than later. But as long as I can take Madame Durand with me every night, since she'd be bored on her own here . . ."

"I don't see why not," said the Palais registrar, delighted with the lovely distraction his colleague promised him.

"She can tell me which nuts to remove," continued citizen Durand.

"And then, from time to time, if tonight's supper wasn't too terrible, you can come and have the same again."

"Yes, but not too often," said the Palais registrar fatuously, "for I must tell you there'd be hell to pay if I came home any later than usual to a certain little house in the rue du Petit-Musc."

"Well then, we've got ourselves an excellent arrangement," said Durand. "Wouldn't you say, darling?"

Madame Durand, extremely pale and extremely sad always, looked up at her husband and answered:

"Let your will be done."

Eleven o'clock struck. It was time to go. The Palais registrar got up and took his leave of his new friends, effusively thanking them for the dinner and expressing his pleasure at getting to know them. Citizen Durand led his guest to the door, then returned to the room.

"Go, Geneviève, go to bed."

The young woman stood up without a word, picked up a lamp, and went into the room on the right. Durand, or rather Dixmer, watched her go, standing lost in thought for an instant with a black scowl on his face after her departure, then he took himself off to his room, which was on the opposite side.

42

THE TWO NOTES

From then on, the clerk from the War Ministry went to work assiduously every evening in the office of his colleague from the Palais. Madame Durand recorded their activity concerning removal of the nuts and bolts on registers prepared in advance, which Durand copied zealously.

Durand examined everything without appearing to notice anything. He had noted that every evening at nine o'clock a basket of provisions was brought by Richard or his wife and dropped at the door. When the registrar took leave of the gendarme with an "I'm off then, citizen," the gendarme, either Gilbert or Duchesne, would come out, grab the basket, and take it to Marie Antoinette.

During the three consecutive nights Durand had remained tinkering later than usual, the basket also remained later in its place, since it was only on opening the door to say good-bye to the registrar that the gendarme would take hold of the provisions.

A quarter of an hour after introducing the new full basket, one of the two gendames would put the empty basket of the day before at the door, in the same place as the other one had been.

The evening of the fourth day—it was the beginning of October—after the usual session, when the Palais registrar had retired and when Durand, or rather Dixmer, had stayed behind with his wife, he let his quill drop and stooped to pick it up, looking around and listening as intently as if his life depended upon it. He then swiftly got to his feet and dashed to the door of the wicket, where he took up the napkin covering the basket and drove a tiny silver case into the soft bread loaf destined for the royal prisoner.

Then, pale and trembling from the emotion that even a man with the most powerful nervous system is rocked by when he has just accomplished some supreme act long prepared and strongly longed for, he went back to his place with one hand on his forehead, the other on his heart.

Geneviève watched him all the while, but without saying a word. Ever since he had taken her from Maurice's place, she always waited for him to speak first. But this time it was she who broke the silence.

"Is it for tonight?" she asked.

"No, tomorrow night," Dixmer answered crisply.

He looked and listened once more, closed the books, and knocked on the gendarme's door.

"Huh?" said Gilbert.

"Citizen," he said, "I'm off."

"All right," called the gendarme from the back of the cell. "Good night."

"Good night, citizen Gilbert."

Durand heard the grinding of the keys in the locks, realized the gendarme was about to open the door, and took off. In the corridor that led from the apartment of old man Richard to the courtyard, he bumped into a clerk coiffed with a fur cap and brandishing a heavy bunch of keys. Fear seized Dixmer; this man, brutal like all men of his station, was about to say something to him, was peering at him, was perhaps about to recognize him. He shoved his hat down, while Geneviève pulled the trimmings of her black mantle over her eyes.

Dixmer was wrong.

"Sorry!" was all the clerk said, even though he was the one that had been knocked into.

Dixmer gave a start at the sound of the man's voice, which was soft and polite. But the clerk was no doubt in a hurry and he slipped into the corridor, opened the door to old man Richard's, and disappeared. Dixmer continued on his way, dragging Geneviève behind him.

"That's odd," he said when they were outside with the door firmly shut behind them and the fresh air had cooled his burning brow.

"Oh, yes! Very odd!" muttered Geneviève.

In the days when they had been close, husband and wife would have communicated the source of their amazement to each other. But Dixmer shut his thoughts away in his mind, battling with them as he would some hallucination, while Geneviève simply threw a backward glance over the somber Palais when they had turned into the pont-au-Change. As she looked back, something like the phantom of a lost friend materialized, stirring up a whole host of memories both bitter and sweet at once.

They reached the place de Grève without having uttered a single word.

During that time, the gendarme Gilbert had stepped out and taken the basket of provisions destined for the Queen. It contained fruit, a cold chicken, a bottle of white wine, a carafe of water, and half of a two-pound loaf of bread.

Gilbert removed the napkin and recognized the normal arrangement of things packed in the basket by citizeness Richard. Then he shifted the screen and spoke loudly to the Queen.

"Citizeness, here is your supper."

Marie Antoinette broke the bread, but scarcely had her fingers made an impression in it than she felt the cold contact of silver and understood that the bread enclosed something out of the ordinary. She looked around, but the gendarme had already withdrawn. For a moment the Queen didn't move, measuring as she was Gilbert's gradual retreat. When she was sure he had gone to sit down next to his comrade, she pulled the case out of the bread.

The case contained a note. She unfolded it and read the following words:

> Madame, be ready tomorrow at the same time as you receive this note, for tomorrow at this time a woman will be introduced into Your Majesty's prison cell. This woman will take your clothes and give you hers; then you will walk out of the Conciergerie on the arm of one of your most devoted servants.
>
> Do not worry about the commotion that will occur in the neighboring room, do not stop at the cries or groans; concentrate only on quickly putting on the dress and mantle of the woman who is to take Your Majesty's place.

"What devotion!" murmured the Queen. "Thank you, Lord! So I am not, as they claim I am, an object of execration for everyone."

She reread the note. The second paragraph suddenly hit her.

" 'Do not stop at the cries or groans,' " she murmured. "Oh! That means they'll strike my two guardians, poor fellows, who've shown me so much pity. Oh, never! Never!"

She tore off the bottom half of the note, which was on white paper, and as she had no pencil or quill with which to reply to this unknown friend who so concerned himself with her, she took the brooch from her fichu and pricked the paper to form the letters that composed the following words:

> I cannot and should not accept the sacrifice of anyone's life in exchange for mine.
>
> M. A.

Then she slipped the note back into the case and drove the case into the untouched part of the broken loaf of bread.

This operation had only just been completed when the clock struck ten. The Queen was holding the piece of bread in her hand and sadly counting the notes ringing out the hours as they vibrated slowly and distinctly, when she heard a jarring noise such as a diamond would make scratching glass at one of the windows overlooking what was known as the Women's Courtyard. This noise was followed by a faint shock at the windowpane, a shock repeated several times and covered deliberately by a man's cough. Then a small piece of rolled-up paper appeared at a corner of the window, slid slowly in, and fell to the foot of the wall. The Queen heard the sound of keys jangling and footsteps ringing on the cobblestones as they moved away.

She realized that a hole had just been made in a corner of the window and that the man moving away had slid a piece of paper through this hole. The piece of paper was, no doubt, a note. This note lay on the ground. The Queen looked longingly at it, all the while listening to hear if one of the guards was approaching. But she could hear them jabbering away together, as was their wont—softly, through a kind of tacit agreement not to disturb her. So she got up as quietly as she could and, holding her breath, retrieved the note.

A thin hard object slid from it as though it were a sheath and rang out with a metallic sound as it fell to the brick floor. This object was a file of incredible fineness, a jewel more than a tool, one of those steel implements with which the feeblest and clumsiest hand can cut through the thickest iron bar in a quarter of an hour.

She read the note:

Madame, tomorrow night at half past nine a man will come and chat with the gendarmes who guard you through the window on the Women's Courtyard. While they are so engaged, Your Majesty will saw through the third bar of her window, cutting diagonally from left to right. . . . A quarter of an hour should suffice Your Majesty; then get ready to go through the window. . . . This note comes from one of your most devoted and faithful subjects, who has dedicated his life to the service of Your Majesty and would be happy to sacrifice it for her.

"Oh!" murmured the Queen. "Is this a trap? But, no, I think I recognize the writing. It is the same as at the Temple; it is the writing of the Knight of Maison-Rouge. Well, well! Perhaps God wants me to escape after all."

With that the Queen fell on her knees and took refuge in prayer, the prisoner's supreme balm.

43

DIXMER'S PREPARATIONS

The next day finally dawned, preceded by a night of insomnia; but the dawn was alarming, appearing as apocalyptic red streaks that could only be described, without exaggeration, as the color of blood. Every day in those days and in that particular year, the most beautiful sun had livid spots.

The Queen hardly slept a wink and what sleep she did get was not restful; barely had she closed her eyes than it seemed to her she could see blood and hear screaming. She had actually fallen asleep with the file in her hand.

She spent part of the day in prayer. The guardians were so used to seeing her praying that they took no notice of the increase in pious devotion.

Now and again the prisoner drew from her bosom the file that had been sent to her by one of her saviors; she would compare the delicacy of the implement with the strength of the bars. Luckily, the bars were sealed into the wall only at one end, that is, at the bottom. The top fitted into a crossbar. With the bottom part sawed through, one had only to yank the bar for it to come away.

But it wasn't the physical difficulties that froze the Queen's blood in her veins; she knew perfectly well that the thing was possible, and it was this very possibility that turned hope into a bloody flame that dazzled her.

But she realized that to reach her her friends would have to kill the men who guarded her, and she would not have consented to their deaths at any cost. Those men were the only ones to have shown her some pity for a long, long while.

On the other hand, beyond those bars she was instructed to saw, on the other side of the bodies of those two men who would bite the dust trying to prevent her saviors from reaching her, were life, liberty, and perhaps vengeance, three things so sweet, especially for a woman, that she asked God to forgive her for desiring them so passionately.

Furthermore, she believed she saw no sign that the guardians were agitated by any suspicion; they didn't even seem to be aware of the trap they hoped to catch the prisoner in, supposing the plot was a trap. These simple men would have given themselves away to eyes as practiced as those of a woman used to sniffing out evil, having suffered so much of it.

And so the Queen almost entirely gave up thinking about the twin openings that had been presented to her like a trap. But the more the humiliation of being caught in a trap faded, the more she became apprehensive about seeing blood shed for her sake.

"Strange fate, sublime spectacle!" she muttered. "Two plots come together to save a poor queen, or rather a poor woman prisoner who has done nothing to lure or encourage the plotters, and they are going to break at the exact same time! But who knows? Perhaps they are one and the same plot. Perhaps it's like drilling two tunnels that are meant to meet up at the same point.

"I would thus be saved—it is up to me!

"But a poor woman sacrificed in my place!

"And two men killed so the woman can get to me!

"God and the future would not forgive me.

"I can't! I can't! . . ."

Yet her mind kept being visited and revisited by those great notions having to do with the devotion of servants for their masters, along with the antique tradition of the rights of masters over the lives of their servants; phantoms almost effaced of a dying royalty.

"Anne of Austria[1] would have said yes," she told herself. "Anne of Austria would have placed the grand principle of the salvation of royalty above all else. Anne of Austria was of the same blood as I am and almost in the same situation as I am in. What madness to have come to pursue the royalty of Anne of Austria in France! And anyway, it wasn't I who came! Two kings[2] said: 'It is important that two royal children who have never seen each other, who do not love each other, who perhaps will never love each other, be married at the same altar, and die on the same scaffold.' "

"And then again, won't my death entail that of the poor child who, in the eyes of my few remaining friends, is still King of France?

"And when my son is dead as my husband is dead, won't their two shades smile with pity to see me stain the throne of Saint Louis with my blood to spare a few drops of common blood from spilling?"

The Queen grew increasingly fretful, her doubts increasingly feverish as the day wore on, until finally, full of the horror her fears engendered, she made it to the evening. Several times she had examined her two guardians; never had they looked more tranquil; and never had the small attentions of these coarse but good men struck her more forcefully.

When darkness came to the prison cell, when the marching feet of the rounds could be heard, when the sound of arms and the howling of dogs gave the echo throughout the somber vaults new life, when, finally, the whole prison showed itself fearful and without hope, Marie Antoinette stood appalled, overcome by an inherently feminine weakness.

"Oh! I will flee," she said. "Yes, yes, I will flee. When they come, when they start to talk, I'll saw the bar and I will await what God and my liberators command of me. I owe myself to my children; they will not kill them, or if they kill them and I am free, oh! Well then, at least . . ."

She did not finish, her eyes closed, her voice was bitten off. It was a frightful dream, the dream of this poor Queen in a room sealed with locks and bolts and iron bars. But soon, in her dream, bars and bolts fell away; she saw herself in the middle of a great army, somber and pitiless; she ordered the flames to burn, the blades to shoot out of their sheaths; she took her revenge on a people who were not, in the end, her own.

Meanwhile, Gilbert and Duchesne chatted quietly as they prepared their evening meal.

Meanwhile, too, Dixmer and Geneviève entered the Conciergerie and as usual set themselves up in the office. After an hour, also as usual, the registrar of the Palais completed his work and left them to it. As soon as the door had shut on his colleague, Dixmer rushed to the empty basket placed at the Queen's door, waiting to be exchanged for that evening's basket.

He seized the bit of bread left over, broke it and found the case with the Queen's message hidden in it. As he read what she had pricked, the color drained away from his face. Geneviève watched as he tore the paper into tiny pieces, which he tossed into the fiery mouth of the furnace.

"It's fine," he said. "Everything's agreed." He turned to Geneviève. "Come here, madame."

"Me?"

"Yes, there's something I don't want anyone else to hear."

Geneviève, as still and cold as marble, shrugged resignation and approached.

"The time has come, madame," said Dixmer. "Listen to me."

"Yes, monsieur."

"You prefer a death that is useful to your cause, a death that will see you blessed by the whole loyalist party and pitied by a whole people, regardless, to an ignominious death enacted only out of revenge, don't you?"

"Yes, monsieur."

"I could have killed you on the spot when I found you at your lover's; but a man who, like me, has sacrificed his life to an honorable and sacred mission has to know how to put his own misfortunes to good use by dedicating them to the cause. This is what I have done, or rather what I count on doing. I have refused, as you see, the pleasure of taking the law into my own hands. I have also spared your lover."

Something like a smile, fleeting but terrible, flickered over Geneviève's ashen lips.

"But as for your lover, you know me well enough to know I've just been biding my time till I could go one better."

"Monsieur," said Geneviève, "I am ready, so why the preamble?"

"You're ready?"

"Yes, you're going to kill me. You're right. I'm waiting."

Dixmer looked at Geneviève with a jolt of shock in spite of himself. She was sublime at that moment, luminous with the most brilliant glow of all, that comes from love.

"I will go on with my plan," said Dixmer. "I've alerted the Queen, she's waiting, though she'll no doubt have a few objections. You'll have to force her."

"Fine, monsieur; your wish is my command—just tell me what to do."

"Shortly," Dixmer resumed, "I'll go and knock on the door and Gilbert will open it. With this dagger"—and here Dixmer opened his coat and flashed a double-edged dagger, pulling the blade half out of its sheath—"with this dagger, I will kill him."

Geneviève shuddered in spite of herself. Dixmer signaled for her to pay attention to what he was saying.

"The moment I stab him, you rush into the back room, the room the Queen's in. There is no door, you know, just a screen; you change clothes with her while I kill the second soldier. Then I'll take the Queen's arm and walk her out through the wicket gate."

"Very well," said Geneviève coldly.

"Do you follow?" Dixmer continued. "Every night you're seen wearing this mantle of black taffeta that hides your face. Put your mantle on Her Majesty and drape it the way you usually drape it on yourself."

"I'll do exactly as you say."

"It now remains for me to forgive you and to thank you, madame," said Dixmer.

Geneviève shook her head with a chilling smile.

"I don't need your forgiveness, monsieur, or your thanks," she said, raising her hand dismissively. "What I am doing, or rather what I am going to do, would erase any crime, and I am guilty of mere weakness. Furthermore, this weakness, if you recall your own conduct, monsieur, was practically forced upon me by you. I removed myself from him, yet you pushed me into his arms. You are the instigator, the judge, and the avenger rolled into one. So it is now up to me to forgive you for my death—and I do forgive you. And it is now up to me to thank you, monsieur, for taking away my life, since that life would have been unbearable separated from the only man I love, particularly once you cut me off from him by your vicious revenge."

Dixmer dug his nails into his chest; he tried to say something but his voice failed. He circled the office.

"Time is passing," he said at last. "Every second counts, so let's get on with it, madame. Are you ready?"

"I've said so, monsieur," Geneviève answered with the calm peculiar to martyrs. "I'm waiting!"

Dixmer gathered all his papers, went to see if the doors were properly shut and to check that no one could get into the office, then began to reiterate the instructions to his wife.

"Save your breath, monsieur," said Geneviève. "I'm well aware what I have to do."

"Well then, adieu!"

With that Dixmer held out his hand, as though, at this extreme moment, all recriminations should subside in the face of the momentousness of the situation and the sublimeness of the sacrifice.

Geneviève shivered as she touched her husband's hand with her fingertips.

"Stay close to me, madame," said Dixmer. "And as soon as I've struck Gilbert, go in."

"I'm ready."

Dixmer then gripped his enormous dagger in his right hand and, with his left, knocked on the door.

44

THE PREPARATIONS OF THE
KNIGHT OF MAISON-ROUGE

While the scene just described was taking place at the door of the Queen's prison cell, or rather of the outer section occupied by the two gendarmes, other preparations were forging ahead on the opposite side of the cell, out in the Women's Courtyard.

A man suddenly emerged like a statue made of stone that had broken away from the wall. This man was followed by two dogs, and while humming the "Ça ira," a song very much in vogue at the time, he had scraped the five iron bars that secured the Queen's window with the bunch of keys he held in his hand.

At first the Queen had jumped; but, recognizing the event as a signal, she had immediately opened her window quietly and got down to the task at hand with a surer method than anyone would have imagined, for more than once, in the locksmith's workshop where her royal spouse used to spend a good part of every day amusing himself, her dainty fingers had handled tools similar to the one on which all her hopes of salvation now rested.

As soon as the man with the bunch of keys heard the Queen's window opening, he knocked on the wardens' window.

"Ah! Ah!" said Gilbert, looking through the glass pane. "It's citizen Mardoche."

"The man himself," replied the wicket clerk. "Well then, looks like we're going about our business, keeping watch?"

"As usual, citizen turnkey. It seems to me you don't often catch us lying down on the job."

"Ah!" said Mardoche. "It's just that tonight vigilance is more necessary than ever."

"Bah!" said Duchesne, who had come over.

"No, I'm serious."

"What's up, then?"

"Open the window and I'll tell you all about it."

"Open it," said Duchesne.

Gilbert opened the window and shook hands with the turnkey, who had already carefully befriended the two gendarmes.

"So what's up, citizen Mardoche?" repeated Gilbert.

"What's up is that the session of the Convention got a bit heated. Did you read about it?"

"No. What happened?"

"Ah! What happened first is that citizen Hébert was onto something."

"What?"

"He found out that the plotters, who were thought to be dead, are very much alive and kicking."

"Ah, yes," said Gilbert. "Delessart and Thierry. I heard about that; they're in England, the rotters."

"And the Knight of Maison-Rouge?" said the turnkey, raising his voice so that the Queen would hear him.

"What! Don't tell me he's in England too, that one?"

"Not at all, he's in France," continued Mardoche, keeping his voice at the same pitch.

"You mean he came back?"

"He never left."

"He's got guts, I'll give him that," said Duchesne.

"That's how he is."

"Well then, we'll have to try to stop him."

"Of course we'll try to stop him, but that's not an easy task, apparently."

At that moment the Queen's file screeched loudly against the iron; fearing that it would be heard despite the efforts he was making to cover it, the turnkey brought his heel down hard on one of the dog's front paws, and it gave a yowl of pain.

"Oh, poor thing," said Gilbert.

"Bah!" said the turnkey. "He should have worn his sabots. Quiet, Girondin, quiet!"

"His name's Girondin, your dog, eh, citizen Mardoche?"

"Yes, it's just a name I gave him, no reason."

"So you were saying," Duchesne said. A prisoner himself, he took as much interest in any bit of news as any other prisoner. "You were saying?"

"Ah, yes, that's right, I was saying that citizen Hébert—now there's a patriot! I was saying that citizen Hébert made a motion to bring the Austrian woman back to the Temple."

"Why is that?"

"Why do you think! He reckons they only took her out of the Temple to stop her being searched pronto by the Commune of Paris."

"Oh! Not to mention to get her away from this damned Maison-Rouge with all his escape plans," said Gilbert. "I believe the underground tunnel exists."

"That's what citizen Santerre said by way of reply; but Hébert said that from the moment they were alerted there was no more danger; that they could guard Marie Antoinette at the Temple with half the precautions they need to guard her here, and, I have to say, the Temple is a lot more solid and secure a building than the Conciergerie."

"And I have to say," said Gilbert, "that I'd love it if they took her back to the Temple."

"I can imagine, you must be bored stiff watching over her all the time."

"No, it makes me sad, that's all."

Maison-Rouge coughed loudly as the file made more and more noise the further it ate into the iron bar.

"And what did they decide?" asked Duchesne when the turnkey's coughing fit had subsided.

"They decided she'd stay here, but that they'd start her trial immediately."

"Oh, the poor woman!" said Gilbert.

Duchesne, whose hearing was no doubt finer than that of his colleague, or who was perhaps less spellbound by Mardoche's tale, cocked an ear in the direction of the compartment on the left, a move the turnkey noticed.

"So, you see, citizen Duchesne," he shouted, "the attempts of the plotters are going to become all the more desperate when they find out they've got less time ahead of them to carry out their plots. They're going to double the guards on all the prisons, given that it's a question of nothing less than an armed insurrection in the Conciergerie. The plotters will kill everyone until they've gotten in to the Queen, until they've reached the Widow Capet, I meant to say."

"Hummph! How can they get in, your plotters?"

"Dressed up as patriots: they'll pretend to be reenacting another second of September, the mongrels. And then, once the doors are open, curtains!"

There was a moment of silence occasioned by the stupor of the gendarmes. The turnkey heard the file grinding away with a mixture of joy and terror. Nine o'clock sounded.

At that same moment, someone knocked on the door of the outer cell. But the two gendarmes were so preoccupied they didn't answer.

"Well then, we'll be extra careful, we'll keep our eyes peeled," said Gilbert.

"And if we have to, we'll die at our post as true republicans," Duchesne added.

"Surely she must soon be finished," the turnkey said to himself, wiping the sweat trickling into his eyes.

"And you be careful too," said Gilbert. "You won't be spared any more than we would be if anything like the event you describe occurs."

"I agree," said the turnkey. "I spend my nights doing the rounds; and I'm at the end of my rope. You fellows, at least you get relieved and you can sleep one night out of two."

There was a second knock on the door of the wicket. Mardoche gave a start; any event, no matter how trivial, could foil his plan.

"What's that, then?" he asked before he could stop himself.

"Nothing, nothing," said Gilbert. "It's just the clerk from the War Ministry letting me know he's on his way out."

"Oh, well and good!" said the turnkey.

But the clerk continued to knock.

"All right! All right!" cried Gilbert without leaving the window. "Good night! Good-bye! . . ."

"I think he's saying something to you," said Duchesne, turning round to face the door. "Answer him, then. . . ."

They heard the voice of the clerk.

"Come here for a moment, citizen gendarme, would you?" he called. "I want to have a word with you."

That voice, altered by strong emotion though it was, caused the turnkey to prick up his ears, for he felt he recognized it.

"What do you want then, citizen Durand?" asked Gilbert.

"Just a word."

"Well then, you can speak to me tomorrow."

"No, tonight; I must speak to you tonight," the voice insisted.

"Oh, no!" murmured the turnkey. "Now what's going to happen? That's Dixmer's voice."

Sinister and vibrant, the voice seemed somehow to borrow something morbid from the distant echo down the long corridor. Duchesne turned back.

"Right!" said Gilbert. "Since he insists . . ."

With that he went toward the door. The turnkey took advantage of the gendarmes' momentary distraction. He ran to the Queen's window.

"Is it done?" he asked.

"I'm more than halfway," answered the Queen.

"Oh, God! God!" he murmured. "Hurry up! Hurry up!"

"Well then, citizen Mardoche," said Duchesne, "where've you got to?"

"Here I am," cried the turnkey, swiftly returning to the window of the front compartment.

At that very moment, as he was about to resume his place, a terrible cry rang out through the prison, followed by swearing and then the sound of a sword sliding out of its metal sheath.

"Oh, you mongrel! Oh, you bastard!" cried Gilbert.

The noise of a struggle in the corridor was heard. At the same time the door swung open, revealing to Mardoche's stunned gaze two shadows glued together in the wicket suddenly giving way to a woman, who shunted Duchesne aside and rushed headlong into the Queen's compartment.

Duchesne did not bother with the woman but ran instead to help his embattled comrade. Mardoche leapt to the other window, where he saw the woman at the Queen's knees, begging her, pleading with the illustrious prisoner to change into her clothes.

He strained, eyes blazing, to make out the woman's face, which he feared he already recognized. All of a sudden he gave a mournful cry.

"Geneviève! Geneviève!" he cried.

The Queen had dropped the file and looked annihilated by yet another aborted attempt at escape.

Mardoche grabbed the iron bar, half sawed off by the file, with both hands and shook it in a supreme effort. But the steel bite was not deep enough; the bar resisted.

Meanwhile, Dixmer had managed to push Gilbert back into the cell and was about to go in after him when Duchesne threw his weight against the door and managed to push it back, though he couldn't quite close it, for Dixmer in his desperation had jammed his arm between the door and the wall. At the end of this arm was the dagger, which, though blunted by the copper guard of his sword belt, had sliced all the way down the gendarme's chest, slitting open his clothes and tearing the flesh.

The two men rallied with all their combined force and managed to raise the cry for help at the same time. Dixmer felt his arm was about to break; he rammed his shoulder against the door and managed to pull his bruised arm out before the door banged shut and Duchesne slid the bolts into place as Gilbert turned the key.

Rapid steps were heard in the corridor, and then it was all over but the shouting. The two gendarmes looked at each other and gazed about them. They heard the noise the phony turnkey was making as he tried to break the bar.

Gilbert rushed to the Queen's cell, where he found Geneviève on her knees, pleading with the Queen to change into her clothes. Duchesne grabbed his rifle and ran to the window. He saw a man hanging by the bars, which he was shaking with rage and trying in vain to scale.

Gilbert took aim. The young man saw the barrel of the rifle being lowered at him.

"Go ahead!" he shouted. "Shoot! Kill me!"

Sublime in despair, the Knight stuck out his chest in defiance of a mere bullet.

"Knight!" cried the Queen. "Knight, I beg you. Stay alive! Live!"

At the sound of Marie Antoinette's voice, Maison-Rouge dropped to his knees. The shot left the gun, but that movement saved him and the bullet flew over his head. But Geneviève believed her friend had been killed and she fell senseless to the hard brick floor.

When the smoke cleared, there was no one left in the Women's Courtyard.

Ten minutes later, thirty soldiers led by two commissioners turned the Conciergerie inside out, paying particular attention to its most inaccessible recesses. But they found nobody. The clerk had sauntered past old man Richard in his armchair, serene and smiling. As for the turnkey, he had run out shouting: "Alarm! Alarm! Sound the alarm!"

The sentry on duty at the entrance had wanted to pin him with his bayonet, but the turnkey's dogs had leapt at the sentry's throat.

Only Geneviève was arrested, interrogated, thrown in jail.

45

SEARCHING

We can no longer leave in the shade one of the principal characters of this story, the man who, while the accumulated events of the preceding chapter were being accomplished, suffered more than anyone, and whose sufferings most deserve to kindle our readers' sympathies.

The sun was high and hot in the rue de la Monnaie and the gossips were all gabbling away at their doorsteps, as gaily as if a cloud of blood had not settled over the city for the past ten months, as Maurice came home in the cabriolet he'd promised to bring back.

He left his horse's reins in the hands of a scrubber in front of the church of Saint-Eustache and ran upstairs to his place, his heart filled with joy.

Love is an invigorating feeling: it can revive hearts dead to sensation; it peoples deserts; it causes the phantom of the beloved to rise before your very eyes; it causes the voice singing in the lover's soul to reveal all of Creation illuminated by hope and happiness; and since, while being an expansive feeling, it's still a self-centered one, it blinds the one who loves to everything that is not the beloved.

Maurice did not see those other women; Maurice did not hear their comments; he saw only Geneviève preparing a departure that would bring them lasting happiness; he heard only Geneviève distractedly humming her favorite song, and that song was buzzing so deliciously in his ears he would have sworn he heard the different modulations of her voice mingled with the sound of a lock clicking shut.

Outside the door, Maurice paused. The door was half open. Normally it was always shut, so this circumstance surprised Maurice. He looked around to see if he could see Geneviève in the hall; Geneviève was not in the hall. He went inside, crossed the anteroom, the kitchen, the salon; he visited the bedroom. Anteroom, kitchen, salon, bedroom were unoccupied. He called. No one answered.

The officieux had gone out, as we know. Maurice imagined that in his absence Geneviève had needed some rope, say, to tie up the chests, or some provisions for the coach trip, that she had gone down to buy these things. Such a course seemed absolutely reckless to him, but although anxiety was beginning to get the upper hand, he still did not suspect anything.

And so he waited, pacing from one end of the room to the other, leaning out of the window from time to time to be hit in the face by gusts of air whooshing in at him, laden with rain.

Maurice eventually thought he could hear footsteps on the stairs; he listened; it wasn't Geneviève's tread, but that didn't stop him from rushing to the landing and leaning over the balustrade, where he recognized the officieux coming up the stairs with the typical insouciance of servants.

"Agesilaus!" he cried. The officieux looked up.

"Ah! It's you, citizen!"

"Yes, it's me; but where is the citizeness?"

"The citizeness?" Agesilaus asked in bewilderment as he continued to climb.

"Who else! Did you see her downstairs?"

"No."

"Then go down again. Ask the concierge and speak to the neighbors."

"Right away."

Agesilaus went back down the stairs.

"Run! Faster!" cried Maurice. "Can't you see I'm on tenterhooks?"

Maurice waited for five or six minutes at the top of the stairs, then, when Agesilaus did not return, he went back into the apartment to hang out the window again. He spotted Agesilaus going in and out of two or three shops, apparently without result.

He shouted to him in his frustration. Agesilaus looked up and saw his master leaning impatiently out of the window. Maurice made a sign for him to come back up.

"She can't have gone out, it's not possible!" Maurice said to himself. And he called out again: "Geneviève! Geneviève!" Everything was dead quiet. The lonely room even seemed to have lost its echo. Agesilaus reappeared.

"Well, the concierge is the only one who's seen her."

"The concierge saw her?"

"Yes; the neighbors know nothing about her."

"The concierge saw her, you say? How come?"

"He saw her go out."

"So she went out?"

"It looks like it."

"Alone? I don't believe Geneviève went out alone."

"She wasn't alone, citizen; she was with a man."

"What! With a man?"

"That's what the citizen concierge reckons."

"Go and get him. I must know who this man is."

Agesilaus took two steps toward the door, then turned around.

"Wait a moment," he said, apparently thinking.

"What? What is it? Say something, you're killing me."

"Maybe it's the fellow who ran after me."

"A man ran after you?"

"Yes."

"What for?"

"To ask me for the key on your behalf."

"What key, you idiot? Tell me, for God's sake, tell me!"

"The key to your apartment."

"You gave the key to my apartment to a stranger?" Maurice shrieked, seizing the officieux by the collar with his two hands.

"But it wasn't a stranger, monsieur—it was one of your friends."

"Oh, right, one of my friends? So it must have been Lorin, then. That's it, she's gone out with Lorin."

Maurice tried to smile through his sick feeling; he mopped his forehead, bathed in sweat, with his handkerchief.

"No, no, no, monsieur, it's not Lorin!" said Agesilaus. "Cripes! I reckon I know Monsieur Lorin pretty well by now!"

"Then who is it?"

"You know, citizen, that man, the one who came round that day . . ."

"What day?"

"The day you were so down in the dumps and he took you off and you came back gay as a lark."

Agesilaus had registered all this. Maurice stared at him in fright. A shiver ran through his entire body. After a long silence, he said:

"Dixmer?"

"Oh, yes, heavens, I think that's it, citizen," said the officieux.

Maurice tottered and fell backward into a chair. His eyes clouded over and he nearly blacked out.

"Oh, my God!" he murmured.

When he opened his eyes again, he looked straight at the bouquet of violets, forgotten, or rather left behind, by Geneviève. He fell upon it, kissed the violets, and then suddenly took in the space where they had been placed.

"Ah, it's all becoming clear now," he said. "These violets . . . her last farewell!"

Maurice spun around then, and only then did he notice that the chest was only half-packed, the rest of the linen lying on the floor or in the cupboard hanging open. No doubt the linen on the floor had fallen from Geneviève's hands when she'd sighted Dixmer.

He could see that moment in all its gruesome detail. The scene loomed up before him, vivid and terrible, between these four walls that had previously witnessed so much happiness. Until that moment, Maurice had sat defeated, crushed. Now his arousal was fearful, the young man's surging anger terrifying.

He shot up, closed the window, grabbed two pistols that were lying on his desk fully loaded for the journey, checked their caps, and, seeing that they were in working order, shoved the pistols in his pockets.

Then he slipped two rolls of louis into his purse—despite his patriotism, he had judged it prudent to keep the louis in the bottom of a drawer—then he grabbed his saber in its scabbard and said:

"Agesilaus, you are quite fond of me, I believe; you've served my father and me for fifteen years."

"Yes, citizen," said the officieux, seized with fright at the sight of a marblelike pallor and nervous tremor he had never remarked in his master before, his master passing rightly for the most fearless and unshakable of men. "Yes, what are you asking me to do?"

"Listen! If the woman who was living here . . ."

He broke off, his voice trembling so much as he said these words that he could not go on.

"If she comes back," he resumed after a moment, "let her in. Close the door behind her. Take this rifle, place yourself on the stairs, and, on your head, on your life, on your soul, do not let anyone in. If they try to break down the door, defend it. Shoot! Kill! Kill! And don't worry, Agesilaus, I'll take the blame."

The young man's tone, his vehement assurance galvanized Agesilaus.

"Not only will I kill," he said, "but I'd get myself killed for citizeness Geneviève."

"Thank you. . . . Now listen. I loathe this apartment now. I never want to climb back up those stairs again—not until I've found her. If she is able to escape, if she comes back, stick that great big Japanese vase at your window, filled with the daisies she loved so much. That's in the day. At night, put a lantern there instead. Every time I go past the end of the street, I'll get the message; as long as I don't see the vase or the lantern, I'll keep searching."

"Oh, monsieur, be careful, be careful!" cried Agesilaus.

Maurice didn't even answer. He dashed out of the room, flew down the stairs and over to Lorin's. It would be hard to describe the stupefaction, the anger, the rage of the worthy poet when he learned the news—we would have to revert to the relentlessly moving elegies Orestes inspired in his friend Pylades.

"So you don't know where she is?" he kept saying, over and over.

"Lost, disappeared!" howled Maurice in a paroxysm of despair. "He's killed her, Lorin, he's killed her!"

"Oh, no, my friend, no, my dear Maurice. He hasn't killed her. No, you don't assassinate a woman like Geneviève after so many days of reflection. No, if he was going to kill her he'd have killed her on the spot and left her body at your place as a sign of revenge. No, don't you see? He's run away with her, all too happy to have got hold of his treasure again."

"You don't know him, Lorin; you don't know him," said Maurice. "That man had something ugly in his eyes."

"No, no, no, you've got it wrong; he always gave me the impression of being a good sort of burgher—that's what I thought, anyhow. He's taken her to sacrifice her. He'll get himself arrested with her and they'll be killed together. Ah! Now that's the danger," said Lorin.

His words threw fat on the fire of Maurice's delirium.

"I'll find her! I'll find her or die!" he cried.

"Well, as for that, we'll find her, that's for sure," said Lorin. "Just calm down. Now look, Maurice, my good Maurice, believe me, you'll waste your time looking if you don't go about it the right way and you can't go about it the right way while you're so worked up."

"Adieu, Lorin, adieu!"

"What are you doing?"

"I'm going."

"You're leaving me? Why?"

"Because this is my concern alone; because I'm the only one who should risk his life to save Geneviève's."

"Are you tired of living?"

"I'll take what comes: I'll go and find the president of the local Surveillance Committee, I'll talk to Hébert, to Danton, to Robespierre. I'll confess all if they'll just give her back to me."

"All right," said Lorin.

Without another word he rose, adjusted his sword belt, clapped the regulatory hat on his head, and, as Maurice had done before him, took two loaded pistols and shoved them in his pockets.

"Let's go," he said simply.

"But you're compromising yourself!" cried Maurice.

"So what?

> When, my friend, the play is done,
> We should go back to having fun."

"Where will we look first?" asked Maurice.

"Let's look in the old quartier first—you know, the old rue Saint-Jacques. We'll watch out for Maison-Rouge; wherever he is, Dixmer won't be far behind. Then we'll go over to the houses at the Vieille-Corderie. You know they're talking about transfering Antoinette back to the Temple! Believe me, men like that won't give up hope of saving her till the very last."

"Yes," Maurice agreed, "actually, you're right.... Maison-Rouge, do you really think he's still in Paris, then?"

"Dixmer certainly is."

"True, true; they must have teamed up again," said Maurice, whose wits were returning with the odd vague flicker.

From that moment, the two pals began to search. Endlessly. In vain. Paris is big and it casts a dense shadow. No fathomless pit is as dark and deep as Paris when it conceals a crime or misdemeanor entrusted to it.

Lorin and Maurice went past the place de Grève a hundred times; a hundred times they unwittingly skirted the cramped house in which Geneviève had most recently lived under Dixmer's constant surveillance, the way priests of yore used to watch girls destined to become sacrificial virgins.

On her side, seeing herself doomed to die, Geneviève, like all generous souls, accepted the sacrifice and wished to die without any commotion. Besides, she feared any publicity that Maurice's revenge would not fail to attract, less for Dixmer than for the Queen's cause. And so she maintained a silence as profound as if death had already sealed her mouth shut.

Yet without saying anything to Lorin, Maurice had pleaded with the members of the terrible Committee of Public Safety; and Lorin, without discussing it with Maurice, had frantically explored the same avenues.

And so, the very same day, a red cross was drawn by Fouquier-Tinville beside both their names, and the word SUSPECT joined them in a bloody accolade.

46

THE JUDGMENT

The twenty-third day of the first month of the year II[1] of the French Republic, one and indivisible, the day corresponding to the fourteenth of October 1793 old style, as they used to say at the time, a curious crowd invaded the galleries of the chamber where the revolutionary *séances* were held, and they stayed there from early morning.

The corridors of the Palais and the avenues of the Conciergerie were overflowing with avid and excited spectators, who passed noises and passions on down the line to one another just as the ocean passes on its roaring and its foam as it surges in to shore.

Despite the frenzied curiosity that had each spectator jumping up and down, and perhaps even because of this curiosity, each wave of the turbulent sea was compressed between two barriers, with the outside pushing in and the inside pushing back. The net result of all this ebb and flow was that everyone remained more or less stationary. But those in the best spots knew that they had to get themselves forgiven for their felicity, and they aimed to do so by telling their less well placed neighbors, who then passed on the original news, what they could see and hear.

But right next to the door to the gallery a group of men all squashed together were battling fiercely over two inches of horizontal or vertical space—for two inches in breadth was enough to see a corner of the room and the faces of the jurors between two shoulders, and two inches in height was enough to see the whole room and the face of the accused over the top of someone's head.

Unfortunately, this passage leading into the room from one of the corridors, this narrow defile, was occupied almost entirely by one man with very broad shoulders who held his arms out like flying buttresses, thereby shoring up the vacillating crowd ready to burst into the room if only they could somehow get past this rampart of flesh.

This immovable rock of a man blocking the door of the gallery was young and handsome. At every ever-more-determined surge of the crowd at his back, he shook his thick hair like a horse shaking its mane; below his hair his eyes shone with a grim and resolute gleam. A living breakwater, every time he repelled the throng—by a look, by a ripple of muscle—he would simply resume his focused immobility.

The compact mass had tried to topple him a hundred times, for he was tall and it was impossible to see anything from behind him; but no rock could have been more immovable, as I think we might have said.

Yet at the other end of the human tide, among the densely packed throng, another man had carved out a path with a determination that bordered on ferocity. Nothing managed to stop him in his relentless advance, neither the kicks of those he left behind, nor the curses of those he winded in passing, nor the tongue-lashings of women, for there were many women in the crowd that day.

He responded to kicks with kicks, to curses with a look that withered the most foolhardy, to complaints with an imperturbability bordering on contempt. Finally, he had gotten as far as the vigorous young man sealing off, so to speak, the entrance to the door. Everyone was keen to see how things would pan out between these two tough antagonists, and so, with everyone holding their breath in expectation, the latecomer tried out his technique, which consisted of wedging his elbows between two spectators and torpedoing bodies that seemed virtually welded together with his own, thereby splitting them asunder.

Yet the man was young and small, with a pale face and spindly legs that revealed a constitution as puny as his fiery eyes revealed an impressively strong will. But his elbow had scarcely brushed the side of the young man planted in front of him than this latter, amazed at such naked aggression, spun round with a raised fist that threatened to come crashing down to crush a man so fearless.

The two antagonists thus found themselves face-to-face; they both let out a stifled cry at the same time, for they recognized each other.

"Oh, citizen Maurice!" said the frail young man in a tone of inexpressible pain. "Let me through; let me see! Please! You can kill me later!"

Maurice, for it was in fact he, felt pierced to the quick with tenderness and admiration for such eternal devotion, for such indestructible determination.

"You," he murmured. "You, here! How can you be so reckless!"

"Yes, I'm here! But I'm exhausted. . . . Oh, God! She's speaking! Let me see her! Let me hear her!"

Maurice moved aside and let the young man through. Since Maurice was at the head of the crowd, nothing now encumbered the view of the man who had suffered so many blows and rebuffs to get there.

This whole episode and the whispering and muttering it occasioned excited the jurors' curiosity. The accused as well glanced in their direction from the front of the court, and she saw and recognized the Knight. Something like a frisson shook the Queen for a moment as she sat in her iron chair.

The examination was conducted by President Herman, interpreted by Fouquier-Tinville and debated by Chauveau-Lagarde,[2] the Queen's counsel; it went on as long as the jurors' strength and that of the accused held out.

During all this time, Maurice remained in his place without moving, though spectators had already come and gone several times over in the courtroom and the corridors beyond.

The Knight had found a column for support and leaned back against it, looking no less pale than the white stucco.

Day had been followed by darkest night: a few candles burned on the jury's tables, a few lamps smoked in sconces on the chamber walls, lighting up with a sinister red reflection the noble visage of this woman who had once looked so beautiful under the splendid lights of parties at Versailles.

She was on her own here, giving short noncommittal replies to the president's questions, sometimes leaning over to whisper a few words in her defense counsel's ear. Her polished white forehead had lost none of its habitual hauteur, and she was wearing the black striped dress of mourning she had refused to change out of since the death of the King.

The jurors adjourned to deliberate. The session was over.

"I hope I wasn't too disdainful, monsieur?" the Queen asked Chauveau-Lagarde. "Was I all right?"

"Ah, madame!" he replied. "You only have to be yourself and you will always be all right."

"Look how arrogant she is!" cried a woman in the audience, as though a stranger's voice were answering the question the unhappy Queen had just put to her lawyer.

The Queen turned her head to look at the woman.

"Yes, you heard me," the woman went on. "I said you're arrogant, Antoinette—and look where it's got you!"

The Queen went bright red.

The Knight turned toward the woman who had pronounced that judgment and replied gently:

"She was Queen."

Maurice grabbed him by the wrist.

"Please!" he said to him in a lowered voice. "Have the courage not to give yourself away."

"Oh, Monsieur Maurice," replied the Knight, "you are a man and you know you are speaking to a man. Tell me, do you think they can condemn her?"

"I don't think it," said Maurice. "I know it."

"But a woman!" cried Maison-Rouge with a sob.

"No, a queen," countered Maurice. "You yourself just said so."

The Knight in turn grabbed Maurice's wrist, and with a force you would not have thought he had in him pulled Maurice down to his level. It was three-thirty in the morning; great empty gaps were visible among the spectators. A few lights went out here and there, throwing whole areas of the chamber into darkness. One of the darkest areas was where the Knight and Maurice were, Maurice totally attentive to what the Knight had to say.

"Why are you here, then, and what have you come to do?" asked the Knight. "You, monsieur, who do not have the heart of a bloodthirsty tiger?"

"Alas!" said Maurice. "I'm here to find out what's happened to another poor unfortunate woman."

"Yes, I know," said Maison-Rouge. "The woman whose husband pushed her into the Queen's cell, isn't that right? The woman who was arrested before my very eyes?"

"Geneviève?"

"Yes, Geneviève."

"So Geneviève is a prisoner, sacrificed by her husband, sent to her death by Dixmer? . . . Oh! I see it all, I understand everything now! Tell me what happened, Knight, tell me where she is, tell me how I can find her. Knight . . . that woman is my life. Do you hear?"

"Well, I saw her; I was there when she was arrested. I too had come to break out the Queen! But Dixmer and I weren't able to communicate with each other, and so we doubled up and our two plans did harm, not good."

"And you didn't save her, at least, your sister, Geneviève?"

"How could I? Iron bars separated me from her. Ah, if you'd been there, if we could have joined forces, that cursed bar would have yielded and we would have saved both women."

"Geneviève! Geneviève!" murmured Maurice.

Then he looked at Maison-Rouge with a frightening expression of rage.

"And Dixmer, what's happened to him?"

"I don't know. He ran one way and I ran the other."

"Oh!" hissed Maurice between clenched teeth. "If I ever get my hands on him . . ."

"Yes, I know. But nothing is desperate yet for Geneviève," said Maison-Rouge, "whereas here, for the Queen . . . Oh, look, Maurice, you're a man with a heart, a powerful man; you have friends. . . . Oh, please, I beg you as one prays to God. . . . Maurice, help me save the Queen."

"You think I would?"

"Maurice, Geneviève beseeches you through me."

"Oh! Don't say that name, monsieur. How do I know you didn't sacrifice that poor woman, just like Dixmer?"

"Monsieur," replied the Knight loftily, "the only person I know how to sacrifice, when I support a cause, is myself."

At that moment the door to the jurors' anteroom opened again, just as Maurice was about to reply.

"Silence, monsieur!" said the Knight. "Silence. The jurors are back."

Maison-Rouge was pale and tottering; he placed his trembling hand on Maurice's arm.

"Oh!" murmured the Knight. "Oh! My heart is failing me."

"Courage; get a grip on yourself or you're finished!" said Maurice.

The Tribunal had indeed returned, and the news of its return spread throughout the corridors and galleries. The crowd surged forward again into the courtroom and the lights seemed to revive all on their own for this decisive and solemn moment.

The Queen was brought back in; she held herself erect, majestically still, regal, her eyes steady and her lips tightly pressed together.

They read her the decree that condemned her to death.

She listened without blanching, without batting an eyelid, without moving a muscle of her face, without giving any appearance of emotion.

Then she turned to the Knight and addressed a long and eloquent gaze to him, as though to thank this man whom she had never seen other than as a monument of devotion. Then, leaning on the arm of the officer of the gendarmerie who commanded the armed forces, she walked out of the tribunal, calm and dignified.

Maurice let out a long sigh.

"Thank God!" he said. "Nothing in her deposition compromised Geneviève. There is still hope."

"Thank God!" echoed the Knight of Maison-Rouge. "It's all over and the struggle is at an end. I didn't have the strength to carry on."

"Be strong, monsieur!" Maurice whispered.

"I will be strong," replied the Knight.

They shook hands and both men moved off through two different exits.

The Queen was taken back to the Conciergerie: the bell of the great clock struck four as she stepped inside.

At the far end of the Pont-Neuf, Maurice was stopped by Lorin's outstretched arms.

"Halt there!" he said. "You can't pass."

"Why's that?"

"First, where are you going?"

"Home. That's just it: I can, now that I know what's happened to her."

"So much the better. But you can't go home."

"What's the reason?"

"The reason is this: two hours ago, the gendarmes came to arrest you."

"Ah!" cried Maurice. "All the more reason."

"Are you mad? What about Geneviève?"

"True. Then where are we going?"

"To my place—where do you think?"

"You've lost me."

"All the more reason. Follow me."

And with that, Lorin dragged Maurice away.

47

PRIEST AND BUTCHER

When she quit the Tribunal, the Queen had been taken to the Conciergerie. When she reached her room, she took a pair of scissors and cut off her beautiful long hair, which had only become more beautiful due to lack of powder,[1] which had been abolished for over a year now. She wrapped her shorn hair in paper and wrote on the outside: *To be divided between my son and my daughter.*

She then sat, or rather fell, on a chair and, broken by exhaustion—the hearing had lasted eighteen hours!—she fell asleep. At seven o'clock, the noise of the screen being moved caused her to wake with a start. She looked around in fright and saw a man whom she had never seen before.

"What do they want of me now?" she said.

The man came closer and greeted her as politely as if she were not the Queen.

"My name is Sanson," he said.

The Queen gave a faint shudder and got out of bed. The name alone spoke volumes.

"You've certainly come early, monsieur," she said. "Couldn't you wait just a little?"

"No, madame," replied Sanson, "I was ordered to come."

These words out of the way, he took a step closer to the Queen. Everything about the man, and about the moment, was dramatic and terrible.

"Ah! I understand!" said the prisoner. "You want to cut off my hair?"

"It has to be done, madame," said the executioner.

"I am aware of that, monsieur," said the Queen, "and I wanted to save you the trouble. My hair is there, on the table."

Sanson looked in the direction the Queen had pointed.

"Only, I'd like it to be passed on to my children tonight."

"Madame," said Sanson, "such niceties do not concern me."

"But I thought . . ."

"All I have to worry about," resumed the executioner, "are the belongings of . . . persons. . . . Their clothes, their jewelery—and then only when they give them to me formally; otherwise it all goes to la Salpêtrière[2] hospital to be handed out to the poor there. It belongs to them after that. A decree of the Committee of Public Safety has ruled that that's how it works."

"Be that as it may, monsieur," Marie Antoinette insisted, "can I count on my hair going to my children?"

Sanson did not answer.

"I'll see to it that it does," said Gilbert.

The prisoner threw the gendarme a look of ineffable gratitude.

"Now," said Sanson, "I came to cut your hair, but since the job's been done, I can, if you like, leave you alone for a moment."

"Please do, monsieur," said the Queen, "for I need to collect myself and pray."

Sanson inclined his head and left the room.

The Queen found herself alone, for Gilbert had only looked in to say what he had said. While the condemned woman knelt on a chair that was lower than the rest and which served her as a prayer stool, a scene no less terrible than the one we have just recounted was taking place in the presbytery of the little church of Saint-Landry, on the île de la Cité.

The priest of that parish had just gotten up and his old housekeeper was laying out his modest breakfast when suddenly someone began hammering violently on the presbytery door.

Even these days, an unannounced visit to a priest always signals some event of moment, whether a baptism, a marriage in extremis, or a last confession. But in those days, the visit of a stranger could signal something even more serious. In those days, in fact, the priest was not God's agent and had to account to men.

But the abbé Girard was among those juror priests[3] who had least to fear from such a knock, for he had taken an oath before the Constitution: in him conscience and probity had got the upper hand of self-esteem and the religious spirit. Doubtless abbé Girard accepted the possibility of progress in government and regretted all the abuses committed in the name of divine power, for he had embraced the fraternity of the republican regime while holding on to his God.

"Go and have a look, Missus Hyacinth," he said. "Go and see who's banging on our door at this hour in the morning. And if, by any luck, it's not some pressing service that's required of me, tell them I've been called to the Conciergerie this morning and that I'm obliged to leave very shortly."

Missus Hyacinth was called Missus Madeleine once upon a time; but she had accepted the name of a flower in exchange for her name, just as Father Girard had accepted the title of citizen in place of that of priest.

At her master's invitation, Missus Hyacinth bustled off down the steps of the small garden where the entrance gate was. She pulled the bolts and a very pale, very agitated young man, but one with a sweet and honest countenance, presented himself.

"Monsieur Father Girard?" he said.

Hyacinth examined the newcomer's disheveled clothes, long beard, and nervous tremor and it all seemed most inauspicious.

"Citizen," she said, "there is no monsieur here and no father."

"Pardon me, madame," the young man corrected himself, "I mean the 'server' of Saint-Landry."

Despite her patriotism, Hyacinth was impressed by the use of the term *madame*, which you wouldn't have used those days to address an empress; yet she answered brusquely.

"You can't see him; he's reading his breviary."

"In that case I'll wait," replied the young man.

"But," said Missus Hyacinth, reverting in the face of his persistence to the initial bad impression of the young man, "you'll be waiting for nothing, citizen; he's been called to the Conciergerie and will be leaving this instant."

The young man went a whiter shade of pale, or rather went from pale to livid.

"So it's true!" he murmured, then added more loudly: "That's exactly why I've come to see citizen Girard, madame."

While he was speaking, he'd managed to get inside, gently, it's true, but firmly, and to bolt the gate behind him; and despite the entreaties and even the threats of Missus Hyacinth, he got into the house and penetrated as far as the priest's room. When the priest spotted him he gave a cry of surprise.

"Pardon me, Monsieur Father," the young man blurted in a rush, "but I must talk to you about something very serious. Could I please speak to you in private?"

The old priest knew great suffering when he saw it. He could read a whole saga of passion in the expression on the young man's face, hear the ultimate anguish in his feverish voice.

"Leave us, Missus Hyacinth," the curé said.

The young man watched impatiently as the housekeeper, who was used to participating in her master's secrets, hesitated to withdraw; when she had finally shut the door, he spoke.

"Monsieur curé, you will first want to know who I am. I will tell you. I am an outlaw; I am a man condemned to death, one who lives only through sheer daring. I am the Knight of Maison-Rouge."

The priest gave a shudder of fear from his great armchair.

"Oh, you have nothing to fear," said the Knight. "No one saw me come in, and anyone who might have seen me wouldn't have recognized me. I've changed a lot in the last two months."

"But what is it you want, citizen?" asked the juror priest.

"You are going to the Conciergerie this morning, are you not?"

"Yes, I've been summoned by the concierge."

"Do you know why?"

"Someone sick, someone dying, someone condemned to death, perhaps."

"You said it: yes, a woman condemned to death awaits you."

The old priest looked at the Knight in amazement.

"But do you know who the woman is?" Maison-Rouge went on.

"No . . . I don't."

"Well, the woman is the Queen!"

The priest gave a cry of pain.

"The Queen? Oh! My God!"

"Yes, monsieur, the Queen! I asked around and found out who the priest was they were going to send her. I learned that it was you and I came running."

"What do you want of me?" asked the priest, alarmed at the Knight's crazed tone.

"I want . . . *Want* is not the word, monsieur! I've come to beg you, to implore you, to beseech you."

"But what for?"

"To get me in with you to see Her Majesty."

"Oh! But you're mad!" cried the father. "You'll get me killed! You'll get yourself killed!"

"You have nothing to fear."

"The poor woman has been condemned and that's it for her."

"I know; it's not to try to save her that I want to see her. It's . . . Just listen to me, Father; you're not listening to me."

"I'm not listening to you because you're asking me to do the impossible. I'm not listening to you because you're acting as though you're deranged," said the old man. "I'm not listening to you because you're frightening me."

"Father, don't worry," said the young man, trying to calm down a bit. "Father, believe me, I haven't lost my mind! The Queen is finished, I know; but if I could just prostrate myself at her knees, for just one second, it would save my life. If I don't see her I'll kill myself, and since you know the cause of my despair, you will have killed both my body and my soul at once."

"Son, son," said the priest, "you're asking me to sacrifice my life! Think about it: old as I am, my existence is still indispensable to many unfortunate souls. Old as I am, to go looking for death myself is to commit suicide."

"Don't refuse me, Father," replied the Knight. "Listen! You need a server, an acolyte; take me along, bring me with you."

The priest tried to rally his firmness, which was beginning to waver.

"No," he said. "No, I would be failing in my duties. I swore an oath to the Constitution and I swore in all sincerity, with my heart, my soul, and my conscience, to support the Revolution. The woman condemned is a guilty queen. I would accept dying if my death were useful to my fellows; but I do not want to fail in my duty."

"But," cried the Knight, beside himself, "I tell you, I repeat, I swear that I don't want to save the Queen. Listen, I swear on this Bible, on that crucifix, I swear I'm not going to the Conciergerie to prevent her from dying."

"Well then, what do you want?" asked the old man, moved by that note of despair that cannot be feigned.

"Listen," said the Knight, whose soul seemed to burst forth from his mouth. "She was my protectress, my liege lady; she has a certain attachment to me. Seeing me in her final hour will be, I'm sure, a consolation for her."

"That's all you want?" asked the priest, his resolve shaken by the irresistible tone.

"Absolutely all."

"You're not cooking up some plot to try to free the condemned woman?"

"None. I am a Christian, Father, and if there's a shadow of a lie in my heart, if I hope for her to live, if I am working toward that end in any way, may God punish me with eternal damnation."

"No, no! I can't promise you anything," said the priest, his mind once more haunted by all the great and numberless dangers of such recklessness.

"Listen, Father," said the Knight in a tone of deep suffering, "I've spoken to you so far as a dutiful son. I've spoken to you only from charitable Christian feelings. Not a bitter word, not one threat has passed my lips, and yet my head is in turmoil; and yet my blood is boiling with fever; and yet despair is gnawing at my heart; and yet I am armed. See? I have a dagger."

And the young man drew from his breast a fine gleaming blade, which threw a livid reflection over his trembling hand. The priest jumped nimbly back.

"Do not fear," said the Knight with a sad smile. "Others, knowing you to be so faithful to your word, would have frightened you into swearing an oath. No, all I did was beg you, that's all; and I beg you again, my hands joined in prayer, my forehead to the floor: do what you can so that I can see her for one moment. And take this—it's your guarantee."

He pulled out of his pocket a note, which he presented to abbé Girard, who unfolded it and read the following words:

I, Armand, Knight of Maison-Rouge, declare, in God's name and upon my honor, that I have, by the threat of death, forced the worthy curé of Saint-Landry to take me to the Conciergerie despite his refusal to do so and his strong repugnance for the task. In witness whereof, I have signed,

MAISON-ROUGE

"All right!" said the priest. "But swear to me again that you won't do anything stupid; it's not enough for me that my life be saved. I'm also responsible for yours."

"Oh! Don't worry about me!" said the Knight. "You agree to do it?"

"I have to, since you want it so badly. You will wait for me down below, and when she goes into the office, you'll see her then. . . ."

The Knight seized the old man's hand and kissed it with the same fervor and respect as if he were kissing a crucifix.

"Oh!" murmured the Knight. "At least she'll die like a queen and the hand of the butcher won't touch her!"

48

THE CART

The moment he obtained the consent of the curé of Saint-Landry, Maison-Rouge dashed to a half-open closet that he recognized as the grooming booth where the priest completed his toilet. There, in a sleight of hand, his beard and mustache fell under the razor, and it was only then that he could see for himself how horribly pale he was. It was frightening.

When he returned he was outwardly calm. And he seemed to have forgotten completely that despite losing the beard and mustache, he could still be recognized at the Conciergerie.

He trotted behind the priest, whom two commissioners had come to get while he had been shut away shaving; and with the audacity that removes any suspicion, with the frantic and distorting bravura fever produces, the Knight entered the gate that at the time led to the court-yard of the Palais de Justice.

Like abbé Girard, he was dressed in a black frock coat, ecclesiastical habits having long been abolished.

Inside the office, they found more than fifty people, either prison employees, deputies, or commissioners, getting ready to watch the Queen pass by—either as attorneys and representatives or out of sheer bloody-minded curiosity.

His heart was beating so hard when he found himself facing the wicket that he no longer heard the priest's conversation with the gendarmes and the concierge. But a man holding enormous scissors and a piece of freshly cut cloth bumped into Maison-Rouge on the landing. Maison-Rouge turned around and recognized the executioner.

"What are you after, citizen?" asked Sanson.

The Knight tried to suppress a shiver that ripped through his veins despite his best efforts.

"Me?" he said. "As you can see, citizen Sanson, I am with the abbé of Saint-Landry."

"Oh, right!" replied the executioner before stepping aside and barking orders at his aide.

Meanwhile Maison-Rouge went into the registrar's office. From there he slipped into the compartment where the two gendarmes were.

Those fine men were distraught. As dignified and arrogant as she had been with others, the condemned woman had been goodness itself with them, nothing but sweetness and light: they were more like servants to her than her wardens.

But from where he was the Knight could not see the Queen: the screen was shut. It had been opened only to allow the priest through and then closed behind him. When the Knight entered, the conversation was already under way.

"Monsieur," the Queen was saying in her shrill and haughty voice, "since you swore an oath to the Republic, in the name of which they are putting me to death, I cannot trust in you. We no longer worship the same God!"

"Madame," replied Girard, deeply moved by this disdainful profession of faith, "a Christian who is about to die must die without hate in her heart, and she must not turn her back on her God, in whatever form He presents Himself to her."

Maison-Rouge stepped forward to move the screen, hoping that when she saw him, that when she understood the cause that brought him, she would change her mind about the priest. But the two gendarmes rose as one.

"But," protested Maison-Rouge, "I'm the priest's acolyte. . . ."

"Since she's rejecting the priest," said Duchesne, "she doesn't need his acolyte."

"But perhaps she will accept me," said Maison-Rouge, raising his voice. "She can't possibly not accept."

But Marie Antoinette was too immersed in her fury to hear and recognize the Knight's voice.

"Go, monsieur!" she said, addressing herself to Girard still. "Leave me, get out! Since we now live under the reign of freedom in France, I am claiming my freedom to die as I choose."

Girard tried to resist.

"Leave me, monsieur!" she said. "I'm telling you to go!"

Girard tried to get a word in.

"It is my wish," said the Queen with a gesture of the hand that was pure Maria Theresa.[1]

Girard came away. Maison-Rouge tried to see into the gap in the screen, but the prisoner had turned her back. The executioner's aide crossed the priest's path; he had arrived bringing ropes.

The two gendarmes pushed the Knight back as far as the door before he could utter a cry or make a move to accomplish his plan, dazed, desperate, and stunned as he was. And so he found himself with Girard in the corridor by the wicket gate. From the corridor they were pushed back as far as the office, where the news of the Queen's rejection of the juror priest had already spread and where Marie Antoinette's Austrian arrogance was already the subject of gross abuse for some, and for others a source of secret admiration.

"Off you go," said Richard to the priest. "Go home, since she's chasing you away. Let her die the way she wants to."

"Listen," said Mother Richard, "she's right and I'd do the same."

"And you'd be wrong, citizeness," said the priest.

"Shut up, woman," muttered the concierge, raising his eybrows. "It's got nothing to do with you. Go, Father, go."

"No," Girard said. "No. I'll go with her whether she likes it or not.

A word, just one single word, if she hears it, will remind her of her duties. Besides, the Commune gave me a mission . . . and I must obey the Commune."

"So be it, but send your sacristan back, then," barked the adjudant major commanding the armed forces, a former actor from the Comédie-Française[2] named Grammont.[3]

The eyes of the Knight flashed like twin bolts of lightning and he automatically went for his chest. Girard knew he had a dagger under his vest and stopped him with an imploring look.

"Spare my life," he said in a very low voice. "You haven't got a chance, don't throw away your own life too with hers; I'll speak to her about you during the procession, I swear to you. I will tell her what you risked to see her one last time."

These words sobered the young man somewhat. In any case, the usual reaction was in operation, with his whole nervous system undergoing a strange kind of collapse. This man whose will was so heroic, whose might so marvelous, had come to the end of his hope, the end of his will. He floated, irresolute and weary, defeated, in a sort of somnolent state one would have taken for an early warning sign of death.

"Yes," he said. "This is exactly as it should be: the cross for Jesus, the scaffold for her. Gods and kings drink the chalice men offer them to the last dregs."

With that thought in mind—so resigned, so passive—the chevalier let himself be pushed and shoved with complete acceptance, without defending himself in any way, though he did make a kind of involuntary groan. He was pushed and shoved right to the outer door without putting up any more resistance than Ophelia,[4] that devotee of death, when she saw herself being washed away by the waves.

At the foot of the doors and gates of the Conciergerie, one of those terrifying crowds was milling, the sort of crowd you can't imagine unless you've see one at close range at least once. Impatience dominated every other passion, and every other passion declared itself for all the world to hear, so that the combined noise was voluminous and immensely prolonged—as though all the noise of Paris and its entire population were concentrated on the quartier of the Palais de Justice.

At the head of the crowd an entire army was camped, with cannon aimed at protecting the procession festivities and making everything safe for those who had come for the entertainment.

There was no way anyone could break through this thick rampart, which was building little by little since news of the Queen's condemnation had spread outside Paris, with patriots from the faubourgs and outlying areas joining in the fray.

Ejected from the Conciergerie, Maison-Rouge naturally found himself in the front row of soldiers. The soldiers asked him who he was. He replied that he was abbé Girard's curate but that, having sworn allegiance to the Republic like his priest, he too had been rejected by the Queen. It was then the soldiers' turn to push him back—to the front row of spectators.

There he had no choice but to repeat what he'd told the soldiers. Then the cry went up:

"This fellow's just left her. . . . He saw her. . . . What did she say? . . . What's she doing? . . . Is she still as arrogant as ever? . . . Has she finally caved in? . . . Is she weeping? . . ."

The Knight answered all these questions in a voice that was weak, gentle, and affable all at once, as though this voice was the final manifestation of the life hanging by his lips.

His response was the simple truth: but this truth was a eulogy to Antoinette's backbone, and what he said with the simplicity and faith of an evangelist threw anguish and remorse into more than one heart.

When he spoke of the little Dauphin and of Madame Royale, of this Queen without a throne, this wife without a husband, this mother without her children, this woman finally alone and abandoned, without a friend among all the butchers, more than one brow, here and there, became veiled in sadness, more than one tear sprang up, furtive and burning, in eyes previously gleaming with hate.

Eleven o'clock rang out from the Palais clock and all noise ceased on the instant. A hundred thousand people counted each stroke of the hour as it called out and was answered by the beat of their heart.

Then the last vibration of the final stroke died in the ether and a great commotion was heard behind the doors at the very moment that a cart, coming from the quai aux Fleurs, where the flower market was, carved its way through the throng of spectators and guards and parked at the foot of the steps.

Soon the Queen appeared at the top of the immense flight of steps. Every possible passion was concentrated in the crowd's eyes; their breathing was shallow and quick.

Her hair was cut short; most of it had gone white during her captivity and this silvery tone made her pearly white skin all the more delicate and luminous, made the beauty of this Daughter of the Caesars[5] almost celestial in this, her final hour.

She was dressed in white and her hands were tied behind her back.

When she showed herself at the top of the stairs with abbé Girard on her right, accompanying her against her will, and the executioner on her left, both men dressed in black, a murmur ran throughout the crowd—one that God alone, who can see into men's hearts, could understand and formulate as truth.

At that moment a man passed between Marie Antoinette and the executioner. It was Grammont, intent on pointing out to the Queen the ignoble cart.

In spite of herself, the Queen took a step back in shock.

"Get in," said Grammont.

Everyone heard him; you could have heard a pin drop in that moment, so great was the emotion.

Then they saw the blood rush to the Queen's cheeks and right to the roots of her hair. Immediately afterward her face became deathly pale again.

Her white lips parted.

"Why a cart for me," she said, "when the King went to the scaffold in his carriage?"

Abbé Girard then said a few words to her in a very low voice. No doubt he was battling this final cry of royal pride in the condemned woman.

The Queen closed her mouth and faltered. Sanson held both arms out to steady her, but she stood up straight and tall again before he could touch her and swiftly descended the steps, while the aide righted a wooden footstool at the back of the cart. The Queen climbed up, the priest climbed up after her. Sanson made them both sit down.

When the cart began to pull away, the people surged forward in one tremendous movement. But since the soldiers weren't sure what the movement meant, they promptly joined forces to hold the crowd back as best they could. As a result, there was a great empty space between the cart and the front rows of onlookers. Within this space a mournful howling rent the air.

The Queen leapt to her feet and scanned the sea of bodies. Then she saw her dog, missing for two months; her little dog, who had not been able to get into the Conciergerie with her and who now hurled himself at the cart, despite all the yelling and kicking and shoving. But almost immediately poor Black, exhausted, emaciated, broken in spirit, disappeared under the horses' hooves.

The Queen watched him; she could not speak, for her voice was drowned by the din; she could not point him out, for her hands were tied; and even if she had been able to point to him, even if she had been able to be heard, she would no doubt have pleaded for him in vain.

She lost sight of him for a moment, but when she spotted him again he was in the arms of a pale young man, high above the crowd, standing on a cannon, who, made taller by some ineffable exultation, saluted her, pointing heavenward.

Marie Antoinette also looked up to the heavens and sweetly smiled.

The Knight of Maison-Rouge gave out a groan, as though this smile had pierced his heart like a knife, and as the cart turned into the pont-au-Change, he fell back into the crowd and vanished.

49

THE SCAFFOLD

At the place de la Révolution, two men were waiting together with their backs against a streetlamp. What they were waiting for, like the rest of the crowd—which had earlier split among those who had gone to the Palais de Justice, those who had gone to the place de la Révolution, and those who had fanned out to line the whole of the route between those two squares—was for the Queen to arrive at the great death-deliverer. That instrument was already worn, by rain and sun, by the hand of the butcher, and—horrible to say!—by contact with its victims; it dominated with sinister arrogance all the heads below as a queen dominates her people.

Noticeably pale and angry-looking, the two men standing there, talking fitfully in subdued voices, were Maurice and Lorin. Oblivious of the crowd, though in such a way as to make everyone envy them, they were quietly continuing a conversation that was not the least interesting of all the conversations snaking through the huddled groups of spectators, who, as though charged with electricity, were swaying in a human sea that ran from the pont-au-Change to the place de la Révolution.

The idea just expressed, of the guillotine's dominating all heads, had struck them both.

"See how the ugly monster raises its red arms!" Maurice said. "You'd think it was calling us and leering through some ghastly maw."

"Ah!" said Lorin. "I must admit I'm not of that school of poetry that sees everything in red. I see things in rose, for my part, and even at the foot of this hideous machine, I'd still sing and have hope. *Dum spiro, spero*—As I live, I hope."

"Do you still have hope now that they're killing women?"

"Ah, Maurice!" said Lorin. "Son of the Revolution, don't renounce the mother who bore you. Maurice! Stay a true and loyal patriot. The woman who is about to die is not just any woman, Maurice. The woman who is about to die is the bad genie of France."

"Oh! It's not her I feel sorry for. It's not her I weep for!" cried Maurice.

"I know: it's Geneviève."

"Ah!" cried Maurice. "You know, there's one thought that's driving me mad, and that is that Geneviève is guillotine fodder in the hands of those bastards Hébert and Fouquier-Tinville: the very men who sent poor Héloïse here and now are sending the high and mighty Marie Antoinette."

"But that's exactly why I still have hope," said Lorin. "When the people in their rage have made a grand meal of both tyrants, they'll be satisfied, for a while at least, like a boa constrictor that takes three months to digest what it has devoured. Then they won't gobble anyone else up and, as the prophets of the suburbs say, the smallest tidbits will put them off."

"Lorin, Lorin," said Maurice, "I'm not as cynical as you are! Just between you and me—though I'm ready to say it out loud—I hate the new queen, the one who looks set to succeed the Austrian woman whom she is about to destroy. It's a sad queen whose purple robe is made of a fresh supply of blood each day and who has Sanson for prime minister."

"Bah! We'll escape her clutches!"

"I don't think that for a second," said Maurice, shaking his head. "You see how to avoid being arrested at home, we have no other recourse but to stay out in the street."

"So what! We can leave Paris, nothing's stopping us. So let's not bewail our fate. My uncle's waiting for us at Saint-Omer—money, passports, the lot. No gendarme is going to arrest us. What do you think? We only stay because we want to."

"No, that's rubbish and you know it, my excellent friend, devoted soul that you are. . . . You stay because I want to stay."

"And you want to stay because you want to find Geneviève. Well then, what could be more simple, more right and natural? You think she's in jail, which is more than likely. You want to look out for her, and to do that you can't leave Paris."

Maurice gave a sigh. It was obvious his thoughts were elsewhere.

"You remember the death of Louis XVI?" he asked. "I can still see myself, wan with emotion and pride. I was one of the leaders of the pack I'm hiding among today. I was higher and mightier at the foot of this scaffold than the King who mounted it ever had been. What a difference, Lorin! Who'd have thought it? And when you think it has only taken nine months to bring about such a terrible turnaround!"

"Nine months of love, Maurice! . . . 'Love, you sank Troy!' "

Maurice sighed once more; his vagabond thoughts took another turn, scanned another horizon.

"That poor Maison-Rouge," he murmured. "This is a sad day for him."

"Alas!" said Lorin. "Do you want to know what I think is the saddest thing about revolutions, Maurice?"

"Yes."

"It's that your enemies are often people you'd like to have as friends, and your friends people . . ."

"There's one thing I have trouble believing," Maurice cut in.

"Which is?"

"That he won't come up with some plan, crazy as it may be, to save the Queen."

"One man against a hundred thousand?"

"I said, crazy as it may be . . . Me, I know that, to save Geneviève . . ."

Lorin frowned. "I say again, Maurice, you're losing the plot. Even if you had to save Geneviève, you wouldn't become a bad citizen. But that's enough of that; people can hear us, Maurice, they're listening. Hey! Heads are starting to sway; wait, there's citizen Sanson's valet standing up on his basket and peering into the distance. The Austrian woman is heading for us."

Indeed, as though to accompany the undulation Lorin had remarked, a prolonged and growing shudder invaded the crowd. It was like one of those gusts of wind that begin by blowing and end by howling.

Maurice increased his considerable height still further by standing on the base of the lamppost and looked toward the rue Saint-Honoré.

"Yes," he said with a shiver. "Here she is!"

They could just glimpse another machine almost as hideous as the guillotine, and that was the cart. To left and right the arms of the escort gleamed, and out in front Grammont responded with the flashing of his saber to the cries of the odd fanatic.

But as the cart drew nearer all cries suddenly died out under the imperious and somber gaze of the condemned woman. Never had a face imposed respect so forcefully; never had Marie Antoinette been greater and more of a queen. She took the pride of her courage to such heights as to strike terror into the hearts of all those who looked upon her.

Indifferent to the exhortations of the abbé Girard, who had stuck with her in defiance of her will, she stood looking straight ahead without glancing either left or right. Whatever thoughts were burning in her mind they shone forth with the rigidity of a conviction in her immutable gaze. The jerky movement of the cart over the uneven cobblestones, by its very violence, further emphasized the inflexible erectness of her deportment; you'd have said a marble statue was being paraded on a chariot; but the royal statue had luminous eyes and her shorn hair was blowing about in tufts in the wind.

A silence like the silence of the desert suddenly battened down on the three hundred thousand spectators of this scene, which the sun shone down upon for the very first time.

Soon, from where Maurice and Lorin were standing, you could hear the screeching of the cart's axle and the snorting of the guards' heavy horses.

The cart stopped at the foot of the scaffold.

The Queen, who had doubtless never imagined this precise moment, snapped out of her trance: she swept her haughty gaze over the crowd and the same pale young man she had seen before standing on a cannon appeared to her again from on top of a milestone.

From this vantage point, he sent her the same worshipful salute he had addressed to her as she was leaving the Conciergerie; then he immediately jumped to the ground.

Several people saw him and, as he was dressed in black, the rumor quickly spread that a priest had waited for Marie Antoinette in order to grant her absolution as she mounted the scaffold. They could say what they liked—the Knight didn't give them a second's thought. In extreme moments, there is a supreme respect for the things that matter.

The Queen nimbly descended the three steps of the footstool. She was supported by Sanson, who showed her the greatest consideration up until the last, all the while carrying out the task he himself seemed condemned to perform.

While she was walking toward the steps of the scaffold, a number of horses reared up; a number of guards on foot and a number of soldiers on horseback seemed to wobble and lose their balance; then something like a shadow could be seen slipping beneath the scaffold. But calm reestablished itself almost in the same instant. No one wanted to leave their place at this solemn moment, no one wanted to miss the slightest detail of the great tragedy that was about to unfold. All eyes were on the doomed woman.

The Queen was already on the platform of the guillotine with the priest still talking at her. An aide pushed her gently from behind; another undid the fichu that covered her shoulders.

Marie Antoinette felt that infamous hand flutter at her neck; she made a sudden movement and stepped on Sanson's foot as he was busy, unbeknownst to her, tying her to the deadly frame. Sanson pulled his foot away.

"Pardon me, monsieur," said the Queen. "I didn't do it on purpose."

Those were the last words uttered by the Daughter of the Caesars, the Queen of France, the widow of Louis XVI.

The quarter hour after midday rang out from the clock at the Tuileries. And at that very moment Marie Antoinette fell into eternity.

A terrible cry, a cry that summed up all that forbearance could possibly contain, such as joy, horror, grief, hope, triumph, expiation, smothered like a hurricane another cry, feeble and lamentable, which came from beneath the scaffold at the same moment.

The gendarmes heard it, faint as it was, and stepped forward. The crowd was thinner now and spread out like a river that has burst its banks, breaking through the hedgerow of soldiers and sending them flying, washing over the foot of the scaffold like a tidal wave and carrying it away.

Everyone wanted to see close up the remains of a royalty they believed forever destroyed in France.

But the gendarmes were looking for something else: they were looking for the shadow that had broken through their lines and slipped under the scaffold. Two of them came back, dragging by the collar a young man who was pressing to his heart a handkerchief stained with blood.

The man was followed by a little spaniel who howled forlornly.

"Death to the aristocrat! Death to the *ci-devant*!" shouted a few men of the people, pointing at the young man. "He dipped his handkerchief in the Austrian woman's blood: put him to death!"

"Good God!" cried Maurice. "Lorin, do you recognize him? Do you recognize him?"

"Death to the royalist!" repeated the maniacs. "Get that handkerchief off him! He wants to keep it as a relic. Take it off him! Take it off him!"

A proud smile fluttered across the young man's lips. He tore his shirt, baring his chest, and dropped his handkerchief.

"Messieurs," he said, "this blood is not that of the Queen; it is my own. Let me die in peace."

And a deep and streaming gash appeared, gaping, under his left breast. The crowd screamed and moved back as the young man slowly fell to his knees, gazing at the scaffold as a martyr would gaze at an altar.

"Maison-Rouge!" Lorin murmured in Maurice's ear.

"Adieu!" murmured the young man, bowing his head with a divine smile. "Adieu, or rather au revoir!"[1]

With that, he expired[2] in the midst of the stunned guards.

"That's what we have to do, Lorin," said Maurice, "before we become bad citizens."

The little dog ran around the corpse, bewildered and yowling.

"Hey, it's Black!" said a man holding a huge baton in his hand. "Well, well! It's Black. Here, boy!"

The dog went over to the man calling him. But as soon as he came within reach the man raised his baton and smashed his skull, bursting out laughing as he did so.

"Oh, the bastard!" said Maurice.

"Quiet!" murmured Lorin. "Quiet, or we're finished. . . . That's Simon."

50

THE HOME VISIT

Lorin and Maurice had gone back to Lorin's place, where Maurice was staying. To avoid compromising his friend too openly, Maurice had adopted the habit of going out early and coming back late.

Moving with the throng, keeping up with events, regularly observing the transfer of prisoners to the Conciergerie, he was daily on the lookout for any sign of Geneviève, not having been able to find out which prison she had been locked up in. For since his visit to Fouquier-Tinville, Lorin had given him to understand that the first move he made in public would be his undoing—and that would mean being sacrificed without having come to Geneviève's aid. Maurice, of course, would have got himself locked up on the spot if it meant being reunited with her; but he opted for prudence for fear of being separated from her forever.

And so every morning he went from the Carmelites prison to Port-Libre, from the Madelonnettes prison to Saint-Lazare, from the prison of La Force to the Luxembourg.[1] Stationing himself in front of the prison gates as the carts came out ferrying the accused to the Revolutionary Tribunal, he'd give the departing victims the once-over before running to the next prison on his round.

But he soon realized that ten men would not be enough to keep an eye in this way on the thirty-three prisons that Paris possessed at that time, and he made do with visits to the Tribunal itself to await Geneviève's court appearance.

This was already the onset of despair. Indeed, what resources remained to the condemned after their arrest? Sometimes the Tribunal, which began its sessions at ten in the morning, had condemned twenty or thirty people by four in the afternoon. The first person condemned enjoyed another six hours' life; but the last, struck down by a sentence at a quarter to four, fell under the ax at four-thirty.

To resign himself to a similar fate for Geneviève was thus to grow tired of living, of constantly doing battle with fate.

If only he'd been told in advance about Geneviève's incarceration, how Maurice would have thumbed his nose at the very blind human justice that then held sway! How easily and swiftly he'd have whisked her out of jail! Never was it easier to escape; never was escape more rare. Once all these nobles were thrown in jail, they set themselves up there as though they were still at the château, making themselves completely at home in order to die. To flee was like evading the consequences of a duel: women themselves blushed for shame at a liberty acquired at such a price.

But Maurice would not have shown himself so scrupulous. Knocking off a few dogs, bribing a turnkey: what could be simpler! Geneviève's was not such an illustrious name that it drew the attention of the world. . . . She would not be doing herself dishonor in fleeing, and besides . . . what if she were dishonored? Who could give a fig!

Oh! With what a bitter taste in his mouth he imagined the gardens of Port-Libre, so easy to scale; the rooms of the Madelonnettes, so convenient for busting out of and hitting the street; the ridiculously low walls of the Luxembourg and dim halls of the Carmes, to which any man with a bit of gumption could so easily gain access by taking out a window!

But was Geneviève in one of these prisons?

Devoured by doubt and worn out by worry, Maurice heaped insults upon Dixmer's head; he threatened him, he savored his hatred for the man whose cowardly revenge cloaked itself in the pretense of devotion to the royal cause.

"And I'll find him," thought Maurice. "For if he wants to save the poor woman, he'll show himself; if he wants to finish her off, he'll insult her. I'll find the bastard and it'll be a sorry day for him when I do!"

The morning of the day on which the facts we are about to lay before the reader occurred, Maurice had gone to set himself up at the place du Tribunal Révolutionnaire. Lorin was still asleep. He was woken up by a great racket at the door composed of women's voices and the butts of rifles. He threw a frightened glance around the room, like any man surprised and hoping to persuade himself that nothing compromising was in sight.

Four sectionaries, two gendarmes, and a commissioner came bursting in all at once. This visit was so momentous that Lorin hastened to throw on his clothes as quickly as possible.

"Are you arresting me?" he asked.

"Yes, citizen Lorin."

"And why is that?"

"Because you are suspect."

"Ah! That's only fair!"

The commissioner scribbled a few words at the bottom of the arrest sheet.

"Where is your friend?" he said.

"Which friend is that?"

"Citizen Maurice Lindey."

"At his place, I guess," said Lorin.

"No, he's not, he's staying here."

"He is? I'll be damned! Do have a look around, and if you find him . . ."

"Here's the denunciation," said the commissioner. "It is quite explicit."

He handed Lorin a piece of paper with hideous handwriting and baffling spelling. The denunciation claimed that citizen Lindey was seen every morning coming out of citizen Lorin's abode and that he was under arrest as suspect. The denunciation was signed: Simon.

"Surprise, surprise! But the cobbler won't be cobbling much longer," said Lorin, "if he keeps moonlighting like this. Two jobs! Stool pigeon and boot-soler both! What a Caesar is our Monsieur Simon. . . ." He burst out laughing.

"Citizen Maurice!" said the commissioner. "Where is citizen Maurice? We order you to hand him over."

"Even when I tell you he's not here?"

The commissioner went into the next room, then climbed up into a small loft where Lorin's officieux lodged. Finally he opened the door of a room below, but there was no trace of Maurice. On the kitchen table, though, a freshly penned letter attracted the commissioner's attention. It was from Maurice; he had dropped it there as he went out that morning without waking his friend, even though they shared the same bed. It read:

"I'm off to the Tribunal; eat without me, I won't be back until tonight."

"Citizen," said Lorin, "as keen as I am to obey you, you understand I can't follow you in my shirttails. . . . Please permit my officieux to dress me."

"Aristocrat!" said a voice. "He has to be helped to put his drawers on. . . ."

"My God, yes!" said Lorin. "I'm like citizen Dagobert,[2] I am. Notice I didn't say *king*."

"Go ahead," said the commissioner, "but make it snappy."

The officieux came down from his loft to assist his master to get dressed. Lorin's aim was not exactly to have a valet de chambre dress him. It was to ensure that nothing that happened escaped the officieux, so that he could later tell Maurice all about it.

"Now, messieurs . . . pardon, citizens . . . now, *citizens,* I'm ready and I'll follow you. But please let me take with me the latest volume of Monsieur Demoustier's *Lettres à Emilie.*[3] I haven't read it yet and it will help me survive the boredom of captivity."

"Your captivity?" erupted Simon, who had now become a municipal officer in turn. He happened to enter at that point with four sectionaries in tow. "It won't be long coming. You feature in the trial of the woman who tried to help the Austrian woman get away. She's being judged today. . . . You'll be judged tomorrow, after you've testified."

"Cobbler," said Lorin with gravity, "you're sewing your soles on too fast."

"Yes, but what a nice leather knife I've got!" replied Simon with a ghastly smile. "You'll see, you'll get yours, my pretty grenadier."

Lorin gave a shrug.

"Well then, are we going?" he said. "I'm waiting for you."

And as everyone had turned to go down, Lorin gave municipal officer Simon a swift kick so hard it sent him rolling and howling the whole length of the shiny steep stairs. The sectionaries couldn't help themselves from laughing. Lorin put his hands nonchalantly in his pockets.

"In the exercise of my duties!" said Simon, livid with rage.

"Oh, for crying out loud!" said Lorin. "Aren't we all exercising our duties?"

They made him get in a fiacre and the commissioner escorted him to the Palais de Justice.

51

LORIN

If the reader will just bear with us while we pay a second visit to the Revolutionary Tribunal, we'll find Maurice at the same spot where we saw him once before; but we'll find him quite a bit paler and a lot more agitated.

As we reopen the curtain on this funereal stage where historical events rather than personal predilection have led us, the jurors are out deliberating, for a certain case has just been heard. Two accused who had already spruced themselves up for the scaffold—one of those brazen maneuvers by which, at the time, defendants tried to win over jurors—were chatting with their defense counsels, who were offering the usual vague words that a doctor despairing of a patient might glibly pronounce.

The mob in the galleries was in a ferocious mood that day, the kind of mood that excites the severity of the jurors: placed under the immediate surveillance of the *tricoteuses*—knitting away—and the working class faubouriens from the suburbs, jurors hold up better, sticking to their guns like actors redoubling their efforts before a hostile audience.

Accordingly, since ten-thirty in the morning, five defendants had already been turned into so many condemned by the same jurors, now rendered inflexible.

The two who found themselves in the dock were thus waiting to hear the yes or the no that would either restore them to life or hurl them into the jaws of death.

The mob in attendance, made ever more ferocious by the habitual nature of this daily tragedy, which had become its favorite spectacle, was warming them up, hectoring and shouting comments that had by then acquired a frightening force.

"Look, look, look! Look at the tall one!" said one of the *tricoteuses*, who, not having a cap, was sporting a tricolor cockade as big as a fist on her bun. "See how white he is! You'd think he was already dead!"

The condemned man looked at the harpie poking fun at him with a scornful smile.

"What do you say to that?" said her neighbor. "He's laughing."

"Yes—with one side of his face."

One faubourien looked at his watch.

"What time is it?" his pal asked.

"Ten to one; this has been going on for three quarters of an hour."

"Just like at Domfront, city of misfortune: arrive at twelve, get hanged at one."

"And what about the little one!" cried someone else. "Look at him, then. Won't he look a sight when he sneezes in the sack!"

"Bah! It all happens so fast, you don't even have time to notice."

"Hey, we'll ask Sanson for his head; we've got a right to see it."

"Notice how he's wearing his best tyrant blue! It's bloody lovely when poor folks like us can cut well-heeled fops like that down to size."

Indeed, as the executioner had told the Queen, the poor inherited each victim's personal effects, the spoils being transported to the Salpêtrière hospital as soon as the execution was over to be distributed among the destitute. That is where the murdered Queen's clothes had been sent.

Maurice listened to these words whirling around in the air without taking a scrap of notice. Every person was at that moment preoccupied with some potent thought of their own that set them apart. For some days now his heart had beaten only intermittently and fitfully; now and again fear or hope seemed to suspend the ongoing pulse of his life, and these endless oscillations had more or less damaged his heart's susceptibility: he felt only numbness now.

The jury returned to the chamber and, as expected, the foreman declared the two defendants condemned. They were taken away and marched out with a firm step. They knew how to die in those days. . . .

The usher's voice rang out, mournful and sinister.

"The citizen public prosecutor versus the citizeness Geneviève Dixmer."

Maurice shivered from head to toe and sweat pearled over his entire face. The small door through which the accused came in opened and Geneviève appeared. She was dressed in white; her hair was done beautifully, for she had parted it and curled it artfully instead of cutting it off the way many women did.

Maurice saw Geneviève and felt all the strength he had carefully built up for the occasion drain from him at once. But he had, after all, been expecting the blow, since he had not missed a single hearing for twelve days now and three times already the name Geneviève on the public prosecutor's lips had struck his ear. But certain kinds of despair are so vast and so deep no one can sound their depths.

All those who saw this woman appear, so beautiful, so childlike, so luminously white and wan, uttered a cry: some of fury—there were, at the time, people who hated all forms of superiority, superiority in beauty as much as superiority in wealth, genius, or birth; others of admiration; still others of pity.

Geneviève no doubt recognized one cry out of all the cries, one voice among all the voices, for she turned to where Maurice was while the president flipped through the accused's file, looking up at her from time to time.

She saw Maurice at a glance, hidden as he was in his great broad-brimmed hat, and turned to face him smiling sweetly; with an even sweeter gesture, she placed her two trembling pink hands to her lips and blew him a kiss that contained her whole soul as well as her breath. The kiss winged its way across the room to the one man in all the crowd who had the right to claim it.

A murmur of interest rippled through the whole chamber. Geneviève was called to the stand and turned back to the jurors; but she stopped midway, her eyes wide with absolute terror, as she fixed on one point of the room.

Maurice stood on the tips of his toes but he could see nothing, or rather, something more important called his attention back to the stage, that is, to the bar. Fouquier-Tinville had begun reading the act of denunciation.

This act held that Geneviève Dixmer was the wife of a committed conspirator who was suspected of having aided the ex–Knight of Maison-Rouge in his successive attempts to save the Queen.

She had, moreover, been caught in the act of kneeling before the Queen, begging her to change clothes with her and offering to die in her place. This stupid fanaticism, said the act of denunciation, might merit the praises of the counterrevolutionaries; but today, the act added, every French citizen owed his life to the nation alone, and sacrificing one's life to the enemies of France was to commit treason twice over.

Geneviève, asked if she acknowledged having been, as the gendarmes Duchesne and Gilbert claimed, caught at the Queen's knees, beseeching her to change clothes with her, answered simply:

"Yes!"

"In that case," said the president, "tell us about your plans, your hopes."

Geneviève smiled.

"A woman can conceive hope, but no woman can devise a plan of the kind I am a victim of."

"How is it you found yourself there, then?"

"I had no choice: I was pushed."

"Who pushed you?" asked the public prosecutor.

"People who threatened to kill me if I didn't do as I was told."

With that the angry gaze of the young woman once again fixed on that point of the room Maurice could not see.

"So to escape from the death with which you were threatened, you braved the death that would surely result from any condemnation."

"I yielded with a knife at my breast, whereas the blade of the guillotine was still a long way from my neck. I buckled under clear and present violence."

"Why didn't you seek help? Any good citizen would have defended you."

"Alas, monsieur!" replied Geneviève in a tone at once so sad and so tender that Maurice's heart swelled to bursting. "Alas! I had no one near me to turn to."

Tender sympathy now took over from interest, as interest had taken over from curiosity. Many lowered their heads, some hiding their tears, others letting them fall freely.

Maurice then saw to his left a head that remained rigid, a face that remained hard. It was Dixmer, standing grim and implacable, not taking his eyes off Geneviève or the members of the Tribunal for a second.

The blood rushed to the young man's temples; anger rose from his heart to his brow, filling his whole being with a wild desire for revenge. He threw Dixmer a look filled with a hate so electric, so powerful, that

Dixmer, as though scalded by burning liquid, snapped his head around toward his enemy. Their eyes crossed like two darting flames.

"Tell us the names of the instigators," the president ordered.

"There is only one, monsieur."

"Who is . . . ?"

"My husband."

"Do you know where he is?"

"Yes."

"Tell us where he is hiding."

"He may be vile, but I will not descend to his level. It is not for me to say where he is hiding; that is for you to find out."

Maurice looked straight at Dixmer.

Dixmer didn't move a muscle. The idea crossed Maurice's mind to denounce the man then and there even if it meant denouncing himself. But he squashed that idea quickly. "No," he said to himself. "That's not the way he should die."

"So you refuse to guide us in our search?" said the president.

"I believe, monsieur, that I cannot do so," replied Geneviève, "without making myself as contemptible in the eyes of others as he is in mine."

"Are there any witnesses?" asked the president.

"There is one," the usher replied.

"Call the witness."

"Maximilien Jean Hyacinthe Lorin!" barked the usher.

"Lorin!" cried Maurice. "Oh my God! What's happened!"

Lorin was arrested the very same day this scene occurred and so Maurice knew nothing about the arrest.

"Lorin!" murmured Geneviève, looking around her, appalled.

"Why doesn't the witness answer the summons?" asked the president.

"Citizen president," said Fouquier-Tinville, "upon a recent denunciation, the witness has been arrested at his domicile; he will be brought in presently." Maurice flinched.

"There was another, more important witness," Fouquier-Tinville went on, "but we haven't been able to find that one yet."

Dixmer turned, smiling, to Maurice: perhaps the same idea that had sprung to the lover's mind had now sprung to the husband's.

Geneviève went deathly white and collapsed, giving out a groan. At that very moment, Lorin entered with a couple of gendarmes in his wake. Behind him and through the same door, Simon emerged, plunking himself down in the front gallery as though this was his local haunt.

"Your full name?" asked the president.

"Maximilien Jean Hyacinthe Lorin."

"Your state?"

"Free man."

"Not for long!" growled Simon, showing him his fist.

"Are you related to the prisoner?"

"No, but I have the honor of being one of her friends."

"Did you know she was plotting to help the Queen escape?"

"How do you expect me to have known that?"

"She could have confided in you."

"In me, a member of the Thermopylae section? . . . Please!"

"You have sometimes been seen with her, however."

"I could well have been seen—often, even."

"Did you know her to be an aristocrat?"

"I knew her as the wife of a master tanner."

"Her husband did not in reality exercise that craft; it was merely the façade behind which he hid."

"That I know nothing about; her husband is no friend of mine."

"Tell us about the husband."

"Gladly! He is a man so odious . . ."

"Monsieur Lorin," said Geneviève. "Have pity . . ."

Lorin continued imperturbably.

". . . that he sacrificed his poor wife, whom you have before you, to satisfy, not even his political imperatives, but his personal hatreds. The man is so low I'd put him almost on a par with Simon."

Dixmer became livid. Simon opened his mouth to speak but the president silenced him with a wave of the hand.

"You seem to know the story rather well, citizen Lorin," said Fouquier. "Tell us more."

"Forgive me, citizen Fouquier," said Lorin, getting up. "I've told you all I know."

He bowed and sat down again.

"Citizen Lorin," continued the prosecutor, "it is your duty to enlighten the Tribunal."

"Let it enlighten itself with what I've just said. As for this poor woman, I repeat, all she did was obey violence. . . . Open your eyes! Look at her! Does she look like a conspirator? She was forced to do what she did, that's all there is to it."

"You think so?"

"I know so."

"In the name of the law," said Fouquier, "I request that the witness Lorin be charged before the Tribunal as a prisoner in complicity with this woman."

Maurice gave out a groan. Geneviève hid her face in both hands.

Simon cried out in a transport of joy: "Citizen prosecutor, you've just saved the nation!"

As for Lorin, without saying a word in reply, he jumped over the balustrade to take a seat by Geneviève's side, took her hand, and respectfully kissed it:

"Hello, citizeness," he said with a composure that electrified the assembly. "How are you doing?"

Then he sat back in the dock.

52

WHAT HAPPENED NEXT

This entire scene had passed like a nightmare vision before Maurice, who stayed the course, leaning on his sword for support, watching his friends fall, one after the other, into that bottomless pit that never releases its victims. The mortal image was for him so overwhelming that he wondered why he, as the companion of his unfortunate friends, still clung to the edge of the precipice instead of just letting go, giving in to the vertigo that was dragging him down in their wake.

Jumping over the balustrade, Lorin had seen the dark smirking figure of Dixmer. When he sat down next to Geneviève, she leaned and whispered in his ear.

"God help us!" she said. "Did you know Maurice is here?"

"Where?"

"Don't look now; you might give him away."

"Don't worry."

"Behind us, near the door. He'll be in agony if we are condemned!"

Lorin looked at the young woman with tender compassion.

"We will be," he said. "Please don't have any doubts. Your disappointment would be too cruel if you were reckless enough to hope."

"Oh, my God!" said Geneviève. "Think of our poor friend, who will be all alone here below!"

Lorin turned round then to Maurice; Geneviève was not able to resist throwing him a quick look, either. Maurice had his eyes fixed on them and he pressed a hand to his heart.

"There is a way for you to save yourself," said Lorin.

"Is there?" asked Geneviève and her eyes sparkled with joy.

"Oh! I can answer for that!"

"If you manage to save me, Lorin, how I would bless you!"

"But the way . . ." Lorin trailed off.

Geneviève read the hesitation in his eyes.

"So you saw him too?" she said.

"Yes, I saw him. Do you want to be saved? Let him have his turn in the iron chair and you will be."

Dixmer doubtless divined what was afoot from the expression in Lorin's eyes as he spoke to Geneviève, for he at first blanched before returning to his sinister calm and his infernal smile.

"It's not possible," said Geneviève. "I couldn't go on hating him then."

"Admit that he knows how generous you are and is exploiting you, throwing down the gauntlet, taunting you."

"No doubt, for he is sure of himself, of me, of us all."

"Geneviève, Geneviève, I'm not as perfect as you; let me drag him down and let him perish."

"No, Lorin, I beg you, I want nothing in common with that man, not even death. I'd feel I was being unfaithful to Maurice if I died with Dixmer."

"But you won't die."

"How will I live when he is dead?"

"Ah!" cried Lorin. "No wonder Maurice loves you! You are an angel and the nation of angels is in heaven. Poor dear Maurice!"

Simon was dying to hear what the two accused were saying to each other, but he couldn't make out their words and had to scrutinize their faces instead.

"Citizen gendarme!" he cried. "How about stopping the conspirators from carrying on with their plots against the Republic—right here in the Revolutionary Tribunal!"

"Right!" said the gendarme. "You know very well, citizen Simon, that plots stop here, or that if people continue to conspire it won't be for long. The citizens are merely talking, and since the law doesn't prohibit talking in the tumbrel, why would anyone be prohibited from talking in court?"

The gendarme was Gilbert, who recognized the prisoner as the woman he caught in the Queen's cell, and was showing, with his usual probity, the sympathy he couldn't help but feel for courage and devotion.

The president had consulted his assessors; at Fouquier-Tinville's invitation, he began his questions:

"Accused Lorin, what was the nature of your relationship with citizeness Dixmer?" he asked.

"What was the nature, citizen president?"

"Yes."

> "A friendship like ours, there was none purer,
> She loved me as a brother, I loved her as a sister."

"Citizen Lorin," said Fouquier-Tinville, "that's not a good rhyme."

"How do you mean?" asked Lorin.

"Obviously there's one too many *er*'s."

"Cut, citizen prosecutor! Cut! That's your job."

The impassive face of Fouquier-Tinville paled slighty at the terrible joke.

"And how did citizen Dixmer look upon the liaison of a man who claimed to be a republican with his wife?" asked the president.

"Oh! That I cannot tell you. I've told you I never knew citizen Dixmer and was more than happy not to."

"But," Fouquier-Tinville went on, "you don't say that your friend citizen Maurice Lindey was the knot that bound you with the accused in such a pure friendship?"

"If I don't say so," answered Lorin, "it's because it seems tactless to me to say so, and I might add I think you should have followed my example."

"The citizens of the jury," said Fouquier-Tinville, "will appreciate this singular alliance of two republicans with an aristocrat, and at the very moment when this aristocrat is convicted of the vilest plot ever hatched against the nation."

"How could I have known about the plot you're talking about, citizen prosecutor?" asked Lorin, more revolted than scared by the brutality of the argument.

"You knew this woman, you were her friend, she called you her brother, you called her your sister, and yet you didn't know what she was up to? Is it thus possible, as you yourself have asked," asked the president, "that she perpetrated on her own the action imputed to her?"

"She did not perpetrate the action on her own," said Lorin making use of the technical jargon employed by the president. "As she told you, as I told you, and as I now repeat, her husband pushed her into it."

"So how is it you don't know the husband," said Fouquier-Tinville, "since the husband was complicit in it with his wife?"

Lorin had only to mention Dixmer's initial disappearance; Lorin had only to mention the love between Geneviève and Maurice; Lorin had only to mention, finally, how the husband had kidnapped his wife and hid her in some secret hideout, in order to exonerate himself from all connivance by clearing up any ambiguity.

But to do that, he would have to betray his two friends' secret; to do that, he would have to make Geneviève blush for shame in front of five hundred people. Lorin shook his head as though to say no to himself.

"Well?" asked the president. "What do you say to the citizen prosecutor?"

"That his logic is overwhelming," said Lorin. "And that he has convinced me of something I wasn't even aware of."

"What?"

"It is that I am, it would seem, one of the most dreadful conspirators ever seen."

This declaration provoked universal hilarity. The jurors themselves couldn't hold out, for Lorin had sent up the prosecutor's tone with perfect accuracy. Fouquier felt the brunt of the general scorn. But since, in his tireless perseverance, he'd managed to ferret out all the secrets of the accused and knew them as well as they knew themselves, he could not help but feel compassionate admiration for Lorin.

"Come now, citizen Lorin," he said. "Speak, defend yourself. The Tribunal will hear you out. For it knows your past, and your past is that of a fearless republican."

Simon tried to speak; the president signaled to him to be quiet.

"Speak, citizen Lorin; we're listening," he said.

Lorin shook his head once more.

"This silence is tantamount to admission," the president continued.

"No, it's not," said Lorin. "This silence is just silence, that's all."

"Once again," said Fouquier-Tinville, "will you speak?"

Lorin turned to the audience to ask Maurice with a look what he should do. Maurice did not signal to Lorin to speak, and Lorin remained silent. Which was the same as condemning himself.

What followed next happened very fast. Fouquier summed up his accusation; the president summed up the debates; the jurors took a vote and brought back a verdict of guilty against Lorin and Geneviève. The president condemned them both to death.

Two o'clock rang out from the great clock of the Palais. The president only took as long to pronounce the death sentence as it took the clock to sound the hour. Maurice heard the two sounds jumbled together. When the double vibration of the voice and the clock's timbre died away, his strength was gone.

The gendarmes led away Geneviève and Lorin, who had offered her his arm. They both saluted Maurice, though in their very different ways: Lorin with a smile, Geneviève, pale and faltering, with one last kiss, blown from fingers wet with tears.

She had kept alive the hope of living until the very last moment and was weeping now not for her life but for her love, which would be extinguished with that life. Maurice was half-demented and did not respond to his friends' adieus; he rose, weak and dazed, from the seat he'd collapsed onto. His friends had disappeared.

He felt that only one thing was still alive in him: it was hate that bit into his heart like acid. Gazing around one last time he spotted Dixmer, who was shuffling out with the other spectators and had just ducked his head to pass through the low arched door into the corridor.

With the speed of a coiled spring, Maurice bounded from seat to seat to reach the door. Dixmer was already through and was disappearing down the dark corridor. Maurice followed behind him. The moment Dixmer stepped onto the flagstones of the great hall, Maurice tapped him on the shoulder.

53

THE DUEL

In those days, being tapped on the shoulder was never a laughing matter. Dixmer swung around and recognized Maurice.

"Ah, hello, citizen republican," Dixmer said, without giving away any emotion other than by an imperceptible jolt that he immediately got under control.

"Hello, citizen coward," replied Maurice. "You were expecting me, weren't you?"

"Let's say that, on the contrary, I was no longer expecting you," said Dixmer.

"Why is that?"

"Because I was expecting you sooner."

"I'm still here too soon for you, you murderer!" Maurice added in a voice, or rather a low rumble, that was frightening because it was the growling of the storm that had built up in his heart, and his eyes blazed lightning.

"If only looks could kill, citizen!" Dixmer scoffed. "You realize we'll be recognized and followed."

"Yes, and you're terrified of being arrested, aren't you? You're terrified of being carted off to the scaffold where you send others? Let them arrest us, so much the better, for it seems to me a certain guilty party is missing from the nation's jail quota today."

"Just as one person is missing from the honor roll, isn't that right? Since your name was struck off, I mean."

"Right! We'll get back to that later, I hope. Meanwhile you've got your revenge, miserable cur that you are—in the worst possible way, on a woman! Since you were apparently expecting to see me, I wonder why you didn't wait for me at my place the day you stole Geneviève away from me?"

"I felt the original thief was you."

"Please, no wit, monsieur, I've never known you to show any; no speeches, I know you're bigger on action than on words. Witness the day you tried to assassinate me: that day, you showed your true colors."

"And I've kicked myself more than once for not paying heed," Dixmer replied calmly.

"Well then," said Maurice, smacking his sword, "I'm offering you a chance to avenge yourself."

"Tomorrow, if you like, not today."

"Why tomorrow?"

"Or tonight."

"Why not straightaway?"

"Because I'll be busy until five o'clock."

"Some other hideous scheme?" said Maurice. "Some other ambush?"

"I'd leave that alone, if I were you!" said Dixmer. "You are indeed most ungrateful. My God! For six months I let you conduct a great romance with my wife; for six months I respected your rendezvous, let your little smiles pass. Never has a man, you'd have to agree, been less of a tiger than I have."

"What you mean is you thought I was useful and you used me."

"No doubt!" Dixmer replied calmly, more and more in control of himself the more Maurice got carried away. "No doubt! Whereas you betrayed your republic and sold it to me for one look from my wife; while you were busy dishonoring yourselves, you by your treason and she by her adultery, I played the wise man and hero. I bided my time and I carried the day."

"Vile man!" said Maurice.

"Oh! Aren't I just! You appreciate your own conduct, I hope, monsieur. You are the vile one, surely! You are disgusting!"

"You are wrong, monsieur; what I call vile and disgusting is the conduct of a man to whom a woman's honor had been entrusted, who had sworn to keep that honor pure and intact and who, instead of keeping his word, used her beauty as bait to hook a hungry heart. Before all else, you had the sacred duty of protecting that woman, monsieur, and instead of protecting her, you sold her."

"I'll tell you what I had to do, monsieur," replied Dixmer. "I had to save my friend, who supported a sacred cause with me. Just as I sacrificed my property to that cause, so I sacrificed my honor. As for me, I completely forgot about myself. I thought of myself only at the very last. Now my friend is no more: my friend was stabbed to death; now my Queen is no more: my Queen died at the guillotine; now, well, now I'm finally thinking of my revenge."

"Why don't you say *murder.*"

"You don't murder an adulteress: in striking her dead you merely punish her."

"You forced her into adultery; it was therefore legitimate."

"You think so?" said Dixmer with a dark smile. "Ask her remorse if she thinks she acted legitimately."

"The man who punishes strikes in broad daylight; you, you aren't punishing her—you're throwing her head to the guillotine while cowering in the dark."

"You think I'm hiding myself! And how do you figure that, dimwit that you are?" Dixmer asked. "Am I hiding by turning up at her condemnation? Am I running away by going as far as the Hall of the Dead to toss her a last good-bye?"

"So you intend to see her again?" cried Maurice. "You are going to say good-bye to her?"

"Really!" said Dixmer, shrugging his shoulders. "You don't know the first thing about revenge, do you, citizen Maurice? In my place, I suppose you'd be happy just to let things take their course, let circumstances dictate the outcome? For example, the woman in adultery having deserved death, the moment I punish her with death I've evened the score with her, or rather, she's even with me? No, citizen Maurice, I've come up with something better than that: I've found a way of paying back that woman for all the wrong she's done me. She loves you—so she's going to die far away from you; she hates me, so she's going to see me again before she dies!"

Taking a wallet out of his pocket, he went on, "You see this wallet? It contains a pass signed by the Palais registrar. With this pass, I can get to where they keep the condemned locked up. Well, I shall go in and find Geneviève; I'll call her an adulteress; I'll see her hair fall under the hands of the executioner and, while her hair is falling, she'll hear my voice repeating over and over: *Adulteress!* I'll go with her by the side of the cart, and when she steps onto the scaffold the last word she'll hear will be the word *adulteress.*"

"Watch out, Dixmer! She won't have the strength to bear so much vileness: she will denounce you."

"No!" said Dixmer. "She hates me too much for that. If she was going to denounce me she'd have done it when your friend whispered to her to do it: since she didn't denounce me to save her life, she won't denounce me in order to die with me. For she knows full well that if she denounced me, I'd slow her demise by a day; she knows very well that if she denounced me, I'd go with her, not only to the bottom of the Palais steps but right up to the scaffold; she knows very well that instead of abandoning her, I'd hop up with her onto the cart; she knows very well that, all the way along, I'd repeat that terrible word to her: *adulteress;* and that on the scaffold I'd go on repeating it, that the moment she drops into eternity the accusation will go with her."

Dixmer was frightening in his rage and his hate. He had grabbed Maurice's hand in his and shook it with a force the young man had never once come across before. It had a sobering effect on Maurice: the more wildly excited Dixmer became, the calmer Maurice felt.

"Listen," said the young man. "There's one thing lacking in your revenge."

"What?"

"It is being able to say to her: 'While I was leaving the Tribunal, I saw your lover and I killed him.'"

"On the contrary, I'd prefer to tell her that you're alive and kicking and that for the rest of your life you will suffer from the sight of her death."

"And yet you will kill me," said Maurice, looking around to check whether he was master of the situation. "Or I will kill you."

Feeling the white heat of his emotion, exalted by fury, his strength doubled by the self-control he'd imposed on himself in order to hear Dixmer's terrible scheme to the end, Maurice seized Dixmer's throat and yanked him toward him, walking backward all the while toward a set of stairs that led to the banks of the Seine.

At the touch of Maurice's hand, Dixmer too felt all the hate rise up like lava.

"Right!" he said. "You don't need to drag me by force. I'm coming."

"Come then, you are armed."

"I'll follow you."

"No, you go first. But I warn you, the faintest hint of movement and I'll split your head in two with my sword."

"Oh! You know very well you don't frighten me," said Dixmer with that smile that the ghastly pallor of his lips made so alarming.

"My sword doesn't frighten you, no," muttered Maurice, "but losing your revenge does. And yet, now that we are face-to-face, you can kiss revenge good-bye."

They had actually reached the water's edge, and if they could still be seen where they were, no one could arrive in time to prevent the duel from taking place. Besides, an equal rage devoured both men.

While they spoke they had descended the small set of steps that lead down from the square in front of the Palais. The quay was virtually deserted at this hour, for it was just past two and, as the condemnations continued, the crowd was still packing the courtroom, corridors, and courtyards of the Palais.

Dixmer seemed as thirsty for Maurice's blood as Maurice was for his. They dived under one of the arches that lead from the prison cells of the Conciergerie to the river, today putrid sewers, but once full of blood and used for carrying more than one corpse far away from the black holes of the dungeons. Maurice stood between Dixmer and the water.

"I really do think it is I who will kill you, Maurice," said Dixmer. "You're shaking like a leaf."

"And I," said Maurice, taking his sword in hand and carefully cutting off any retreat, "on the contrary, Dixmer, think that it is I who will kill you and, having killed you, will remove from your wallet that pass from the Palais registrar. Oh! Never mind about buttoning up your coat; I can tell you now my sword would tear it open even if you were wearing an antique bronze breastplate."

"You intend to take the pass?" said Dixmer.

"Yes!" said Maurice. "I'm the one who'll get to use it, your little pass; I'm the one who'll get to flash the pass and go in to Geneviève; I'm the one who'll sit next to her on the cart; I'm the one who'll murmur in her ear for the time remaining to her to live: I love you. And when her head falls: I loved you."

Dixmer made a move with his left hand to transfer the pass from his right and throw it with the wallet into the river. But, quick as a flash of lightning, slicing like an ax, Maurice's saber came down and severed that hand entirely from the wrist.

The mutilated man gave out a cry, shaking his bleeding stump and moved into the en garde position as a terrible battle began under the arches in this dark and hidden recess of the Seine. Confined to such a narrow space that blows could not be aimed freely from off the line of the body, so to speak, the two men slipped on the wet stones and clung with difficulty to the sewer walls. Every slip only enraged both men further, and they threw themselves all the more frenziedly into the fray.

Dixmer felt his blood run out of him and knew his strength would flow out with it. He charged at Maurice with such violence that Maurice was forced to take a step back. As he broke away, his left foot slipped and the point of his enemy's sword grazed his chest. But with a movement as speedy as thought, on his knees though he was, he flipped the blade back up with his left hand and held the point at Dixmer, who surged forward, airborne with anger, on sloping ground, fell on his sword, and impaled himself.

A terrible curse was heard, then the two bodies rolled together out from under the vault.

Only one man got up again and that man was Maurice, Maurice covered in blood, but the blood was the blood of his enemy. He plucked his sword from the body and, as he did so, he seemed to suck out the rest of the life that still quivered through Dixmer's limbs in a nervous tremor.

When he had thoroughly assured himself that Dixmer was dead, he leaned over the body, opened the dead man's coat, took the wallet out, and dashed off.

Giving himself a rapid glance, he could see that he wouldn't go four steps in the street without being arrested, for he was covered in blood. He went and crouched down at the water's edge and washed his hands and clothes. Then he bounded back up the stairs, casting one last look behind him. A steaming red thread was coming out from under the arches and streaming toward the river.

When Maurice had almost reached the Palais, he opened the wallet and found the pass signed by the Palais registrar.

"Justice exists! Thank you, God!" he murmured.

And on that note he swiftly mounted the steps that lead to the Hall of the Dead as the clock struck three.

54

THE HALL OF THE DEAD

You will recall that the Palais registrar had opened his registers of nuts and bolts for Dixmer and enjoyed relations with him that the presence of Madame Dixmer did nothing to sour.

This man, as you may well imagine, was frightened out of his wits when the revelations about Dixmer's plot got out. Indeed, for him, the issue was no less grave than whether he looked to others like he might be one of Dixmer's phony colleague accomplices—thereby being condemned to death as surely as Geneviève.

Fouquier-Tinville had summoned him to appear before him.

You can understand the pains the poor man took to establish his innocence in the eyes of the public prosecutor. He succeeded, largely thanks to Geneviève's confession, which established the man's ignorance of her husband's plans—and partly thanks to Dixmer's flight, but above all thanks to the interests of Fouquier-Tinville who wanted to keep his administration free from taint of any kind.

"Citizen," the registrar had said, throwing himself on his knees, "forgive me, I let myself be hoodwinked."

"Citizen," the public prosecutor had replied, "an employee of the nation who lets himself be hoodwinked in times such as these deserves to be guillotined."

"But a person can be stupid, citizen," the proud registrar went on, dying to call Fouquier-Tinville *monseigneur*.[1]

"Stupid or otherwise," said the public prosecutor, "no one should allow themselves to doze off in their love for the Republic. The geese on the Capitol[2] were stupid, too, mere creatures, yet they managed to wake up in time and save Rome."

The registrar had nothing to say to such an argument; he merely groaned and waited.

"I pardon you," said Fouquier. "I'd even go so far as to defend you— I don't want one of my employees suspected for a second. But just remember, at the slightest word that reaches my ears, at the slightest reminder of this business, it's off with your head."

There is no need to say with what enthusiasm and solicitude the registrar ran to get the newspapers, which are always keen to say what they know and sometimes what they don't know, even if ten men's heads were to roll as a result.

He looked everywhere for Dixmer to caution him to remain silent, but Dixmer had quite naturally moved and could not be found.

Geneviève was brought to the chair of the accused, but she had already declared during the preliminary hearing that neither she nor her husband had any accomplices. So you can imagine how he beamed his thanks at the poor woman when he saw her go by on her way to the Tribunal. But after she had gone by and he had popped back into the office for a moment to retrieve a file citizen Fouquier-Tinville had requested, he suddenly saw Dixmer coming toward him, looking cool, calm, and collected. The vision petrified him.

"Oh!" he cried as though he'd seen a ghost.

"Don't you recognize me?" the vision asked.

"Of course I do. You are citizen Durand, or rather citizen Dixmer."

"So I am."

"But are you dead, citizen?"

"Not yet, as you can see."

"I mean you're going to be arrested."

"Who do you think's going to arrest me? No one knows who I am."

"But I know who you are and I only have to say the word and you'll be guillotined."

"And I, I only have to say two words and you'll be guillotined with me."

"That's horrible, what you're saying!"

"No, it's logical."

"But what's this about? Come on, tell me! Hurry up—the less time we spend talking together the less danger for either of us."

"The situation is this. My wife is going to be condemned, right?"

"I'm afraid that's right! Poor woman!"

"Well then, I want to see her one last time to say good-bye."

"Where?"

"In the Hall of the Dead!"

"You'd dare go in there?"

"Why not?"

"Oh!" said the registrar, goose bumps sprouting at the very idea of such a thing.

"There must be a way," Dixmer persisted.

"To get into the Hall of the Dead? Yes, no doubt."

"How?"

"You get yourself a pass."

"And where do you get these passes?"

The registrar went pale as a corpse and stammered:

"The passes, where do you get them—is that what you asked?"

"I'm asking where you procure them," replied Dixmer. "I think the question is clear enough."

"You procure them . . . here."

"Oh, really! And who usually signs them?"

"The registrar."

"But you are the registrar."

"Yes, I know, it's me."

"Fancy that! What a stroke of luck!" said Dixmer, helping himself to a seat. "You will sign a pass for me."

The registrar gave a start.

"You're asking me for my head, citizen," he said.

"No I'm not! I'm asking you for a pass, that's all."

"I'm going to have you arrested, you miserable creep!" said the registrar, gathering all his energy.

"Go ahead!" said Dixmer. "But the instant you do, I'll denounce you as my accomplice, and instead of going into the infamous Hall all on my own, I'll take you with me."

The registrar went white.

"Oh, you mongrel!" he said.

"There's no mongrel about it," said Dixmer. "I need to speak to my wife and I'm asking you for a pass so I can reach her."

"Come now, is it really so essential that you speak to her?"

"It would seem to be, wouldn't it, I'm risking my neck to do it."

The reasoning seemed plausible to the registrar; Dixmer could see that the man was rattled.

"Come on," Dixmer said, "don't worry, no one will be any the wiser. For Christ's sake, there must be other cases similar to this from time to time, surely."

"It's rare. There's not a lot of competition."

"Well then, we can change that. That's all I'm asking for—if it can be done."

"It can be done, all right. You enter through the door of the condemned; you don't need a pass for that. Then, when you've spoken to your wife, call me and I'll escort you out."

"Not bad!" said Dixmer. "Unfortunately, there's a story doing the rounds."

"What?"

"The story about a poor hunchback who took the wrong door and, thinking he was entering Archives, wound up in the room we're talking about. But since he came in through the door of the condemned instead of through the main door, and as he didn't have a pass that would confirm his identity once he was inside, they wouldn't let him go. They argued that since he had come in through the door of the other condemned, he was condemned like the others. He protested in vain, cursed, yelled his head off—no one believed him, no one came to his aid, no one got him out. So, despite his protests, his curses, his shouts, the executioner first cut off his hair and then his head. Is the story true, citizen registrar? You would know better than anyone."

"Alas! Yes. It is true!" said the registrar, shaking visibly.

"Well then, you see that with precedents like that, I'd be mad to walk into such a death trap."

"But I'll be there, I tell you!"

"And what if you're called away, what if you're busy elsewhere—or if you *forget*?" Dixmer ruthlessly emphasized the last word: "What if you *forget* that I'm there?"

"But I promise . . ."

"No. Besides, that would compromise you: you'd be seen talking to me, and then again, in the end, I just don't like the idea. I'd definitely prefer a pass."

"Can't be done."

"Then, my friend, I will talk, and we will go and take a little turn of the place de la Révolution together."

In a delirious, catatonic state, the registrar signed a pass, one for "a citizen." Dixmer threw himself upon it and rushed out to grab a seat in the courtroom, as we have seen.

You know the rest.

From that moment, to avoid any accusation of complicity, the registrar stuck close to Fouquier-Tinville, leaving the management of his office to his chief assistant.

At ten minutes past three, Maurice, armed with the pass, crossed a hedgerow of wicket clerks and gendarmes and reached the fatal door without mishaps of any kind. When we say fatal we are exaggerating a bit, for there were two doors: the main door, through which carriers of passes came and went, and the door of the condemned, through which only those people entered who would be leaving only to walk to the scaffold.

The room into which Maurice had managed to penetrate was divided into two sections. In one section sat the employees whose job it was to register the names of arrivals; in the other, furnished only with a few wooden benches, were placed both those who had just been arrested and those who had just been condemned—which amounted to the same thing.

The room was dark, lit only by the windows of a glass partition taken from the office.

A woman dressed in white reclined in a corner, motionless and semiconscious, with her back to the wall. A man was standing before her, arms folded, shaking his head from time to time and hesitating to speak to her, for fear of bringing her back to a consciousness she seemed to have vacated.

Around these two characters you could see the condemned stirring in bewilderment, sobbing or singing patriotic hymns. Others paced the floor, taking long strides as though seeking some release in movement from the thoughts that devoured them.

This was indeed death's antechamber, and the furnishings saw to it that it lived up to its name. You could see caskets filled with straw, half-open as though beckoning the living: these served as beds, provisional tombs.

A huge cupboard stood against the wall opposite the glass partition. One of the prisoners opened it out of curiosity and reeled back in horror. The cupboard held the bloodstained clothes of the previous day's beheaded, and long locks of hair hung here and there: these were the executioner's perquisites, his tips, which he sold to the relatives when not required by the authorities to burn such precious relics.

Maurice was out of breath and panting in great distress when he opened the door and took in the whole scene at a glance. He took a few steps into the room and then rushed and fell at Geneviève's feet.

The poor woman gave out a cry that Maurice smothered on her lips. Lorin hugged his friend in his arms, weeping; those were the first tears he had shed.

What was strange was that all the unhappy people gathered together, all of whom were to die together, barely glanced at the moving tableau offered to them by these three unhappy people, their fellows. Everyone had too much on their own mind to think about what others were going through.

The three friends remained momentarily locked in an embrace that was silent, ardent, almost jubilant. Lorin was the first to pull away from his sorrowing friends.

"So you are condemned too?" he said to Maurice.

"Yes," Maurice replied.

"Oh! How wonderful!" murmured Geneviève.

The joy of people who only have an hour to live can't even last as long as they live.

Maurice, after contemplating Geneviève with the deep and burning love he had in his heart, after thanking her for her at once extremely egotistical and extremely loving outburst, turned to Lorin.

"Now," he said, enfolding Geneviève's hands in his, "let's talk."

"Ah, yes! Let's talk!" replied Lorin. "I mean, if we still have any time left, it's only right. What do you want to say to me? Let's have it."

"You were arrested because of me, condemned because of her, having broken no laws. As Geneviève and I are paying our debt, it isn't right that you be asked to pay as well."

"I don't understand."

"Lorin, you are free."

"Free, me? You're mad!" said Lorin.

"No, I'm not mad; I repeat, you are free: look, here's a pass. They'll ask you who you are. Tell them you're employed in the registry office in the Carmes prison; you came to speak to the citizen registrar of the Palais. You asked him for a pass to see the condemned out of curiosity. You went, you saw, you're satisfied, and now you're leaving."

"I hope you're joking?"

"Not at all, my friend. Here's the pass, for God's sake use it. You're not in love. You don't need to die just to spend a few more minutes with the woman who is your heart's desire and not to lose a second of eternity together."

"Now listen, Maurice!" said Lorin. "If one can get out of here, which I swear I would never have thought, why not save Geneviève first? As for you, we'll see what we can do."

"No, no, impossible," said Maurice with a dreadful clutch at the heart. "Look, you see, on the pass is written *citizen,* not citizeness; and anyway Geneviève wouldn't want to leave me here, to live knowing I was to die."

"Well then, if she wouldn't want to, why would I? Do you think I have less courage than a woman, then?"

"No, my friend, I know, on the contrary, that you are the bravest of men. But nothing in the world could excuse your pigheadedness in the circumstances. Please, Lorin, profit from the moment and give us the supreme joy of knowing you're free and happy!"

"Happy!" cried Lorin. "Are you kidding? Happy without you? . . . What on earth do you want me to do in this world, without you, in Paris, without my old habits? Without seeing you ever again, without annoying you ever again with my poetry? No, for pity's sake, no!"

"Lorin, my friend! . . ."

"Exactly, it's because I am your friend that I must insist: if I were a prisoner, as I am, I'd knock down walls if it meant seeing the two of you again. But to escape from here all alone, to drift about the streets weighed down with something like remorse moaning incessantly in my ears: 'Maurice! Geneviève!,' to wander past certain places and certain houses where I've seen you both and where I will see no more than your shades from now on, to finally wind up hating Paris, which I've always loved so much: no, thank you! I believe they were right to outlaw kings, if only because of Dagobert."

"And what's King Dagobert got to do with what's happening to us?"

"What's he got to do with it? Didn't that frightful tyrant say to the great Eloi:[3] 'No one is such good company you can't leave them'? Well, I'm a republican! And I say: You should never leave good company for anything, not even the guillotine. I like it here and I'm staying."

"My poor friend! My poor friend!" said Maurice.

Geneviève said nothing but she gazed at Lorin with eyes bathed in tears.

"You regret life, don't you?" said Lorin.

"Yes, because of her!"

"Me, I don't regret it because of anything. Not even because of the Goddess of Reason, who—I forgot to tell you—recently wronged me greatly, which won't even mean she goes to the trouble of consoling herself like that other Artemisia, the ancient one who built her husband a mausoleum. So I'll have got off as gay as a lark. I'll put on a show for all the scoundrels that run after the cart; I'll whip up a nice quatrain for monsieur Sanson and then it'll be curtains. That is, wait a minute . . ."

Lorin broke off.

"Ah, that's right, that's right," he said, "that's right, I do want to get out. I knew very well I didn't love anyone, but I forgot there's someone I hate. What does your watch say, Maurice? The time!"

"Three-thirty."

"I've got time, by jiminy! I've got time."

"Of course," cried Maurice. "There are nine accused left today, it won't finish before five o'clock. So we have nearly two hours before us."

"That's all I need; give me your pass and lend me twenty sous."[4]

"Oh! My God! What are you going to do?" murmured Geneviève.

Maurice shook his hand; all that mattered to him was that Lorin got out.

"I have an idea," said Lorin.

Maurice pulled his purse out of his pocket and put it in his friend's hand.

"And now the pass, for the love of God! I mean, for the love of the Eternal Being."

Maurice handed him the pass. Lorin kissed Geneviève's hand and, taking advantage of the moment when a batch of condemned were being brought to the office, leapt over the wooden benches and presented himself at the main door.

"Hey!" said a gendarme. "Here's one trying to get away, looks like."

Lorin stood straight and presented his pass.

"Here, citizen, gendarme," he said. "Try to be a better judge of people, next time."

The gendarme recognized the registrar's signature, but he belonged to that class of civil servants generally lacking in trust, and as it just so happened that the registrar was returning from the Tribunal at that very moment, shaking with a tremor that hadn't left him since he had so recklessly risked his signature, the gendarme appealed to him.

"Citizen registrar," he said, "here is a pass that an individual wants to use in order to leave the Hall of the Dead. Is the pass in order?"

The registrar went white with fright and, convinced that he would see the terrible figure of Dixmer if he looked up, he snatched the pass and hastened to reply.

"Yes, yes, that's my signature, all right."

"Well then," said Lorin, "since it's your signature, hand it back."

"Not on your life," said the registrar, tearing the pass into a thousand pieces. "Not on your life! These sorts of passes can only be used once."

Lorin stood for a moment, undecided.

"Ah, too bad!" he said. "The main thing is that I kill him."

And he raced out of the registrar's office without further ado.

Maurice had gazed after Lorin with an emotion only too easy to imagine. As soon as Lorin had disappeared he said to Geneviève, "He's saved!" with an exaltation akin to joy. "They tore up his pass, he can't come back. And anyway, if he were to get back in somehow, the Tribunal session is nearly over; at five o'clock he'll come back and we'll be dead."

Geneviève gave a sigh and shivered.

"Oh! Hold me in your arms," she said. "We'll never leave each other again. . . . God! Why can't we be struck with the same blow and let out our last breath together!"

They withdrew to the remotest corner of the dark room; Geneviève snuggled close to Maurice and wrapped both arms around his neck;

thus entwined, breathing the same breath, silencing in themselves all noise and thought, they reached a numb out-of-body state together through force of love, at the approach of death.

Half an hour ticked away.

55

Why Lorin Left

Suddenly a great commotion was heard and gendarmes rushed in from the low door, trailing Sanson and his assistants behind them, carrying bundles of ropes.

"Oh! My friend, my friend!" cried Geneviève. "The fatal moment has come, I can feel myself faltering."

"But you are wrong to," broke out the ringing voice of Lorin:

> "You are wrong, it seems to me,
> For death itself spells liberty."

"Lorin!" wailed Maurice in despair.

"That wasn't so good, was it? I'm with you. Since yesterday I've been coming up with the most pathetic lines. . . ."

"Ah! As though that's the issue. You came back, you poor idiot! . . . You came back!"

"We had a deal, I thought. Listen, for what I have to say concerns you as much as Geneviève."

"My God! My God!"

"Let me speak, then, or I won't have time to tell you. I wanted to leave to go and buy a knife, rue de la Barillerie."

"What did you want a knife for?"

"I wanted to kill the good Monsieur Dixmer with it."

Geneviève shuddered.

"Ah!" said Maurice. "I understand."

"I bought it. This is what I said to myself, and you'll see what a logical mind your pal has. I'm beginning to think I should have been a mathematician instead of a poet. It's too late now, unfortunately. So this is what I said to myself—try to follow my reasoning. I said, 'Monsieur Dixmer has compromised his wife; Monsieur Dixmer came to see her be judged, Monsieur Dixmer won't deny himself the pleasure of seeing her get on the cart, especially with the two of us on it with her. I will therefore find him in the front row of spectators: I'll slip in close beside him, I'll say to him: "Good day, Monsieur Dixmer," and I'll plant my knife in his guts.' "

"Lorin!" cried Geneviève.

"Don't worry, dear friend, Providence has done things properly. Just think of it: instead of standing facing the Palais, as is their wont, all the spectators had turned halfway around to the right and were lining the quai. Fancy that, I said to myself, no doubt there's a dog drowning: why wouldn't Dixmer be here? A drowning dog always helps to pass the time. So I approached the parapet and I see all along the riverbank a bunch of people raising their arms in the air and leaning down to look at something on the ground, saying *alas* so many times it was nearly enough to flood the Seine. I went closer. . . . That something . . . Guess who it was. . . ."

"It was Dixmer," said Maurice in a grim voice.

"Yes. How did you know? It was Dixmer, dear friend, Dixmer! He'd ripped open his guts all by himself. The poor man no doubt killed himself by way of atonement."

"Ah!" said Maurice with a somber smile. "Is that what you think?"

Geneviève held her head in both hands. She was too feeble to bear such a rush of emotions.

"Yes, I did think that, given that his bloody sword was found nearby; unless somehow . . . he met up with someone. . . ."

Without saying a word and taking advantage of the fact that Geneviève could not see him, overcome as she was, Maurice opened his coat and flashed Lorin his bloodstained vest and shirt.

"Ah! That's something else," said Lorin.

He gave Maurice his hand.

"Now," he said, leaning to whisper in Maurice's ear, "they didn't search me, you know, because I told them I was in Monsieur Sanson's party when I came back in, so I still have the knife—if the guillotine is repugnant to you."

Maurice grabbed the weapon with glee.

"No," he said, "it would hurt her too much."

He handed the knife back to Lorin.

"You're right," said Lorin. "Long live the machine of Monsieur Guillotine![1] What is the machine of Monsieur Guillotine? One nick to the neck, as Danton said. What's a nick?"

With that, Lorin threw the knife into the group of condemned. One of them grabbed it, rammed it into his chest and instantly fell down dead.

At the same moment, Geneviève made a move and gave out a cry. Sanson had placed his hand on her shoulder.

56

Long Live Simon!

Hearing Geneviève shriek, Maurice realized the battle was about to begin.

Love can lift the soul to heroic heights; love can defy natural instinct and propel a human being to desire death; but it does not extinguish in that being the fear of pain. It was clear that Geneviève accepted death more patiently and more religiously from the moment Maurice was going to die with her. But resignation does not exclude suffering, and leaving this world means not only hurtling into that abyss we call the unknown but suffering on the way down.

Maurice glanced around and in his mind embraced it all, and all that was to follow.

In the middle of the room was a body from whose chest a gendarme had rushed to extract the knife, for fear that it would serve others. Surrounding him, men dumb with despair scarcely paid him any attention; they were busy scribbling disjointed words in pencil on a wallet, or shaking each other's hands; some were repeating a cherished name over and over again, without respite, like mad people do, or bathing a portrait, a ring, or a lock of hair in tears; others were spitting out furious curses against tyranny, that banal property everyone always likes to curse—even, at times, tyrants themselves.

Amid all these poor unfortunates, Sanson, weighed down less by his fifty-four years than by the gravity of his lugubrious office; Sanson, as gentle, as consoling as his mission allowed him to be, gave this one advice, that one sad encouragement, and found Christian words to respond to despair as much as to bravado!

"Citizeness," he said to Geneviève, "we'll have to take off your fichu and put your hair up or cut it off, if you don't mind."

Geneviève started trembling uncontrollably.

"Come, my friend," said Lorin gently, "have courage."

"May I put her hair up myself?" Maurice asked.

"Oh yes!" cried Geneviève. "Let him do it, I beg you, Monsieur Sanson."

"Go ahead," said the old man, turning his head the other way.

Maurice undid his cravat, which was dripping wet with the heat of his neck; Geneviève kissed it and placed herself on her knees before him, offering him her lovely head, more beautiful in pain than it had ever been in her joy.

When Maurice had finished the doleful operation, his hands were trembling so hard, there was so much pain in the expression on his face, that Geneviève cried out:

"Oh! I have courage, Maurice!"

Sanson turned back.

"Don't I, monsieur, don't I have courage?" she said.

"Certainly, citizeness," replied the executioner in a moved voice. "Real courage."

Meanwhile, the first assistant had run through the list sent by Fouquier-Tinville.

"Fourteen," he said.

Sanson counted the condemned.

"Fifteen, including the dead man," he said. "How can that be?"

Lorin and Geneviève counted after him, stirred by the same thought.

"You say there are only fourteen condemned and yet we are fifteen?" she said.

"Yes, citizen Fouquier-Tinville must have made a mistake."

"Oh!" said Geneviève to Maurice. "You lied! You weren't condemned."

"Why should I wait till tomorrow when you are dying today?" Maurice replied.

"My friend," she said smiling, "you reassure me: I see now how easy it is to die."

"Lorin," said Maurice, "Lorin, for the last time . . . No one recognizes you here. . . . Say you came to say good-bye. . . . Say you got locked in by mistake. Call the gendarme who saw you leave. . . . I'll be the real condemned man, I who have to die; but you, we beg you, friend, do us the joy of living to keep our memory alive. There's still time, Lorin, we beseech you!"

Geneviève joined her hands together in sign of prayer. Lorin took those hands and kissed them.

"I said no, and I meant no," he said in a firm voice. "Not another word about it or you'll make me feel I'm in the way."

"Fourteen," Sanson repeated. "And there are fifteen of 'em!" Raising his voice, he went on, "Let's see, is there someone with a special claim? Is there someone who can prove they're here by mistake?"

Perhaps a few mouths opened at this question, but they closed again without uttering a word. Those who would have lied were ashamed of lying; the man who would not have lied did not wish to speak. There was a silence that lasted several minutes, during which the assistants went about their mournful business.

"Citizens, we are ready," came the flat and solemn voice of old Sanson finally.

A few sobs and a few groans greeted him.

"Well then," said Lorin, "so be it!

> "Let's die for the Nation,
> It's the finest fate! . . .

"Yes, when you die for the nation; but, really, I'm beginning to think we're only dying for the pleasure of those watching us die. Good Lord, Maurice, I'm coming round to your opinion, I'm also beginning to be disgusted by the Republic."

"Order!" barked a commissioner at the door.

Several gendarmes came into the room and thus sealed off the exits, placing themselves between the condemned and life, as though to prevent them from returning to it.

The call was sounded.

Maurice, who had seen the man who killed himself with Lorin's knife judged, answered when his name was called. So it transpired that only the dead man was de trop. He was ferried out of the room. If they'd managed to find his identity, if they'd managed to recognize him as having been condemned, dead as he was, he'd have been guillotined along with the rest.

The survivors were pushed toward the main exit. As each person came up to the wicket, his hands were tied behind his back. Not a word was spoken between the sorry souls for ten minutes. Only the butchers spoke and acted.

Maurice, Geneviève, and Lorin couldn't hold out any longer and pressed together so as not to be separated. Then the condemned were pushed out of the Conciergerie and into the courtyard. There the spectacle became alarming.

Several condemned faltered at the sight of the carts and had to be helped up by the clerks.

The gates of the Conciergerie were still shut; behind them you could hear the muffled voice of that great animal, the crowd, and you could tell by the volume of noise that the crowd was vast.

Geneviève climbed up onto a cart with alacrity, with a little help from Maurice, who had hold of her elbow, and Maurice hoisted himself up behind her. Lorin took his time, selecting his seat—on Maurice's left.

The gates opened: in the front row was Simon. The two friends saw him straightaway; he saw them. He stood up on a boundary stone close to where the carts had to pass; there were three of them. The first cart rattled on its way. This was the one the three friends were in.

"Hey! Good day, beau grenadier!" Simon called out to Lorin. "You're going to try out my blade, it looks like?"

"Yes," said Lorin, "and I'll try not to make it too blunt so it's still sharp enough to cut through your thick hide when it comes your turn."

The other two carts rattled away behind the first. An appalling storm of cries, bravos, groans, curses exploded around the condemned.

"Courage, Geneviève, courage!" murmured Maurice.

"Oh!" she answered. "I don't regret life, since I'll be dying with you. I regret only that I don't have my hands free to hold you in my arms before I die."

"Lorin," Maurice said, "Lorin, root around in my coat pocket, will you; you'll find a penknife there."

"Oh, thank Christ!" said Lorin. "I could do with a penknife! I was somewhat humiliated at having to go to my death trussed up like a baby calf."

Maurice brought his pocket down to the level of his friend's hands; Lorin took the penknife and together they managed to get it open. Then Maurice took it in his teeth and cut the ropes tying Lorin's hands. Lorin did the same for Maurice as soon as his hands were free.

"Hurry up!" said Lorin. "Geneviève has fainted."

Indeed, to accomplish the rope operation, Maurice had turned his back for a moment from poor Geneviève, and as though all her strength came from him, she simply closed her eyes and dropped her head to her chest.

"Geneviève," called Maurice. "Geneviève, open your eyes, my darling; we only have a few minutes left to see each other in this world."

"The ropes are hurting me," she murmured.

Maurice untied her. Instantly she opened her eyes and sprang to her feet, galvanized by an exaltation that made her resplendently beautiful.

She wrapped one arm around Maurice's neck, seized Lorin's hand with the other, and all three, standing tall in the cart, with the other victims at their feet shrouded in the stupor of anticipated death, launched a greeting and a look of gratitude to the heavens, which allowed them to freely prop one another up.

The people who had insulted them when they were seated shut up when they saw them on their feet.

The scaffold came into view.

Maurice and Lorin saw it. Geneviève did not, she was looking only at her lover.

The cart pulled up.

"I love you," Maurice said to Geneviève. "I love you!"

"The woman first, the woman before the rest!" cried a thousand voices.

"Thank you, people," said Maurice. "Who said that you were cruel?"

He took Geneviève in his arms and their lips pressed together; he carried her and placed her in Sanson's arms.

"Courage," said Lorin. "Courage!"

"I have," replied Geneviève. "I have!"

"I love you!" murmured Maurice. "I love you!"

It was no longer a matter of victims having their throats cut; this was friends turning death into rejoicing.

"Adieu!" Geneviève cried to Lorin.

"Au revoir!" Lorin cried back.

Geneviève disappeared under the fatal blade.

"Your turn!" said Lorin.

"Your turn!" said Maurice.

"Listen. She's calling you."

Indeed, Geneviève gave out her last cry.

"Come," she beckoned.

A great roar riffled through the crowd. The beautiful, graceful head had fallen.

Maurice rushed forward.

"Wait a moment," Lorin was saying. "Let's stick to logic. Do you hear me, Maurice?"

"Yes."

"She loved you, they killed her first; you aren't condemned, you die second; me, I did nothing, and as I'm the biggest criminal of all three, I go last.

> "That's how everything is explained
> With the logic of the brain.

"Sorry, citizen Sanson, I promised you a quatrain but you'll have to make do with a distich."

"I loved you!" murmured Maurice, tied to the fatal block and smiling at his lover's head. "I lov . . ."

The steel blade truncated the rest of the word.

"My turn!" cried Lorin, bounding up to the scaffold. "And be quick about it! For I truly am losing my head. . . . Citizen Sanson, I robbed you of two lines; but I'm offering you a pun instead."

Sanson tied him up in turn.

"Let's see," said Lorin. "It's the done thing to call out 'Long Live' something or other when you die. Once upon a time they used to cry 'Long Live the King!' but there is no more king. After that, they cried 'Long Live Liberty!' but there is no more liberty. Why not 'Long Live Simon,' who has joined all three of us together."

With that the head of the generous young man fell next to the heads of Maurice and Geneviève!

Notes

1. The Recruits
   1. *death of Louis XVI:* The execution of the deposed king took place on January 23, 1793.
   2. *France cut its ties:* The execution of Louis XVI led most of Europe's monarchies—under the leadership of Pitt's England (*see note 6, p. 402*)—to declare war on the new French Republic.
   3. *enemies it had already defeated:* The Revolutionary armies had won great victories over the Prussians and Austrians in late 1792.
   4. *Austro-Hungarian Empire:* The Holy Roman Empire, which had by the end of the eighteenth century become virtually synonymous with Austria and the domains of the Hapsburg family.
   5. *watching Catherine II tear up Poland:* Catherine the Great of Russia, along with Prussia and Austria, carved up and claimed Polish territory three times in the late eighteenth century, the final partition taking place in 1796.
   6. *September massacres:* Violent mobs invaded the prisons of Paris in early September 1792 and murdered thousands of prisoners.
   7. *Maczinski . . . Dampierre:* All of these generals served with varying degrees of success in the Revolutionary and Imperialist armies. Of particular interest is Francisco de Miranda (1750–1816), a Venezuelan patriot who joined his Revolutionary brothers in France before returning to fight for

independence alongside Simón Bolívar. He was captured by the Spanish and died in prison in 1816.

8. *the Convention:* unicameral legislature that governed France after the final collapse of the Monarchy in August 1792. *See also Glossary, p. 418.*

9. *Dumouriez:* Charles-François du Périer Dumouriez (1739–1823) was an aristocratic officer and diplomat who joined the Revolutionary cause as a successful general under the Convention. *See also Glossary, p. 419.*

10. *Danton:* Georges-Jacques Danton (1759–94), celebrated orator, influential member of the Convention and the Committee of Public Safety, also Minister of Justice. Dumas is referring to Danton's call for a massive levee of troops to face encroaching foreign armies. *See also Glossary, p. 418.*

11. *sections:* the administrative divisions of Paris instituted by the Revolutionary government.

12. *Girondins . . . Montagnards:* The Girondins were the moderate republicans of the National Assembly who came to dominate the Convention after the fall of the Monarchy. They were eclipsed by the more radical faction known as the Montagnards in 1793. The Montagnards, taking their name from the high seat where they grouped in the national assemblies, were the radicals of the Revolution.

13. *Jacobins:* a political club that became increasingly radical as the Revolution progressed; the most famous member was Robespierre. *See also Glossary, p. 420.*

14. *mayor of Paris:* Jean-Nicolas Pache (1746–1823) began as a Girondin then allied himself with the Montagnards, as the latter group became more powerful. His new friends made him mayor of Paris, in which position he helped carry out the purge of May 31–June 2 that left the Montagnards firmly in control of the Convention.

15. *Commune:* the governing body of Paris under the Revolution, the Commune in 1793 was under the influence of Jacques-René Hébert (1757–94), then an ally of the Jacobins before he judged them too moderate.

16. *Robert Lindet:* Robert Lindet (1796–1825), member of the Convention and of the Committee of Public Safety, wrote the indictment of "Louis Capet," as the king was called by Revolutionaries.

17. *Féroud:* a backbencher of the Convention.

18. *Collot d'Herbois:* an extremist and member of the infamous Committee of Public Safety. He eventually turned on Robespierre.

19. *Cordeliers:* a radical political club founded by Danton in 1791. Other prominent members were Hébert and Marat. *See also Glossary, p. 418.*

20. *Louvet:* Jean-Baptiste Louvet de Couvray (1760–97) was a leader of the Girondin who had denounced Robespierre as early as November 1792.

21. *the Temple:* The fourteenth-century headquarters of the Knights Templar became a prison for the Royal family after the coup of August 10, 1792.

22. *citizeness:* Revolutionary egalitarianism and civic spirit demanded that the terms *madame* and *monsieur* be replaced by *citizeness* and *citizen.* As the reader will note, such political jargon was taken very seriously, especially under the Terror; a lapse in political correctness could be dangerous, even lethal.

23. ci-devant: this adjective, meaning "former," became almost exclusively associated with officially abolished aristocracy. It came to be used as a noun.

24. *Palais-Egalité:* the rebaptized Palais-Royal, the Paris residence of the Orléans family. The last duke of the Old Régime joined the Revolution with fervor, taking the name Philippe-Egalité and, as a member of the Convention, voting for the execution of his cousin Louis XVI, before going to the guillotine himself.

25. *National Guard:* this corps was formed as a citizens' militia in 1789; the National Guard was a frequent actor in the violent politics of Paris, usually siding with the populace against Royalist forces. *See also Glossary, p. 421.*

26. *carmagnole:* the short, close-fitting jacket favored by revolutionaries.

27. *tenth of August:* on this day in 1792, riots in Paris drove the Royal family from the Tuileries Palace to seek the protection of the National Assembly. The abdication of Louis XVI and the collapse of the monarchy soon followed. A republican government was established on September 21.

28. *Frères et Amis section:* the name of Maurice's *section*—literally "brothers and friends"—reflects the *fraternité* of the Revolution.

29. *"slaves are marching":* that is, subjects of tyrannical monarchs. Such jargon was typical of the Revolutionaries.

2. THE STRANGER

1. *Soeurs et Amies:* literally, "sisters and friends."

2. *cavaliers:* literally a synonym for knight; for Lorin, chivalry is not necessarily an aristocratic virtue.

3. *Pindus and Parnassus:* twin mountains of Greece traditionally associated with poets.

4. Le Moniteur: Beginning in 1789, the newspaper *Le Moniteur* published the proceedings of the successive Revolutionary governments.

5. *sans culottes:* literally, "those without breeches," or the common people of Paris.

6. *Pitt's men:* William Pitt the Younger (1759–1806), Prime Minister of Great Britain from 1783 to 1801 and from 1804 until his death. Pitt became an implacable opponent of Revolutionary France and then of the Napoleonic Empire.

7. *Thermopylae club:* from the name of the site of a fierce but doomed resistance the Greeks put up against the invading Persian armies of Xerxes I. Allusions to the ancient republics and heroes of classical Greece and Rome were common in the propaganda and imagery of the Revolutionary generation. Political clubs of all ideologies, less famous than the Jacobins and Cordeliers, abounded in the Revolutionary years.

8. *the* Marseillaise: taking its name from the troops from Marseille who sang it while storming the Tuileries on August 10, 1792, this violent revolutionary song—"Let impure blood wash over our furrows"—quickly spread throughout Paris and the whole country. "La Marseillaise" is now the French national anthem.

9. *Dorat, Parny, and Gentil-Bernard:* all French poets of the eighteenth century, known for their love poetry. The verse-spouting Lorin—would-be poet, gallant lover, fearless soldier, and fiercely loyal friend and comrade-in-arms—represents a traditional ideal of French culture.

10. *cockades:* The colors of these small badges, usually worn in hats, were a declaration of political principle and affiliation; Lorin's cockade is no doubt the politically correct red, white, and blue tricolor. In 1793 it would be declared a crime to wear the white cockade, a sign of royalism.

11. Gaul and Lutetia: the Roman names of France (Gaul) and Paris (Lutetia).

3. RUE DES FOSSÉS-SAINT-VICTOR

1. *pont-Marie . . . pont de la Tournelle: pont* means bridge; the pont-Marie connects the Right Bank to the île Saint-Louis; the Pont de la Tournelle then crosses to the Left Bank. Maurice and his companion are working their way south through the heart of Paris.

2. *the Bièvre River:* this small river once flowed into the Seine near the île de la Cité and the île Saint-Louis. The banks of the Bièvre were the site of many manufactures such as tanneries and tapestry makers. The Bièvre was covered to form an underground canal in the late nineteenth century.

3. *chevalier:* the French word for "knight"; the mysterious lady is complimenting Maurice's chivalric manners.

4. THE CUSTOMS OF THE DAY

1. *the Capet woman:* from Hugues Capet, the tenth-century founder of the French royal dynasty and ancestor of the Bourbons. Louis XVI and Marie Antoinette were called Citizen and Citizeness Capet—among other things—by the revolutionaries.

2. *chasseurs:* the name used for many different divisions of the cavalry and infantry in the French armies.

3. *Madelonnettes prison:* a former convent dedicated to the rehabilitation of young prostitutes, converted to a prison by the Revolution.

4. *Agesilaus:* known as Agesilaus II, King of Sparta (399–360 B.C.) at the time of the battle of Marathon.

5. *Phrygian cap:* the red cap that was especially popular with the *sans culottes;* in ancient Rome, the Phrygian cap was worn by freed slaves.

6. *Paris himself:* the Trojan prince; the ancient country of Phrygia was near Troy.

7. *"You sleep, Brutus":* from *The Death of Caesar,* by Voltaire.

8. *Eucharis:* From Homer's *Odyssey,* Eucharis is the beautiful nymph with whom Telemachus falls in love, but the young hero must leave her to continue his quest to find his father. The scene inspired a famous painting by Jacques-Louis David (1748–1825).

9. *Demoustier:* Charles-Albert Demoustier (1760–1801), author of *Lettres à Emilie sur la mythologie* (1788), a popular book that was part of the vogue of antiquity in late-eighteenth-century France.

10. *Cythera:* according to Greek myth, this island was the site of Aphrodite's birth from the waves, thus sacred to the goddess of love.

11. *Knight of Maison-Rouge:* Knight, or *Chevalier,* was the title given to younger sons of noble families; the word has the same associations—medievalism, chivalry, etc.—as *knight* in English. Maison-Rouge, which literally translates as "Red House," was the name given to corps of guards attached to the person of the king under the Ancien Régime, named for their brilliant scarlet cloaks. The name also alludes to Alexandre de Rougeville (1752–1814), who inspired the character of Maison-Rouge. A self-styled marquis of dubious origins but unquestionable loyalty to the Royal family, Rougeville was a member of the Order of Saint-Louis and was even rumored to have been the Queen's lover. He was also the chief conspirator in the so-called "Carnation Plot," which inspired an important aspect of this novel.

12. *Proteus:* son of Poseidon, this demigod had the power to change his form at will.

13. Pastor Aristaeus fugiens Peneia Tempe: From Virgil's *Georgics*, Book IV:317: "The shepherd Aristaeus fled Peneian Tempe"; when the shepherd Aristaeus was struck by a series of unexplained misfortunes, his mother advised him to leave his home in Tempe to seek out and capture Proteus, who would then reveal the divine source of Aristaeus's bad luck. Proteus, for obvious reasons, proved difficult to catch.

14. *Barnave:* the politician Antoine Barnave (1761–93), one of those selected to escort the Royal family back to Paris after their attempted escape was foiled at Varennes. The Queen and the Revolutionary—who favored a constitutional monarchy—rode back to Paris in the same carriage and found each other surprisingly sympathetic.

15. *Diafoirus:* A character in Molière's *Le Malade imaginaire* (*The Imaginary Invalid*), Diafoirus is a pretentious and incompetent doctor who exploits his hypochondriacal patient.

16. *Washington:* the great citizen-soldier of the new American Republic was a hero to the Revolutionary and Romantic generations of Europe.

17. *muscadin:* scornful nickname given to fashionable young men during the Revolutionary era.

18. *"wear a wig":* Like breeches, wigs were considered a sign of aristocratic sympathies, frowned on by good patriots like Maurice and Lorin.

19. *Chloris:* the name given to the object of love by some eighteenth-century poets, in imitation of the Greeks.

5. What Sort of Man Maurice Lindey Was

1. *the Robe:* the *noblesse de robe* formed a second tier of nobility between the upper nobility, the *noblesse de l'épée* (nobility of the sword) and the bourgeoisie. The offices of magistrates were handed down from father to son for generations.

2. *Versailles on the fifth and sixth of October 1789:* On the evening of October 5, a violent mob, stirred up by agents of various anti-royalist factions and led by the market-women of Les Halles, arrived from Paris to demand the return of the Royal family to the capital. Louis XVI and his Queen never saw the palace again.

3. *as many patriots:* i.e., Maurice was seeking to impose order on the violent chaos of that night.

4. *Swiss Guards:* The troop of Swiss Guards at the Tuileries palace in Paris were the Royal family's last line of defense in the assault of August 10. Most were killed.

5. *Jemmapes:* the site of an important victory of the French—led by Dumouriez (*see Glossary, p. 419*)—over the Austrians on November 6, 1792.
6. *The people's representative:* political officers attached to military units to ensure the proper adherence to Revolutionary dogma.
7. *son of Saint Louis:* King Louis IX (born 1214, reigned 1226–70), a direct ancestor of the Bourbons, was cannonized for his efforts in the crusades. The Bourbon kings frequently referred to themselves as "sons of Saint Louis."

6. THE TEMPLE

1. *Marie:* Marie Thérèse de Bourbon, daughter of Louis XVI and Marie Antoinette, known as Madame Royale.
2. *Santerre:* Antoine-Joseph Santerre (1752–1809), commander of the National Guard, was appointed to command the soldiers posted at the Temple to guard the Royal family. *See also Glossary, p. 422.*
3. *Elisabeth:* the sister of Louis XVI, known as Madame Elisabeth.
4. *Citizeness Capet:* Marie Antoinette (*see note 1, p. 403*).
5. *Dauphin's bed:* Dauphin is the official title of the eldest son and heir of the King of France. The boy mentioned is Louis-Charles de Bourbon. *See also Glossary, p. 419.*
6. *the Austrian woman:* Marie Antoinette was born an Austrian Archduchess. The French word *autrichienne,* meaning "Austrian," contains the word *chienne,* "bitch"; this was one of the first epithets used against the Queen as her popularity deteriorated.
7. *Tison:* The Tison family was appointed by the Convention to wait on the Royal family in the Temple.
8. *Madame Royale:* the title given to the princess Marie Thérèse (*see note 1 above*).
9. *Agrippina:* Vipsania Agrippina (c. 14 B.C.–A.D. 33), the legendarily cruel and manipulative mother of Nero (*see also ch. 38, note 1, p. 413*).
10. *"I appeal to any mother . . .":* Dumas here echoes Marie Antoinette's appeal to the spectators at her trial when she denied the most outrageous charges of sexual abuse leveled at her: "I appeal to any mother who may be present."
11. *"two poor mothers":* i.e., the children's aunt considered herself a second mother.

7. A Gambler's Oath

1. *Committee of Public Safety:* the twelve-member commission that came to control the entire Convention, while Robespierre eventually became the dominant member of the Committee. *See also Glossary, p. 418.*

2. *emigrés:* the aristocrats who fled France due to the Revolution; they were considered traitorous criminals and their property was confiscated. Emigrés who attempted to return to France were arrested, tried, and usually executed as traitors and/or spies.

3. *Osselin:* Charles-Nicolas Osselin (1752–94), a leading member of the Convention who sponsored most of the anti-emigré laws. *See also Glossary, p. 421.*

4. *the Terror:* the name given to the reign of the Jacobins and the Committee of Public Safety when thousands of people were executed, mostly by guillotine. *See also Glossary, p. 423.*

5. *eighteen centuries of monarchy:* The French Royal family dated their family's reign back to Hugues Capet [or Clovis?].

6. *Simon:* a failed cobbler who established a reputation for political fervor and was appointed guardian of the former Dauphin Louis-Charles de Bourbon. He was instructed by the Convention to "toughen up" the boy. *See also Glossary, p. 422.*

7. *the Mountain:* name given to the most radical members of the Convention, the Montagnards derived from the high seats they occupied. (*See note 12, p. 400.*)

8. *place de la Révolution:* the former place Louis XV, where the guillotine was set up for public executions, including those of the King and Queen; today the place de la Concorde.

8. Geneviève

1. *"two hundred percent":* Dixmer's gray-market traffic; the harsh economic laws imposed by the Convention drove many people into the sort of gray-market transactions that Dixmer describes here.

9. Supper

1. *Robespierre:* Maximilien de Robespierre (1758–94), the fanatic leader of the Terror. He was in fact known to his allies and supporters as "l'Incorruptible." *See also Glossary, p. 422.*

2. *the Vendée:* a region in western France that gave its name to the popular Royalist uprisings that were centered there and in Brittany.

10. SIMON THE COBBLER

1. *Madame Veto:* "Monsieur and Madame Veto" were epithets used against Louis XVI and Marie Antoinette; the Constitution of 1791 gave the King veto power over legislative action. Louis's attempts to use the veto were enormously unpopular and provoked riots in Paris, including the storming of the Tuileries on June 20, 1792.

11. THE NOTE

1. *Lorient:* a port on the southern coast of Brittany.

12. LOVE

1. *de:* The so-called nobiliary particle, *de* and its variants—*d', de l', de la, des, du*—usually but not always indicated noble birth, e.g., the Marquis de Lafayette. *Du* was fairly common among bourgeois, hence Geneviève's reassurance to the good patriot Maurice.

2. *Blois:* small city on the Loire, known for its Renaissance palace.

3. *Auteuil:* Auteuil to the west and Rambouillet to the south of Paris were country villages at the time. Auteuil is now part of the city of Paris.

4. *Tarquin:* Tarquin the Proud, last king of the ancient kingdom of Rome, was known for his cruelty and despotism.

5. *the Invalides:* The golden-domed Hôtel des Invalides was established as a military hospital and home for wounded veterans by Louis XIV.

6. *the thirty-first of May:* the civil unrest fomented by the Montagnards began on May 31, 1793, and led to the June 2 arrest—and subsequent execution—of many leaders of the more moderate Girondin party.

7. *Brunswick's threatening words:* Duke of Brunswick, commander of the Prussian army moving against Paris; in July 1792, he issued a public proclamation warning of dire consequences for the Parisians if the Royal family came to any harm. The news of the proclamation provoked violent reaction in Paris, and helped precipitate the August 10 attack on the Tuileries.

8. *Longwy and Verdun:* these losses were military and political reverses for the previously successful Revolutionary armies.

9. *departments:* these administrative districts were created by the Revolutionary government to replace the traditional provincial divisions.

10. *Marat:* Jean-Paul Marat (1743–93); the brutal invectives of *L'Ami du peuple,* Marat's newspaper, were too much even for the Revolutionary era,

and he was arrested, but soon acquitted due to his enormous popularity. *See also Glossary, p. 420.*

11. *Hanriot:* François Hanriot (1759–94), a merchant who became a general in the National Guard, and took part in the September massacres. *See also Glossary, p. 419.*

13. THE THIRTY-FIRST OF MAY

1. *tricolor scarf:* the Revolution adopted the tricolor in opposition to the white flag of the Bourbons.

2. *Curtius . . . Cassius: Curtius*—Marcus Curtius, a young Roman patrician who threw himself into the crevice created by an earthquake in order to appease the gods; *Fabricius*—Gaius Fabricius Luscinus, the general and Consul of the Roman Republic, known for his simplicity and probity in power; *Brutus*—Lucius Junius Brutus, the Roman hero who drove the last Tarquin king out of Rome and established the Republic, his order to execute his sons when they were discovered taking part in a royalist plot was held up as an example of patriotism; *Cassius*—Gaius Cassius Parmensis, the Roman general who plotted Julius Caesar's assassination when the latter became overly ambitious.

3. *Brissotin:* prominent Girondin leader Jacques-Pierre Brissot de Warville (1754–93). Followers of Brissot were referred to as "Brissotins."

4. *Rolandists:* Followers of the Girondin leader Jean-Marie Roland de La Platière (1734–93). *See also Glossary, p. 422.*

15. THE GODDESS OF REASON

1. *The Goddess of Reason:* The Revolution briefly adopted the image of a Goddess of Reason as part of a campaign of de-Christianization.

2. *abbé Maury's cruets:* Jean-Siffrein Maury (1746–1817), a priest who established a reputation for his eloquent sermons before taking his oratorial skills to the National Assembly, defending the monarchy and religion in vigorous debates with Mirabeau. His differences with a fellow priest, the radical populist abbé Fauchet, led them to fight a duel with pistols. The "cruets" refer ironically to the small vessels used to hold the wine and water during the Catholic Mass.

3. *the Supreme Being:* Robespierre instituted the cult of the Supreme Being as part of his campaign to restore moral order—without the superstition and institutional tyranny of the Catholic Church—to the new Republic.

4. *Artemisia:* Actresses and dancers—Lorin met his love at the Opera Ball—frequently took extravagant stage names; Théroigne de Méricourt was born Anne-Josephe Terwagne. Artemisia's namesake was a queen in ancient Halicarnassus, wife of Mausolus, for whom she built a famous tomb, the Mausoleum.

5. *Mausolus:* a provincial ruler (satrap) of the ancient Persian empire.

6. *Saint-Just:* a gifted orator and radical revolutionary who became Robespierre's closest ally. He was guillotined with Robespierre in July 1794.

16. THE PRODIGAL SON

1. *Théroigne de Méricourt:* (1762–1817) known as the Amazon of Liberty, this opera singer and courtesan placed herself at the head of the mob that marched to Versailles on October 5, brandishing a sword and riding a black horse. She later became an ardent advocate of women's rights. A supporter of the Girondins, she was violently attacked by a group of market-women who supported the Montagnards. Apparently suffering permanent brain damage in the assault, she was committed to an insane asylum for the rest of her life.

2. *Madame Roland:* the wife of the Girondin leader, she hosted an important salon and was an influential figure in her own right. She was arrested and guillotined in the May 31 purge.

3. *Varennes:* small city in northeastern France where the Royal family was arrested following their attempt to escape control of the Revolutionary government in Paris.

17. THE MINERS

1. *assignats:* the paper money issued by the Revolutionary government, backed by the confiscated properties of the Church and emigrés.

18. CLOUDS

1. *décadi:* the Revolutionary government sought to create a new calendar beginning in the year 1 (1792), when the Republic was established. Décadi was, so to speak, the new Sunday.

19. THE REQUEST

1. *boudoir:* small drawing room where women received their lovers.

2. *savant:* here, one who is erudite and well read.

3. *he's shot up ... in no time:* Santerre's rise in rank had more to do with politics

than with military ability, but rapid advancement of talented officers—Napoleon Bonaparte being the most famous—was common in the Revolutionary armies.

21. THE RED CARNATION

1. "A stone-cutter": i.e., a mason. There is a possible play on words here. The Freemasons were suspected of all sorts of plots in the Revolutionary era. Dumas himself was suspicious of the Masons.

2. *"sneezes in the sack":* one of the many darkly humorous euphemisms for death by guillotine.

22. SIMON THE CENSOR

1. *It had disappeared:* Dumas based this plan on a real plot involving Rougeville (*see note 11, p. 403*). Rougeville managed to gain access to Marie Antoinette in the Conciergerie (*see also Glossary, p. 418*)—not the Temple—and hand her a bouquet of carnations with two notes hidden in it, as in the novel. The first note informed the Queen that she would soon receive money with which to bribe her guards, the other detailed the plan for her escape. Marie Antoinette did manage to respond, in pencil, not in pinpricks. The plot was discovered and added momentum to the already determined execution of the Queen. It also led to stricter surveillance for the royal prisoner. Rougeville managed to escape from Paris and then from France.

24. MOTHER AND DAUGHTER

1. *Conciergerie:* prison and former royal palace on the île de la Cité; the prison was the last holding place of prisoners condemned to death. *See also Glossary, p. 418.*

25. THE NOTE

1. *"Ah, things will all . . . the lampposts":* "Ça ira" was one of the most popular Revolutionary songs; its lyrics celebrated the practice of hanging aristocrats from the *lanternes* (lampposts) in the streets of Paris.

2. *Barbaroux's:* Charles-Henri-Marie Barbaroux (1767–94) had been a radical, but allied himself with the Girondins when the Montagnards became too extreme. He paid with his life, but he did not kill himself, as Roland did.

3. *the Princesse Lamballe looming up on a pike:* Following her brutal murder

during the September massacres, the head of the Princesse de Lamballe was stuck on a pike and taken to the Temple to be shown to her friend Marie Antoinette through a window.

26. BLACK
1. "Aux armes, citoyens! . . . impur": Madame Tison sings a verse from "La Marseillaise"; now the French national anthem, the "Marseillaise" was a Revolutionary song associated with troops from the Marseilles region. (*See note 8, p. 402.*)

27. THE MUSCADIN
1. *"no more châteaux":* Dumas is playing with the Revolutionary jargon.

28. THE KNIGHT OF MAISON-ROUGE
1. *Cromwell's:* The English revolutions of the seventeenth century were a constant reference point for the Revolutionary and Romantic generations in France. Oliver Cromwell (1599–1658), leader of the anti-Royalist Puritan faction, was the chief proponent of the execution of King Charles I; he then became the leader of the country with the title of Lord Protector.

29. THE PATROL
1. *Racine:* Jean Racine (1639–99), one of the greatest playwrights of the seventeenth century. Racine's verse tragedies (*Phèdre, Andromaque*) are among the greatest works of the Classical period.
2. *Molière:* Molière was the stage and pen name of Jean-Baptiste Poquelin (1622–73), the great comic playwright (*Tartuffe, Le Misanthrope*) of the seventeenth century.
3. *Amadis: Amadis de Gaule* was a Spanish medieval romance that told the story of a heroic knight who, in spite of his virtue, is rejected by his lady. The spurned, brooding young lover was described as the *beau ténébreux*, a popular image in Romantic literature.

32. FAITH SWORN
1. *Enceladus:* In Greek mythology, the many-armed Enceladus was one of the Titans who rose up in rebellion against the gods of Olympus.
2. *Monsieur Latude . . . ladies of Les Halles:* an adventurer who called himself the Chevalier de Latude, he had been imprisoned in the Bastille and Vin-

cennes prisons. He became a popular hero based on his three escapes from prison, and in the propaganda of the Revolution was portrayed as a victim of despotism. He was an honored guest at a ceremony commemorating the fall of the Bastille; *the ladies of Les Halles*—The market-women of Les Halles—called the *poissardes*—often played a part in the violence of the Revolutionary years. It was these women who led the march from Paris to Versailles on October 5, 1789.

3. *Osselin . . . marquise de Charny:* the revolutionary politician Osselin, who proposed some of the harshest anti-emigré laws, fell in love with the beautiful Marquise de Charny. Probably under her influence, he began assisting certain prisoners and was expelled from the Jacobin club and then arrested. Osselin was eventually guillotined.

4. *"a tyrant who knew the fair sex well":* a reference to the very gallant Francis I (born 1494, reigned 1515–47).

34. THE CONCIERGERIE

1. *the old palace of Saint Louis:* the Conciergerie (for Saint Louis, *see ch. 5, note 7, p. 405*).

2. *the place de Grève:* historically the site of public tortures and executions in Paris; the placement of the guillotine in the place de la Révolution was a temporary political calculation.

3. *Richard:* The sympathetic M. et Mme. Richard were the concierges of the Conciergerie prison when Marie Antoinette arrived there. They were replaced by more "patriotic" guardians after the discovery of the Carnation Plot. Their maid later published her memories of looking after the Queen.

4. *Widow Capet:* There was in fact some confusion about how the *ci-devant* royal prisoner should be registered on her arrival at the Conciergerie.

5. *fleur-de-lys:* the three lilies against a blue background was the traditional heraldic symbol of the Kings of France.

6. Le Voyage du jeune Anarcharsis: immensely popular 1788 work by the priest Jean-Jacques Barthélemy; the *Voyage* recounted the fictional travels of a young Greek in the time of Plato, as a device for presenting ancient Greece to contemporary readers.

35. THE HALL OF LOST FOOTSTEPS

1. *Fouquier-Tinville:* Antoine Fouquier-Tinville (1746–95), the relentless chief prosecutor of aristocrats during the Terror. He was executed in 1794 with Robespierre and the other leaders of the Convention.

2. *"Nero's confession to Narcissus":* from Racine's *Britannicus,* the young Emperor, not yet the monster of legend, confesses to the scheming servant Narcissus his love for Junia, the beloved of Britannicus, Nero's cousin and rival for the Imperial throne. Narcissus encourages the Emperor to eliminate Britannicus as a romantic and political rival.

36. CITIZEN THÉODORE
1. *sabots:* heavy wooden shoes worn by peasants.
2. *Gracchus:* another name taken from the Classical era; the Gracchus family rose from the plebeian class to the aristocracy in the last years of the Republic; several were known as patriots and reformers.

38. THE ROYAL CHILD
1. *Messalina ... Agrippina:* Two legendary Roman empresses to whom Marie Antoinette was frequently compared in anti-Royalist propaganda. Messalina, first wife of the Emperor Claudius, was made a legend by Tacitus and Suetonius for her lusty immorality. After Claudius had her killed, he married Agrippina, who is said to have used poison to assassinate her enemies—including her husband—to advance her son, Nero, to the throne. Nero had her killed anyway.
2. *Hébert:* Jacques-René Hébert (1757–94), journalist and politician, his newspaper, *Le Père Duchesne*—named for a popular figure in French theater—was the organ for the most radical elements in Revolutionary politics. Hébert was arrested after accusing Robespierre of an excessive moderation, and sentenced to death.

39. THE BOUQUET OF VIOLETS
1. *Carmes:* a former convent turned into a prison by the Revolutionary government.
2. *Boulogne ... Abbeville:* Boulogne is a port on the English Channel; nearby Abbeville is an inland town on the Somme River.
3. *louis:* the *louis d'or* was a gold coin worth 24 francs at the end of the eighteenth century.
4. a Marseillais: Revolutionary troops from the Marseilles region that had a reputation for excessive zeal, even among other Revolutionaries.

40. THE PUITS-DE-NOÉ BY NIGHT
1. obole: an insignificant amount of money.

41. THE CLERK FROM THE WAR MINISTRY

1. *Sanson:* The Sanson family were the chief executioners of France for almost two hundred years.

43. DIXMER'S PREPARATIONS

1. *Anne of Austria:* from the Spanish branch of the Hapsburgs, Queen of Louis XIII and mother of Louis XIV. When her husband died, she found herself Regent for the five-year-old king. With the help of Cardinal Mazarin, she fiercely defended the royal prerogatives against the aristocratic and parliamentary revolts known as the *Fronde*.

2. *Two kings:* Apparent references to Louis XV—her husband's grandfather—and her own father, Holy Roman Emperor Francis I, who arranged her marriage to the future Louis XVI.

46. THE JUDGMENT

1. *year II:* Seeking to wholly re-create society, the Revolutionary government instituted a new calendar beginning with the establishment of the Republic. The year II indicated the second year of the Republic, starting in September 1793.

2. *Chauveau-Lagarde:* Claude Chauveau-Lagarde (1756–1841), lawyer who defended Marie Antoinette and many other doomed aristocrats before the Revolutionary tribunal. *See also Glossary, p. 417.*

47. PRIEST AND BUTCHER

1. *powder:* One of Robespierre's laws was a ban on wigs and powder, which were considered aristocratic. Robespierre never applied the law to himself and, like an aristocrat, continued to wear a powdered wig and the formal suit, with cravat and breeches, of the lawyer that he had been before entering politics.

2. *la Salpêtrière:* a hospital established in 1656.

3. *juror priests:* Priests were required to swear an oath of loyalty to the Constitution rather than to Rome. This measure provoked a serious split among the French people, especially in the provinces.

48. THE CART

1. *Maria Theresa:* Marie Antoinette's formidable mother, Holy Roman Empress and Queen of Hungary and Bohemia (born 1717, reigned 1740–80).

2. *the Comédie-Française:* the state theater of France, founded early in the reign of Louis XIV.

3. *Grammont:* from a famous family of actors, Grammont joined the Revolution with fervor.

4. *Ophelia:* a reference to Hamlet's lover, who went mad and drowned herself.

5. *Daughter of the Caesars:* The Hapsburgs claimed actual descent from the Roman Caesars.

49. THE SCAFFOLD

1. *"Adieu . . . au revoir!":* Formally, *adieu* was used for final farewells, *au revoir* suggests "till we meet again."

2. *he expired:* unlike his fictional counterpart, Rougeville (*see note 11, p. 403*) survived Marie Antoinette's execution and the Terror. He escaped to Brussels, where he was eventually captured and imprisoned. Released after the fall of the Convention, he offered his services to Napoleon, but remained a Royalist. In 1814, he was accused of treason by the Imperial government for allegedly offering to serve with approaching Russian armies. He was executed by firing squad in March 1814, just weeks before the collapse of the Empire.

50. THE HOME VISIT

1. *Carmelites . . . Luxembourg:* The policies of the Terror required many prisons in Paris alone.

2. *Dagobert:* Dagobert I, King of the Franks from 629 to 639. He reinforced royal authority and confirmed the borders of the Frankish kingdom.

3. *Demoustier's* Lettres à Emilie: *See note 9, p. 403.*

54. THE HALL OF THE DEAD

1. monseigneur: literally, "my lord," a form of address reserved for bishops and archbishops, and under the Ancien Régime, for princes of the Royal family.

2. "The geese on the Capitol": according to Roman legend, the sacred geese of the Capitol hill began honking when they sensed the approach of a silent army of Gauls in the fifth century BC.

3. *Eloi:* Saint Eloi, Bishop of Noyon (died 660), served as treasurer and adviser to Dagobert.

4. *sous:* a coin worth twenty *centimes;* five *sous* equaled one franc.

55. WHY LORIN LEFT

1. *Monsieur Guillotine:* Joseph-Ignace Guillotin (1738–1814), physician and deputy to the Estates-General, promoted the use of the machine that bears his name—but which, contrary to popular belief, he did not invent—as a humanitarian measure. Prior to 1789, decapitation was reserved for aristocrats, commoners were hanged.

GLOSSARY OF
HISTORICAL PERSONS AND TERMS

AUGUST 10, 1792: The ultimate collapse of the Bourbon monarchy, when the mobs stormed the Tuileries Palace, forcing the Royal family to seek asylum from the Legislative Assembly and the subsequent abdication of Louis XVI.

BAILLY, JEAN SYLVAIN (1736–93): Mayor of Paris from 1789 to 1791, Bailly supported a constitutional monarchy. He was forced to resign after ordering the NATIONAL GUARD to fire on a group of *sans culottes*. He was arrested and guillotined in 1793.

BARBAROUX, CHARLES-JEAN-MARIE (1767–94): leading GIRONDIN guillotined in ROBESPIERRE's purge.

BARNAVE, ANTOINE (1761–93): a gifted young orator who quickly became one of the leaders of the National Assembly in 1789. An advocate of constitutional monarchy, Barnave was one of the first victims of the TERROR.

BRISSOT (DE WARVILLE), JACQUES-PIERRE (1753–94): journalist and politician, became one of the leaders of the moderate GIRONDIN party in the CONVENTION. His followers were known as *Brissotins*.

CAPET: From Hugues Capet, the traditional founder of the French Royal family, the imprisoned Bourbons were called Capet by the anti-Royalist press and then by the governments of the Revolution.

CARMAGNOLE: the short, close-fitting jacket favored by revolutionaries.

CHAUVEAU-LAGARDE, CLAUDE (1756–1841): lawyer who defended Marie

Antoinette and MADAME ELISABETH before the Revolutionary Tribunal. His other clients included BRISSOT and Charlotte Corday.

CHÉNIER, MARIE-JOSEPH (1764–1811): a poet and playwright as well as a politician, Chénier survived the TERROR and continued to wield influence under the Directory.

CI-DEVANT: this adjective, literally meaning "former," became charged with political significance during the Revolution when it came to be used—often as a noun—to refer to members of the legally abolished nobility.

CLAVIÈRES, ETIENNE (1735–93): Genevan banker inspired to democratic idealism by the writings of Rousseau; served briefly as Minister of Finance.

COLLOT D'HERBOIS, JEAN-MARIE (1750–96): member of the COMMITTEE OF PUBLIC SAFETY, one of the chief architects of the TERROR. He turned on ROBESPIERRE in 1794 and was exiled in 1795.

COMMITTEE OF PUBLIC SAFETY: a committee of twelve members of the CONVENTION formed in April 1793 to deal with foreign and domestic threats to the new Republic; the Committee soon became the real political power in France. Its influential members included DANTON, SAINT-JUST, and the increasingly powerful ROBESPIERRE. It was the Committee, and especially Robespierre, who enacted and executed most of the brutal measures associated with the TERROR.

CONCIERGERIE: massive medieval edifice on the île de la Cité, a royal palace until the fourteenth century, when the kings moved to the Louvre and the Conciergerie became a prison; as a Revolutionary prison, the Conciergerie loomed large as the last stop for those condemned to the guillotine.

CONVENTION: or *Convention nationale,* the unicameral legislature that governed France after the official abdication of Louis XVI and the declaration of a Republic in September 1792. At first dominated by the (relatively) moderate republican GIRONDINS, the more radical MONTAGNARDS became increasingly powerful, ultimately taking power in a bloody coup that sent most of the Girondin leaders to the guillotine. The Convention government is now chiefly associated with the TERROR. The armies of the Convention were successful for a time, repelling Austrian and Prussian armies and conquering such territories as Belgium and Savoy.

CORDELIERS: Radical Revolutionary club—officially "The Society of Friends of the Rights of Man and the Citizen"—that met in a former monastery. Founded by DANTON in 1791, its most famous members included MARAT and HÉBERT.

DANTON, GEORGES-JACQUES (1759–94): Powerful orator and republican politician, Danton became Minister of Justice for the Republic in 1792, and helped form the Revolutionary Tribunal and the COMMITTEE OF PUBLIC SAFETY. His rhetoric inspired both the SEPTEMBER MASSACRES and the AUGUST 10 storming of the Tuileries. DANTON split with the increasingly powerful ROBESPIERRE over the policies of the TERROR, and was arrested and convicted on charges of corruption, which later proved to be true. He was guillotined with a number of his followers in April 1794.

DAUPHIN: The formal title given to the eldest son and heir of the King of France. The Dauphin in this novel—Louis-Charles de Bourbon (1785–95), known as "Charles Capet" to the Revolutionaries—is traditionally known as Louis XVII. The boy died while still imprisoned in the Temple.

DUMOURIEZ, CHARLES (1739–1823): born Charles-François du Périer du Mouriez, became a successful Revolutionary general after having served as a diplomat under Louis XV and as the last Minister of War under Louis XVI (1791–92). Dumouriez won such significant victories as Valmy over the Prussians and Jemappes against the Austrians, and successfully conquered and occupied modern Belgium for the Republic. When Dumouriez was relieved of command and summoned back to Paris after losing the battle of Neerwinden in March 1793, he understood the order to be a death sentence and defected to the Austrians. Dumouriez's treason precipitated the MONTAGNARD reaction and the arrest and execution of many GIRONDIN leaders.

FABRE, PHILIPPE (1750–94): known as Fabre d'Eglantine, he was DANTON's secretary and ally.

FOUQUIER-TINVILLE, ANTOINE (1746–95): the relentless chief prosecutor of aristocrats during the TERROR. He was executed after the fall of ROBESPIERRE and the CONVENTION.

GIRONDINS: Moderate republicans, enemies of the more radical JACOBINS and MONTAGNARDS, led by ROLAND and BRISSOT. The Girondins steadily lost power to the Montagnards; many eventually were condemned to death by the COMMITTEE OF PUBLIC SAFETY.

HANRIOT, FRANÇOIS (1759–94): General of the Parisian National Guard, successor to SANTERRE, Hanriot took part in the SEPTEMBER MASSACRES. A close ally of ROBESPIERRE, Hanriot attempted to defend him during the coup of 9 Thermidor, but ultimately was arrested and executed.

HÉBERT, JACQUES-RENÉ (1757–94): Journalist and politician, his newspaper, *Le Père Duchesne*—named for a popular figure in French theater—was the organ for the most radical elements in Revolutionary politics. Hébert was arrested after accusing ROBESPIERRE of excessive moderation, and sentenced to death.

JACOBINS: Taking their name from the former monastery that was their headquarters, the Jacobins were, with the CORDELIERS, the most radical of the political clubs that proliferated in Revolutionary Paris. The most famous Jacobins were ROBESPIERRE and SAINT-JUST. The word *jacobin,* in French and English, became a political epithet for *radicals* throughout the early nineteenth century.

LAMBALLE, PRINCESSE DE: Marie Thérèse de Savoie-Carignan (1749–92), by birth a member of the Royal House of Savoy and by marriage a Princess of the Blood Royal of France, the Princesse de Lamballe was one of Marie Antoinette's closest friends. Having fled to Italy at the outbreak of the Revolution, she returned to Paris out of loyalty and friendship to her Queen. Brutally murdered in the La Force prison during the SEPTEMBER MASSACRES, her head was stuck on a pike and carried to the Temple prison to be shown to Marie Antoinette through the windows.

LANJUINAIS, JEAN-DENIS (1755–1827): a founding member of the JACOBIN Club, with whom he split as they became more radical. His moderate positions earned him a death sentence, but he went into hiding and managed to outlast the TERROR. He survived to serve both Napoleon and the Bourbon Restoration.

LEBRUN, CHARLES-FRANÇOIS (1739–1824): More famous as one of three Consuls of Napoleon Bonaparte's first government, and then archtreasurer under the Empire, Lebrun briefly served as the GIRONDIN Minister of Foreign Affairs.

MADAME ELISABETH (1764–94): the younger sister of Louis XVI, she remained in France to share prison and ultimately death with her brother and his family.

MADAME ROYALE: Marie Thérèse de Bourbon (1778–1851), daughter of Louis XVI and Marie Antoinette. After the execution of her parents, she was sent to Austria in exchange for French prisoners of war in 1794. She returned to France with her uncle, Louis XVIII, in 1814. She became one of the chief supporters of the reactionary ultraroyalists, and was forced to flee France again when the Bourbon branch fell in July 1830.

MARAT, JEAN-PAUL (1743–93): physician, writer, and politician, he founded the newspaper *L'Ami du peuple* (*Friend of the Common Man*), an organ of extremist positions. A MONTAGNARD in the CONVENTION, he helped to instigate the SEPTEMBER MASSACRES and to bring down the GIRONDINS. He was assassinated in his bath by Charlotte Corday, as famously depicted by Jacques-Louis David (1748–1825) in his painting *Marat assassiné*.

MONGE, GASPARD (1746–1818): better remembered as a mathematician, Monge was also a politician and member of the JACOBIN Club. He was Minister of the Marine in the first year of the CONVENTION.

MONTAGNARDS: taking their name from the "Mountain," the high seats they occupied in the legislative assemblies of the Revolutionary governments, the Montagnards were the most radical members of the CONVENTION.

NATIONAL GUARD: the Paris civil militia, founded in 1789 under the command of Lafayette, became a major factor in the factional battles of the Revolution, frequently used against Royalist forces. On AUGUST 10, 1792, the Garde Nationale aided in the taking of the Tuileries that brought down the monarchy.

OCTOBER 5 AND 6, 1789: In the evening of October 5, a violent Parisian mob, led by the market-women of Les Halles, marched to Versailles to demand the return of the Royal family to Paris. The mob led the King and his family back to the Tuileries the next day; the Bourbons never saw their palace again.

OSSELIN, CHARLES-NICOLAS (1752–94): an ally of DANTON who became an influential member of the CONVENTION. He wrote some of the harsh anti-emigré legislation before he fell in love, ironically, with a beautiful young aristocrat, the Marquise de Charny. Probably at her instigation, he began aiding many political prisoners. When this was discovered, he was expelled from the JACOBIN Club and subsequently arrested and condemned to deportation; when he was found to be plotting in prison, he was sent to the guillotine.

PATRIOT: during the Revolution, the term was appropriated by republicans.

PÉTION (DE VILLENEUVE), JÉRÔME (1756–94): Mayor of Paris from 1791 to 1793, and president of the CONVENTION in 1792, Pétion was a leader of the GIRONDINS. When the MONTAGNARDS took power, he fled Paris and eventually killed himself in order to escape arrest.

PHRYGIAN BONNET: the red cap, popular among the sans culottes, modeled after the hat worn by freed slaves in ancient Rome.

RICHARD: Richard and his wife were the concierges—chief attendants—at the CONCIERGERIE when Marie Antoinette first arrived at that prison. They were judged to be overly solicitous of the CI-DEVANT queen, and were replaced by more "patriotic" staff after the failure of the Carnation Plot.

ROBESPIERRE, MAXIMILIEN DE (1758–94): legendary leader of the JACOBINS and the MONTAGNARDS, and chief architect of the TERROR. His harsh laws led to the deaths of thousands deemed traitors throughout Paris. Robespierre solidified his grasp on power by outmaneuvering political enemies to the left (HÉBERT) and right (the GIRONDINS, DANTON) to become virtual dictator of France. He remained in power for just over a year before his own allies turned on him and brought him down in the coup known as 9 Thermidor, the date of his downfall according to the Revolutionary calendar. He was executed, along with his closest followers, in July 1794.

ROLAND, JEAN-MARIE (1734–93): Leader of the GIRONDINS, Roland opposed the execution of Louis XVI and was eventually forced to flee Paris. His highly cultivated and influential wife, Jeanne-Marie (1754–93)—known as Manon—hosted an important salon where Girondins and their political allies gathered. She was arrested and executed with the other leaders of the *Rolandiste* party. Hearing of her death, her husband killed himself in Rouen.

SAINT-JUST, LOUIS-ANTOINE-LÉON DE (1767–94): a gifted orator and radical revolutionary who became ROBESPIERRE's closest ally. He was guillotined with Robespierre in July 1794.

SANSON: The Sanson family were the chief executioners of France from 1688 to 1848. Charles-Henri presided over the execution of Louis XVI in January 1793; his son Charles-Henri guillotined Marie Antoinette and Madame Elisabeth the following October.

SANTERRE, ANTOINE-JOSEPH (1752–1809): a wealthy brewer of the faubourg Saint-Antoine. Popular for his charity, Santerre became active in Revolutionary politics and the NATIONAL GUARD. On AUGUST 10, he led his batallion in the assault on the Tuileries. Appointed commander-in-chief of the National Guard by the CONVENTION, he was also commander of the Temple when it became the prison of the Royal family.

SEPTEMBER MASSACRES: from September 2 to 6, 1792, mobs enraged by news of the Prussian invasion of France, and spurred on by the rhetoric of DANTON and MARAT, murdered thousands of prisoners in the Revolutionary prisons of Paris.

SERVAN, JEAN-MARIE-ANTOINE (1752–1808): onetime minister of war who returned to power, briefly, after AUGUST 10. He managed to survive the TERROR.

SIMON, ANTOINE (1736–94): The illiterate Antoine Simon was a failed shoemaker who made a name for himself in Revolutionary politics, first in the Paris Commune and then in the CONVENTION. He was appointed, with his wife, guardian of the former DAUPHIN as part of an effort to give the boy a popular upbringing, that is, to undo the influence of his tyrannical parents and the courtiers that surrounded them.

TERROR: beginning with laws enacted in September 1793 until the fall of ROBESPIERRE in July 1794, the increasingly ruthless dictatorship of the COMMITTEE OF PUBLIC SAFETY sought to purify France of those deemed Royalists and traitors. Best remembered for mass executions by guillotine, the TERROR was also a time of draconian, and disastrous, economic policies.

TISON: the Tisons were appointed to look after the Royal family in the Temple prison; the participation of the Tison daughter in the Carnation Plot—or any other Royalist activity—is an invention of Dumas.

VALAZÉ, CHARLES-ELÉONORE DUFRICHE (1751–94): a pamphleteer who became associated with the GIRONDINS; he opposed the execution of the King. Arrested and condemned to death in the JACOBIN reaction, he killed himself in prison. The leader of the CONVENTION ordered that his body be brought to the scaffold with the other Girondin prisoners.

VARENNES: town in northeast France where the Royal family was arrested on June 22, 1791, after they tried to flee the control of the Revolutionaries in Paris.

VERGNIAUD, PIERRE VICTURNIEN (1753–93): an eloquent orator of the GIRONDIN party, guillotined as part of ROBESPIERRE's purge.

Reading Group Guide

1. *The Knight of Maison-Rouge* is set in a time of great historical unrest. Does Dumas make his characters seem more authentic because of their position alongside historical figures, or do they suffer from the technique?

2. In chapter 22 Dumas writes that "genetic differences" between Lorin and Simon "easily explain" their animosity, and goes on to list Simon's unattractive qualities. Does this nasty depiction of Simon allow you to cheer when Lorin condemns him with his last breath? What does Lorin's condemnation reveal about him?

3. Dumas writes in chapter 26 that "there are fatal periods in history in which prayer, the natural hymn God has planted firmly in mankind's heart, becomes suspect in the eyes of men, for prayer is an act of hope or gratitude" (p. 197). Does the Queen ever really believe she will escape? Which events indicate she may eventually be saved, and which prove that her fate has been sealed?

4. In chapter 5, "What Sort of Man Maurice Lindey Was," our "startlingly good-looking" hero is credited with storming the Bastille,

fighting like a lion in numerous battles, jumping in front of cannons, and leading the charge into the Louvre—"all of which had helped to forge a reputation worthy of the great days of Rome or Greece." Is Marcus too good to be true? What later incidents flesh out this hyperbolic depiction?

5. Given Geneviève's litany of sorrows, is it possible that her love for Maurice is not nearly as deep as hers for him? If not for the guillotine, would they have lasted? Why or why not?

6. Early in the novel, Lorin informs Maurice that "worship of the nation doesn't exclude worship of love." Do the actions of the novel prove this point, or disprove it?

7. How does Maurice come to sympathize with the Revolution? If not for Geneviève, would he ever have done so? Does this demean his commitment to the cause?

8. Dumas, especially through Lorin, demonstrates remarkable comedic timing. For instance, after much protesting, Lorin leaves Maurice and Geneviève saying, "I knew very well I didn't love anyone, but I forgot there's someone I hate." How does Lorin's poetry and wit counter Maurice's more conscious chivalry? Is either Lorin or Geneviève the better friend to Maurice? Why?

9. Lorin's final poem states "That's how everything is explained / With the logic of the brain." Does Lorin believe in logic, or does his good nature remain with him until the very end? Can he be both a hopeless romantic and a pragmatist?

10. In the Biographical Note, André Maurois is quoted as saying "Dumas was a hero out of Dumas. As strong as Porthos, as adroit as d'Artagnan, as generous as Edmond Dantès. . . . He turned his own existence into the finest of his novels" (pp. vii–viii). Do Maurice Lindey and the Knight live up to these classic characters? Is it true that the heroes of modern novels are less heroic and more subtle, and that these two would be better suited to the silver screen?